LEARNING TO FLY
ALIEN SPACECRAFT
THE SHANTIVIRA BOOK TWO

FAY ABERNETHY

First published in 2023 by
Fay Abernethy
c/o autorenglück.de
Franz-Mehring-Str. 15, 01237 Dresden, Germany
www.fayabernethy.com

German National Library Cataloguing in Publication Data
A catalogue record for this book is available from the German National Library (*Deutsche Nationalbibliothek*). More details available at http://dnb.d-nb.de.

Cover design and illustration © Patrick Knowles
www.patrickknowlesdesign.com
Formatting by BB eBooks Co., Ltd. www.bbebooksthailand.com

ISBN: 978-3-949516-04-7 (ebook)
ISBN: 978-3-949516-05-4 (paperback)
ISBN: 978-3-949516-06-1 (hardcover)

Paperback edition

This book is dedicated to all those who, for whatever reason, have left the country of their birth and made their home elsewhere.

FREE NOVELLA

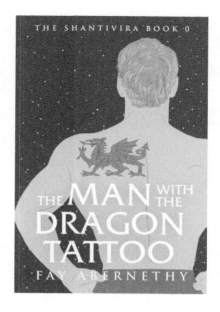

Get your FREE no-obligation download from
www.fayabernethy.com today. Yours to keep, forever!

PROLOGUE

DAN, JANUARY 2015

THE SOYUZ CAPSULE had separated from the International Space Station, survived the sizzling plasma stream and re-entered the Earth's atmosphere, all without incident. When the parachutes deployed, Dan allowed himself to relax. Almost home. They'd be on the ground in ten minutes. He'd done it.

Against all odds, he'd smuggled hard evidence that aliens existed down to the planet. He couldn't wait to see the expression on his senior officer's face when he handed it over. They'd award him a medal, for sure. His folks were going to be so proud of him.

Valentin, the Soyuz commander, reached across and shook his hand, congratulating him on a successful re-entry. Dan grinned back at him and did the same with Tatiana, the co-pilot. They all had the same sparkle in their eyes: a heady mixture of relief and joy to be returning to the Earth. Dan's heart swelled with elation and anticipation.

AN UNKNOWN RED-HEAD materialised directly on Dan's lap, making him yell with shock. She said nothing, but her iridescent yellow eyes flashed with utter contempt as she pulled out a knife and sliced open his spacesuit with brutal efficiency. In a single swift movement, she reached inside and ripped away the stolen *zana* he'd taped to his body for safekeeping.

Dan yelled again, this time with pain. For an instant, a shaft of sunlight illuminated the translucent communication device and the dark chest hairs still stuck to the tape. Then the woman vanished.

Immediately grasping Dan's betrayal, Tatiana opened her mouth to speak. Valentin caught her eye and she shut it again. The loudspeaker crackled, breaking the horrified silence.

'This is Ground Control. Are you OK? The cockpit camera failed, then we heard screams. Report!'

Valentin responded, 'Flight Engineer Simpson has torn his suit. I didn't see what happened.'

'Flight Engineer Simpson? What happened?'

Dan hesitated. What could he say? Not, 'an irate space demon with a very sharp knife,' or Ground Control would have people in white coats ready to cart him off the minute they landed.

'Flight Engineer Simpson, report!'

'I don't know!' he lied feebly. 'I just looked down and my suit was ripped.'

'Board Engineer Markovich?'

'I was looking at the instruments. I didn't see anything.'

'Ground Control?' said Valentin. 'We must prepare for landing. There'll be time for questions later.'

Except for essential communication, the cockpit was

uncomfortably quiet for the rest of their descent. The retrorockets fired and the Soyuz capsule came to a standstill with a violent jerk. 'Soft landings,' they say, Dan thought. He'd been in softer car crashes.

The cosmonauts continued with the silent treatment while they waited for the team outside. The open audio feed meant he was spared the full force of their disapproval. But, in their way, they were telling him he was on his own.

After a long few minutes, the hatch opened and helping hands pulled them out into the beautiful fresh air. Dan took in great lungfuls of it; he'd never smelt anything as good as the Earth smelt that day. The journey back from space was over. Now they'd be under constant observation by the space agencies and wouldn't be able to speak privately for weeks or even months. The cosmonauts stayed in Kazakhstan; Dan travelled back to the US, alone.

PART ONE

1. A NEW FRIEND

HANNA, JANUARY 2015

I N HER LOWEST gear, Hanna crested the hill and gasped as the icy breeze hit her full on, blasting the warmth out of her jacket. She stopped pedalling and admired the view over Essoona to the rolling waves out at sea. High, fluffy clouds scudded across the winter-blue sky.

She turned and cupped her hands round her mouth, yelling, 'Come on, Lucy!' Unlikely she'd be heard, but never mind. She dropped her bike and found a sheltered spot to wait in. Out of the wind, the pale morning sunshine felt almost warm.

To the west, the sun climbed the sky above a ridge of mountains. The forbidding white peaks slashed with dark stripes of rock reminded Hanna of last month's disastrous trip to Switzerland. Once again, she thanked her lucky stars she'd reached Syenitia on time and in one piece.

The teleports on the *Shantivira* had stopped working when Kitty, the Earth's resident shape-shifting space demon, had gone into self-imposed exile. Kitty's sister Rowan, the only other space demon in the galaxy, had temporarily reactivated them so Hanna and the rest of the second-year trainees could travel to Syenitia.

Hanna's mind returned to yesterday's *zana* call with

Irion. Mary and Irion, her unofficial adoptive parents who ran the *Shantivira's* secret language school in London, had been rushed off their feet since the arrival of the latest intake of first-years. As the students couldn't access the space station for flight training, they were having additional classroom sessions. Irion was working flat out teaching the new recruits Kawaida, the interstellar language Hanna and her classmates had learned last year.

'Things will calm down when Kitty returns,' Irion had said. 'Once the teleports are up again, it'll be Tima and Valeri putting in the extra hours on the simulators and I can have a break.'

Hanna had waited as the holographic projection of the silver alien took a delicate sip of tea from an Elizabeth II Diamond Jubilee mug. Behind her, Hanna could see the brown 1980s kitchen units in Mary and Irion's basement flat. Arguably hideous, but familiar and therefore comforting. The first place she'd felt safe and loved since her parents had died. Knowing she could always go back there gave her the confidence to face the challenges the coming year would bring.

'Anyway, in other news,' Irion had continued, 're-member that SD card Lucy gave Mary before Christmas?'

Hanna had nodded. How could she forget? The SD card holding details of the prototype weapon Nestor and David had built, ostensibly to protect the Earth, but which Nestor had highjacked and fired at Kitty. The SD card included a list of everyone who'd worked on the *Shantivira*, right back to the 1970s. Through it, they'd discovered Nikolai's mother had also been a Shantiviran. A fact Hanna suspected Nikolai would have preferred to keep to himself.

David had pressed the card into Lucy's hand moments before his death; Lucy had handed it to Mary, who would give it to Joe as soon as the teleports came back online. They'd all agreed deciding what to do with it was a job for the *Shantivira's* captain.

'Well it's gone!' Irion had said, tucking a lock of lime-green hair behind her ear. 'I'm still hoping it'll turn up, but Mary's convinced it's been stolen.'

Hanna's stomach had swooped, leaving her nauseous. Only she and her closest friends knew about the card. Was one of them a thief? She couldn't bear the thought there might be *another* traitor in their midst, not after last year's dramas.

'Any idea how long it's been missing?' she'd asked.

'No. Mary hid it under a loose floorboard in our bedroom. Then we forgot about it, to be honest. I disturbed the floorboard while vacuum cleaning yesterday; when I looked, it wasn't there!'

'Could it have slipped out of sight?'

'I don't think so. It could have been gone for weeks already.'

'That's disturbing.'

'Yes. Could you have a gentle probe, Hanna? All the people who know about it are with you in Essoona. Perhaps there's a perfectly rational explanation.'

WAITING IN HER sheltered nook on the hillside, Hanna gazed at the jagged horizon as she mulled over the problem. Someone who knew about it. Her. Her boyfriend, Hassan. Her best friend, Farida. Her arch rival and (after a bumpy start) good friend, Lucy. Lucy's boyfriend, Felix. Saïd. Nikolai. All people she trusted with her life. Not Hassan. Not Farida. Not Lucy, not this time. Hmm.

Lucy appeared, pink-cheeked and panting as she pedalled up the last few metres to where Hanna sat. 'Phew!' she said, throwing her bike down beside Hanna's. 'I'm so unfit after Christmas! I'm not sure I'd have made it up here without the reduced gravity.' She looked round at the scrubby hillside. 'D'you reckon the story's true?'

Hanna knew which story she meant: the Syenitian fairytale, *The Princess and the Dragon*. The story that this hill was the ancient remains of a gigantic space spirit who'd died and turned to stone while defending the planet, his Syenitian wife and their twin daughters. Few Syenitians knew that Rowan and Kitvian, the unique half-Syenitian, half-space spirit daughters, were not only real, but still around today, with a telepathic link enabling them to communicate over any distance. Syenitian mythology referred to them as the 'space demons': Verndari, or 'Protector', who traditionally shielded Syenitia from harm, and Reika, or 'Wanderer', who had left Syenitia to roam the galaxy.

'Well,' Hanna said, 'it *is* called Dragon Hill. I don't see why not.'

They sat watching some hikers they'd overtaken earlier plod past towards the summit. The hill was rumoured to have sacred healing powers, which meant it attracted tourists of all shapes and sizes.

'Do you think Kitty will ever die?' asked Lucy.

'In the story, Ahmitor only stops being immortal because he became a father. So no, not unless she has some children tucked away that we don't know about.'

'I think there's a lot we don't know about Kitty,' said Lucy.

'What *I* want to know is, when will she come back?' Hanna sighed.

Lucy grinned. 'You mean, when will the teleports work again, so you can see Hassan? You've only been apart a fortnight!'

Unusually perceptive for Lucy. Hanna smiled shyly. It might have only been two weeks, but it was the longest she and Hassan had been separated since they'd met, nearly eighteen months ago. Hassan was a year ahead of them on the programme, living aboard the *Shantivira* for his final phase of training. The worst was not knowing when they'd meet again in person. They couldn't even make plans. Still, they called each other every day on their *zanas*, so it wasn't all bad.

Hanna changed the subject. 'How are you finding Dunia House?'

Dunia House was the one place in the Syenitian capital – and on Syenitia – where you were sure to meet other humans. A place where the furniture was the right size, where the media streams were tuned to Earth channels and where the books were in Earth languages. It acted as an unofficial embassy and a hall of residence for second-years like Hanna and Lucy. Hanna knew it well from visiting Hassan last year.

Lucy shrugged. 'I like the kitchen. And Mrs Park's cool. I'm quite getting into her K-Dramas.'

Dunia House was managed by an elderly Korean couple. During the week, Mrs Park, the housekeeper, prepared an evening meal which they ate together at the long kitchen table. Her husband, Mr Park, worked in the garden and on the Dunia House allotment, providing them with most of their fruit and vegetables. The enormous kitchen was Mrs Park's domain, the walls lined with wooden cupboards crammed full of equipment and hand-labelled jars of pickled *everything*.

Whenever they got home, her first question was always, 'Have you eaten?' She'd serve them a bowl of whatever bubbled on the hob, or fetch plates of deep-fried yumminess from the pantry. Hanna's waistband already felt tighter.

Mrs Park loved watching television while she worked and had a wall-mounted screen showing back-to-back Korean dramas. When not alone, she turned down the sound and switched on the Hangul subtitles. Hanna constantly found herself trying to work out the plot with only the actors' theatrical expressions to go on.

'I'm glad I have my own room,' continued Lucy, 'especially as Felix is sharing with Saïd.'

'The lounge is nice, isn't it?' replied Hanna absently, her mind drifting back to Hassan. She picked up a flat stone and placed it on a larger one near her feet. She found another and balanced it on top of that. Another six months and he'd be a qualified *Tumba* pilot. Thinking of him gave her a warm glow inside.

'Yeah, very comfy,' conceded Lucy. 'Are you and Farida getting on each other's nerves yet?'

Hanna shook her head. 'I'm pleased we're sharing. We always have plenty to talk about when she gets back from university.' Carefully, Hanna positioned another stone on her little tower. How high could she go before it collapsed?

'Syenitian Mathematics.' Lucy shivered. 'Ugh. Rather her than me. How's she doing?'

'Finding it tough, being the first ever human to go there. But you know Farida: never happier than when she's studying.'

'She'll miss us next year, when we're home on the *Shantivira* and she has another two years to go.'

Hanna pursed her lips. She'd miss Farida too, but they had a whole year together first. 'She'll have made new friends by then.'

'You think? They're not as snooty up at the uni as the Academy lot?'

'Oh, they're not that bad!' But Hanna knew Lucy's experience was different to her own. The humans lagged far behind their alien classmates at the elite Essoona Pilots' Academy. The native Syenitians were merely patronising, but some trainees from other Galaksi Alliance planets were openly hostile, saying the humans were only there because of their physical resemblance to young Syenitians. Those with pale skin, like Lucy, Felix and Nikolai, bore the brunt of this antagonism. Nikolai suffered particularly because, as well as being white, he was considerably overweight. Even Saïd had shaved off his beard in an attempt to blend in; Hanna thought it suited him.

'I can see *why* they hate us,' said Lucy, philosophically. 'We need to show them we've earned our place here. Shall we do some extra navigation later?'

'OK,' Hanna said, cautiously adding another rock to her pile. It was respectably high now, but distinctly wobbly. 'I wish they'd let us practise on the simulators outside class times,' she said. 'I'm nervous about tomorrow.' Oh. Damn. The stack tumbled to the ground, scattering stones. Lucy giggled and Hanna set about collecting them. She'd have another go, this time aiming for stability rather than height.

Lucy helped Hanna gather more rocks. 'I'm nervous, too. They're all so much more experienced than us.'

'Are you worried you'll be in the bottom ten per cent and get thrown off the programme?'

Lucy screwed up her face. 'A bit. I'm more worried about Felix.'

She had a point. Hanna focused on positioning her next stone correctly. Felix had many talents, but he was one of the worst pilots in their year. Tomorrow's races – their first time flying in space proper – would be insanely competitive. The Academy's policy was to take on excess students at the start of the year and weed out the slowest after a fortnight's training. Nobody wanted to be one of the fifteen who'd have to leave the course tomorrow.

'I'm sure he'll be fine,' Hanna said, trying to sound reassuring. They'd all miss Felix if he had to return to Earth.

The flight training was incredibly demanding. Hanna and Lucy had been stunned to find themselves flying real *Tumbas* on their very first morning. They'd practised over the sea every day since, for hours at a time. Hanna longed for Tima, who'd taught them to fly on the *Shantivira's* simulators. Their new Syenitian trainer, Kalarran, expected perfection at all times. If he *didn't* criticise you, you could consider yourself highly praised. His chiselled features reminded Hanna a little of Aldeman, Joe's

Syenitian boss, but he lacked the politician's charm.

From outside, the one-person fighter craft looked like giant horse chestnuts. The prickly green shells were grown on farms; the flight systems were added after they matured. *Tumbas* were cybernetic organisms with low-level consciousness and they had distinct personalities. Flying them was a different experience to flying simulators.

Each student had been assigned their own *Tumba*; Hanna's was called 'Tulu'. She'd no idea if Tulu was a he, she, they or an it but, after a few hours flying, she chose the pronoun 'her'. Hanna had been tense that first day and Tulu had responded badly: flying erratically and not reacting immediately to instructions. Then Hanna's training had kicked in and she'd realised she knew what she was doing. Once she'd relaxed, Tulu had become more cooperative. Soon Hanna found herself talking to her, having whole one-sided conversations.

Now it was crunch time. Tomorrow, she'd see new stars, without the glare of the city lights. If Tulu crashed, it would be Hanna's fault. And if they finished in the slowest ten per cent, well, that would be Hanna's fault, too.

She completed her stone-stack and sat back on her heels with satisfaction. That should last a while, she thought.

'Good job,' said Lucy. 'What do you reckon? Shall we push on to the top?'

'I'm not sure I can be bothered,' said Hanna. She closed her eyes and directed her face towards the sun. It might be winter, but it still offered a pleasant warmth. 'It's so nice, sitting here.'

But Lucy was not to be dissuaded. 'Come on, it can't be much further.'

THEY FOLLOWED THE dirt track upwards until they reached an exposed ridge. The track became so narrow, one wobble of Hanna's handlebars would send her plummeting down the hillside. Ahead, a lone walker approached. It would be impossible to pass. This was beyond Hanna's comfort zone.

Thankfully, Lucy agreed. 'This is no good,' she said, dismounting. 'We'll turn back. We can come another day on foot.'

They were heading off when a shout from behind made them pause. The walker was closer now and waving at them. 'I thought it was you!' she shouted in Kawaida. 'Maybe you don't recognise me, but we just started flight school together? I'm Aneira.'

Aneira was not a Syenitian. Instead of towering over them, she was roughly the same height as Hanna. Had her eyes been brown and not pale violet, she'd have passed for a South Asian human. Her straight black hair was bobbed short and, when she smiled, her teeth were pleasingly crooked.

'Sorry, I don't know your names.'

They introduced themselves and walked down the hill, Hanna and Lucy wheeling their bikes. 'What are you doing up here on your own?' asked Hanna.

'I often come.'

'Often?' said Lucy. 'Have you been on Syenitia long?'

'I grew up near Aldina, up the coast. My brothers and

my dad still live there. My parents divorced a few years ago and I came to Essoona with my mum.'

Hanna phrased the question as sensitively as possible. 'But your ancestors aren't from Syenitia originally?'

The crooked smile reappeared, a toned-down version this time. 'You mean, why am I small and brown, instead of tall and pale like the natives?'

'I suppose I do, yes,' said Hanna.

'My family's from Amra, which isn't an Alliance planet, but we moved to Syenitia for my dad's work. He has an import-export business with my uncle, who's still on Amra. I could apply for an Academy scholarship because I'm a Syenitian citizen now. But tell me about you. I'd never heard of humans until you turned up at school. Where's your planet? What's it called?'

'Earth,' said Lucy. 'It's not an Alliance planet either.'

'But we don't know where it is,' said Hanna.

Aneira blinked. 'What do you mean? You must know, roughly. How many days did it take you to get here? What kind of ship did you travel in? Where did you stop on the way?'

Hanna looked at Lucy. Were they allowed to talk about the teleports?

As usual, Lucy missed the hint and opened her mouth without thinking. 'We teleported,' she blurted out before Hanna could stop her. 'It would've taken us weeks otherwise.'

'Teleported?' Aneira echoed. 'How are you authorised for teleports? I thought only senior government officials could access them.'

Hanna shrugged. 'We got lucky. There's no interstellar

travel on our planet; we're just starting out. Most people back home don't realise there's intelligent life outside our solar system.'

'A primitive planet? Goodness. Why are you being allowed to train?'

Hanna explained about the *Shantivira*. How Aldeman Varpushaukka, the head of the Syenitian Council and Syenitia's Galaksi Alliance representative, had set up the space station more than forty years ago in the hope that humans would eventually contribute to intergalactic peace. The *Shantivira's* day-to-day mission was to protect the Earth from hostile species – without revealing the existence of aliens to the general population.

They stood to one side as another group of hikers passed them on the path.

'Tell me about humans,' said Aneira as they continued downwards. She jerked her head at Lucy. 'How come she looks like an adolescent Syenitian and you don't?'

Before Hanna could answer, Lucy said, 'Skin tone varies all over our planet: Hanna's ancestors lived in a region with strong sunshine, so her skin has more of the special pigment which protects us from UV light than I do. My ancestors come from a region with far less solar radiation. They evolved pale skin to get enough of a vitamin which our skin can synthesise from sunlight.'

Aneira nodded. 'That's nice – that looking different to each other is normal on your world. It must be easy to fit in wherever you go there.'

Lucy caught Hanna's eye and Hanna shook her head. No need to admit what life on Earth was really like. Time to change the subject. She asked Aneira, 'Do you know anyone else in our year?'

The path widened into a track, broad enough to walk side-by-side. It wasn't so steep now; soon they'd reach the bottom of Dragon Hill.

'I know a couple of the Syenitians,' said Aneira. 'I went to school with Briavan in Aldina. Stay away from her, she's nasty. There's a guy from Essoona who takes the same tram as me. We chat sometimes. And now I know you two.'

Hanna thought of the twenty humans she lived with at Dunia House. Lived with, ate with, studied with, spent her free time with. A warm cushion of friends who insulated her from the strangeness outside. However much she missed Hassan – not to mention Irion and Mary – she'd never be lonely here like Aneira obviously was. She had a flashback to her former life as a cleaner: an Ethiopian in the UK illegally, working for a fraction of the minimum wage. Years of loneliness she wouldn't wish on anyone else.

'Come back to ours for lunch,' she said, putting her hand on Aneira's arm. 'Then you can meet the rest of us.'

2. LEARNING TO FLY (I)
HANNA

T HE FOLLOWING DAY dawned bright and clear, a good omen. For the third time, Hanna checked her backpack: a fresh hygiene balaclava to wear under her helmet, her trusty *zana* (she'd decorated hers with glittery stickers to prevent it from getting mixed up with the others), a packet of tissues, a pencil and a notebook, a bottle of water, sandwiches and some *omena* fruit from the Dunia House allotment. It would be a long day. Then she left to catch the tram.

The flying trams formed the backbone of Essoona's public transport system, blanketing the city in a dense and frequent network. Passengers paid nothing; you hopped on and off as you wished, never having to worry about what sort of ticket you needed. Three separate tiers ran above the street-level roads (which were reserved for the pay-as-you-go private pods).

The platforms, located over the pedestrian walkways and cycle tracks, housed a multitude of tiny kiosks selling refreshments to commuters. Hanna could pick out the meaning of the signs and menus written in Kawaida, but many were in Syenitian with no translation, making her feel illiterate.

Hanna had often travelled on the trams with Hassan, but he'd always avoided peak periods. Now she understood why. Aliens of every shape and colour jostled for space in the morning rush hour and she never knew who or what she'd be pressed up against. Since Hanna was shorter than most of the locals, sometimes even breathing was tricky. When the weather got warmer – which Mrs Park promised it would – Hanna vowed she'd do the trip by bike. Assuming she made it through today and didn't get thrown off the programme.

At the stop for the Academy, Hanna glimpsed a familiar black bob on the stairs below. 'Aneira!' she called. The head turned – it *was* her – but the current of people swept her onwards. When Hanna, Lucy and the other Dunia House residents reached the street, they found Aneira waiting for them. They walked through the leafy suburb together, towards the coast and the day ahead.

Kalarran was at the gate, making sure they went straight to their *Tumbas*. There'd be no sitting in the classroom today. To get to theirs, Hanna, Lucy and Aneira had to walk past Elian, a Syenitian who radiated confidence and behaved as if he were the natural leader of the group. Maybe he was: the other Syenitians all deferred to him and he'd come top in every test so far. His chestnut hair was plaited into a single waist-length braid, ready for the active day ahead. He faced away from them, talking to a pretty Syenitian female who was mirroring his body language.

'That's Briavan, who I went to school with,' said Aneira.

Briavan showed no awareness of their presence, but as

they passed, she jabbed her leg into Aneira's path, sending her sprawling to the ground.

'Wow. What a *bitch*,' Lucy said.

Elian helped Aneira up. 'Are you all right?' he asked with genuine concern. 'What happened?'

'You didn't see?' Hanna half-shouted. She turned on Briavan, intending to give her a piece of her mind, but Aneira placed a restraining hand on her arm.

'It was an accident, Hanna,' she said, her eyes begging her not to say anything. 'I tripped.'

Briavan stood motionless, her arms folded across her chest. Her lips twitched into a thin, triumphant smile.

Elian was still holding Aneira's hand. 'But you haven't hurt yourself?'

'No, no, I'm fine,' said Aneira, backing away. 'Thank you.'

'Good luck in the races,' he said. Behind him, Briavan's expression flashed thunder.

Hanna was relieved to climb into Tulu's warm interior, the all-round screen still blank. Despite being naturally gregarious, she relished the solitude of her own independent spacecraft. She put on her helmet, fired up the control panel and initiated the launch sequence.

In her earpiece, Kalarran's voice announced the rendezvous coordinates. Tulu's screen showed a location two thousand kilometres beyond Syenitia's atmosphere. A safe distance from the main transport routes but not too close to the satellite orbits. It was the furthest Hanna had ever flown away from Essoona. As the light from the planet faded, her screen filled with stars: a view as clear as from the *Shantivira's* biomes, but with unfamiliar constellations. She ought to be able to identify them; they'd covered the star charts of this region in their first week. Looking closer, she recognised a couple of shapes, but couldn't remember their names. More studying was required.

'We'll do some warm-up exercises first,' said Kalarran. 'Find a space and practice your standard manoeuvres. Return to these coordinates in thirty minutes.'

Tulu seemed perkier out here. Normally sluggish in the morning, she zipped about cooperatively at Hanna's slightest command. 'You like it up here, don't you?' she said. A bubble popped up at the side of her screen: Aneira requesting a connection. Hanna accepted, and a small version of Aneira's cheerful face appeared.

'How are you getting on?'

'Good, thanks. Tulu likes it up here.'

'Oh, yeah, all *Tumbas* prefer being in space. Listen, I've set up a private group for you, me and Lucy. So we can talk outside the open channel.'

'Is that allowed?'

'Everyone does it. How would you form flight teams, otherwise?'

'Flight teams?'

'You don't know *anything*, do you?'

Lucy's face materialised below Aneira's. 'Hi, Hanna. This is fun, isn't it? Permin's doing what I ask him for once.' Permin was Lucy's *Tumba*. 'Aneira, will you show us how to link with the others? I want to bring some of the boys in too.'

'Afterwards, on the planet. I'd rather keep the group small. I'm not sure it's permitted, officially. Come on, it's time to head back to the rendezvous.'

On the way, Hanna repeated her question, 'What's a flight team, Aneira?'

'When you connect your *Tumbas* so you can cooperate as a smaller unit. Otherwise, we can only talk to Kalarran or everyone at once. This way, we can work together.'

'Work together on what?' said Lucy.

Kalarran interrupted before Aneira could answer. 'Time for the races. You've been split into groups of ten and issued with start and finish coordinates.'

As Hanna programmed the locations, she asked Aneira, 'Are we in the same group? How do I know who I'm competing against?'

'Ask Tulu,' came the reply.

Hanna did. Tulu displayed the positions of the *Tumbas* in her group and showed a live feed of the pilots' faces down the side of the screen, each identified by their *Tumba's* name. The only person she recognised was Nikolai.

'Can they see me?'

'If they know how to switch on the feed,' said Aneira. 'Some will.'

'Can they hear us?' Lucy asked.

'If you invite them into a group. Kalarran's closed the open channel for the races; officially, we can only communicate with him.'

'Good luck, you two,' said Hanna.

'Good luck,' Lucy answered.

Aneira said, 'I'm going to switch off for the race, so we don't distract each other. Good luck.'

Aneira's and Lucy's faces disappeared and Hanna

focused on the task ahead. At the bottom of her screen, the clock counted negative numbers up to the start time. The route overview showed a rectangle, with the start and finish at the lower right corner. She switched to navigation mode and waited.

Ready.

Go.

She threw herself forwards into her harness and Tulu accelerated. She was among a knot of leaders: in her peripheral vision she saw a *Tumba* close on each side. So close, she was aware of their shields repelling hers as she tested how far she could move left and right. She didn't dare turn to look back, or Tulu might turn with her. The *Tumbas* on either side rolled around her exterior to join in front, blocking her path. What an evil trick! Were they working together? On the overview she saw they were the only two ahead of her. Another pair had moved up to her sides, three more bunched up at her rear.

Corner approaching. The pack lurched into it, still in a tight cluster. One of the *Tumbas* directly behind was edging its way above her, she sensed its shields shoving her downwards. At the same time, another was trying to move below her. She must escape this trap right now, or she'd be stuck. This was all harder, faster and more aggressive than anything she'd experienced. OK, she thought. If that's how you want to play it.

She told Tulu her plan, unsure how much the pod understood beyond direct commands. On the straight, she punched the little ship down, briefly pushing away the lower competitor before it shoved up into the gap, helping to drive her out of the pack.

Hanna kept pressing forwards, keeping a close eye on the approaching marker for the next bend. In space, it was harder to judge which line to take: she had to rely on her instruments absolutely.

'Now, Tulu!' she shouted.

She flung herself sideways and Tulu responded sweetly. 'Good girl!' Hanna yelled.

She was below the left-hand leader now, the cluster of spacecraft still pelting along at maximum speed. The coming curve would decide everything. She needed to arrive at the finish coordinates, not some point beneath them. When should she come up level with the others again? Before the curve? After it? Time was running out. Don't do two things at once, she thought. 'Now, Tulu!' she shouted again, hurling herself to the left. Wow. Tulu activated the exterior thrusters in the same millisecond. A perfect right angle at hundreds of kilometres per hour.

'Well done, Tulu! Now, up to the same level as the others, while we're still in front.' Hanna pushed against the floor, the harness digging into her shoulders. This was the home stretch. 'Don't let up, girl,' she said as she leaned forward to keep the speed. 'Stay on this line, as fast as you can.'

She felt the pack jostling behind her, trying to creep past. But there was no time. Almost there. Almost … yes!

Hanna yelled with exhilaration and relief, lavishing Tulu with exuberant praise. Then she flopped back in her seat, trembling with exhaustion.

In her earpiece, Kalarran's voice said. 'Congratulations, Hanna. Your cornering was satisfactory. You have fifteen minutes to reach the coordinates for the final.'

Again? She had to do it all again? Hanna wasn't sure she could. Her legs were like jelly. 'Take it easy on the way over, Tulu,' she said. 'Give us a chance to recover.'

Aneira's face flickered into view again, followed by Lucy's. 'How'd you do?' Aneira asked.

'I won!' Hanna said, beaming.

'Congratulations! What about you, Lucy?'

'I won too,' said Lucy, with an ear-to-ear smile. 'It was awesome; like Permin could read my mind. He wanted to win as much as I did.'

'Well done, Lucy!' said Hanna. 'Nikolai came fifth in my group. And you, Aneira?'

'Yeah, piece of cake. Your friend Felix came eighth.'

'Did he?' said Lucy, her voice hopeful. 'So he'll stay on the programme with us?'

'Should do,' said Aneira. 'It'll depend on his times, but usually it's just the slowest person in each group who has to leave.'

That's a relief, thought Hanna. 'So we're in the final together?' she said.

'See you in ten minutes.'

FIFTEEN TUMBAS LINED up, the clock ticking towards zero for the second time. Hanna could see her rivals on her screen: Lucy, as always, Aneira, Saïd, one Sayari male with skin as silver as Irion's but darker green hair, one four-armed Wadudu (gender unknown); the rest were ethnic Syenitians. Two she recognised: Elian and Briavan.

Aneira had left their communications on this time, saying they might be able to help each other. But they were all silent, totally focused on the start.

And they were off.

This course was a convoluted sequence of markers in 3D space, testing their manoeuvring skills rather than their ability to fly fast. The last race had been a warm-up in comparison. A dense pack of Tumbas formed ahead, with Elian in front beyond it and Briavan hot on his heels. Hanna was in eighth place, with the new and unwelcome sensation of not being the best pilot in the group. At least she was ahead of Saïd, who had a secondary pack building up behind him. Lucy clung to the rear of the head pack; Aneira had the inside pole position.

Time to do something while she was still free of neighbours. Tulu clearly had a talent for cornering. That was how to catch up. 'We'll do what we did last time, Tulu. Take a line just below them, then we'll have space to move.'

The next corner was approaching fast. 'Ready?' she said, her voice loud in the small cockpit. 'Go!' Tulu fired the thrusters to change direction as Hanna threw herself into the bend. She checked their position. Good. The lead pack was still in front, but closer, since cornering tightly was impossible while flying in a group.

'Ready? Go!'

Now she was with the pack, directly under Lucy. 'Hi Lucy!' she said.

'Where've *you* been? It's not like you to let me get so far ahead.'

'I'm making up for it now though. Come on Tulu, next one!'

Now she was below Aneira. 'Hello Aneira!'

'Hanna, glad you caught up! Now we can have some fun.'

Fun? thought Hanna. How is there time for fun? It was all she could do to stay on course at this speed.

'All right, ladies,' said Aneira, 'here's the plan. On the next corner the three of us will break away from this cluster and form our own, just beneath it. It's a drop, so it should be easy to pull away. Then we'll catch up with Briavan.'

'And teach her a lesson?' asked Lucy hopefully.

'No. We'll just be faster than her. That'll be enough, believe me. Hanna, you're lowest. You lead. OK?'

'OK. Ready, Tulu? Go!'

Hanna squatted and pulled her knees to her chest simultaneously, her feet in the loops attached to the floor. Her seat telescoped down and Tulu changed direction abruptly, closely followed by Aneira and Lucy. Tulu swivelled to face forward, and Hanna threw herself into her harness, going for maximum acceleration. They'd done it! Briavan's *Tumba* was nearer now.

'Great work, you two!' said Aneira. 'Don't relax, keep pushing.'

Aneira led the next corner. Hanna launched herself upwards in a desperate attempt to keep up. On the feed, she heard Lucy grunt with physical effort. Now they were right behind Briavan with a straight stretch ahead.

'OK,' said Aneira. 'Hanna, go on her right, Lucy on her left. I'll go above. Let's block her view.'

Flying at top speed, they crept closer. Briavan must have seen them, but they were too fast for her to pull away. Now they were level with her *Tumba*, rolling slowly round its exterior to meet in a triangle at the front. If Hanna hadn't been concentrating so hard, she'd have laughed at Briavan's furious expression.

'We did it!' Aneira sounded delighted. 'Watch out for the upcoming bend, keep it tight, Lucy, you lead.'

'OK,' said Lucy, 'Did you hear, Permin? One, two, three … go!'

They cornered as a single unit, giving Briavan no opportunity to slip past.

'The leader isn't far ahead,' said Hanna.

'Can we catch him?' said Lucy, a new confidence in her voice.

'Let's find out,' said Aneira. 'Briavan'll stick to us like a *takiainen* burr, though, whatever we do. Hanna, you lead the next corner.'

'OK,' said Hanna, 'Ready Tulu? One, two, three … go!'

Not bad. They accelerated along the straight, edging nearer to Elian.

'I'll lead the next corner,' said Aneira. 'Ready? Go!'

They went.

Now they were right behind him, the triangle of friends sandwiched between Elian in front and Briavan at the rear.

'OK, same like we did to Briavan, before the next bend. Lucy left, Hanna right, me below.'

Painfully slowly, they edged in front of Elian.

'Ready for the corner?' shouted Aneira. 'I'll lead. One, two, three … drop!'

They plunged down. Briavan used the chance to creep up beside Elian, but Hanna, Lucy and Aneira managed to pull away as a pack.

'What now?' asked Lucy. 'We're coming to the finish.'

'Thanks for your help, ladies,' said Aneira.

'Thanks for yours,' said Hanna. 'Now we're ahead, I'm going to try and come first, OK?'

'Of course!' said Aneira, grinning. 'So am I!'

'May the best woman win,' said Lucy, pulling away. Sneaky.

I'm not having that, thought Hanna. 'Come on, Tulu, catch her!' she cried. But Aneira was faster and overtook Lucy on the last bend.

'Aaargh!' yelled Lucy in frustration as Aneira surged ahead on the final stretch, putting lengths between them and her. She passed the final marker first, followed by Lucy, then Hanna, milliseconds later.

Hanna pulled up with relief. 'Well done, Tulu!' she said, patting the console. 'We came third on our first day in space!'

Lucy groaned, 'We'll be stiff all over tomorrow. My thighs are on fire!'

'Mine too,' said Hanna. 'And my stomach muscles.'

When all fifteen *Tumbas* had finished, Kalarran said, 'Good. Next, some flying in formation.'

Would it never end? Hanna wanted to return to Dunia House and crawl into bed. Instead, she ate her sandwiches while Tulu flew back to the rendezvous.

Lucy asked, 'Where did you learn to fly like that, Aneira?'

Aneira shrugged modestly. 'I've been racing deactivated *Tumbas* since I was a teenager. I was Syenitian Junior Champion six years' running.'

Hanna laughed. 'That explains a lot.'

'I'm astonished we could keep up,' said Lucy.

'You were both excellent, considering your lack of experience,' said Aneira. 'You have an unusual rapport with your ships, which is more important than people think. It'll be fun trying to stay ahead of you.'

3. EXILED
DAN, FEBRUARY 2015

D AN SAT IN the empty waiting-room, his right knee twitching to its own private rhythm. This was the point of no return. In a few moments, that door over there would open and he'd reveal the whole *Shantivira* story to the NASA debriefing panel. The lack of evidence made things so much harder. Would they hear him out, or laugh in his face?

Despite mounting pressure, he'd managed to postpone speaking about the damage to his spacesuit. Instead, he'd focused on reporting on his time aboard the ISS and doing the standard tests for recently landed astronauts.

The past weeks had been a lonely emotional roller coaster. After being caught red-handed with the stolen *zana*, he'd initially suffered from guilt and regret, doubting whether he should speak up at all. But, as time went on, his thoughts settled into a loop of resentment and self-justification.

He knew he was going against the wishes of his fellow ISS crew members – and the promise of temporary secrecy made to Joe Llewellyn, the captain of the *Shantivira*, when he'd pulled the ISS in for emergency repairs after a debris strike. But it was Dan's duty to inform the authorities. America had a right to know.

A MOVEMENT IN his peripheral vision alerted him: he was no longer alone. An unwelcome figure had appeared beside him, a head taller than him even sitting down. Her medieval dress creased where it touched the marble floor, covering her feet in folds of green velvet. Dan took in the braid of red hair over her shoulder; her sparkling yellow eyes with vertical slits for pupils; her flawless skin and slightly pointed ears. He knew if she parted those perfect ruby lips, he'd see the wickedly curved canines of a predator. He was certain: she was a space demon, like Kitty. How many of these terrifying beauties were there? He'd thought Kitty was the only one.

Shock is a physical reaction. It hit him in the stomach first, then icy splinters extended to his heart, spreading cold fatigue through his limbs. He froze in his seat, incapable of movement. Who are you? he wanted to ask, but all he managed was, 'Uh-oh.'

The woman took his hand. 'Time to go, Dan.'

Instantly, a roaring sound filled his head, as if he'd fallen into deep water. Flickering lights rushed past his eyes, disorienting him and making him want to vomit. A second later it stopped; Dan's body felt strangely heavy. Or weak, he wasn't sure which. The atmosphere was suddenly humid, thick with heat and moisture. When he drew breath, the air had a slightly bitter, astringent taste.

As his eyes adjusted to the strong sunshine, he saw they were standing on a scrubby hillside, overlooking a city. The only visible highway passed directly above the buildings in the centre: a fat ribbon of densely packed air traffic. A wide, brown river separated the town from an industrial zone on the plain beyond. Dan thought he saw an airport, although the aircraft appeared to be all shapes and sizes.

The woman released his hand and grinned at him, revealing her demon's teeth. Dan gulped. He'd played fullback at college, but she towered over him. Terror locked his knees, rooting him to the spot. His heart thumped so hard, he was sure she heard it too.

'I heard you were curious about teleporting,' she said, studying him like a scientist evaluating an interesting specimen. Her eyes were like a snake's, with an added unearthly glitter. 'Now you know what it's like.'

'Who—Who are you?' he stammered, managing to take a step back. 'Where are we? Are you going to kill me?'

'Don't be so melodramatic. Of course I'm not going to kill you. I'm Rowan.' She held out a pale hand for him to shake. Dan stared numbly at her black fingernails and, after a moment, she dropped it again.

'Fine,' she shrugged. 'Be like that. You met my sister, before she went away.'

'Kitty?'

'Yes. Kitty.'

'Is she all right? Is she still … big?' said Dan, remembering the last time he'd seen Kitty, just after she'd ripped an invading spacecraft to pieces with her bare hands.

'Bored out of her skull and missing Joe, but she's got her size down to normal, now. She'll need another month until she's safe to be near people again. I've been feeding from her a lot myself. That helps. We speak every day. I'll tell her you asked after her.'

'Are you … like her?'

The reptilian eyes narrowed and Rowan tilted her

head to one side. 'Do you mean, am I a giant, shape-shifting space monster, masquerading as a harmless Syenitian? Or am I an instinct-driven crazy woman who spends unhealthy amounts of time with primitive species?'

'Um—'

Rowan sighed. 'Do you have siblings, Dan?'

'Er, yeah, a younger brother. Mark.'

'Are you alike?'

'Not really. Actually, no, not at all.'

'Well, I'm nothing like my sister, either. We're twins: physically we're alike, but our similarity stops there. I'm the sensible one. The reliable one. The one who steps in to clean up the mess.'

'You mean me,' said Dan, his shoulders slumping. He looked at the ground. The dust and small stones by his feet were a vibrant shade of orange.

Rowan's voice softened. 'Oh, not just you, Dan. But my workload's doubled since Kitty's been out of action. As hard as I try, I can't be everywhere at once.'

Dan looked up at her. 'So what did you bring me here for? And *where* is here?'

'This is Amra, three hundred light years from Earth. It's bigger than your planet, so the gravity's stronger. You'll feel tired until you acclimatise. But it'll make you strong. I picked it because it's safe and peaceful and its development level is similar to Earth's. They're rather ahead of you, in fact. It might look chaotic, but they have space travel and technology you'll find interesting. It's not an Alliance planet yet, but the Amranese are very keen to join. They have two arms, two legs and one head, like us. That city is Laro, an important trading post for the planet—'

'Wait! You're going to *leave* me here?' Dan interrupted, almost shouting. 'Three hundred light years from home? Take me back! Please! I won't say anything, not ever, I swear.'

Rowan shook her head. 'It's too late, Dan.' Her jawline hardened as she looked down at him. 'You've broken our trust, twice. We respect your patriotism, but we can't allow one country to learn about the *Shantivira* before the others. We're simply putting you out of harm's way until the negotiations start. Your crewmates are bright enough to keep quiet. Why couldn't you? Joe will approach the UN when Kitty returns. You can go home a few weeks later.'

'You can't do this to me!' said Dan. His voice came out shriller than expected. 'I demand you take me back! I have rights!'

Rowan sighed again. 'It's not for ever. Regard it as an opportunity. Look, I have to be somewhere else in two minutes. So shut up and listen. There's stuff you need to know.'

Her mouth twisted into a rueful smile as she pulled a *zana* from behind her back, seemingly out of thin air. 'Ironically, I'm now authorised to give you your own *zana*. You can use it for communication, but access to the Earth networks is blocked. There are programs on it to help you learn Kawaida, and enough *fedha* per month to stop you from starving. Don't lose it, it's your lifeline. If you want more luxuries, you'll need a job. They're always on the lookout for pilots. You have flying experience, don't you?'

He nodded, speechless. She really intended to leave him here.

'What else? Oh yes.' She turned and disappeared. Before Dan could react, she was back again, carrying a rucksack and a guitar case. Both belonged to Dan. 'I hope I packed the right things,' she said, dumping them at his feet. She pulled out a small bottle of green pills. 'Take one of these every day until they're gone. They'll help with the bacteria shock.'

Zombie-like, Dan took the bottle. Bacteria shock? The lump in his throat prevented him from asking for more details.

Rowan looked at the sky and sniffed the air. 'If you get going, you might make it to shelter before the afternoon rains. Watch out for the mosquitoes here. They're nasty.' She bent down and kissed his cheek. The scent of her skin was surprisingly pleasant. Subtly citrussy. 'Good luck, kiddo. Sorry it came to this, but you only have yourself to blame.'

In a swirl of green velvet, she was gone.

Dan touched his cheek where she'd kissed him. This couldn't be real. He sank to his knees and sobbed, his tears splashing into the rust-coloured dust. Moments later, his inner voice halted his outburst: on your feet, Simpson, it said. No going to pieces. Work the problem. He stood up straight and wiped his face on his sleeve. Taking a deep breath, he shouldered his rucksack, picked up his guitar and set off down the hill.

HE FOLLOWED A stone-paved road which led him through a residential area with luxurious dwellings carved into the rocky hillside. At least, from the widely spaced, understated entrances, he assumed they were luxurious. The lower he went, the humbler they became.

At the bottom, the ground levelled out. The low houses here were built of stone, crammed together and laid out without any obvious strategy. There were no roads between them, just a maze of twisting, flagstoned paths, wide enough for two people to walk abreast and worn smooth by the passage of many feet. The overhanging roofs kept the streets dark and cool. Dan only realised it was raining when water began gushing down a drainage gully at one side.

He threaded his way through the alleyways, trying to head in the direction of the highway he'd seen from the hillside. Even when he couldn't see it, he heard the hum of the traffic. The closer he got, the shabbier the neighbourhood became. The buildings – brick tenements rather than stone houses now – were taller and more ramshackle, painted long ago in cheerful, ice-cream colours. Lines of washing hung across the street and unkempt children played between the houses. As he passed, they stopped to stare at him.

The few adult Amranese he saw made no attempt to speak to him. They didn't seem hostile, more … uninterested. Apart from their weird purple eyes, their appearance was human: dark-skinned with short, straight black hair. Dan couldn't distinguish the men from the women; all wore similar clothes. He didn't see a single person whose head reached beyond his shoulders.

The alleyway opened into a large square, filled with food stalls crowded by shoppers. The rain shower had passed and the sun's glare accentuated the market's vibrant colours like a camera filter. Out of the shade, the oppressive heat hit Dan in a body blow; every pore prickled instantly with sweat.

Shadows cast by vehicles passing overhead flashed over the wet flagstones; the square was directly beneath the highway. This was a pedestrian city, so where did the traffic come from? In one corner, he observed a tower of driverless pods hovering one above the other, and a line of people waiting, laden with shopping bags. When one pod was full, it rose to join the highway and the next descended to pick up passengers.

Dan's stomach rumbled, reminding him of his basic needs. He had no local currency and nowhere to stay the night. The few phrases of Kawaida he'd learned on the ISS weren't going to cut it.

Not knowing where to go or how to find a lodging, Dan decided to try something he hadn't done since his teenage years in Boston – busking. Perhaps someone would give him something to eat, at least. He found a spot on the edge of the square and got out his guitar. Sitting on his rucksack, he began to strum. The familiar melodies returned swiftly to his fingertips: Tom Petty, Don McLean, The Eagles, Bob Dylan. The old favourites. Gaining confidence, he started to sing.

IT DIDN'T TAKE long for a crowd to form, although it was like playing to a wall. Dan couldn't detect any emotional response on their faces. Nobody threw a donation into the guitar case he'd laid out so hopefully. But he persevered and his silent audience grew.

Among the Amranese, he saw the occasional 'alien' face peering at him. Others not from these parts, like him. All sizes and colours, all humanoid. Some hairy, some entirely bald. A movement in the back row caught his eye – a single figure was swaying in time to the music. Female and taller than the locals, with silver skin and tightly braided electric-blue hair.

As he watched her dance, a heavy hand descended on his shoulder. Dan turned: the hand belonged to a police officer (he presumed), one of a pair sporting fuchsia body armour. He couldn't understand a word they said, but guessed he was in trouble for performing without a licence. Dan gathered his things and accompanied them to the police station.

They threw him into a cell with a dumpy creature covered in green fur. He was surprised at how strong they were for their size, until he remembered what Rowan had said about the gravity. Probably everyone here was stronger than him.

He eyed the green creature cautiously. When Dan had entered the cell, it had taken one look at him and rolled over in its bunk with its back to him. It obviously didn't regard Dan as a threat, or find him interesting.

Rather than being frightened, Dan was furious with Rowan, the *Shantivira* and the shadowy Galaksi Alliance for putting him in this situation. Rage at his powerlessness churned his stomach, sending his mind into a destructive spiral. He fantasised about revenge.

+ + +

THE DOOR TO Dan's cell opened with a rusty creak. A beaming officer beckoned to him and Dan sat up, confused by the officer's sudden friendliness. He followed him (her?) along a dingy corridor to a room where more magenta-clad officers were scrutinising his belongings. One bowed to Dan respectfully and touched the screen of Dan's new *zana*.

It projected a holographic figure in formal robes, speaking a pre-recorded message. Dan had no idea what the message was, but he recognised Aldeman, the leader of the Syenitian Council. The police officers must know Aldeman too, seeing as their attitude to Dan had changed so dramatically. It seemed it was in their interests to look after him.

When the message had finished, the officer placed the *zana* in the top pocket of Dan's rucksack and the others repacked Dan's stuff. He noticed they handled his guitar with particular reverence. Perhaps they'd enjoyed his playing after all.

They escorted Dan to the roof and climbed into a hot pink transport pod. The officer in front tapped coordinates into a screen and the pod rose to join the flow of traffic. It was unlike any road Dan had ever seen. The pods rafted up and sped through the air so fast his eyes could barely focus on his surroundings. Above and below, rows of vehicles rocketed past on multiple levels: the highway was thicker than it was wide.

After a few minutes, their pod peeled away and struck out across the city. The aerial perspective helped Dan understand it better: the buildings all had a landing pad on top, with the remaining roof space filled by flashing advertisements and shop signs. From the ground it had appeared medieval – now he saw this was a modern civilisation after all.

The pod flew on autopilot, jerking and swooping as it avoided other aircraft. By the time they landed on a nondescript roof, Dan felt distinctly nauseous. He followed the officers down countless stairs to the ground floor, where they stood before a door, waiting.

Waiting for what? After a moment's awkward silence, an officer pulled Dan's shoulders down so his head was level with what he'd assumed was the intercom. He blinked as a pulse of light scanned his face, then the door clicked open. Oh! The officers pushed him gently through the door and, without saying goodbye, trooped back up to the landing pad.

His new home was a narrow, high-ceilinged room with plain white walls. Glass doors at the far end opened onto a small courtyard shared with the other buildings on the block. A compact kitchen with a table and two chairs made the most of the natural light. No sofa, no entertainment system.

A wide ladder accessed a double bed on a platform above the entrance area. Below, sliding white doors revealed a tiny shower room and a generous cupboard. All was spotlessly clean. A glow of relief spread through Dan's chest. Things were looking up.

4. A RESCUE AND A REUNION
JOE, MARCH 2015

J OE WAS IN the control room of the *Shantivira* going through the daily report with Delius, the space station's main computer, when the heavyweight cyborg paused, motionless, as he processed an incoming signal.

'What is it, Delius?' said Joe.

'The DSV *Ariane* has lost contact with Björn Cederlund's diving bell, Captain. The *Ariane* has been blown off course in a storm and is still travelling away from the dive site. It's not looking good for the divers. They're 180 metres below the surface. If they've no hot water supply, hypothermia will set in in minutes.'

The *Shantivira* didn't usually monitor staff's family members, but since her husband's job as a saturation diver was so dangerous, Tima had talked Joe into making an exception.

'Don't tell me,' said Joe, 'they didn't see the storm in the forecast.'

Last December, during their desperate battle to prevent a Ranglatiri pirate frigate from surviving to tell other Ranglatiri about the Earth's riches, a piece of its wreckage had destroyed a major weather satellite. Now forecasts were less reliable than they had been.

Delius said, 'I would imagine so, sir.'

Of course, they were lucky it hadn't been worse. The frigate's shields had been utterly impenetrable: some new technology, still being analysed at the government labs in Essoona. Joe had had to persuade Kitty to break the enemy ship apart from the inside. This had involved her absorbing the life energy of everyone onboard the frigate – including a cargo hold packed with prisoners. The energy rush had caused her to revert to her original space demon form and grow uncontrollably, giving her an insatiable appetite and driving her temporarily insane. He still felt guilty about it, but he hadn't seen another way to protect the Earth. As it was, once she'd lost her self-control, their telepathic connection had almost fried his brain. *And she'd nearly consumed the* Shantivira's *fleet of fighters.* Only a miracle had saved them.

She'd been drifting through the galaxy for months, keeping away from all life until she could regain control. Their telepathic conversations (always in Welsh) were no substitute for his wife's physical presence. They hadn't been apart this long since his army service. He missed her terribly: a permanent dull ache in his chest during the day and a chilly, empty bed at night.

Joe closed his eyes and reached out with his mind, smiling as he made contact.

Cath? he said. *Time to come back. You're needed.*

Needed? asked Kitty.

Björn's at the bottom of the North Sea and his support ship's been blown off course. The Ariane's *lost contact with the bell, so either it's detached or they're being dragged along behind the ship.*

Not good, either way.

Do you need the coordinates?

Kitty paused, locating Björn's individual biosignature. *No. I have him. You can watch through my eyes.*

Joe opened his eyes and looked at Delius. 'I've called her back.'

'Won't she still be too volatile, sir? It's only been a few months.'

'It's worth the risk to help Björn. Anyway, she was getting bored. A bored Kitty's worse than a volatile one.'

'Shall I contact Tima, sir?'

'Wait ten minutes. I don't want to worry her unnecessarily.'

Joe's eye's glazed over as he tuned into what Kitty was seeing. It had become a regular habit: every time she spotted some amazing astronomical sight, she'd share it with him. Through her eyes, he'd seen things the Hubble telescope operators could only dream of. All he saw now was darkening brownish water.

Are you shrinking? he asked, as the light faded to blackness.

As fast as I can, she said. *Look—there's a light. Shit, it's worse than I imagined.*

One diver stood by the diving bell, his neck craned up at Kitty. Not Björn: he was smaller and slighter than Joe's friend. The helmet prevented Joe seeing his face, but he assumed the man was petrified by the appearance of the space demon's monstrous red feet, disembodied in the darkness. Kitty was shrinking rapidly, so the diver must be able to see up to her hips. Which meant he'd see her tail, too. Twice as long as her scaly legs, this had knobbly scutes running down to the tip, like on a crocodile. Or, indeed, a dragon. Poor sod, he thought, recalling his own terror the first time he'd seen the 'real' Kitty.

Joe knew saturation divers worked in threes: a pair in the water, inspecting or repairing underwater infrastructure such as oil pipelines, with one person staying in the bell. So where was the other diver? Oh.

Is that Björn?

It is.

Is he still alive?

Unconscious. The cold will help.

Björn lay on his back, his right leg trapped under the diving bell's frame. The bell must have detached from the *Ariane* and fallen, pinning the unfortunate diver to the seabed.

At least it's below the knee, said Kitty.

Can you fix him?

Maybe. First things first.

Kitty stretched out a black-clawed hand and picked up the diving bell as if it weighed no more than a can of fizzy drink. She put it down gently – beside Björn, instead of on top of him – then shrank until she was no taller than a Syenitian.

Kitty scooped up Björn's limp form and made for the opening under the diving bell. She shoved him headfirst through the cramped hole and, when the other diver came to help, teleported inside. In one fluid movement, she pulled Björn up and sat him on a coiled-up cable. The bellman yelled in shock.

'Help the other one,' she barked at him in a low-pitched growl, and focused on removing Björn's helmet.

Joe was surprised to hear her speak aloud. In her original form, her physical voice usually emerged as infrasound: lower than humans could hear.

He remembered diving bells were filled with a mixture of helium and oxygen, making the divers' voices high-pitched and squeaky. It must be doing the same for her, bringing her voice into the audible range.

Kitty used Björn's dive knife to cut away his suit and boot from the damaged leg, revealing a bloody mess of crushed tissue between the knee and foot. Eew.

Can you save it? he asked silently.

Don't know. It's worth a try. You can watch, but don't distract me, OK?

JOE HEARD THE other diver explaining to the bellman how this creature had appeared and lifted the bell off Björn's leg. Whatever she was, she was here to help. The bellman calmed down enough to say they'd lost contact with the *Ariane* and were running on emergency supplies. The diver confirmed, 'Yeah, after you sent the call to abort, the bell moved, dragging us behind. The main umbilical and the lift wire must've snagged 'cause the bell shot up and we dangled beneath. There was this terrible creaking, groaning noise the whole time, then the cables snapped. I got clear before the bell hit the seabed; Björn wasn't so lucky.'

'Was it her?' said the bellman. He must mean Kitty, thought Joe.

'She came after. I stood there like a lemon before she showed up, wondering what the hell to do. If it *was* her fault, it was an accident. Look, she's trying to help him. One thing's for sure, we've detached from the ship and we're on our own.'

'I'll get the survival packs; we need to put our thermal suits and scrubbers on.'

Hearing this, Kitty's head snapped round. 'Just the scrubbers,' she growled. 'You're in no danger of hypothermia – I'm radiating heat – but I can't prevent CO_2 build-up. Leave the bell scrubber on for Björn. We'll give him his personal one when he regains consciousness.'

'Do you think he will?' asked the diver.

'Why are you helping us?' asked the bellman.

'Björn's a friend. Of course I came, the minute I heard you were in trouble. He's going to be fine. Maybe I can save his leg, but I need to work fast – and I must concentrate or I'll join up the wrong blood vessels and it'll be for nothing. So stay quiet and don't ask questions until I'm done.'

The bellman cleared his throat nervously. 'Ma'am? You should wear the extra scrubber. We need to keep the CO_2 down or in a few hours it'll poison us.'

'Not me,' she said, and Joe assumed she'd treated them to a toothy grin because the bellman and the diver jumped back in alarm. 'I only breathe to speak or smell stuff. I'm not changing the atmosphere in here. You,' she pointed at the bellman, 'help me remove Björn's suit. I'll lift him … that's it.'

When they'd stripped Björn down to his undersuit, she sat back on her heels. 'Thanks,' she rumbled. 'Now, stay out of my way. Help your colleague with his kit and put your scrubbers on. Tell me if the thermometer goes above 34 °C.'

Kitty sat cross-legged, very still, touching Björn's leg with one hand and his foot with the other. Joe sensed her mental effort as she tried to channel her excess life energy along the right pathways. Slowly, the bones began to reform, growing down from the knee and up from the foot. Then came an intricate web of veins, arteries and blood vessels, suspended in the air by an invisible force. It took hours. Joe tuned in and out, planning next month's duty roster and giving Björn's wife Tima progress reports.

OK, moment of truth time.

Joe watched as the blood began to flow, spreading through the reassembled network like a time lapse film of tree branches growing. After a few minutes, it was clear the blood was circulating normally.

Thank you, thank you, thank you, said Kitty and, far above on the *Shantivira*, Joe could sense her relief and satisfaction. *That was the tricky bit,* she said. She flicked her tail, hitting the diver behind her in the face.

Clearly more relaxed in her presence than he had been a few hours ago, he pulled away his mask and said, 'Oi, Godzilla, watch it, will you?'

Joe sniggered. *Godzilla! I'm so going to start calling you that!*

Kitty didn't react, except to lay the offending append-age across Björn's shoulders, like a warm scarf. Deep in concentration, she continued her work, adding a network of nerves, then muscles, fat and skin, layer by layer. Björn's foot twitched and his eyes opened. He grinned at Kitty.

'*Hej,*' he said in his native Swedish, 'you're back from your vacation?'

Up on the *Shantivira*, Joe punched the air, ecstatic.

You did it! Well done, babe! Tell him welcome back from the dead from me, will you?

Kitty laughed: a gravelly rockfall sound. Björn noticed his crewmates recoiling at the sight of her canines, and tried to reassure them by touching his thumb and forefinger in the divers' signal for 'OK'. He patted the tail around his neck.

'You're scaring my buddies, Kitty. Can't you get changed?'

'Sorry. I was busy,' Kitty grunted in English, shifting into her Syenitian form. The slightly pointed ears and waist-length black hair stayed, but the tail disappeared and milk-pale skin replaced the red scales. Whichever form she took, she couldn't disguise her space demon nature entirely: the pupils of her iridescent green eyes were always vertical slits and she could only hide her predator's teeth by keeping her mouth almost closed. This explained why, if she didn't want to talk to anyone except Joe, she generally chose to appear as a black jaguar.

'Clothes, Kitty, clothes!' Björn chuckled, also switching to English. 'Wait until I tell Joe my workmates saw his missus in the altogether!'

'Oh. Good point.' Kitty's familiar medieval red dress materialised around her: her default choice of clothing, but entirely inappropriate for a diving bell. Or, indeed, the modern world. That's my girl, Joe thought, imagining the flowing velvet brushing against his skin. Not much longer. Soon they'd be together again.

Kitty said, 'Joe's been watching and listening in. He says hi.' Now her voice was high-pitched and squeaky, like the rest of them. She turned to the other two. 'I'm Kitty.

Sorry I didn't introduce myself before.' She extended a slender hand for them to shake, which they did, hesitantly. 'I forgot my manners. Anyway, the news from topside is a huge storm blew your ship off course. That's why you got detached. But the storm has passed and they're coming back for you.'

The diver took off his mask. 'Who are you?' he asked.

'*What* are you?' said the bellman. 'Where did you come from? Why are you helping us?'

Kitty said nothing, leaving Björn to fill the silence. 'Let's say ... my wife has friends in low places.'

Joe felt Kitty smile. She reached behind her back and, as if by magic, a *zana* appeared in her hand. She offered it to Björn. 'Do you want to make the call?'

He looked at her blankly.

'You should tell the *Ariane* you're coming back up,' she said. 'They need to be ready for you.' She handed him the device. 'It's dialling the dive control room now. Audio only.'

'Hello?' said a voice.

'Gordon! It's Björn Cederlund.'

'Björn! Thank God! Are you OK? How are you talking to us?'

'Oh, we've been having adventures, but we're fine. I just wanted to tell you we'll be on our way up soon.'

'I'm afraid it'll take a bit longer; we're waiting for the support team to come from the mainland and reattach your cable. They need another twelve hours. Can you hold on that long? Are you keeping warm? You've been offline for six hours. What's the bell temperature?'

'That's what I'm saying: we don't need to wait. Cancel

the team – we'll be up within the hour.'

'What? Björn, how are you talking to us? I don't understand.'

'Just be ready. Goodbye.' Björn disconnected before Gordon asked more questions.

Kitty took the *zana* and stood up. 'Right, I'll be off.' She kissed Björn on the cheek. 'See you soon, no doubt. I'm looking forward to going home.'

The bellman was confused. 'Where are you going? How will we get back up?'

'Not your problem,' Kitty winked. 'I'll bring you up slowly; monitor your seals. If anything leaks, bang on the walls and I'll stop your ascent.'

Björn reached up and squeezed her hand. 'Thanks,' he said.

'Anytime,' she said. 'Watch your depth gauge. Bye, guys.'

JOE'S VISION WENT black. *You've teleported outside?* he asked.

Yeah. Back to nearly full size, standing up as slowly as I can. How far is the Ariane? *And in which direction?*

Five kilometres east.

The black water turned brown as Kitty's head neared the surface. Cradling the diving bell and its precious cargo against her stomach, she began to walk. *I can hear the engines,* she said. *Not long now.* Ten minutes later a dark shape loomed ahead. *There it is. Where's the moon pool?*

Joe watched as she slotted the bell into the access hole in the bottom of the ship. She pushed it upwards slowly, waiting for feedback that the crew were attaching the crane. At last, the bell lifted away from her hand. By the time it cleared the water, she'd materialised on the *Shantivira*, her arms around Joe and her lips against his.

+   +   +

THEIR TONGUES REACQUAINTED themselves: warm, moist, exploratory. Eyes closed, Joe inhaled the luscious scent of her skin, simultaneously stroking her hair, her neck, working his way down the soft contours of her body. Eventually, he broke away to draw breath.

He held her at arm's length, studying her. *How are you?* he asked. *Are you safe?*

I think so. Still fizzy, but I can keep a lid on it. I won't need to feed for weeks.

Welcome home, cariad.

Sorry I missed your birthday.

Can't be helped.

Kitty turned, aware of Tima standing behind her. Beaming with tear-stained relief, Tima threw her arms around Kitty's waist and hugged her fiercely, mumbling, 'Thank you! Thank you!' into the red velvet of her dress. Kitty returned the embrace and kissed her friend's black curls. 'Happy to help,' she said out loud, her physical voice strange to Joe's ears after their long separation.

Touching is nice, she said in a private aside. *I'd forgotten how good a cuddle feels.*

Let me remind you. He encircled her from behind, pressing himself against her.

Tima released Kitty. 'You two must have a lot of

catching up to do. You should take some holiday, Joe.'

'I should. Not until after the staff meeting, though. I have news for you all.'

WITH KITTY'S RETURN, there was a celebratory atmosphere at the senior staff meeting. The *Shantivira's* conference room was in traditional Japanese style, with paper screen walls and *tatami* mats. A water feature trickled at the far end, but the space was otherwise unfurnished. The crew sat on the floor in a large oval.

Joe watched, amused, as Kitty – in her favourite black jaguar form – worked her way round the circle, affectionately nuzzling her colleagues. She was a tactile person, better able to express her pleasure at being home again non-verbally. This worked both ways: the team's natural response was to stroke her and scratch her head. In her Syenitian form, Kitty frequently came across as alien and formidable, even to those who knew her well. As an Earth creature she was more approachable – despite her obvious wildness.

Her circuit complete, Kitty flopped down beside Joe and rested her head on her paws, listening attentively as each department head made their report. After the general update, it was Joe's turn. He ran his hand along Kitty's spine and patted her flank. 'Now Kitty's home, our teleports are working again. We can get back to business as usual.'

After the team's cheers, whistles and applause had died down, Joe cleared his throat.

'You all know I've spent the last few months negotiating with the Syenitian Council for permission to approach the UN. Those negotiations are now complete. We're authorised to inform them of our existence and offer a limited technology transfer, enabling the Earth to develop its own shield generators and gravity generators for space travel. I'm preparing to initiate contact as soon as possible.'

A murmur rippled around the room.

'I have a question, Captain.'

'Yes, William?'

'Are you aware Dan Simpson has disappeared?'

The rumour mill had been working efficiently. No surprise there.

'Yes, I am.'

'Do we have anything to do with it?' William asked bluntly.

Joe knew he wouldn't survive one of his friend's cross-examinations for long. Before joining the *Shantivira*, William had been a disability rights lawyer in New York; being 130 cm tall himself had motivated him to help others who struggled in a society designed for the able-bodied. He was skilled in asking penetrating questions.

Joe wasn't supposed to discuss it, but he owed his colleagues as much truth as he could give them. 'Dan's safe and well. Unfortunately, we had to remove him for his own protection.' Joe pursed his lips, still regretting how things had turned out. 'He planned to reveal details of our operation to NASA, before we could approach the United Nations – in direct violation of our agreement. He'll be returned as soon as the UN knows as much about us as the ISS astronauts do. I can't say any more, I'm afraid. He has no partner or children, but I'm sure his parents are worried.'

I should check up on him, shouldn't I? came Kitty's voice in his mind. *Rowan told me she left him on Amra, in the Elegua sector. A bit harsh, if you ask me.*

Yes, said Joe. *Do that. But stay and help me out with the UN first. I need you to get me past their security systems. Give Dan a chance to settle in. It might be the making of him.*

There was a thoughtful silence, broken by Hagar asking, 'What about the ISS? The three newest crew members only know us from your *zana* calls with Takeshi. Shouldn't we re-establish fresh food deliveries, now Kitty's back? We need to maintain good relations with the ISS so they can speak well of us when they return to Earth.' She paused. 'After it's official with the UN, I mean.'

Is she still doing the long-distance relationship thing with Simon-the-ISS-climatologist? Kitty asked.

Yup. He's due to go home soon. They'll be able to meet in person.

And in private.

And in private, Joe agreed.

We can start this Friday if you like, said Kitty.

Joe looked across the circle at Maneewan, their head of catering. Last year, she'd relished the challenge of preparing a weekly picnic basket for consumption in microgravity.

'Maneewan?' he said out loud. 'You up for it?'

The creases around Maneewan's eyes deepened as she smiled. 'Just let me know when you need it.'

'Champion,' said Joe. 'I'll talk to Takeshi.' He stood to

indicate the meeting was over. 'Right. I'm taking the rest of the day off. Tomorrow too. I don't want to be disturbed unless it's an emergency. I must reacquaint myself with Mrs Llewellyn.'

TOGETHER, THEY STROLLED back towards Docking Bay 3 and *The Pride of Essoona*, Joe's liveaboard spacecraft. When the dragonfly-shaped vessel came into view, the jaguar at his side shifted to her Syenitian form and rested her hand on his shoulder.

Joe, wait. Before we get ... distracted, I want to visit the memorial for the pilots we lost.

The orchard? Sure. He turned on his heel to head for the lift, but Kitty's hand pulled him back. He heard the familiar rushing in his ears and clamped his eyes shut just in time to prevent the nausea. When he opened them, they were standing among the fruit trees in the temperate biome; the grazing flock of ducks scattering with outraged quacks at their sudden appearance.

I thought you disapproved of teleporting walkable distances? he said.

She shrugged. *I have all this excess energy to burn off.*

I have some ideas how to do that, Joe said with a smirk.

Kitty gave him a playful shove. *Patience! Show me the trees first.*

Ten saplings were dotted in gaps between the mature trees and along the edge of the field. Apples, pears, plums and cherries. On each, a wooden plaque hung from a coloured ribbon, carved with the name of the person the tree was dedicated to. Joe waited while Kitty moved from tree to tree, caressing the bark with a faraway expression. Below the hem of her dress, he observed her bare toes wriggling in the soil. He suspected she was channelling some of her surplus life energy into the trees and they'd have a burst of growth in the coming weeks.

I've known most of these people since they were teenagers, she said. *I recruited them, watched them grow up, grow older, fulfil the potential I knew they had. They were part of my family and now they're gone.*

Joe put his arm around her waist. *They knew the deal. They chose this life. If you hadn't stepped in, well, it doesn't bear thinking about.* He imagined the *Shantivira's* forests on fire, humanity enslaved and the green Earth reduced to a dusty wasteland. That was the only future a planet had if the Ranglatiri got hold of it. *You saved us*, Cath. *You kept your promise. Thank you.*

Kitty looked away. *It didn't cost me my life though, did it?*

Just as well. The Earth needs you, cariad.

I killed thousands of innocent people along with the Ranglatiri crew, Joe. Whole families, destroyed in an instant. When I consume someone, I feel them intimately: their hopes, fears, their connections to the people around them.

No wonder she'd lost it that day. He'd asked too much of her. He was as responsible for their deaths as she was.

They were prisoners, he reminded her. *Their situation was hopeless. You saved them from a worse fate: slow death by slavery, being eaten alive by those monsters, who knows. We'd tried everything else. We had no choice.*

There's always a choice, said Kitty. *We chose the Earth.*

That was the right thing to do. We did our jobs. But it doesn't stop me feeling it. She sighed and pulled down a cherry branch to smell the blossom. *I never asked,* she said, *how did you inform their families when you couldn't get down to the planet?*

The pilots we lost? he said. *Mary did most of it: she knew them from their time at the language school.*

Tough job.

Tough lady. Full of Yorkshire grit. I'm sure she made a better job of it than I would have. Now you're back, we'll be able to invite the friends and relations up here for a proper memorial service. Although, he paused and pursed his lips with disapproval, *a couple had never told their families what they really did for a living. Can you believe it?*

Kitty's jaw dropped, then she snorted with laughter. *Pot. Kettle. Black, Joe!*

That's different.

It is not.

My mother is not *my family.*

One of us would have to inform her, though, if something happened to you. You need to tell her the truth, Joe.

Not this again. Time to change the subject. *Hey, do you want to hear something funny? When I did the birthday phone call last week, she told me she has a boyfriend!*

A boyfriend! Like, a toyboy? Kitty allowed herself to be deflected.

My impression is, he's the same age as her. Mr Evans he's called. A Welsh speaker. She didn't say much, but she sounded perkier than usual. She was waiting for him to take her out for lunch. At Peterstone Court, no less.

Kitty raised her charcoal eyebrows. *Oooh. Grace is going up in the world.*

I think he might be quite rich. He must be insane, voluntarily spending time with the passive aggressive empress.

You have to forgive her, Joe.

You always say that. Joe turned and started walking away from her.

And I'll keep on saying it. I understand why you feel the way you do, but it's not good for you, carrying all that hatred. Put it down, love.

I can't, he insisted. *The best I can do is not ever think about her unless I have to. Cath, let's forget it for now, OK? I don't want Mam spoiling our reunion. Let's go back to the* Pride *and have sex until bedtime.*

5. ESSOONA WEEKEND
HANNA

H ANNA STRETCHED OUT her arm. The paintbrush just reached the corner; she wouldn't need to climb down and shift the stepladder over after all. Her brush dripped, depositing a crimson blob on Lucy's head.

'Aargh, watch it, Hanna!'

Aneira and Farida, working at a safe distance, giggled.

'Sorry!' said Hanna, not particularly repentant. Lucy had wisely come wearing overalls, but hadn't covered her hair. She ought to have borrowed an old hijab from Farida, Hanna thought. Out loud, she said, 'It matches the green nicely.'

'Yeah, you look like a traffic light!' Farida chuckled.

'Ha ha. Anyone got some orange?'

Aneira stepped back to admire their handiwork. 'Not bad for a morning's work, ladies. Four more to go, then we can go to yours for lunch.'

Now they'd settled into a routine, they had more energy to enjoy life in Essoona. They'd wanted to paint a *maalaus* – street art on giant panels provided by the city for citizens to express their creativity – since their first visit. After much discussion, they'd split their canvas into twenty-four squares to create an eye-watering patchwork reminiscent of the skirts Hanna used to make. Hanna was doing white polka dots on a red background, Lucy green and white stripes, Farida yellow triangles and Aneira sine waves in shades of purple. You could see the clashing colours from the end of the street.

'Hey,' said Lucy. 'That reminds me, I found out how Mr and Mrs Park came to Dunia House.'

'Oh?' said Hanna, descending the stepladder.

'Don't tell me,' said Farida, 'they're from the North and they ran away from the regime.'

'You knew?' said Lucy.

'Suspected. I asked Mrs Park if they'd ever go back to Korea or the Earth in general, and all she'd say was they could never go back or "they" would find them. That nowhere on the planet was safe from "them". Then she got all flustered and changed the subject.'

'I don't think they ever talk about it,' said Lucy. 'I found out from Aussie Ozzy's girlfriend.'

'Jangmi's back?' said Hanna. Hassan's best friend's girlfriend was a green-skinned, plant-based gardener from Echanua, who'd returned to her parents' farm last autumn to spend the cold months in hibernation. During spring and summer, she helped Mr Park grow food to supply Dunia House. They weren't self-sufficient, but their efforts contributed to the household significantly.

'I met her on the allotment last weekend, when Felix and I were planting peas. She doesn't know much Earth history, but she said they tried to swim from the "dangerous" part of their country to the "safe" part.'

'In the open sea? Isn't that whole coastline heavily guarded?' said Hanna, beginning her final square. You might as well commit suicide, she thought. 'They must have been desperate.'

'They were,' said Lucy. 'They had no wetsuits or floatation devices. Jangmi assumes their families were executed or sent to labour camps. If they'd been caught, the same would have happened to them, so they swam for it. But a current dragged them far from the coast. They'd have drowned, but Kitty was mermaiding nearby and found them. She brought them to Essoona and they were too traumatised to ever return to the Earth. Not even for a visit.'

'That's so sad,' said Hanna, thinking: more of Kitty's waifs and strays. Like her and Hassan, like the Pweza (the giant octopuses who'd tried to invade the Earth last year and had been rehomed on Syenitia instead) and who knew how many others.

'Sounds like they got lucky,' said Aneira.

'Depends on your definition of lucky,' said Farida, looking at Hanna, clearly thinking about Hanna's own history. 'They lost their family and can never go home. Will you hold the ladder for me, Aneira?'

They kept going until all the squares were filled. They ought to have come back later, after the paint had dried properly, but when Farida suggested this, none of them had the patience. They peeled off the masking tape and stood back to absorb the full effect. A glow of satisfaction spread through Hanna's belly. Not perfect, but close to what she'd been trying to achieve.

'Wow,' said Lucy. 'That's the most impressive piece of art I've ever done.'

'Me too,' said Farida.

Hanna caught Aneira's eye. She'd done a number of *maalaus* and had been an invaluable source of practical tips. Aneira tilted her head. 'It's the most *vibrant* one I've done. Should've brought my sunglasses.'

Farida pulled out a paper bag of *jelimbegu* and passed them round. Hanna took a handful and chewed, letting the delicious fruity flavour spread through her mouth. The first time she'd tried them, she hadn't believed they were the seeds of the yellow *auringukka* flower which grew anywhere it could take hold. They were as sticky and sweet as one of her Earth favourites: jellybeans.

'We should celebrate,' said Lucy. 'Not just this, but in general. It's been a tough few months and we haven't had a proper party yet. Anyone got a birthday coming up?'

'Mine's on 15 April,' said Hanna, 'but I've never had a birthday party. Last year was the first time anyone gave me presents.'

Lucy looked stricken. 'You've never had a birthday party? Not one?'

Hanna shook her head and Lucy enveloped her in a lung-crushing hug. Letting go, she said, 'We'll have to do something about that. How old will you be?'

'Twenty-one.'

Lucy goggled. 'Twenty-one? You're coming of age? Getting the keys to the house?'

Confused, Hanna said, 'I already have the keys to the house. What's special about turning twenty-one?'

'It's when society considers you an adult. Traditional-ly.'

Hanna sniggered. She'd considered herself an adult since her periods had started. Since the orphanage had trafficked her to the UK to work as a cleaner with no payment except bed and board – effectively a domestic slave. She bit her tongue, managing not to say *Do the British take that long to grow up?* out loud. Luckily, Lucy wasn't one to notice the subtleties of human reactions and was still in full flow.

'The fifteenth ... we could have it two weeks from today. Not much time, but I'm sure Mrs Park will help. We should keep the guest list below a hundred ... You'll need to tell me who you want to come, Hanna, but you can leave the rest to us. Right, girls?' she said looking at Farida and Aneira, who agreed enthusiastically.

A hundred guests? Hanna wasn't sure she even knew a hundred people. 'Lucy, wait. Nothing too big, all right? Just our year, and Hassan and Aneira. Irion and Mary if they can make it. Don't go overboard, promise me?'

Lucy pushed out her bottom lip. 'OK. I'm not sure where I'd find a marquee and a bouncy castle here at short notice anyway.' Seeing Hanna's face, she said, 'Joke! Hanna, this is going to be amazing. Relax. You won't have to lift a finger.'

THEY RETURNED TO Dunia House, going round the back to put away their painting gear in the shed and wash their brushes in the big sink in the utility room. They trooped into the kitchen, ready to raid the fridge for lunch. Mrs Park normally let them fend for themselves at weekends, so they were surprised to see the table laden with colourful delicacies, including Hanna's personal favourite, *Haemul Pajeon*: seafood and spring onion pancakes.

At the head of the table sat a blond giant, head bent over his bowl, shovelling in noodles with chopsticks. Hanna recognised him instantly: Tima's husband, Björn. Mrs Park sat beside him, watching him eat like a proud mother. What was *he* doing here?

He looked up and smiled a welcome. '*Hej*, guys,' he said in Kawaida. 'Would you like to join us? Song-Yi's made far too much food. Again.'

'I didn't know humans came that *big*,' Aneira whispered.

Björn roared with mirth. 'We haven't met, have we?' he said. He stood and offered Aneira the traditional Syenitian hand-press greeting. 'I'm Björn. I used to come here all the time when my wife was in her second year. Years ago now, but Song-Yi hasn't forgotten me.' He winked at Mrs Park, who tittered like a teenager, hand over her mouth.

'How could I, the amount you put away?' she scolded. 'And you and Tima still drop by occasionally. When are you going to bring the children again? Isn't Sören starting school soon?'

'He's at *förskoleklass*,' said Björn. 'He'll start proper school in August.'

'They grow up so quickly, don't they?' said Mrs Park with a sigh.

'What are you doing here, Björn?' asked Lucy, with characteristic directness.

'Got a job interview on the west coast tomorrow. They need divers to act as intermediaries between the Pweza and the folks on land while they're building their new city.'

'You're not staying in the oil industry?' asked Farida.

'No. I've chucked it in. It was time. The fossil fuel industry isn't future-proof. And I can't square it with my conscience anymore.'

THAT AFTERNOON, HASSAN came to pick her up for one of their regular walk-and-talks. They'd begun them last year when Hassan had lived at Dunia House, updating each other on their lives and exploring the city at the same time.

After a long kiss hello, Hassan said, 'I have a surprise for you. A magical mystery tour.' When alone, they always spoke Nuer, their shared mother tongue.

'But I wanted to show you the *maalaus* we did this morning!'

'I'll look at it later, before I go back. I've booked us a pod; it's waiting outside.'

'Ooh, fancy,' said Hanna. Individual transport pods were expensive to rent, so usually they went everywhere by tram or bike. 'Are we going out of town?'

Hassan nodded. 'Further than I can walk.'

Hanna followed him out of the grand front entrance. In the street, a strip of long grass and shrubbery bordered the wide pavement, separating them from a busy cycle track. More grass and flowers fringed the main carriageway beyond. Hanna saw a stationary pod directly opposite them, identical to the others swooshing past.

Would they be sensible and walk to the pedestrian crossing at the end of the block and back up the carriageway shoulder to their pod? Or take their chances and cross the cycle track right there?

Hassan shot her a mischievous grin. 'Let's make a run for it.'

'No risk, no fun,' Hanna said, quoting Joe's infamous motto.

'After these guys,' said Hassan, jerking his head at a rapidly approaching pack of Syenitians. They sprinted to the middle line and waited for a gap in the flow, then they were over and standing on the grass. Hassan waved his *zana* at the door handle and the lock clicked. He held the door open for Hanna. 'Your carriage awaits, Madam.'

Hanna giggled and climbed in. The pod contained two upholstered benches, with space for six average-sized life forms to sit facing each other. As soon as Hassan shut the door, the pod lurched into the flow of traffic, docking onto a platoon of four pods.

Hanna studied the route marked on the screen. Their destination was several kilometres north-west of the city boundaries. Travel time: forty-two minutes. 'You're still not telling me where we're going?'

Hassan smiled and shook his head. 'You'll see. Do you mind if I take my feet off? I had a long shift dematerialising space junk this morning.'

'Sure.'

He unfastened his black and silver boots and tossed them on the floor. With a sigh of relief, he swung his stumps up into Hanna's lap and she began massaging them.

'So what's everyone else up to this afternoon?' he asked.

'Farida's studying of course. We'll go to the baths later, after you've gone. Lucy's on a bike ride. The others have gone rock climbing, you know, the ones who used to climb in London. Nikolai's started going with them; he's lost loads of weight.'

'How's he getting on, not smoking?'

'Tough initially, but he's traded the nicotine rush for endorphins. I don't think he's ever been properly fit before; he's enjoying it. Doesn't spend as much time on his *zana* as he used to.'

'Are you any closer to finding out who took the SD card?'

Hanna shook her head. 'I haven't dared confront anyone. There's no proof and I don't want to falsely accuse anyone. You think it's Nikolai, don't you?'

'I can't see anyone else taking it. Not you, me or Farida. If Lucy had wanted it, she'd have just kept it. Felix isn't interested. Possibly Saïd; he's tech-curious. And I remember the look on Nikolai's face when he handed the chip to Lucy. Reluctant, you know? It's only a hunch, but yes, he's my chief suspect.'

'Hassan?'

'What?'

'I still have nightmares about David sometimes. That hole in his chest.'

Hassan swung his legs down and put an arm round her shoulders. 'Like Ibo?' he asked, understanding immediately that David's murder had awakened the long-suppressed trauma of her brother's death. Hanna buried her face in Hassan's jacket. 'Sometimes I dream it's Ibo that Nestor shoots, instead of David. And there's nothing I can do to stop him,' she sniffed.

'There was never anything you could have done, Hanna. For either of them.'

She sat up again, dragging the back of her hand across

her eyes. 'I know. In my head, I *know* that. But still …'

'Yeah.' Hassan put his arms around her, and she leaned into him. They sat in silence, watching the colourful wooden tenement blocks flash past, their exteriors covered in solar panels and greenery: different mosses, grasses and ivy, depending on the way the building faced. Hanna said, 'I also wonder what happened to Nestor and his sidekick.'

'I expect he's licking his wounds somewhere. He's not our problem, Hanna. Leave him to Joe and Kitty.'

The built-up zone ceased abruptly and now they were travelling through fields and orchards. Like the *Shantivira's* biomes, they were planted with a seemingly haphazard combination of crops and trees, which Hanna knew was carefully calculated to maximise the long-term yield from that particular area. The dense planting meant most agricultural work had to be done by hand. Luckily, finding seasonal manual labour wasn't an issue. City dwellers received a fortnight's paid leave a year to work on a farm of their choice, staying on-site in state-sponsored accommodation. At busy periods, the farms had a holiday-camp atmosphere, with people frequently returning to the same place to work with friends they'd made in previous years.

Essoona itself wasn't at all like London, the only other city she knew well. There were no suburbs with individual dwellings and large gardens. All the U-shaped residential buildings were six storeys high, arranged in eight pairs around a large central square closed to motorised traffic, except for deliveries. Each pair of apartment blocks shared a secluded outdoor space between the facing open ends of the two 'U's, as well as a generous 'village green' for all sixteen buildings. The edge of this public zone was taken up by allotments and the centre held an amenity for the wider community: a school, a park, a sports centre or, in Dunia House's case, a bathhouse.

This grid pattern continued to the city limits. No two squares were alike and exploring them was one of Hanna's favourite pastimes. Essoonians did most of their shopping locally, their daily needs catered for by small businesses in the tenements at street level: bakeries, grocers, fishmongers, small supermarkets, banks, post-offices, cafés, restaurants, second-hand shops and repair centres. It was like a village: you saw the same faces each day. Mr Park knew *everyone*. People passing the Dunia House allotment stopped to chat so often, he'd worn a smooth patch on the wooden fence from leaning on it.

'Nearly there,' said Hassan, putting his prosthetic feet back on.

They crested a hill and Hanna gasped at the view of undulating meadows filled with rows of prickly green balls. 'It's a *Tumba* farm!' she squealed in delight. Ever since she'd learned *Tumba* hulls were organic, she'd wanted to see them growing.

Hassan beamed. 'I knew you'd like it.'

The pod halted outside the gate to the visitors' centre and Hassan programmed it to wait.

He showed his ID to the Syenitian female at the reception and explained he'd reserved a place on the next tour.

'It's a military facility, so it's a tour or nothing, I'm afraid,' he told Hanna.

The ten others in their group were all Syenitians. The

tour leader was a weathered male, his pale skin tanned from a life outdoors. They followed him into the fields and stopped beside an almost full-sized shell. The man launched into a detailed and enthusiastic explanation – of which Hanna understood not a word, because he was speaking Syenitian. Damn. A look at Hassan told her he wasn't getting any of it either, despite months of learning the language in his spare time. 'His accent!' muttered Hassan. 'Excuse me,' he said more loudly, 'would it be possible to do the tour in Kawaida? We don't speak Syenitian.'

The tour guide looked troubled. 'Sorry! Me ... Kawaida ... notverygood.' He said something to the other guests and a female stepped forward. 'I'll interpret for you. My name is Tirivan.'

'Thank you!' Hanna treated the woman to one of her widest smiles and introduced herself and Hassan. Slowly they proceeded along the path, with Tirivan summarising the guide's minutes-long description at each station.

The spiky shells were all different sizes, planted in no discernible order. Each plant had a similar growing area, big enough for an adult *Tumba*. After a few medium-sized ones, they came to a patch with a tiny *Tumba* at the centre, perhaps twenty centimetres across.

'A baby!' exclaimed Hanna. 'It's so *cute*! But it looks lonely with all that space around it.'

Tirivan explained the *Tumbas* were networked underground via ancient fungal cables. 'They're not lonely: they're communicating all the time.' She pointed to a larger version. 'See that thick stem going into the ground? Not only does it draw water and nutrients from the soil, it shares them with its brothers and sisters, along with information: weather reports, parasite alarms, who knows what else. When a *Tumba* is fully grown the whole stem area is removed – that's where the spacecraft door goes – and they're shipped to Aldina to have their electronics fitted. Afterwards, they can communicate with almost anything, but not with their younger siblings back in the nursery.'

'Do they know what's going to happen to them?' asked Hassan. 'It must be traumatic, being cut off from their family.'

'Good question,' said Tirivan, and put it to their guide. He shook his head and Tirivan translated his answer. 'All attempts to connect retired *Tumba* fighter craft with the fungal network have been unsuccessful. So no, they have no idea what will happen to them. The period when they're not connected to anything is kept as brief as possible, otherwise they wither and die and can't be used as spacecraft.'

Retired *Tumbas*. Hanna had a vision of Tulu at the end of her life, her green skin withered and wrinkly, relaxing in the sunshine with her aged *Tumba*-colleagues.

Curious, she asked, 'What happens when a *Tumba* reaches the end of its service life?'

'The electronics are removed and they're mulched, generally as fuel for their home space station.'

'Oh.' Poor Tulu. Then again, that *was* the circle of life. Her thoughts turned to Samuel, resting in peace beneath his Wanza tree on the *Shantivira*. The tree had grown more than half a metre since they'd planted it, not even two years ago: it was comforting to think of her miniature baby's remains being part of a new life.

THEY WALKED ON to a hollow in the hillside and entered a dark wood which hadn't been visible from the road. Gnarled, wild trees jostled for space, life bursting forth everywhere Hanna looked. This was no plantation but primeval forest: an ancient green-canopied eco-system with a tangy, moisture-laden microclimate. Hanna had an uncanny sensation that the trees were watching them.

'This is where the parent trees live,' said Tirivan. 'Where the *Tumba* seeds come from. *Kastanja* are very rare and not easy to grow. That's why the nursery is located here: *Tumbas* will only grow if they're linked to the family fungal network.'

There was no path. Hanna glanced at Hassan, but he seemed to be doing fine on the uneven ground. Noticing her concern, he squeezed her hand wordlessly. They picked their way along the mossy bank of a fast-flowing stream until their guide took a sharp left turn. After a few metres struggling through the undergrowth, they stopped in front of a mighty trunk, scarred and pitted with age. The tour leader pointed upwards and, among the broad leaves, Hanna spotted clusters of miniature *Tumbas* dangling from the branches.

'They don't pick them,' translated Tirivan. 'They wait until the seeds fall off the tree and collect them before they take root. His team comes to search for them every morning.'

The tour finished. They headed back the way they had come without stopping for more explanations. Just as well, because Hanna's head buzzed with all the new input. She wondered if Tulu had grown up here and, if so, which tree she'd come from.

They thanked Tirivan and the guide, and returned to their transport pod. Hanna programmed it to take them to her *maalaus*. There were plenty of cafés round there; they could have a cup of *saiju* before they went home.

+ + +

AFTER DINNER, THEY said goodbye and Hassan stepped into the teleport in the first-floor stairwell of Dunia House. From outside, it looked like a wooden door decorated with traditional Syenitian carvings of interwoven plants and insects. If an ordinary visitor opened it, they'd find a broom cupboard stacked with dusty junk. But if your biosignature registered you as belonging to the *Shantivira*, you'd see the space station's bright white cylindrical lift, which doubled as a point-to-point teleport to Dunia House.

After he'd gone, Hanna stood gazing out of the window at the trees encircling the ornamental pond in the courtyard below. Were they talking to each other too? Did the trees on Earth do the same? Probably. She checked her *zana*. Time to find Farida for their trip to the bathhouse.

She was just turning to go when the teleport door swung open, narrowly missing her shoulder. A stocky, blond man in jeans and a motorbike jacket strode out, almost bumping into her. Joe.

He pulled up short and apologised with a blue-eyed twinkle. 'Sorry Hanna, had my head in the clouds, as usual. How are you?'

'Good, thanks.' She told him about her excursion to the *Tumba* farm, while an idea uncurled in the back of her brain. 'Joe, do you have time to talk?'

He flipped out his *zana* and checked the time. 'Not really. I'm meeting Aldeman at a bathhouse five blocks from here. Unless you want to walk and talk? Is it important?'

'Yes,' said Hanna. 'Can you wait five minutes while I get Farida? We were going to the bath in our square, but it would be good to try a different one. It … um … does have separate parts for men and women, doesn't it?'

Joe's face crinkled into a grin. 'It does. Like all the others. Two minutes. I'll be by the front door.'

Hanna ran up to her room, where Farida was packing away her homework. She grabbed their bath rucksacks and told Farida her plan. Together, they hurried to the entrance hall where Joe was leaning against the wall, staring into the middle distance: the expression he habitually wore when speaking to Kitty. According to Irion, Kitty's telepathic link was with just two people: her sister, Rowan, and her husband, Joe. Rowan could only talk this way to Kitty and her own husband, Aldeman. It was so rare for the space demons to find a mortal whose mind they could connect with, Hanna understood why they'd married.

'Wow,' he said, 'that actually was two minutes. I'm impressed.'

He held the door open for them and they went out into the night. 'So, what's this about?'

'David Wang's SD card.'

'Oh. *That.*'

'Did Mary tell you it was missing?'

'She did.'

'Irion asked me to try and find out who took it.'

'Ah. And have you?' He turned to look at her, studying her face.

'Well, no. There's no proof. I have a chief suspect, but I don't want to stir things up unnecessarily.'

'A chief suspect?' Joe's lips twitched, as if trying not to laugh. Suddenly serious, he said, 'Don't tell me.' Hanna opened her mouth to argue, but he held up a hand to stop her. '*Really,*' he insisted. 'I don't want to know. It doesn't matter who took it. Kitty knows where it is and swears it's in safe hands. Sometimes it's best not to ask too many questions. Don't worry about it. And don't pursue it: that's an actual order from me to you both. I mean it, Hanna. Drop it.'

Hanna glanced at Farida, who raised her eyebrows. 'OK. Sure.'

6. TURNING 21

HANNA

A S HER BIRTHDAY drew closer, Hanna couldn't help feeling nervous. Of course she'd been to parties before, but never one held in her honour. What should she say? How should she behave? Would they expect her to make a speech?

Lucy and Aneira had been on overdrive and, all week, whenever she'd wandered into the kitchen, Mrs Park had shooed her out again, saying she didn't want to spoil the surprise. But Hanna didn't *like* surprises. What were they up to?

As a distraction, she found time to experiment with new hairstyles: eventually settling on a few inches of cornrows above her forehead, with the rest of her hair fluffing out behind in its usual halo. She'd worn it in a plain afro since shaving her head for Samuel's funeral. After almost two years, she had enough length to be more creative.

Finally the big day came. Lucy had banned her from the lounge and Mrs Park had banned her from the kitchen, so she spent a pleasant morning on the allotment, planting potatoes with Mr Park. Hassan arrived, boosting her confidence by complimenting her new hairdo. They lunched at the local noodle bar, then teleported back to the *Shantivira* for a swim.

Afterwards, they strolled hand-in-hand through the temperate biome forest to Samuel's grave, where Hanna laid some white *asmini* flowers she'd picked during their walk. As was their habit, they sat in quiet companionship at the foot of the Wanza sapling.

Hanna had come here daily after losing her pregnancy, five months after being raped by her former landlord. Eventually, time and the soothing atmosphere of the clearing had worked their magic. Despite the circumstances of his conception, she still mourned the child who had never been. Then again, Samuel's death had brought her to her new life with Irion and Mary, the *Shantivira* and Hassan. Maybe it was meant to be.

Hassan squeezed her hand. 'Can I give you my present now, while I have you all to myself?'

'Please do.'

He pulled a gold-edged red leather box out of his pocket. It was the wrong kind of box for a ring: too big and too flat.

'Here,' he said, pushing it gently into her hands.

She opened it.

Inside a bed of dried moss nestled a golden oval locket, engraved with an ornate letter 'H', on a fine gold chain. It glinted warmly in the sunlight.

'Do you like it?' asked Hassan eagerly, studying her face.

Carefully, she took it out and let it dangle from her hand. 'It's beautiful!' She leaned over and kissed him. 'Thank you!'

Hassan reached out and clicked a tiny catch on the side of the locket. 'Look,' he said, 'it has space for two photos.'

'One of you, one of Irion and Mary,' she said, deciding. 'I *love* it.' She closed it and weighed it in her palm: heavy enough to be solid gold. 'Is it an antique?' she asked.

'It's second-hand,' said Hassan. 'No idea how old it is. I bought it on the Portobello Road.'

'Will you help me put it on?'

'Sure,' he said, and did. 'So, Birthday Girl, they don't want us back until after sunset. Any idea what you want to do until then?' He waggled one eyebrow suggestively, making her giggle.

'Actually, I do. Not *that*,' she said, patting his knee. 'I want to go to *Laulaahaalia*. I've haven't been since last year.'

Hassan was astounded. 'Why ever not?'

'I didn't want to go without you.'

Hassan's face creased into a smile. He checked the universal clock on his *zana*. 'We'd better get going, then. Will you help me up?'

Hanna stood and pulled Hassan upright. They hurried along the forest paths, across the fields and through the farmyard. On the horizon, the Earth was rising: a semicircle of swirling blue, green and white. However much of a rush she was in, it always stopped Hanna in her tracks. Syenitia might be pretty to look at from space, but the Earth was in a different league. There wasn't another planet like it.

They returned to the main space station through the exterior hatch in the hull, crossing the accommodation deck to access the lift in the central column. The lift ran pole to pole through all seven levels of the space station, but they didn't need it to move a centimetre. Hassan keyed in the command for the Dunia House teleport, pressing his palm on the screen to authorise it.

Seconds later, they stepped onto the first-floor landing, going straight downstairs and out into the street, heading for the community centre two blocks away. Unlike the roofs of most buildings in Essoona, which were covered in a mixture of solar panels and rooftop gardens, the single-storey community halls had a glass dome as their only source of natural light. *Laulaahaalia* was a beloved Syenitian custom, marking the transition from day to night with communal singing. Irion had taught them some popular songs last year.

They were bang on time: the bells announcing the service were already ringing. Holding hands, Hanna and Hassan joined the queue and filed in, taking their places in the snail-shell spiral marked on the floor. This was divided into different colours to match the text which would soon be projected on the wall. As always in a crowd of seven-foot-tall Syenitians, Hanna felt particularly short. The only place to look was up at the sky: still blue, but the light visibly draining away. A session generally lasted half an hour, depending on the weather and the time of year.

Hanna's unknown Syenitian neighbour bowed a polite greeting and took her free hand. She still found it hard to tell the men from the women, but she guessed he was male. On the other side of Hassan was a slender Sayari female, silver like Irion, but with her pink hair twisted into Bantu knots, reminding Hanna of the flowers which grew from Jangmi's head. Hassan greeted her respectfully and held her hand.

Once the coiled chain of people was complete, the hubbub died down. The person at the centre began to sing, joined by other voices to build rhythmic waves of sound. There was no accompanying music and no audience; the sole purpose was the spiritual experience of singing in a group.

Hanna wasn't sure she recognised the tune until she saw her own part high on the opposite wall, scrolling down in purple. Oh, that one. OK. She started singing and let the melody transport her as she watched the sky above darken into a starlit indigo night.

When the last voice faded away there was a moment of perfect silence, then the room filled with chatter. Hanna's neighbour said goodbye and released her hand. Hassan leaned down and murmured, 'Party time!' in her ear.

They returned to Dunia House and went straight to the lounge on the first floor. The high-ceilinged, wood-panelled room was packed with friends: her cohort from Dunia House, others from their year including Aneira and Elian, a couple of Farida's classmates, Aussie Ozzy and Jangmi, as well as Mr and Mrs Park, Tima, Björn and their three kids, Kitty and Joe (an unexpected honour) and—

Hanna squealed with joy and flung herself into Irion's waiting arms, burying her face in her soft white robes. Then she did the same to Mary's mustard-coloured jumper. 'It's so good to see you!' Although the teleports had been up and running again for a month, what with one thing and another, they hadn't found time to meet up.

Someone thrust a glass with a pink paper umbrella

into her hand and the humans plus Irion and Kitty sang 'Happy Birthday', followed by cheering and laughter.

The sofas and chairs had been pushed back to the edges of the room, making space for a dance floor and a buffet. A rather wonky birthday cake took pride of place on the table, liberally coated with yellow butter icing and decorated with blue and pink sugar flowers. Hanna counted the candles: twenty-one.

'Do you like it?' asked Lucy, 'Me and Felix made it. It doesn't look very professional, but it should taste OK.'

Hanna was touched. 'That's so sweet of you! I look forward to trying some.'

She hugged Lucy and Mrs Park. 'Thanks for setting all this up. You must have worked so hard!'

'It was our pleasure, dear,' said Mrs Park. 'We all need a good get-together every so often.'

Lucy said, 'You're popular, Hanna; everyone wanted to help. Hey, that's new, isn't it?' She pointed at Hanna's locket. 'It's lovely.'

Hanna smiled modestly. 'Hassan gave it to me.'

'He has good taste, hasn't he?' Hanna detected a slight wistfulness in Lucy's voice. 'I wish Felix was romantic like Hassan. Do you know what he got me for my last birthday?'

Hanna shook her head.

'A pair of those cowhide clogs from the Allgäu, like he wears round the house here. You know the ones?'

Hanna nodded. Like in Ethiopia, cows were an essential part of the culture in Felix's alpine region of Germany. Traditionally, no part of the cow was wasted. Felix's clogs always made her smile. The thick brown-and-white hair made his feet look like two furry creatures, scuttling across the floor.

'I mean, they're fabulous,' said Lucy, 'handmade and *so* warm. They'll last forever. But they're not exactly sexy.'

Hanna thought Lucy fortunate to be given such a gift. But, on reflection, she liked her new locket more.

DJ ROBERTO HAD selected a mix of old and new Ethiopian music, from 1970s jazz to modern pop – including Yegna, Hanna's favourite band. People were already dancing and she felt her own hips twitching with the rhythm, but Hanna knew she ought to greet her guests first.

After an in-depth catch-up with Irion and Mary, she took a moment to enjoy some deep-fried chicken with pickled radishes – another Mrs Park speciality, best enjoyed with cold beer. As she ate, she watched Elian teaching Aneira to dance. Hanna knew the Amranese had zero music culture and Aneira really wasn't getting the idea. He was uncharacteristically close to her, one hand on her shoulder, the other on her hip. Aneira couldn't stop giggling and Hanna detected a spark of chemistry beginning to work its magic.

'Happy Birthday, Hanna,' said Kitty's voice behind her. 'Love the new hair.'

Hanna turned away from the dance floor: Joe stood there too, holding a plate of fried chicken.

'Thank you both for coming,' she said politely.

'I wasn't going to miss out on Song-Yi's *chimaek*,' said Joe. 'Happy Birthday, Hanna.' He twinkled at her and took another bite.

Kitty looked round at Hanna's guests. 'You're obviously integrating. How do you like life on my home planet?'

'School's tough, but I'm learning a lot. I love the way everyday things are organised here: how they prioritise quality of life and interactions with people, you know?'

Joe swallowed his chicken. 'Having experiences rather than stuff? Yeah. Although actual stuff is so expensive here, going shopping is like bleeding money through your nose.'

Kitty gave him a playful shove. 'When do *you* ever go shopping? You hate shopping.'

'Fair point,' he said, winking at Hanna. 'But the ability to delegate is an important skill.'

'It's the right way round though, isn't it?' said Hanna swiftly, before Kitty could announce she bought most of Joe's clothes, including his underwear (something Hanna knew from Tima). She had an embarrassing habit of oversharing. 'I mean, that information's cheap and physical products are expensive. I've downloaded so many books and videos; I'm never going to run out of stuff to read or watch. And local shops are cheaper if you pay with Essoona pounds instead of Alliance *fedha*.'

'True,' said Joe. 'I'm not much of a reader, but I've built up quite a music collection. And the repair shops are great. I still use the same *zana* from my first days on the *Shantivira*. It's had a few upgrades since then.'

Björn and Tima joined them. 'Happy Birthday, Hanna,' said Tima. 'How's your course going?'

Hanna pulled a face. 'Our flight instructor's not as nice as you. Astro-geography is a *nightmare*. Otherwise, fine, thanks. What about you? Did Björn get the job?'

Björn beamed. 'I did! I begin next month. They're short-handed for the construction work. Most Syenitians aren't willing to give up their urban lifestyles and rough it on the west coast. But it'll be like a vacation for me. There's a thought: is there anyone here with diving experience who'd be interested in helping out at weekends? It's only ninety minutes away by train.'

'Lucy's a qualified diver,' said Hanna. 'You could ask her.'

'Nikolai, too,' said Kitty. 'Make sure you ask him.'

'I will,' said Björn. 'Thanks.'

Hassan's friend Ozzy came over, his arm around Jangmi's green shoulders. Echanuans were plant-based, photosynthesising their energy from the sun. They tended to be agricultural workers as they needed extended periods outside, in daylight. Hanna and Hassan had privately nicknamed Jangmi 'the flower fairy', due to the pink blossoms growing from her scalp and her scanty outfit of oversized leaves. In fact, the leaves weren't clothes, but part of her body.

'Hi, Joe,' said Ozzy. 'You've met Jangmi?'

'Of course,' said Joe. 'Hello, Jangmi.'

Jangmi laughed, a sound like miniature wind chimes on a breezy day. 'Jangmi is what Mr and Mrs Park call me. My real name is—' Jangmi emitted a high-pitched, ululating tone which lasted for several long seconds. Hanna resisted the urge to cover her ears.

'Right,' said Joe, his eyes widening. 'Do you mind if we stick to "Jangmi"?'

She laughed her tinkly laugh again and Ozzy said, 'Joe,

would it be possible for Jangmi to come and work in the *Shantivira's* biomes?'

'Well, there's no actual vacancy at the moment,' said Joe, rubbing his stubble. 'And what would Min Joon do without you here?' Kitty flashed him a look and Joe nodded. 'Good idea,' he said. 'Jangmi, I'll organise an exchange. There must be someone who'd enjoy a spell helping on the Dunia House allotment.'

'Thank you! Thank you!' Jangmi squealed.

Hanna had supposed their relationship wouldn't last beyond Jangmi's winter hibernation, but she was happy to be proven wrong. Next year, she too would be on the *Shantivira* with Hassan and their two years of long-distance relationship would be over. There'd be no separating them then.

Kitty reached for Hanna's hand. 'We can't stay, I'm afraid. Joe's meeting Aldeman at the bathhouse and I'm seeing my sister.'

'Oh, that's a shame,' said Hanna. 'Say "hi" to Rowan from me.' A thought occurred to her. 'Will the teleports stop working while you're away from our solar system?' She didn't want to advertise it, but she'd been planning to spend the night with Hassan in his cabin on the *Shantivira*.

Understanding immediately, Kitty winked at her. 'Don't worry, Hanna. There's a day's time lag before the system notices I've gone. I can visit other places without causing chaos.'

'It was great to see you both.'

'Bye, Hanna,' said Joe. 'Enjoy the party.'

They left the room holding hands and Hanna looked

round for Hassan. He was on the dance floor with Roberto, Farida, Saïd and Felix. Behind them, Aneira was getting the hang of moving to the music.

Hanna watched them, intending to join in once she'd finished her drink. Nikolai appeared at her shoulder.

'They make a nice couple, don't they?' he said, jerking his head at Aneira and Elian.

Hanna looked up at him. 'Do you think so? I heard he was going out with Briavan.'

Nikolai snorted with amusement. 'Briavan pestered him into going on one date with her – total disaster. She talked non-stop about herself and he had to get a mate to send him an "urgent message" so he could escape. He's been avoiding her ever since. He'd rather be with Aneira, if she'll have him.'

'I'm surprised he came, to be honest,' said Hanna. 'I had the impression he felt humans were a bit beneath him.'

'He's cool, Hanna. Give him a chance.' Nikolai took a swig of his beer and Hanna followed his eyes to Hassan and Roberto, who were dancing a theatrical comedy tango. Roberto even had a flower clamped between his teeth. Amused, Nikolai grinned at her. She grinned back.

Should she ask him? No. She definitely shouldn't. But she might not get another chance like this. Whatever Joe said, she must know, for herself. She didn't have to tell anyone else.

'Nikolai?'

'Yes?'

'You remember that SD card from David Wang?'

'Yes?'

'It's missing.'

'Missing?' He sounded surprised. 'What do you mean, missing?'

'Gone. Someone took it from its hiding place. One of us.' She took a deep breath. 'I hate to ask, but was it you?'

He turned to face her; his frown so deep his dark eyebrows almost touched.

'No! Hanna, why would you think that?'

She examined his grey eyes for signs he wasn't telling the truth. He held her gaze without flinching.

'I swear it wasn't me. I haven't got it, OK?'

Either he was telling the truth, or he was a much better liar than Lucy had been last year.

'OK,' she said. 'Sorry. I just wonder what happened to it.'

'How long's it been gone?'

Hanna finished her drink and placed the glass on a nearby table. 'Irion doesn't know.'

'Perhaps it got mislaid,' he said. 'I can't believe one of *us* took it.'

'No,' said Hanna, slowly. 'Neither can I.'

A shadow fell over them and she turned to find Björn standing behind her. 'Do you mind if I borrow Nikolai for a minute, Hanna?'

'He's all yours,' she said, shooting Nikolai an apologetic smile. 'I'm going to dance.'

THE MUSIC HAD switched to a rhythmic ballad; Hanna took Hassan's hand and swung his body towards her. His eyes sparkled as he pulled her close, matching his hip movements to hers. Hanna pressed her head against his chest and inhaled his familiar, calming scent. The whirling in her head slowed a little. She *wanted* to believe Nikolai. He'd almost convinced her. But if he wasn't the thief, who was? She knew Nikolai was good at concealing things; he hadn't told anyone his mother was an ex-Shantiviran until Farida had spotted her name on David Wang's list – the list with the identities of everyone who'd served on the *Shantivira*. All though last year, he'd been lying about his mum by omission, apparently at her request. Perhaps secrecy ran in the family. Hanna didn't know *what* to think.

'You OK?' asked Hassan.

She closed her eyes and let the music guide her. Joe said the SD card was in safe hands and he'd actively ordered her not to pursue it. It wasn't her problem. Everything was OK. The people around them faded away: it was just her, Hassan and the music. She'd missed his physical presence terribly during their long separation. Knowing she'd be in his arms every weekend gave her the strength to handle anything life threw at her. It's all good, she told herself. It's all good.

'Yes,' she said. 'I'm OK.'

WHEN SHE OPENED her eyes, Aneira and Elian were dancing close together nearby. They'd be a couple before the end of evening or Hanna would eat her socks.

Eventually they retreated to the big sofa, where Roberto was listening to Nikolai's discoveries about Syenitia's parallel virtual world. In London last year, via their *zanas*, they'd been able to access the books, films, music and games offered by the Library in Essoona. Nikolai had always been more digitally adventurous than the rest of them; now he was cruising the unofficial corners of the planetary network too – the gambling sites (commercial gambling was forbidden on Syenitia, but the authorities turned a blind eye to 'unofficial arrangements' between 'friends'), the markets for illegal products and substances, and dubious forms of entertainment not sanctioned by the Library authorities. 'Just to see what's out there,' he'd argued when Saïd had challenged him.

That didn't mean Nikolai had stopped visiting the Library. He dropped by in person several times a week, researching the technologies different species had added to the Syenitian store of knowledge over the centuries and making handwritten notes in the black A4 notebook he carried everywhere with him.

Hanna suspected there was something driving him: it was as if he meant to learn as much as he could while he had the chance. Last year, he'd taught himself Syenitian in addition to studying Kawaida, so he also understood the information the Syenitians didn't bother translating for the wider interstellar community. Could someone be *too* curious? She hoped it wouldn't lead to trouble.

Aneira and Elian pulled up chairs and joined them. Aneira gulped her drink. 'Thirsty work, dancing,' she said. 'And more fun than I expected.' Her eyes locked onto Elian's; he sipped his beer and gazed back at her. Hanna raised her eyebrows at Aneira, who responded with a Mona Lisa smile.

Nikolai was still talking, saying how hard it was to get

on a tour of the Library tower. 'I heard there are as many storeys below ground as there are above. And it must be the tallest building in Essoona!'

'It is,' said Elian. 'Have you been to the restaurant at the top? The view's fantastic.'

Nikolai shook his head. The *Shantivira* might pay well, but their budget didn't stretch to the Library restaurant.

'I'm afraid it's not true about the lower levels,' Elian continued. 'But the deeper underground floors do extend below Kirjasto Square.'

'Even under the tree?' said Hanna, thinking of the ancient white *tammi* tree at the square's centre.

'Even under the tree.'

'How come you know so much about it?' asked Hassan.

Elian looked at Hassan. 'You're not in our year, are you? I haven't seen you before.'

'No,' said Hassan. 'I'm on active duty already. A couple more months and I'll be fully qualified.'

'Ah. Well.' Elian cleared his throat. 'Merian, the Head Librarian, is my mother.'

Aneira stiffened. 'Seriously?'

'You honestly didn't know?' he said. 'I did wonder if you were politely not mentioning it.'

'*That's* why the others suck up to you so much. Your mum's the actual Minister for Knowledge.' Aneira muttered something in Amranese which Hanna guessed was a swear word. 'Do you know the other Council members?'

'She tries to keep her family life separate from her work. I know them by sight. I want nothing to do with politics – I just want to be the best pilot I can be.' Elian grinned. 'I think that's why I enjoy hanging out with you and your friends, Aneira. I can be myself without worrying about people's hidden agendas. I hope that's not going to change?'

'Don't worry, Elian. We won't hold it against you,' said Hanna.

'So, Elian,' said Nikolai, leaning forward with a glint in his eye, 'can you get us on a behind-the-scenes tour?'

'The server levels and the deep archives? Leave it to me.'

7. AFRA

DAN

I T WAS TWO months since Dan had arrived in Laro. He'd adapted to the heat and no longer noticed the extra effort the increased gravity required. It had been a steep learning curve, but he was finally settling in.

He'd spent the first few weeks exploring the narrow streets between his flat and the river, and studying Kawaida on his *zana*. Thanks to his astronaut training, perpetual learning was an ingrained habit and he picked up the language quickly. Soon Dan was having conversations with his neighbours about what to do with his rubbish and the best places to buy food.

Shopping was a revelation. He scanned the items with his *zana* and that was it. If only he'd realised how to pay for things on the day he'd first arrived, he could have saved himself a run-in with the police. He'd been so shocked and disoriented, he hadn't understood Rowan: the Syenitians were funding his stay here. An easy life. Until one day, it wasn't. The green light that flashed when he bought something turned red, and the shopkeeper snatched back her wares contemptuously. He'd used up all his *fedha* for that month. Dan would have to find a job.

After a confusing visit to the job centre, Dan went to

the post office and became a door-to-door delivery person. Piled high with packages, his trolley hovered above the ground, making it easy to push. Special goggles with a head-up-display showed him the route he should take to deliver the next parcel and the allotted time to do it. His new uniform consisted of pastel pink shorts and a matching T-shirt. From what he'd seen, the Amranese used shades of pink to identify representatives of the State: the darker the pink, the more important the official.

The maze of streets in downtown Laro soon became familiar territory. Even when off duty, people in Dan's neighbourhood would recognise him and nod hello. The work was physically demanding: he often had to jog to the next set of coordinates to keep within the allotted time. This, combined with the effort needed to overcome the extra gravity, meant Dan was stronger and fitter than he'd been in years.

The hours outdoors had tanned his skin several shades darker and, lacking a supply of razors, he sported a neatly trimmed beard. His military haircut was a distant memory. Rather than attempting to explain what he wanted to a hairdresser, Dan had let his hair grow. Dark curls already covered his ears.

One morning he was making deliveries in an unfamiliar part of town, close to the river. When the door opened he recognised her immediately: the silver alien who'd danced to his music the day he'd arrived in Laro. Close up, he saw her shoulder-length blue hair was flecked with green. She was as tall as he was, her appraising brown eyes meeting his, head-on. She obviously remembered him too. She didn't smile but, from the sparkle in those eyes, he thought she was pleased to see him. And now he could talk to her.

'Hello.'

'Hello.'

'I'm Dan. What's your name?'

'Afra.'

'That's a beautiful name. Can I invite you out to dinner, Afra?'

She said nothing, but her ears began to waggle violently.

Ignoring his question, she asked, 'Are you still playing your music?'

'Not publicly. That didn't end too well the last time. Just at home, on my own.'

'That's a waste. The Amranese don't have much of a music culture. You should try some of the bars around the spaceport. You might have more luck there. In fact,' she paused as she scribbled a set of coordinates on a scrap of paper and handed it to him, 'try this place. Tell them I sent you. It's a bit rough, but you look like a man who can handle himself. You don't want to be a delivery boy for the rest of your life, do you?'

'Thanks,' Dan said, surprised, looking at her curly handwriting.

'So, do you have anything for me?'

'Huh?'

'I'm expecting a package, about this big?'

'Oh. Yes, of course. Sorry. Here you go.'

'Thanks Dan. See you around.'

Without waiting for a reply, she shut the door in his face. Dan pocketed the scrap of paper thoughtfully and resumed his round.

Dan hadn't yet been to the spaceport, which stood on drained marshland beyond the river. After work, he plugged Afra's coordinates into a taxi pod, curious to see where it took him.

Situated on the route between many of the planet's major cities, Laro's wealth had always come from commerce, and now it was an outpost for trading goods from other worlds. The spaceport was the town's main employer. It covered a huge area, its warehouses and gantry cranes reminding Dan of the Conley container terminal back home in Boston. Like any other port, the area around the docks was full of people from faraway places, looking for a good time.

Now he found himself in a deserted backstreet, outside an establishment with peeling yellow paintwork called *The Garden*. Dan couldn't see an actual garden or any greenery at all. Picture panels on the walls showed scantily clad females doing strange things with snakes. What was this place? The lights on the neon sign flickered permanently. There must be a faulty connection. As his pod rose in the air to return to the taxi rank, he experienced a frisson of physical fear. This didn't look like a place for law-abiding citizens. Taking a deep breath, he pushed open the door.

It was dark inside. Apart from a few solitary drinkers, the bar was empty. The Amranese bartender was emptying the dishwasher and Dan waited until he stood up.

'Yeah?'

'Um. I'm a musician? Afra said you might be able to give me a job?'

'Afra Azu who loves the colour blue?'

Was there another Afra? 'Yes,' Dan said.

'Well, we do have a couple of free slots. Our last band got blasted for being too boring. You can have their nights until they're out of hospital, starting tonight.'

Dan's pulse quickened. Was he ready for this? 'Gee, that's great, thanks! What do you mean, blasted?'

'What I said. Blasted.' The bartender mimicked shooting a gun with his hand.

Dan gulped. 'Er. Don't you want me to play a demo for you?'

'Na. If Afra Azu says you're OK, you'll do. The customers'll let you know if they don't like your stuff. We can talk about money if you make it through the evening.'

What am I getting into? Dan wondered, but it was too late to pull out now. Four hours later, he stepped onto the lonely, lonely podium. He had no idea what kind of a reception he'd get. The bar was full of people, most of them not Amranese. Some were familiar aliens, others were … alien aliens. Disturbingly, many carried weapons and wore body armour.

He needn't have worried. When he did his hastily prepared set, none of them turned on him. In fact, they ignored him entirely. Dan persevered, began to relax and enjoy himself. Soon he almost forgot about the crowd and played for his own pleasure. During the second half of his performance, he looked up to see Afra at one of the tables near the back, deep in conversation with a shadowy figure in a hooded grey cloak. She too wore body armour, blue to match her hair. Her boots were also blue: knee-high with rugged soles. Minutes later, the figure departed. Afra remained at the table, staring introspectively at her beer.

When Dan finished (to a total lack of applause or any sign of appreciation), she joined him at the bar and bought him a drink. Now he saw that, to go with her armour, she had a weapon strapped to each thigh. Who was this woman?

'Congratulations! They loved you!'

'They did?'

'Nobody even threw a glass at you! I've never seen it so calm in here. Not a single fight. It's like you hypnotised them.'

The bartender appeared in front of them. 'Hey kid, the job's yours if you want it. You can call me Uras.' He held out his hand, but Dan didn't take it.

'What are you going to pay me?'

'Two hundred *fedha* a night.'

Dan shook his head. 'Try doubling that and I'll consider it.'

Uras made a face. 'Three hundred. My final offer.'

Now Dan held out his hand. 'You've got yourself a deal. Call me Dan.'

They shook hands and Uras returned to work.

'You're a bit of a hustler, aren't you?' Afra said. 'I like that.'

Dan raised his glass to her in thanks. 'Where are you from, Afra?'

'I'm a Sayari from the Sungura sector. I've been based here for three seasons.'

'And what do you do for a living?'

'Oh, this and that,' she said vaguely, waving a slender hand. 'Same as you really, delivering stuff. My ship's waiting for spare parts, so I'm having a holiday.'

'You're a pilot?'

'Like everyone here, yes. What about you? Why are you in a backwater like Amra? Are you a Cylf on the run?'

Dan's cheeks flushed. 'A *Cylf*?' he choked. 'A cybernetic life form?' He wasn't sure whether to be amused or offended. 'Why would you think I'm a cyborg? And why on the run?'

'The beard, obviously,' said Afra. 'They all have beards. On the run because you're trying to blend in with the organics. Cylfs normally stick together and don't like leaving their data sources.' She leaned forward and took his chin between her fingers, examining it. 'But you don't talk like one,' she murmured, almost to herself. 'Are you a Syenitian in disguise? I've never seen a Syenitian with facial hair before. Is it real?'

Experimentally, she pushed her fingernails against the grain, making the hairs stand up. Dan jerked back, frowning. Who did she think she was, touching his face like that? Afra's hand dropped calmly back into her lap.

'I'm not a computer and I'm not a Syenitian, all right?' he said. 'They're the ones who dumped me here, miles from home. I'm no friend of the Galaksi Alliance.'

Afra straightened up and gave him an appraising look. 'Good,' she said. 'I try to stay off their radar myself. So what are you and where are you from?'

8. UN APPROACH

JOE

O N A FRIDAY afternoon, high in the Earth's upper
atmosphere, Joe was keeping the *Pride of Essoona* in
a geostationary orbit above Vienna. As he waited for
Kitty's signal, his mind returned to the report Councillor
Dalian, the Syenitian Defence Minister, had sent him
about the Ranglatiri wreckage samples he'd delivered to
her in Essoona three months ago.

The frigate had been equipped with centrally generated magnetic shielding to protect against physical impacts
from debris, projectile weapons, etc. Boringly standard.
The thing getting Dalian's minions at the Ministry of
Defence all hot under the collar was the mesh of superconducting cables covering the exterior, like a sort of
chain mail for spacecraft. This could instantly absorb and
disperse excess energy, channelling it to the ship's main
energy tanks and making the frigate impenetrable against
conventional energy weapons. At the same time, it
functioned as a full-surface solar panel, extending the
frigate's range.

The engineers had no idea what the superconducting
material was, or where it had come from. They assumed
the Ranglatiri had acquired it as spoils from one of their

raids. But they were thrilled by its potential applications, both military and civilian. Tests were ongoing.

Dalian's message accompanying the report had been typically to the point. 'I hope they do not have a lot of this material, or the Galaksi Alliance planets are doomed.'

KITTY TAPPED AT his consciousness, requesting a connection. Joe switched away from the disturbing topic and opened their private channel.

She said, *It's just the two of them left. Everyone else has gone for the weekend. Now's your moment.*

Cheers, love. Down in a minute.

He fired the top thrusters and descended as fast as he dared. Speed was essential to minimise the likelihood of being spotted, but crashing into the roof of the Vienna International Centre would scupper his mission before it started. Still, with Delius blocking all radar in this sector, he felt safe enough.

Once he reached the cloud layer, he switched on the exterior projectors. Anyone looking in his direction would only see an image of what was behind the *Pride*. Not as effective as the in-orbit cloaking device, but a lot better than nothing. He landed sweetly on the rooftop and lowered the steps. Kitty was waiting for him outside.

Well here goes nothing, he said silently. *Wish me luck.*

Kitty kissed him firmly on the lips. Good luck. I'll get you inside, as close as I can, then I'll guide you from up here.

✦   ✦   ✦

JOE PADDED ALONG the empty corridor. *Nice carpet.*

Isn't it? Take the next left, said Kitty, *then it's the third door on the right.*

Joe obeyed and read the sign on the door. Director, Susan Omondi. United Nations Office for Outer Space Affairs.

Bingo. Laters, babe.

This was it. Now or never. He took a calming breath – and knocked.

'Come in.'

Joe stuck his head around the door and saw a black woman in her late fifties sitting at a desk, her greying hair scraped back in a no-nonsense bun. He flashed her what he hoped was his most disarming smile. 'Susan Omondi?'

The Director studied him over the top of her glasses. 'Yes. And you are?'

He shut the door and held out his hand for her to shake. She didn't respond. Her eyebrows drew together in a frown.

'I'm Joe Llewellyn.' Not waiting for permission, Joe took the seat in front of her desk. He smiled at her again. 'Sorry,' he said. 'I'm just relishing the historic moment. Is it "a historic" moment or "an historic" moment? "An historic" sounds weird to me. Anyway. You're wondering who I am and what I'm doing here.'

'You don't have an appointment.'

'No.'

'Where's your security pass?'

'I don't have one. I snuck in.'

Director Omondi picked up her phone.

Joe leaned forward. In a low voice he said, 'Susan. May

I call you Susan? Call Security if you like. But you're in no danger from me. Please, give me ten minutes of your time and I'll tell you why it's a historic moment.'

He leaned back in his chair, trying to look as unthreatening as possible. 'Would you like to call in someone else so you're not on your own? It would be better to have a witness.'

Susan considered briefly, then made a call, keeping wary eyes on Joe. 'Valentin? Good, I hoped you'd be working late. Would you come along to my office? Right now? Thanks.'

They waited in uncomfortable silence until they heard a knock at the door. Valentin Ivanov entered the room and bellowed with hearty laughter when he saw Joe.

'You're finally making good on your promises?' he said, pumping Joe's hand up and down in a bone-crushing handshake. 'What took you so long?'

'I needed to get it all sewn up at the other end first,' said Joe, grinning back at him.

Valentin turned to Director Omondi. 'Has he told you, Susan? Do you know now?'

'Know what?'

Joe touched his arm. 'Mate, I haven't said anything yet. Pull up a chair.'

Valentin beamed. 'We're making history today!'

'A historic moment, you say?' Susan replied wryly. 'Would you *please* tell me what this is all about? Valentin, did you let this man in? Who is he and how did he get past Security?'

'This is my good friend, Joe. I haven't seen him for months; I had no idea he was coming today.'

'Coming today? But you thought he might be coming sometime?' Without waiting for an answer, she turned to Joe. 'You set me up. You know each other. You knew Valentin was on secondment here and he'd be the last to leave apart from me.'

Joe sat down again. 'Yep. Sorry. But we need Valentin. Now I can give you some answers. Valentin, have you got your phone? You should record this.' He waited until Valentin was ready, then said, 'My name's Joe Llewellyn. I work for the Galaksi Alliance, which is a union of intelligent life from thirty-three different planets located in this galaxy, promoting peace, trade and the exchange of ideas. I'm the captain of the *Shantivira*, the Syenitian space station which protects the Earth from extra-terrestrial threats.' Seeing Susan's incredulous expression he said, 'I know. You're thinking, "Oh God, there's a complete nutter in my office." But this is real. This is Earth's official moment of first contact with aliens. Hey, don't look at me like that! I'm as human as you and Valentin here. But my boss wants to talk to you. He's not.'

Joe reached inside his motorbike jacket and pulled out his *zana*. He placed it on the floor, the screen facing upwards. Apprehensively, Susan rolled her chair backwards. Her eyes widened as the *zana* projected several icons in the air, which Joe manipulated with practised ease to activate the communication link. He leaned back in his seat, watching the life-sized hologram he'd conjured up.

Tall and slender, Aldeman had braided his long black hair for the occasion, choosing to reveal his pointed ears. He wore heavy turquoise robes, embroidered with a sparkling thread which glittered as he moved. Joe hoped

Susan wouldn't find his brother-in-law too intimidating.

The ghostly image bowed and began to speak. The sound quality was perfect; Aldeman might have been in the room with them. Susan's jaw dropped.

'Director Omondi, I greet you on behalf of the Galaksi Alliance. Thank you for taking the time to hear what I have to say. My name is Aldeman Kivinen Estrelor Varpushaukka, I am the leader of the Syenitian Council. The *Shantivira* is one of our projects to safeguard the development of primitive civilisations.'

Susan covered her mouth with her hand, suppressing a snigger. She must think this was a hoax. Or perhaps she was nervous.

'Do I amuse you?' said Aldeman. 'Do you believe I would reveal the identity of my best human operative to you for an elaborate joke?'

Susan stared at Joe. 'This isn't a recording?'

Joe shook his head.

Aldeman said, 'Director Omondi, this is a two-way conversation.' The tone of his voice told Joe he was amused rather than annoyed. Susan dropped her hands in her lap, embarrassed. 'At this stage, I would rather you do not take me seriously and I need to persuade you this is real, than convince you straightaway but terrify you in the process. It is hard to communicate rationally with frightened people.'

'What do you want from us?' Susan asked, her voice quivering.

Aldeman sighed. 'This is not a business transaction, Director Omondi. This is a formal initiation of diplomatic relations. As is our tradition, it is we Syenitians who come bearing gifts. Let me tell you about my organisation.

'The Galaksi Alliance began as a trade federation.' He gestured with his hands and was instantly surrounded by pin pricks of white light: a star map.

'This is my home, Syenitia,' said Aldeman, pointing to a spot close to his right knee. He crouched to touch an icon on his *zana* and the planet glowed blue. A series of coloured dots appeared at the same time, in random clusters. 'These yellow lights show the Alliance member planets. The red ones show systems where we know there is intelligent life. This star over here,' he stretched his left arm outwards and upwards, 'is your sun.'

'Our civilisation is very old. We have refined our strategies for dealing with beings from beyond Syenitia over many centuries. I must emphasise we are not interested in acquiring new territory. Trade networks are important to us, but knowledge and the exchange of ideas even more so. We believe life is sacred; we have made it our mission to protect intelligent life wherever we find it.'

'Knowledge and ideas? If you're so advanced, what can you hope to learn from us?' said Susan.

'Humans are one of the most interesting and unpredictable species I have come across. Your inventiveness and adaptability are your greatest assets. We hope, when you have developed sufficiently, you will help us promote peace throughout the universe.' Aldeman smiled at Susan's cynical expression.

'We are patient. Our lifespans are many times longer than yours. Since you began sending signals into space and drawing attention to yourselves, it was agreed you should be shielded from other intelligent life so you could develop at your own pace. We put one of our space stations into orbit around the Earth four of your decades ago. It is staffed almost entirely by human personnel recruited from your planet. These humans named their space station the *Shantivira*. I believe it means 'the strength to choose the path of peace' in one of your Earth languages.

'I cannot emphasise enough the bravery of these people and the sacrifices they have made to protect their planet.' Aldeman turned to Joe. 'How many invasions did the *Shantivira* prevent last year, Captain Llewellyn?'

'Just two,' said Joe. 'One was nasty. I lost ten pilots in a matter of minutes.'

'Why this "official" first contact now?' Susan asked. 'Surely we're not ready?'

'Many on the Syenitian Council and in the wider Alliance would agree with you, Director Omondi,' said Aldeman. He looked at Valentin. 'We would have preferred to wait until you were safely past your purely capitalist era and had established a sustainable society. But our hand has been forced. Captain Llewellyn made a snap decision recently and, because of his actions, our existence is no longer a secret. Commander Ivanov, perhaps you would explain?'

'Me?' said Valentin, surprised.

'Wait,' interrupted Joe. 'I'll take the camera.'

'Um, OK. Well, back in October, the ISS was hit by orbital debris, as was one of our Soyuz re-entry capsules. So we couldn't all abandon the space station. You know that, Susan, it's in the reports. What you don't know is the strike was more serious than we made out. We were severely punctured and depressurising. Simon Rosenthal was badly wounded by a splinter that pierced the hull. I honestly thought he'd bleed out right in front of us. Even if we'd sent him home in the remaining Soyuz, he wouldn't have survived the trip. Then our communications cut out. There's a gap of several hours in the protocol. We told Mission Control we'd been repairing the wiring to re-establish communications. But that's not what actually happened.' He glanced over at Joe. 'Sure you want to do this?'

'Tell her. It's time.'

Valentin cleared his throat. 'So, the *Shantivira* pulled us into dry dock with her tractor beam. We were terrified. But Simon received immediate medical attention: he doesn't even have a scar. Then they started plugging the leaks.' He looked at Susan head-on. 'What I'm telling you is ... the ISS already carries Syenitian materials and technology. We won't give them up. They make life in orbit safer and more pleasant.'

Susan frowned. 'What kind of technology?'

'Well, apart from the materials used for the repairs, and that everyone on board has their own *zana* – that's one of those,' he said, pointing to the unit projecting the image of Aldeman, 'the main additions are the shield generators. They protect us from further debris strikes and from cosmic radiation. So future cosmonauts on the ISS won't suffer from long-term eye damage or reduced fertility. The deal was to keep the *Shantivira* a secret until Joe got approval from the Syenitians to reveal its existence to the UN.'

Susan rose abruptly and left the office, stony-faced. Confused, the three men looked at each other. Joe stopped the recording.

'Is she all right?' asked Aldeman.

Valentin said, 'I'll go check.' He returned almost immediately, looking more cheerful. 'She's punching the wall in the ladies' restroom and swearing. But I think she'll be back in a minute.'

They waited in silence until Valentin asked, 'Joe, what happened to Dan? He tried to steal a *zana* and someone like Kitty – but not Kitty – came to get it back before we landed. There's a rumour going round he's disappeared.'

Joe shifted in his chair.

Aldeman met Valentin's gaze. 'He was going to the American authorities, before we were ready. He broke his promise, more than once. You see how hard this is – you observed Director Omondi's reaction. Remember how you felt when you first found out about us? Imagine if you told ROSCOSMOS, without our backup. How would they treat you? Are you sure they would let you continue living as a free man?

'For the sake of peace on Earth, this *must* go through the UN, safely packaged in bureaucracy. No one country should have this knowledge before the others. Major Simpson is alive and well and safe. He will be returned when the information he intended to reveal is common knowledge among the Earth space agencies. I will not speak of this again. Joe will deny all knowledge if you ask him about it directly.'

The door opened and Susan reappeared. 'Sorry about that,' she said. 'Please continue.'

'We have no interest in going public to the wider world,' Joe said. 'We don't want to trigger a mass panic. But there are opportunities which shouldn't be missed. We propose teaching representatives from all the space agencies how a shield generator works. We can't give you ours: Syenitian technology uses a power source we can't access on Earth. But we can give you enough information for you to build your own. It wouldn't be alien technology, then, would it? There'd be no fighting over it, if it was available everywhere simultaneously.'

Joe clasped his hands in his lap. 'If that works out, we'd follow up with a gravity generator. Then you'd have the two technologies essential for interstellar travel. Of course, the more people who know about us, the harder the secret will be to keep. But that's OK. If knowledge about the *Shantivira* and the Syenitians trickles out slowly, people will have time to get used to the idea without having to confront the reality directly.

'So you see why we came to UNOOSA. I want to speak at the next meeting of the Committee on the Peaceful Uses of Outer Space and make this proposal to them. But if they're going to take me seriously, I'll need your help, Susan.'

'I have a question,' said Susan. 'You say your space station is defending us from alien invasion. I presume you have weapons. Why approach us instead of the Conference on Disarmament, in Geneva? If I tell my superiors about this and they believe me, that's where they'll want to send you.'

Joe's lips twitched. 'Playing hot potato? Our weapons point away from the Earth, not towards it.'

Aldeman said, 'You will receive no help from us with weapons development. We must insist the information we give you is used for peaceful purposes only. I understand why the idea of the *Shantivira* would make people nervous. We must build a working relationship over time, so we can begin trusting each other. Trust works both ways. You must earn our trust as much as we must earn yours. Otherwise, my human staff and former employees – and their families – could be at risk.'

His expression darkened. 'I have a duty of care towards them and I will protect them by all means necessary. If you want to perceive that as a threat, you can. We look after our own. Any attack on or abduction of associates of the Galaksi Alliance will have consequences.

'The Earth authorities must choose: either work with us, or pretend we don't exist and we all carry on as we are, or ask us to leave and, sooner or later, this planet will be overrun by other, less benevolent species. But you should not take any decisions until you have gathered the information you need. Remember, our long-term goals are trade and friendship. We do not want to live here. You might get the occasional tourist, but Syenitians will not settle here en masse.'

'Why didn't you go to SETI?' Susan asked.

'The people who search for extra-terrestrial intelligence?' Aldeman's mouth twitched, as if he found the idea amusing. 'Because these negotiations will be taking place between humans – there will be no Syenitians landing on this planet anytime soon. Not officially, anyway,' he said, with a sidelong glance at Joe. 'Any problems arising will be human problems, to be dealt with by human institutions. We have centuries of experience in dealing with less-advanced societies. The UN is the only Earth organisation it makes sense for us to contact. Director Omondi, if you can persuade them to deal with us discreetly, in a civilised way, you will be doing your planet a great service.

'So, I have said everything I wanted to. No doubt you will need time to digest what you have learned.' He looked from Susan to Valentin. 'I have the feeling my presence is hindering a full and frank discussion. I will leave you to it. Director Omondi, it was a pleasure to make your acquaintance. You can contact me at any time via Captain Llewellyn.' He bowed low again, and the holographic image flickered and disappeared.

A furious Susan rounded on Valentin. 'How dare you make such a decision without consulting your superiors? And keep it secret all this time! What were you thinking? This isn't first contact! It's a fait accompli!'

'Hey,' said Joe, 'go easy on him. He made the best decision he could in the circumstances. So did I. We just have to deal with the consequences. It's a new situation for all of us.'

Susan kept up her tirade for a few more minutes: venting the anger she'd suppressed while Aldeman had been speaking. When she paused for breath, Joe asked, 'Would you like to visit the *Shantivira*? It'd answer a lot of your questions.'

'Are you serious? I haven't had any astronaut training.'

Joe laughed. 'You don't *need* any training.'

'Well, let me look in my diary. I might have a few days free in a couple of weeks' time.'

Joe shook his head and grinned at her. 'You misunderstand me. I mean: let's go now. My ship's on the roof. Come and have dinner with us and meet some of the team.

He looked at his watch. I can have you home before midnight, easy. Valentin? Want to come too?'

'The *Pride's* on the roof? I thought your cloaking device didn't work in an atmosphere?'

'It doesn't. But I have a camouflage system.'

'You're telling me there's an alien spacecraft parked on the roof and no one's noticed?' said Susan.

'Well, I *hope* no one's noticed,' said Joe.

'But there'll be awkward questions if we don't check out with Security after work,' she said.

'You're right.' Joe stared out of the window. 'There's a building outside, much taller than the others? By the river?'

'The DC Tower,' said Valentin.

'I'll meet you at the top in half an hour.'

9. GUIDED TOUR

JOE

JOE WAITED FOR Kitty to pick the lock on the door between the DC Tower's roof and the public viewing platform on the fifty-eighth floor. Within seconds, it clicked and popped open.

They're walking by, she said, and dematerialised.

Joe stuck his head through the door marked '*Zutritt für Unbefugte verboten!*' He gave a low whistle and beckoned to Valentin and Susan. 'Hurry,' he whispered. 'I don't want to get caught.'

They climbed the metal staircase to the roof, past the paraphernalia for cleaning the skyscraper's windows, up to uninterrupted sky and a panoramic view across Vienna to the hills beyond.

Close up, the *Pride*'s camouflage projectors warped the light around it. You could see something big was there, but not what it was. Joe issued a command and the steps lowered with a pneumatic hiss, floating disembodied in the distorted rooftop scene.

Valentin bounded up without hesitation, disappearing at the top. But Susan's misgivings had caught up with her. 'Am I going to regret this, Mr Llewellyn?' she asked. 'Are you going to hold us hostage? Am I being incredibly stupid coming with you?'

Joe held up his hand in a mock Boy-Scout salute. 'I swear I'll have you home safe and sound by midnight. Come on, Susan. Don't chicken out now.'

'Midnight?'

'Midnight. Or I'm a pumpkin.'

Valentin was waiting in the cockpit, a large transparent ball with a control panel at waist height. 'Please, sit down,' said Joe, taking the centre of the three seats. They were saddles with backrests, designed to be straddled. 'Watch out for the automatic safety harnesses,' he warned.

Susan and Valentin jumped as the harnesses snaked across their hips and chests, securing them to their seats. 'The first time's the worst,' Joe apologised. 'Next time you'll be expecting it.'

Without touching the control panel, he uttered a string of commands in melodic Syenitian, and the ground began to fall away. They glimpsed the *Prater* with its Ferris wheel and funfair, then it disappeared beneath the clouds. The European continent diminished and Africa came into view. Now they were in space proper, looking back at the little blue orb that was home. Such a familiar image: but the original was infinitely more impressive. He said, 'Beautiful, isn't it? You're from Kenya, Susan, right?'

Susan nodded, not turning away from the window. 'Mombasa. My sisters all still live there. I haven't seen them for months. I'm a great aunt now – one of my nephews recently became a father.' Keeping her eyes on the Earth, she said, 'What about you, Mr Llewellyn? I can't place your accent, but I'm guessing you're British?'

'That's right. South Wales.'

She remained silent as the Earth shrank to the size of the moon in the night sky. Then she asked, 'Why were the g-forces so mild during take-off? Why don't I feel sick?'

'Gravity generators,' said Joe. 'They compensate the extreme accelerations during take-off and manoeuvring, and the lack of gravity in space. Do you want a quick tour of the Solar System before we go to the *Shantivira*?'

'Quick?' asked Susan, folding her arms across her chest. 'Neptune's four and a half billion kilometres away. You promised to have us home by midnight!'

'Oh, come on, Neptune's a fraction of a milliparsec away. Ten minutes, tops.'

'Please, Susan,' Valentin pleaded. 'When will we get this chance again?'

Susan pressed her palms together, her fingertips touching her lips. 'All right,' she said, dropping her hands back into her lap. 'Show us what your spacecraft can do.'

'You won't regret it, Susan. Relax. Enjoy yourself.' Joe issued a command and the stars around them dimmed and blurred. Everything outside went black.

'Would you like a cup of coffee, Susan? Or tea?' Joe asked.

'A coffee would be marvellous, thank you. Black, no sugar.'

'Valentin, would you make us all a cuppa? Or there's beer in the fridge, if you'd prefer.'

'Sure, no problem.' Valentin rose and left the cockpit.

'You have a kitchen on board?' said Susan.

'Everything I need to live comfortably. It's a fast ship, but most journeys still take weeks.'

'Where do you travel to?'

'Nowhere at the moment. I can't leave work and go swanning off for months on end. But I travelled all over the galaxy before I became captain of the *Shantivira*.

'What's the orbit of the space station?'

Joe chuckled. 'Sorry Susan, I can't tell you. Don't worry about bumping into us. We stay out of the way.'

She pursed her lips. 'I'm assuming this space station of yours is disguised like this spacecraft? Otherwise it would have been spotted years ago.'

'All our spacecraft are cloaked,' said Joe. 'Nobody sees us unless we want them to.'

VALENTIN RETURNED WITH a tray holding two mugs, a bottle of beer for himself and a plate of chocolate biscuits.

'Champion,' Joe said, taking a mug. 'Thanks, Valentin.' Outside, the stars pricked back into view and there was a sensation of gentle deceleration. Joe checked the timer on the head-up display. 'As promised. Eight minutes and forty-three seconds to Neptune.'

He twisted in his seat to rotate the spacecraft ninety degrees. When the turquoise planet appeared, Susan gasped and took pictures on her phone. Valentin did the same.

What did Valentin have to say? he asked Kitty privately as he waited.

Oh, nothing, really. I was cat-shaped on the sofa and he stroked me under my chin.

You old softie. He felt her smile.

I shifted while he was getting the drinks and told him we don't want Susan knowing about me yet. Or teleporting.

She's got enough information to absorb. So I'm going to stay hidden. Right?

Right. Thanks for the biscuits. I thought I'd scoffed them all.

Kitty laughed. I guessed we might be having visitors, so I kept a secret stash.

OVER THE COURSE of an hour, Joe took them back towards the Sun, pausing at Uranus, Saturn, and Jupiter so his guests could take more photos. After Mars, he took them to Venus. Churning clouds of sulphuric acid hid the planet's surface. 'I won't land,' he said. 'The shields would hold, but I can't justify the power it would need, just for showing off.' In orbit around Mercury, Joe checked his instruments. 'We can land here, if you like? I'll find somewhere not too hot.' The grey planet grew until featureless rocky plains were all they could see. Joe set the *Pride of Essoona* down gently and gave them time to look out of the window.

As he waited, his *zana* emitted a bleep. Joe accepted the call and it projected an ethereal image of Takeshi Yamashiro, the current ISS commander, above the control panel. 'Hey, Joe, is she going to go for it, or are we all in the shit?'

Joe looked at Susan. 'You know what, mate, I'm not sure. You'd better ask her.' He widened the camera angle so Takeshi could see the whole cockpit. The commander grimaced when he realised Susan had been listening.

'Hello, ISS,' said Susan, a smile belying her stern tone. 'You're all in on it, aren't you? I'm not committing to any decisions right now. I need time to think. And I'd have to research the legal position to decide if you're "in the shit".'

While Susan and Valentin chatted with Takeshi, Joe headed back to the *Shantivira*. So far so good. He suspected Susan was enjoying herself, despite her reservations.

WHEN THEY LANDED in Docking Bay 3, a huge hall shaped like a quarter of a circle, a small group of crew members awaited them. 'Our welcoming committee,' said Joe, grateful for the moral support.

Susan stared up at the *Koppakuoria*. Shaped like a gigantic black beetle, the spacecraft towered over the *Pride of Essoona*.

'What's *that*?' she asked.

'That's their cargo ship,' said Valentin.

They only needed the *Koppakuoria* a few times a year for supplies which wouldn't fit in the teleport. Otherwise it just sat there, taking up precious space and causing work for the maintenance team. Joe knew they ought to make better use of it, but how?

The door hissed open and Joe introduced Susan to the line of people at the bottom of the steps, like a visiting dignitary on a diplomatic mission. Which, he supposed, she was.

'This is Yisheng, my second-in-command. Dipesh, our head of maintenance, who installed the shield generators on the ISS. Flight instructors Tima and Valeri. And some of our senior pilots: Nkosi, Kazembi, Shakila, William and Latika.'

Susan greeted them graciously, not missing a beat as she bent low to shake William's hand. Behind them, the team welcomed Valentin back with much hugging and laughter.

At the end of the line, Susan looked back at the *Pride of Essoona*, seeing the dragonfly spacecraft properly for the first time. It stood lightly on six legs, with fearsome weaponry jutting from its glistening blue-green hull. Behind the bulbous transparent head – the cockpit where they'd just been sitting – the filigree wings were folded neatly along its back to save space in the docking bay. Susan's hands dropped to her sides and she gaped, open mouthed.

Joe grinned. 'Pretty, isn't she?' he said.

'*Not* what I was expecting,' said Susan. 'That must be the most stylish piece of kit I've ever seen.'

'Yeah. My pride and joy, that ship. So, we'll have dinner first, then I'll show you round before taking you home. Follow me, please.'

Joe led Susan towards the apex of the docking bay, past the control room, heading for the canteen. As they passed the *Tumbas* in Docking Bay 2, she craned her neck to view the rows of prickly green spheres.

'All right, we'll do a quick stop off. You go on ahead, guys,' he told the others.

'These are *Tumbas*, our standard one-person fighter craft,' he said, striding over to the nearest one and placing his hand on it to open the door. As the steps lowered, Susan peered inside at the single seat, the low-lit control bank and the 270° screen.

'The ports for the thrusters and the weapons system

are inside these pointy bits,' Joe said, tapping one of the spines on the exterior. 'That makes it highly manoeuvrable. If you want to change direction, you swing your seat around to rotate the craft on its axis. If you want to fire at something, you don't have to be facing it.'

'What's the power source?' asked Susan.

Joe hesitated, wondering how much to reveal. 'Organic waste. Like the *Shantivira*, and the *Pride of Essoona*. The Syenitians are more ... aware of their connection to the universe than we are. They've found a way of extracting residual life energy from organic matter: far more than we get from burning it.'

'Would they be willing to share that information with us?'

'No,' said Joe in a flat voice. He patted the *Tumba* to close the door again. 'Syenitians never share information about their power source. We'll have to solve our energy problems ourselves.'

He took her round the central post to the canteen. Susan marched straight across the hall to the supersized curved window and gazed at the Earth: a perfect swirl of blues, greens and browns, streaked with pale cloud.

'How do you ever manage to eat anything, with that view?' she asked.

'We never take it for granted; it reminds us why we're up here,' said Joe. 'You should come again when there's a solar wind: we see both sets of polar lights at once. Stunning.' He turned to head back to the table. 'Come and have something to eat,' he called over his shoulder.

The others were serving themselves from steaming dishes. Maneewan had organised a Kenyan meal in

Susan's honour: fish cooked in coconut stew with *ugali*. Maneewan's husband Vijay had spent all afternoon making *samosas* and *chapatis*.

Joe left space for Susan next to Kazembi and sat by Valentin, who was having an animated conversation with Valeri in Russian. Opposite them sat the odd couple: flamboyant Shakila, dressed elegantly in black, and the reserved and respectable Yisheng. Alike as chalk and charcoal, with a deep friendship which had evolved during their decades on the *Shantivira*. Yisheng's hair was grey now, but Shakila's glossy black mane hinted at regular visits to an expensive salon, keeping the ageing process at arm's length with a firm and determined grip. Tonight she wore a considerable amount of gold jewellery and even more black eyeliner than usual.

Once they'd filled their plates, Susan asked Kazembi, 'So how long have you been on the *Shantivira*?

'Eleven years,' said Kazembi. 'We do two and a half years' training and two and a half years' service; then decide if we want to stay on longer. I love it here. We're a family, you know? Literally. You met Nkosi just now: he's my husband. We have two little girls, Thandiwe, who's seven, and Flora, who'll be ten soon.'

'Isn't it hard to be so far away from them, my dear?'

'Far?' said Kazembi, confused. Then she laughed. 'They're running around outside with their friends. They go to school in Windhoek, where my mother lives, but they're here with us for evenings and weekends – or we're home with them.'

Joe could see the questions bubbling up in Susan's expression. Time for a diversion before someone let slip about the teleports. 'Try some *saiju*, Susan,' he said, pouring her a cup.

'*Saiju?*'

'It's a kind of tea, very popular on Syenitia,' said Shakila.

Susan took a cautious sip. 'Most refreshing, Shakila, is it?'

Shakila nodded.

'And where are you from, originally?'

'Baghdad,' said Shakila, selecting a *samosa* with perfectly manicured fingers. 'You're from Mombasa? I had a marvellous vacation there once, long ago. Magnificent beaches.'

'They are, aren't they?' Susan turned to Yisheng. 'And you're the deputy commander? When did you join the *Shantivira?*'

Yisheng smiled politely and Shakila said, 'He doesn't speak English. I'll interpret for you.' She switched to Kawaida and repeated the question.

Yisheng answered and Shakila translated, 'I joined in 1975. I was one of the first humans to train as a *Tumba* pilot – the *Shantivira's* history is my own history – and my family's history. My daughter Qingqing qualified last year.'

'A family-friendly organisation,' Susan remarked before turning back to Kazembi. 'Tell me about the alien invasions you've prevented.'

'Well, they're mostly not invasions,' said Kazembi. 'People generally send probes first, so we send them away with a message that the planet is protected by the Galaksi Alliance. But there were two attempts last year. One was some refugees who we managed to re-home on Syenitia.

The other was Ranglatiri pirates looking for resources to strip and sell. We threw everything we had at them.'

Joe said, 'You know that weather satellite which went down before Christmas?'

Susan frowned at the apparent non sequitur. 'Yes?'

'It got hit by wreckage from that battle. That's something we do a lot of – dematerialising space debris – especially in the orbits of the terrestrial space stations. But it's less work now the ISS has shield generators.'

'Dematerialising?'

'That's how our weapons work. You can't go around blowing stuff up in space – that would cause more problems than it solves. But I'm not authorised to tell you more.'

'You mean by the—' Susan tried out the new word, '—Syenitians?'

'That's right,' said Joe. 'It took me months of persuasion to get us this far. If first contact is a disaster, it'll be my fault. Some say I should've kept our operation secret and left the ISS crew to die. But I couldn't do that. And Aldeman trusts my instincts. I think we can do this.'

Susan asked, 'Do all Syenitians speak English?'

Joe laughed. 'No. Only Aldeman. Space-voyaging species use Kawaida for interplanetary communication. Kawaida's the official language of the *Shantivira*; you can hear it now, around this table. Some say it sounds like Earth-Swahili.'

He pulled out his *zana* and checked the screen. 'Time's getting on. Have you had enough to eat?'

'Yes, thank you.'

'Then let's go outside,' he said.

'Outside?'

'Follow me.'

ACCOMPANIED BY KAZEMBI, Nkosi and Tima, Joe took Susan to the lift in the central column and pressed the button. When the curved doors slid open, the lights flickered on to reveal the main warehouse. He said, 'This is our maintenance and storage level. Dipesh's kingdom.'

He led them towards the perimeter in a straight line. Lights came on as they approached and switched off again as they moved away. Each direction appeared the same: rows of neatly labelled shelves, cupboards, drawers and large pieces of equipment under dust covers, fading from a pool of brightness into darkness.

Susan shivered. 'Has anyone ever got lost down here?'

'Most of us, at one time or another,' Joe admitted cheerfully. 'Just give the computers a shout and they'll guide you out. Or you can keep walking in one direction.'

THE SMALL GROUP stopped at the nondescript metal door in the hull. Joe saw Susan looking at the line of rubber boots on the doormat but offered no explanation; instead he pulled open the hatch and waited for her reaction.

Face-to-face with outer space, Susan gasped. There was nothing out there but bright sunshine in a pitch-black sky. She peered over the edge and stepped back instinctively when she saw the gleaming white hull of the space station curving away beneath her. Joe chuckled and gently took her arm. 'I'm sorry. I couldn't resist. Go ahead, you

127

lot, we'll catch up in a minute.'

Susan boggled as she watched Tima, Kazembi and Nkosi stride confidently through the door, each giving a practised hop. Nobody fell or screamed. Instead, they changed plane, standing nonchalantly on the exterior of the *Shantivira*. They turned and walked above the door, disappearing from view.

'Gravity generators,' said Joe. 'They pull us onto the closest surface. Hold my hand.'

'But—how can we breathe?'

'Multiple layers of magnetic shields. It's perfectly safe. I'll count to three and we'll jump, OK?'

Susan bit her lip. 'OK.'

'One. Two. Three!'

Susan jumped and almost lost her balance, but Joe caught her easily. 'Gotcha!'

'Thank you,' she said, pulling her jacket straight. 'Where did the others go?'

'To the tropical biome. This way.'

He led her along the convex hull until they arrived at a bamboo fence with a gate. Beyond it, a crazy patchwork of crops and trees stretched to the horizon. Susan was gratifyingly speechless.

Joe said, 'This is how the *Shantivira* generates its atmosphere. We control the temperature and the humidity by varying the shield thickness. We grow a lot of our food here. There's a temperate biome on the other side of the base, where we also have some livestock.'

As they strolled along the rough track, Susan took in their surroundings. Banana and papaya trees grew between plots of sweet potatoes, pineapples and breadfruit, interspersed with ginger and turmeric, chickpeas and avocado trees, and the classic three sisters: maize, beans and squash. Narrow footpaths threaded erratically through the flourishing vegetation. In the distance, coconut trees bordered rice fields.

'We're big on companion planting here,' said Joe. 'If we mix the crops, we have fewer problems with disease and pests, and we can exploit the symbiotic relationships between species. We harvest by hand anyway, so having everything together in a single area isn't important.'

'You harvest everything manually?' said Susan. 'Isn't that a lot of work?'

Joe smiled. 'We're never short of volunteers willing to work outside in their free time. The farm isn't very big.'

Susan looked up at the sun shining fiercely in the black sky above. 'What about rain?'

'No rain. All the irrigation is buried at root level, along with sensors to provide real-time data. It's more hi-tech than it looks. Not a drop of water is wasted.'

They walked on.

After a brief silence, she pointed at the *Shantivira's* thrusters and demat beam ports, which rose out of the ground at intervals. 'What are those white cones?'

'A larger version of the prickles on the *Tumbas*,' said Joe.

'The weapons system?'

'And for manoeuvring, yes.'

They were interrupted by the sound of children's voices. Two boys and three girls ran towards them, followed by Kazembi and Nkosi, with Tima and Björn bringing up the rear.

'Round-up time,' said Joe. 'They should be in bed, but hey, tomorrow's the weekend.'

Tima's husband wore only an ancient pair of shorts and flip-flops, showing off his colourful collection of sea-creature tattoos. Björn was having a holiday on the *Shantivira* before starting his new job. Fair play to him, taking on a new challenge so soon after his accident. Joe wondered what the Pweza would think of the red octopus stretching down Björn's left arm. Would they like it? Disapprove? Think it was supposed to be Kitty? Hopefully it wouldn't cause a diplomatic incident.

Tima introduced him to Susan, who clearly hadn't expected an oversized, semi-naked Scandinavian on her first trip to space. 'Are you a pilot too?' she asked, looking up at him.

Björn laughed. 'No!' he said. 'Babysitter extraordinaire, that's me. We've been playing hide and seek for hours.'

Kazembi clasped Susan's hand. 'It was lovely to meet you. I hope you enjoy the rest of your evening.'

They said goodbye and Joe and Susan continued along the path towards the rainforest. As it loomed ahead, Joe explained, 'Each biome has a wild region at the centre to generate an oxygen baseload and provide a home for the insects we need to pollinate the crops. Want a look?'

'Yes please.'

Under the canopy it was darker and cooler, thick with life. Plants grew over each other, jostling for light in a tangled jumble.

Susan said, 'It's quiet for a rainforest, isn't it? Are there no birds or animals?'

'Some birds,' said Joe. 'Small mammals only. Our focus is on having enough insects to pollinate the plants. We don't have space for a full eco-system.'

He glanced upwards and glimpsed a pair of green eyes glittering behind the foliage. Jaguar-Kitty lay along an overhanging branch, one large paw dangling. He quickly looked at the ground so Susan wouldn't follow his gaze.

Shit, Cath, don't let her spot you. Too many awkward questions.

I won't. Don't fuss. How's it going? Is she softening yet?

Maybe. A little. You have to hand it to her, she's very professional. Cool as a cucumber. I like her.

Perhaps you need to lay on the charm more, get her adrenaline pumping.

Flirt with her, you mean? Joe smirked. *You shock me, babe! Although … she is a lot younger than you.*

Cheeky! You taking her home soon? I'll wait on the Pride.

IT WAS NEARLY eleven o' clock by the time Joe and Susan returned to Docking Bay 3.

Valentin was reluctant to go back with them, because Friday night was poker night. 'Can I stay over?' he asked.

'Sure,' said Joe. 'My sofa's your sofa. I won't play though; I'll be home too late. Don't let William rip you off!'

'But you'll be back in the office on Monday morning?' enquired Susan.

Valentin saluted. 'Eight a.m. sharp, Ma'am!'

SUSAN CLIMBED INTO the *Pride of Essoona* and took a seat in the cockpit, waving goodbye to Valentin as they flew out of the docking bay. As the Earth came nearer, she asked, 'What language are you using to operate this ship? It's different to the other one, what was it called?'

'Kawaida,' said Joe. 'The *Pride* only understands Syenitian. It's a sort of anti-theft feature.'

'So you speak more than one alien language?'

'I do.'

'How? What's your story, Joe?'

'The short version? I'm from a long line of Welsh coal miners. Thatcher closed the mines, so I joined the army. The Royal Regiment of Wales. The Royal Welsh, it's called now. Then I got recruited to the *Shantivira*.'

'And now look at you.' Susan leaned back in her seat and sighed. 'I think I'd sell my soul for a ship like this. That's how they operate isn't it? The Syenitians, I mean. They make you an offer you can't refuse and reel you in like a fish.'

'You noticed, huh?' said Joe. 'Classic Aldeman, that is. That, and getting a local to make the offer, so you don't feel patronised. That doesn't make the Syenitians a threat, Susan. They can help us, if we let them. I reckon if people had the chance to visit other planets, they'd stop taking the Earth for granted pretty quick. The Syenitians *want* us to thrive. We have a lot in common, more than many species they work with.'

'I'll need proper evidence, Joe, if I'm going to convince anyone in the UN. They'll say the video could have been faked. That they can't initiate first contact without solid proof that aliens exist.' Susan pressed her lips together.

'There's no telling how people will react.'

They entered the Earth's atmosphere and plummeted towards the lights of Europe. Joe set the *Pride* down in a forest clearing north of Vienna and activated the camouflage system. Outside, it was completely dark.

'Where *are* we?' asked Susan, peering into the night.

Joe chuckled. 'Well, I couldn't land in your street, could I? Come with me.'

He led Susan past the sofa, through the galley kitchen and down the stairs to the utility room. Susan laughed when she saw the tumble dryer stacked on top of the washing machine and the drying rack covered with laundry. 'This is where it all happens, right? I wasn't expecting such … domesticity.'

'Man's gotta wash,' said Joe. He pointed at a door to one side of the small room. 'The engine room's through there and this,' he announced, opening the opposite door with a flourish, 'is where I keep all my crap.'

The lights flickered on and Susan took in the contents of what Joe thought of as his garage. It even smelled like a garage. Surfboards, skis and a mountain bike were mounted on one wall. A long workbench and shelves full of tools filled the other wall. His trusty off-road touring bike took up most of the floor.

Joe patted the black saddle fondly. 'This is how we get you home, Susan. Are you up for it?'

Susan gulped. 'I haven't ridden a motorbike in years.'

'Then it's about time you did,' he said, unfastening the straps holding it in place.

'What the hell,' she said. 'When I think of everything else I've done today, I shouldn't worry about going on a motorbike.'

Joe laughed and passed her a spare jacket, a helmet and a rucksack for her handbag. She clambered up behind him and he called the command to open the rear door. As the ramp extended, the light from the spacecraft illuminated the trees outside. The air was fresh, with a chill suggesting winter had only recently loosened its grip on the landscape.

He revved the engine and Susan squealed as he released the brakes and shot down the ramp. The hull door closed behind them and they were enveloped in darkness, his headlamp the only light. They bumped along a rough track towards the road, the forest looming dark on either side.

Susan gripped Joe's waist so hard, he could feel the plates of body armour in his jacket crushing against him. Once they reached tarmac she relaxed, leaning into the hairpin bends with him as they rode down the hill. Soon street lights and houses sprang up around them and Joe slowed to read the street names. He stopped outside Susan's house and switched off the engine.

'Nice part of town you live in,' he said, pulling off his helmet.

'God, I feel seventeen again!' cried Susan, taking off her helmet and passing it to Joe. 'That was fan*tas*tic!'

Joe took her wrist and turned it to see her watch. Five to midnight. 'What did I tell you?'

'I won't ask how you knew where I lived. Would you like to come in for a drink?'

'Thanks,' he said, stuffing her jacket and helmet into the rucksack and swinging it onto his shoulders, 'but I'd better get back. Mrs Llewellyn'll be waiting.'

Susan raised her eyebrows. 'There's a Mrs Llewellyn?'

'Oh yes,' said Joe, smiling.

'And does she know about … your work?'

'Oh yes,' said Joe again. 'She's my recruitment officer. And occasional bodyguard.'

'Children?'

'No.' His answer came out more abruptly than intended. He softened it by adding, 'No children. I don't think we'll ever be able to.' He took the glistening white ring from his right thumb and held it up. 'This is my wedding ring and I want it back. You could have it analysed as evidence the Syenitians exist. It's made of *valkoinium*, the same metal used to make the *Shantivira*. It's stronger than any material we have on Earth.'

He placed it in her palm and reached into his pocket for a card. 'This is my direct line. Call me any time. Will you help us, Susan? Can you get me into a COPUOS session?'

'You're very persuasive, aren't you? I don't know. I need time. I'll call you next week, OK?'

'Fair enough.' Joe held out his hand for Susan to shake. 'Goodbye for now. I hope you enjoyed your evening with us.'

'Goodbye, Joe. It was … unforgettable.'

10. NOT COMING BACK

DAN

D AN WHISTLED CHEERFULLY as he moved around his tiny kitchen, wearing nothing but a pair of shorts. Almost done. After weeks of meeting Afra semi-regularly at *The Garden*, she'd accepted an invitation to dinner, marking a new phase in their relationship. She was the first person he'd experienced a real connection with here – his first friend. Perhaps because they were both aliens, but he thought it went deeper. Of course, it helped that he found her so attractive.

Although she never smiled, he had the distinct impression she found him amusing. Dan burned with curiosity to find out more about her. She was very reserved, only referring to her occupation in the vaguest of terms. He thought she probably operated on the wrong side of the law, but that bothered him less than it once might have done.

He knew nothing about the law here and had no desire to find out. There were too many other things to learn. Like astro-geography and navigation, for example, which he was studying at evening classes. He hoped to shake off his ignorance and follow the conversations between the pilots at *The Garden*.

The doorbell rang. He danced barefoot to the door and flung it open, the words 'You're early!' on his lips. His shoulders slumped when he recognised his visitor. 'Oh shit,' he muttered.

Kitty stood on the doorstep. 'Goodness, Dan,' she said, taking in his changed appearance with a humorous twitch of her eyebrows, 'you're looking well.'

'You haven't come to take me home, have you? I'm not ready!'

'Can I come in?' She pushed past him and sat at the table. 'I came to tell you Joe's begun negotiating with the UN. You don't need to come with me right now, but pack up and say your goodbyes. I'll return in a few days to take you home.'

Dan returned to the hob and took a pan off the heat. 'I'm learning so much here. I'd like to stay for longer.'

'The Alliance won't pay your rent forever. But if you can support yourself without its help, they won't mind if you stay.' Kitty gazed around the minuscule apartment. Dan knew it was exceptionally clean and tidy for a bachelor pad.

'Do my parents know I'm OK?'

'They only know what NASA's told them. Basically nothing. Write them a letter. Don't mention the Alliance. I'll deliver it myself.' She eyed the table set for two. 'Are you expecting a visitor?'

'Any minute now. Kitty, I don't want to be rude, but she mustn't see you here. She's not the Alliance's biggest fan.'

Kitty's mouth flicked upwards at one corner. 'And you haven't mentioned we're paying your rent?'

'Nope.'

'So how did you meet?'

Dan updated her on his life in Laro. Kitty laughed like a drain when he told her how he made his money. 'That I have to see! When are you on next?'

He told her, and they arranged to meet a few days later at *The Garden* so she could pick up Dan's letter to his parents. She also agreed to bring him a stock of guitar strings and some disposable razors: Dan was fed up with being mistaken for a Cylf. As Kitty stood up to go, the doorbell rang. Dan's eyes widened, but Kitty – well-versed in subterfuge – patted his arm and pointed at the French doors. He opened them hurriedly and felt a breeze on his cheek as black feathers rocketed past his head, up into the cloudless sky.

The doorbell rang again. Someone was impatient. As usual. Dan grinned and went to answer it. Keep it cool, Dan, he reminded himself. Don't come over all eager puppy and scare her off.

He opened the door and leaned against the warm frame. 'Hey.'

'Hey, yourself,' said Afra. She wore strappy sandals today, and a blue sundress short enough to permit easy access to the guns strapped to her thighs. 'Something smells good. Gonna let me in?'

He stood back, making an ushering motion with one hand.

'Nice,' she said, looking round at the high white walls. 'Big. Must be costing you a packet.'

'I manage,' he shrugged modestly. 'The *Garden* money helps. Take a seat. Dinner's almost ready.'

But Afra wouldn't sit until she'd explored every corner of the tiny apartment. It didn't take her long, but she seemed genuinely impressed. Dan thought of his parents' six-bedroom house in a leafy suburb of Boston, with its garden, swimming pool and games room. What would she think of *that*? What would his parents think of *her*?

He busied himself at the worktop, clearing away the vegetable waste and slicing a loaf of home-made bread. It had taken some experimenting (particularly learning to culture his own yeast from fruit peelings), but he was proud of the result.

Afra sat at the table, watching him spoon his make-it-up-as-you-go-along goulash into two bowls. 'You did this all from scratch? Is there no end to your talents?'

Dan smiled as he set Afra's bowl down in front of her. 'Your dinner, ma'am.'

She attacked the goulash at breakneck speed, slurping and gulping. Her bowl was half-empty before Dan managed to join her.

'I like a woman with an appetite.'

'I don't have a kitchen in my apartment,' said Afra, wiping her mouth on the back of her hand. 'I just eat the stuff you pour hot water on. Or eat out. This is a real treat. I haven't had a home-cooked meal for years. What's this?' she asked, pointing at the still-warm loaf.

'Bread,' he said, picking up a slice. 'Look, you dip it in, like this.'

She copied him. 'Wow! Fantastic! The texture! The flavour! And you *made* this? I've never seen it at the market.'

As they ate, they chatted about people they knew from

The Garden, what Dan had learned on his astro-geography course, places Afra had been to or would like to see. As always, they stayed carefully in the present, never getting too personal. Apart from a few polite enquiries about humans as a species, the Earth and its location – which Dan couldn't answer – Afra had never asked him about his life before coming to Laro. Not even why he felt so hostile towards the Galaksi Alliance. Either she wasn't interested or she hoped if she didn't ask Dan about himself, he wouldn't ask her about herself. She allowed Dan do most of the talking, skilfully deflecting any unwelcome questions.

For his part, Dan was embarrassed to admit to the Earth's level of development and focused on discovering as much as possible about life as an interstellar pilot. The more he talked with the pilots in *The Garden*, the more he wanted to train as one. Learning to fly an alien spacecraft had become a life goal, if not an obsession. If Kitty returned him to his old life as an astronaut, he'd never get the chance.

'Would you like to see my ship?' asked Afra, once she'd finished eating.

Dan almost choked on his beer. That was unexpected. He'd dropped a few brick-sized hints over recent weeks, but she'd never responded. 'Yes, please!'

'The repairs are all done. We can go now, if you like. Before it gets dark.'

Dan sat up straight. 'OK. Are you sure, Afra?'

'Sure, I'm sure.' She stood up. 'Come on.'

Dan didn't need telling twice. 'Let me find a T-shirt.'

They walked to the river and paid a ferrywoman to

take them across. Afra was silent, but when Dan held on to the railing, she put her hand on his. Her skin felt slightly rubbery, like neoprene. Warm and dry.

The small boat docked at a long boardwalk, the planks rotten in places and flanked by crumbling warehouses and workshops. Afra took his hand and guided him to a gap between two of the buildings: a long, dark corridor with high rusty walls on either side. Then a dogleg through an overgrown alleyway behind another warehouse, its paintwork flaking from years of neglect.

Dan felt suddenly vulnerable. He knew nothing about this woman and suspected she was involved in something shady. Had he already found out too much? Was visiting her ship a ruse to get him somewhere deserted? Was she going to shoot him and leave his body for the rats? He shivered. The rats on Amra were huge. It wouldn't take them long to dispose of the evidence.

Another sharp bend and they emerged into sudden sunshine. 'Short cut,' said Afra, succinctly.

Dan gasped. In front of them towered a curving blue … what? '*That's* your ship?'

Afra nodded, the pride on her face clear to see.

'She's *beautiful.*'

Though on the ground, its flowing lines gave the impression of joyful movement, like an oversized dolphin leaping above the sea.

'It's called the *Gezi Urdina*. Sayari for Blue Arrow.'

'Is she fast?'

'There's no hyperdrive, but it handles well. It's good at getting out of tight spots. Do you want to look inside?'

She pulled a controller from a pocket on her thigh

holster and pointed it at the ship. A gangway began to lower from the underbelly.

'Come on.'

He followed her along a plain corridor to the cockpit at the front. Two seats at a bank of controls, switches and screens covering every surface. A spartan metal bench was bolted to the back wall, softened by a solitary blue silk cushion.

'For your passengers?' Dan asked, nodding his head at the bench.

'I never carry passengers,' she said. 'Come and see the engine room.'

She led him back along the corridor to a door marked 'No Entry'.

'It's an old ship,' said Afra, opening the door, 'but that makes it easy to repair, *if* you can find the parts. Laro's good for that; it's one of the reasons I based myself here.'

What Dan saw made no sense. A giant reflective cylinder filled the long room from end to end and top to bottom. It smelled of static electricity or burnt marshmallows, Dan couldn't decide which.

'What's *that*?'

'The reactor, duh-brain. You don't know anything, do you?'

'I know I want to kiss you.'

She touched his cheek. 'Do you?' She pushed him back until he was pressed up against the curved surface. He felt a tingling vibration where he touched it: strange, but not unpleasant. 'Go on, then,' she said.

Dan closed his eyes and stretched his face towards her. Her lips were warm and dry, like her hand had been, her tongue longer and stronger than a human's. She probed his mouth with it, back to the gaps where his wisdom teeth had once grown. He drew her to his chest, the peculiar vibration now travelling through both of them.

Afra pulled away and switched to running her tongue up and down his neck, making him go weak at the knees. 'Aaaahhh,' he moaned as she thrust its tip into his left ear. At the same time, she slid her hand beneath his T-shirt, rubbing his chest rhythmically. He wondered if she could feel his erection growing. How could she not? Would she understand what it was? Would their bodies even fit together that way? He'd been so entranced by her beauty and her air of mystery; he hadn't actually thought that far ahead.

'Dan?' she murmured.

'Mmmm?'

'I'm going away. Tomorrow.'

'Forever?' said Dan, stricken. His erection wilted and died.

Afra's ears waggled in amusement at his expression. 'Just for a couple of weeks. Now the *Gezi Urdina* is ready, there's nothing to keep me here.'

'Thanks very much!'

'That's not what I meant. I enjoy your company, Dan. And you're a great cook. But I have a delivery deadline to keep. You understand about delivery deadlines, don't you?'

'Take me with you.'

Her ears waggled again, as if his suggestion were hilarious. 'No! Carry on playing your music and I'll be back soon. Now, would you like a guided tour before you head back?'

Dan nodded, although his initial excitement about the ship had faded in the light of her news.

'I'll take you back to the ferry afterwards,' she said. 'Can you find your way home from there? I need to run some checks and I don't want you getting under my feet.'

As she showed him the galley kitchen, two shower rooms and two plain cabins with narrow bunk beds, his mind whirled with disappointment and resentment. Was that all she thought of him? A pleasant distraction when she came into port, to be dropped like a stone the minute her work took her elsewhere? Did she have a man in every spaceport? He wouldn't put it past her.

It hadn't escaped him that she hadn't shown him where she kept whatever it was she needed to deliver. She might like him enough to fool around with, but she clearly didn't trust him. No woman had ever treated him so dismissively. Not during high school, not during his time at Princeton, not in the Air Force and certainly not since training as an astronaut. He remembered all the perfectly styled, parentally approved blondes who'd regarded any time he deigned to spend with them as an honour. He'd sailed through life protected by a halo of wealth, an influential family and a glamorous job. Here on Amra, he had nothing except his wits. Right then. He'd better put them to the test and find out what Afra-Azu-who-loved-the-colour-blue was up to.

THREE DAYS LATER, after work, Dan met Kitty at a table in the darkest corner of *The Garden*.

'Here are your guitar strings,' she said, passing him a

stack of little packets.

'Wow, thanks,' he said. 'They should keep me going for a while.'

Kitty produced a flat wooden box, ten inches square, and pushed it across the tabletop.

'What's this? It's not my birthday.'

'Open it and you'll see.'

He lifted the lid and put it to one side. The box contained a selection of soaps, a leather strap, a sharpening stone, a shaving brush with silver bristles, and a cut-throat razor. He lifted it out and pulled the blade from its pearl handle. It glinted in the soft light: beautiful and deadly.

'This is an antique! What is it? Victorian?'

Kitty shrugged. 'Perhaps. Still in good condition. I've sharpened it for you; it's ready to use.'

Dan stared at the blade. Shit. He'd asked for *disposable* razors. After all he'd been through, accidently slitting his own throat would be *so* embarrassing. 'I have no idea how to use this,' he admitted.

'Then *learn*. I've uploaded instructions to your *zana*.'

'Where did you get it? It must have cost a bomb.'

Again, Kitty shrugged. 'Na. S'just something I had lying around. Better someone gets some use out of it. Look after it and it'll last several human lifetimes.'

'I don't know what to say. What an awesome gift. Thank you.'

'No worries. Now, didn't you have a letter for me to deliver?'

Dan closed the razor and placed it reverently back in its box. Reaching into his jacket pocket, he pulled out the letter for his parents. 'There you go,' he said, sliding it across the table. As Kitty tucked it into her sleeve, he produced a second envelope. 'Do you mind delivering another one?'

Kitty looked at the address and raised her eyebrows in a silent question.

'I'm resigning from my job with NASA,' he said. 'I've been doing some thinking since you stopped by. I'm not coming back.'

'Anything to do with a certain Sayari?'

Dan's eyes narrowed. 'You stayed to watch, didn't you?'

Kitty was unrepentant. 'So sue me. I was curious.'

'Maybe. Partly, if I'm honest. It's early days. But romance aside, I can't go back yet. I want to put myself through pilot school and travel the galaxy. If you give me the Earth's coordinates, I'll find my own way home. Don't worry about me.'

'OK, Dan. If that's what you want.' Kitty shook his hand. 'Good luck. I hope it works out for you.'

PART TWO

11. THE LIBRARY
HANNA

H ANNA SAT BESIDE Hassan on the tram into town, her thigh pressed against his. It'd been weeks since she'd travelled by tram; now it was warmer, she preferred commuting by bike. She twirled her locket, burning to share her news with him. She wouldn't discuss it in front of the others – but it was such a milestone, she couldn't keep it to herself for long. How would he react? Would he feel the same way?

They disembarked at the intersection above the fish market and took the Kalakaivo Square / Kirjasto Square exit. Hanna rarely came to central Essoona; her daily life revolved around the blocks near Dunia House and the Essoona Pilots' Academy in the north of the city. She'd forgotten how imposing the groups of official buildings were, with their severe lines and glossy black stone.

The two main squares were back-to-back, with the Council Chambers (the administrative headquarters for the planet) forming the connecting side. She could see Kirjasto Square with its white tree, the ageing limbs propped up by wooden supports. Behind it, the Library tower cast a shadow over the square's white flagstones. Syenitian architects avoided high-rise buildings: partly because they felt more than six storeys negatively affected quality of life, and partly to prevent overshadowing of rooftop food production and the ubiquitous solar panels. The Library was a notable exception.

As the friends crossed the square, Hanna dropped back until she and Hassan were at the back of the group. She gathered her courage to speak, but it failed her when she saw Elian already waiting at the front entrance. Now wasn't her moment after all. Drat.

The public area of the Library was light and welcoming – less forbidding than it appeared from outside – more like a cross between a forest and a cathedral. The main hall was an open, triple-height space, extending across the whole ground floor. White columns of glistening *valkoinium* supported the upper storeys. These columns were shaped like trees, with the branches merging and interlocking in organic patterns on the ceiling. In between, intricate paintings of leaves, birds and animals decorated the remaining space.

At ground level, on the walls beneath the high circular windows, life-size images of historically important Syenitians were painted in the gaps between the columns. As with real Syenitians, Hanna found it difficult to tell the males from the females.

Throughout the hall, clusters of height-adjustable white posts sprouted like mushrooms out of the wooden floor, like mini versions of the surrounding columns. These were docking stations to connect your *zana* to the information within the Library. Much of the Library's data could be accessed remotely, but not all of it. You had to come in person for some of the more specialist reference data – and get permission to download your findings.

There were no chairs, or anywhere to sit down. Syenitians could stand for long periods without discomfort and designed their public spaces accordingly. Not being able to do the same, Hassan had always brought a folding chair with him, passing it on to Hanna when he left. She hadn't thought to bring it today; hopefully they wouldn't need it.

They followed Elian to the information desk, where they scanned the ID chips in their *zanas* as he announced their arrival. The Cylf on duty stared blankly past them for an instant, then refocused on Elian. 'Your guide will be here shortly,' he rumbled. Like all cybernetic life forms, his voice was several tones lower than a Syenitian's or a human's.

Hanna knew from Delius and Gambrinus on the *Shantivira* that the cyborgs communicated silently via a common network. They only used audible speech for 'organic life forms'. The Library was a popular employer with Cylfs, as it gave them access to their heart's desire: data. Strangely, she saw no Cylf visitors, only staff.

Apart from their facial hair, Cylfs looked like heavyset Syenitians and, despite being genderless, species with biological sexes generally referred to them as male. Under their pale skin, a *valkoinium* chassis protected their internal components. They could perform heavy-duty lifting work and talk to any computer system. No complex operation – including the *Shantivira* – functioned without cybernetic life forms.

While they waited, Elian explained who some of the people in the paintings were. 'Here are Amalaran and

Inisan, the scientists who discovered the key to our bio-based power source. You know, the one we don't tell other species about. I *can* tell you they were both pregnant at the time and incorporated their experience of pregnancy into their research.' He moved to another picture. 'This guy here, Sevan, set up what later became the Galaksi Alliance, by negotiating a far-reaching trade agreement with the Sayari, the Mhasibu and the Tarumbets. And this is the great poet Baionan, who wrote many of the songs we still sing during *Laulaahaalia*, tens of thousands of years after his death.'

The next image was of a solemn character, wearing a mustard-coloured velvet dress in the style of Kitty and Rowan, instead of the conventional unisex tunic. For that reason, Hanna guessed the figure was a female.

Elian said, 'This one is from the olden days. Kehvesan is the grandparent of long-distance space travel. They invented the hyperdrive.'

A deep voice behind them made Hanna jump.

'Greetings, Group 10:24 a.m. My name is Isedolus and I will be your guide this morning. Our tour will take approximately two hours, starting at the lower levels and finishing at the restaurant, where the Head Librarian cordially invites you to join her for lunch. Please follow me.'

The red-bearded Cylf pivoted away from them and strode towards the lift at the south-east corner. He wore the same uniform as the Cylf at the information desk: a burgundy tunic and leggings in the Syenitian style, with black lace-up boots.

They hurried to follow him. With the exception of

Nikolai and presumably Elian, none of them had ever gone beyond the main hall. Nikolai had only been to the access points among the archives on the upper levels – after booking a slot weeks in advance. He'd never been downstairs before. Hanna detected a distinct spring in his step.

The service lift was large enough to carry them all without having to crush together. Judging by the control panel, there were twelve levels below ground. The doors shuddered open and a wave of heat hit Hanna in the face, making her forehead prickle with sweat. Wall lamps flickered on in front of them, triggered by the doors' motion. A featureless grey corridor stretched as far as the lights allowed Hanna to see, with none of the decorative touches the Syenitians were so fond of.

'This is the uppermost server level,' said Isedolus, stepping out of the elevator. 'The server levels extend underneath the *Laulaahaalia* building at the other end of Kirjasto Square. The servers must be cooled, so we pump away the heat and distribute it around Essoona via the district heating system. For example, we heat the main city baths and the official buildings on the central squares.'

Lucy asked, 'What about in summer? Surely buildings need cooling then, rather than heating?'

'Correct. In summer, the district heating system becomes a district cooling system, pumping cold water instead of hot. Heat is removed from buildings and stored for the winter in underground tanks located around the city. In addition, Essoona has a network of solar collectors. By the end of the warm season, the temperature in the tanks is above 80°C. If the district heating system does not require the thermal energy from our servers, it goes to the tank under Kalakaivo Square. We always have enough heat to keep the organic life forms cosy through the cold season.'

They stopped outside a heavily insulated industrial door. Isedolus touched the panel and it rolled upwards rapidly. 'Please come through quickly. We must minimise the warm air entering the server room.'

Hanna stepped into a hall filled with row upon row of metallic boxes. Behind them, the door rattled shut. Thanks to her sweaty T-shirt, the air felt icy. Isedolus noticed Hanna shiver.

'We will not stay long. I am aware organic beings risk malfunction if exposed to temperature fluctuations. We Cylfs prefer lower temperatures. We spend much time here doing checks and replacing faulty units.'

Nikolai asked, 'How are the servers protected from flooding?' Clearly, he was still thinking about the thermal storage facility under the neighbouring Kalakaivo Square. 'What if the tank sprang a leak? Could the systems for the whole planet go down?'

Isedolus shook his head. 'The tank is deeper than our servers. The water could never penetrate the Library structure.'

'What if something else happened down here?' asked Hassan. 'How likely is a data outage?'

'We have many backup systems, located at intervals around the planet. No more than a few hours' data could ever be lost.'

'Do you keep all your data forever?' asked Farida. 'Won't you run out of space one day? Isn't that a waste of energy?'

'Space is always an issue. Energy usage also. We are responsible for Syenitia's historical archives, including all our information on alien civilisations. Our algorithms suggest data for deletion, but nothing goes without permission from the Syenitians. The Head Librarian makes those decisions, not Cylfs. Less popular or less important data is stored at remote locations. The information is available, but takes longer to access as the systems are only connected to the network for an hour each day. Come with me please, we will take the stairs to the next level.'

They exited to the warm corridor and followed Isedolus up the spiral stone staircase. They came out into a low-ceilinged hall with the same footprint as the main tower above. Like the level below, it was filled with rows of floor-to-ceiling racks, but the similarity ended there. A jumble of disparate items crammed the shelves: different-sized wooden boxes and crates, bulging sacks, external hard drives, old *zanas* in various states of repair, curious mechanical objects, transparent plates, even some paper books and scrolls. Hanna wondered how they ever found anything.

'This and the floor above are our chaotic storage levels,' said the Cylf. 'We keep items awaiting documentation here, or those which are not frequently accessed.'

'Chaotic storage?' asked Saïd.

'Using the space with maximum efficiency,' Elian said. 'It looks disorganised, but it isn't. You'll see it in the archives upstairs, too. The Library is a random location warehouse. Each item has a code, and without that code you'll never find it.'

'Yes,' said Isedolus, 'you use specific search terms to find an item in the master database and look up its code. That code is linked to a shelf location.'

Hanna's bit her lip in disappointment. That would make it impossible to browse. Surely browsing was half the fun of going to libraries?

They left and climbed the stairs to Level −2. Isedolus stood outside a plain metal door, waiting for them to assemble in the corridor. 'I've been told organic life forms find the next two levels creepy. I assure you this is where my people are happiest. Do not be alarmed.'

He opened the door and Hanna saw hundreds of Cylfs, standing motionless with their eyes open and their index fingers plugged into sockets on a series of rails which criss-crossed the room. It *was* creepy. 'What are they *doing*?' she whispered.

Elian said, 'They don't need a *zana* to access the Library network. They jack straight in. The system shuts them out after six hours or they'd never go home. These levels are always packed.'

So this was where Delius and Gambrinus came on their days off, thought Hanna. Were they looking for something in particular?

Isedolus turned to leave. Back in the corridor, he said, 'Now we will take the elevator again and visit the archives on the fifteenth floor.'

The fifteenth floor was more library-like, Hanna felt. Full-length windows flooded the space with light, the walls and ceilings decorated in the Syenitian style. Beyond the row of network access posts, Hanna saw actual shelves with actual books.

'These are historical records, from before the digital age,' said Isedolus. 'You may walk among the shelves and look, but please do not touch anything.'

Hanna and Hassan followed the others into an aisle at random. It smelled like a proper library. 'Books you can't touch,' said Hanna. 'That's just wrong.'

'Syenitians don't regard books as objects made of paper,' said Hassan. 'To them, a book is a file on a *zana*. These archives are like a museum for them.'

Ahead of them, Lucy was attempting to convince Elian paper books were better than electronic ones.

'I love the smell,' she said. 'And I like to look at my bookshelves and remember all the stories I've read.'

Elian frowned. 'Bookshelves? You have shelves full of books? Is there a lot of space on your planet?'

'There's always space for books,' said Lucy.

'But why can't you remember the stories when you look at your *zana*?'

'Well, I could, if I opened it up and looked for them. But books are there with you, in the room. It's different. Anyway, paper books are better for reading in the bath. I'm always scared I'll drop my *zana* in the water and kill it.'

Now Hanna was sure Lucy was winding Elian up on purpose.

'You'd take a *paper* book into the *bath* with you?' he said, scandalised. 'Surely it's preferable to destroy a *zana* than a priceless artefact? At least you can have it repaired. Anyway, *zanas* aren't allowed in bathhouses, Lucy, you know that, right?'

There wasn't going to be a better opportunity. Hanna

pulled Hassan away from the group, between a row of shelves offering them some privacy. 'Do you want to go swimming later?' she asked.

He blinked at the seemingly random question. 'I thought you had your period?'

Hanna smiled shyly. 'Well ... I do. But I managed to get my cup in at last.'

Before they'd departed for Essoona, Mary had given the women a menstrual cup, explaining that because Syenitians didn't menstruate, sanitary products were hard to come by. But Hanna's vaginismus meant that, after her first painfully unsuccessful attempt to use it, she'd put it away in a drawer and gone back to using her trusty home-made sanitary towels – cut-down squares of old towels which were wonderfully soft on her skin. With some refolding, one towel would last her most of a day; then it would soak with the others in an old ice-cream tub until her period finished and she hot-washed them all at once.

Now she only saw Hassan at weekends, missing swimming with him one week in four was getting annoying. So she kept trying. This morning – finally – it had gone in.

Hassan's face split into a broad grin and he hugged her tightly. 'Well done, Hanna! That's fantastic! Was it very difficult?'

'To begin with. But I really wanted to go swimming with you today.'

'Then you shall. We'll go this evening.'

Hanna took a deep breath. Now for the real question. 'Maybe ... when my period's over, we could have another go at sex? You know, the penetrative kind?'

His liquid brown eyes studied her face. He took her hand in both of his and squeezed it. 'Are you sure?'

She shrugged, attempting to appear casual. 'No harm in trying.'

Hassan held her hand up to his mouth and kissed it. 'No harm at all.'

12. REVELATIONS

HANNA

A T LUNCHTIME THEY took the lift to the top floor, where Merian was waiting for them. Despite her plain robes and apple cheeks, the Head Librarian radiated authority and confidence. She appraised the newcomers swiftly, welcoming them with a sincere smile. Her faded chestnut hair hung loose to her waist and crow's feet bordered her intelligent eyes. Hanna wondered how old she was.

Merian greeted Aneira with familial warmth; Hanna knew they'd already met several times. Then she turned to the rest of them.

'Welcome, Dunians,' she said, using the Kawaida name for Earth. 'I asked Elian to bring you because I wish to learn more about your kind. I have only had dealings with your employer, Llewellyn. I am curious to discover if all Dunians are like him.'

'Like him in what way, my lady?' asked Hassan.

'Call me Merian, dear. I am not one for formality.' She considered for a moment. 'Impatient. Stubborn. Loud. Blunt. Quick-tempered. Focused on the present rather than the future. Brave. Generous. Funny. Infuriating.' She smiled to soften her criticism. 'As I said, I am curious.'

They followed her into the restaurant, to a long table at the edge of the room. The square hall had the same footprint as the rest of the tower; mature trees in enormous pots broke the space up into smaller, more intimate zones. The roof was a gigantic glass pyramid, providing an all-round view of Essoona as spectacular as Elian had promised. The apex was so high, Hanna felt dizzy looking at it.

Hassan nudged Hanna, pulling her attention back to floor level. 'Look!'

A few tables away, Aldeman was eating with a Sayari male. Hanna imagined this kind of establishment was Aldeman's natural habitat and tried not to feel like an imposter. He noticed them and raised his hand in a friendly wave. Hanna waved back shyly, reassured.

They sat down and served themselves from a large bowl of what Hanna thought of as 'Syenitian jollof', a soft, orangey grain with a spicy, nutty flavour. She eyed the different sauces on offer, many of which she didn't recognise. She meant to try them all.

Hanna poured herself a drink from the glass jug at her end of the table. An acquired taste: at mealtimes, Syenitians always drank water with a dash of *omena* vinegar in it.

Lucy and Nikolai were telling Merian about their weekends diving with Björn and the Pweza. They'd been working alongside Björn's team and the giant blue octopuses, helping build long-term underwater accommodation for the hundred thousand Pwezan refugees who'd arrived on Syenitia last year. The Pwezans' home planet had been plundered by the Ranglatiri until its eco-system had broken down entirely and even the oceans had become uninhabitable.

'We're only unskilled helpers on the building site,' said Lucy. 'Fetching and carrying. I'd love to do an underwater welding course, but we don't have the time with all our pilot training. It's fascinating, though.'

'I'm just enjoying the chance to be underwater,' said Nikolai. 'And using a whiteboard to communicate with the Pweza is improving my written Kawaida no end.'

Merian said, 'Remind me, how do you communicate with them? They have language but no speech, correct?'

'That's right,' said Nikolai. 'You need four arms to speak their language. But they can display Kawaida characters on their foreheads, so we talk like that. It takes forever; our dive-time is always over too soon. It's frustrating for Björn that he can't stay on the seabed for weeks at a time, like he used to in his old job. But he holds most of the planning meetings just below the surface, so he can use a snorkel and the Pwezans don't have to come on land.'

'Can they do that?' asked Elian.

'They have special exoskeletons,' said Lucy. 'Like a spacesuit. But it's easier for them if we come into the water.'

They finished the main course and the conversation paused as the staff cleared away the dishes. No Cylfs working up here, Hanna observed. Syenitians only.

'Merian,' she asked, 'I didn't see any Syenitians or other organic beings working in the Library. Are there any, or is it all Cylfs?'

She shook her head. 'Many Alliance species work here,

curating the data for their own societies. But they are in the offices on the floors below us. Cylfs provide the technical support, but we also need people who understand the value and context of the data we safeguard.'

Saïd asked, 'So a Cylf could never be Head Librarian, for example?'

Merian didn't seem offended by the question. 'It is a different job,' she said. 'I am the interface between the data management systems and the decisions about what data we choose to manage.'

'That's a big responsibility,' said Hassan.

'It is a shared responsibility. The important decisions are voted on by the wider committee, whose members are selected at random, like the Council. I am just the representative reporting to the main Syenitian Council.' She looked past them and smiled. 'Talking of which, I believe most of you know Aldeman.'

Hanna swivelled round and saw Aldeman approaching. He pulled a chair from another table and inserted himself between Hanna and Farida. 'Hello everyone, did you enjoy your meal?'

They answered politely and Aldeman looked around the table. 'All familiar faces ... except you,' he said, his gaze resting on Aneira. 'What is your name, my dear?'

'A ... Aneira, my lord,' stumbled Aneira, starstruck. It wasn't every day you met a planet's senior official.

'Ah. You are the student who has been giving Elian here a run for his money. It is a pleasure to meet you, Aneira.'

Aneira mumbled a shy response. Hanna recalled the first time she'd met Aldeman and sympathised. He had a presence you couldn't help responding to. She wasn't surprised he knew her name. Knowing about people wasn't only part of Aldeman's job: he was genuinely interested – especially if they came from beyond Syenitia.

'So, Roberto,' he asked. 'How are you finding life on Syenitia?'

'Great, thanks. The quality of life here is awesome. Way better than in Brazil.' He glanced at Nikolai. 'I've been getting to know some of my classmates better too.'

Hanna noticed the glance. Was there something going on she didn't know about? Nikolai had been hanging out with Roberto a lot since he'd started rock climbing. Last year they'd barely spoken to each other.

'Why would you say our quality of life is better than in your country?'

'Essoona's infrastructure is amazing: your daily needs are all within walking distance, free public transport for when you do need to travel. Everything is clean and works. Rent-controlled accommodation, a universal basic income. Brazil doesn't have the money for all that.'

'As I understand it, Brazil is able to issue its own currency. Brazil's central bank could create the necessary funds with a few taps on a keyboard.'

'But Aldeman, sir,' said Felix. 'That would result in runaway inflation!'

Aldeman raised a charcoal eyebrow. 'Would it? Surely it depends what you spend the money on?'

'What is *Brazil*?' asked Merian. 'I thought humans came from Dunia?'

'Dunia is divided into territories, Merian,' said Aldeman. 'They will not have a planetary government anytime soon.'

'Goodness. How quaint.'

Aldeman continued, 'Inflation only becomes a problem when the demand for products and services outstrips an economy's ability to provide them. An economy's limiting factor is always its real resources – its skilled workers, its physical resources and, of course, the available time – not the amount of money it has. Your John Kennedy understood that when he initiated America's space exploration programme. As long as a government invests sensibly in its economy and keeps within its actual resources, inflation will not be a big issue.'

'Money is merely a concept, a promise: a tool for the fair exchange of products and services,' said Merian. 'The minute people forget this and acquire it for its own sake, it becomes a many-headed monster, eating away at the fabric of society. Countless civilisations have failed this way.'

'Indeed,' said Aldeman. 'This is why our planetary currency, the Syenitian shilling – and all our smaller local currencies, like the Essoona pound, or the Aldina dinar, for example – differ from the *fedha* the Galaksi Alliance uses for interplanetary trade. Our local currencies are designed to lose value if you keep anything above a certain amount for longer than three months.'

'So people spend money instead of saving it?' asked Lucy.

'That's right, Lucy. The money earned on Syenitia remains in circulation within our planetary economy and local communities. There is almost no capital flight. That is the reason for our planet's perceived wealth.'

Felix's jaw dropped. 'Negative interest rates? For a

whole planet? That's crazy! People need to able to save money.'

'Ah, yes. *Interest.* Joe explained the concept to me.' Aldeman looked at Merian. 'On *their* planet, they "grow" money from money. If they hoard it, their hoard increases in value, even though by doing so they pull the wealth generated by the efforts of many out of the economy and exacerbate inequality.'

Merian looked stunned. 'Making money out of money is illegal throughout the Galaksi Alliance!'

'And on Amra,' added Aneira, with just a hint of smugness in her voice.

Aldeman smiled to dispel the sudden cooling of the atmosphere at the table. 'Tell me, Lucy, why do people hoard money?'

Why did people want to be rich? thought Hanna. All *she'd* ever wanted was enough to live on. Plus some savings to cover unforeseen expenses. Was hoarding money a kind of addiction?

Lucy pursed her lips. After a pause, she said, 'To feel safe.'

Aldeman rubbed his chin. 'Hmm. That's what Joe said, too. So, why do they *not* feel safe? Surely their communities should make them feel safe? A community's strength is in the relationships between its members. People in a community take care of each other.'

Hassan said, 'A person is a person through other persons.'

'Very *good*, Hassan.'

'Not me, my lord,' said Hassan, 'Desmond Tutu.'

'But our governments – our communities – *can't* be

relied upon to look after us. We have to look after ourselves,' argued Lucy.

'Indeed,' said Aldeman. 'The structural prioritisation of growth has dismantled many of your communities and Dunia's society has become caught in a vicious circle. We are watching with interest – no pun intended,' he winked, 'to see if you escape it.'

Hanna began to understand. 'So here, people don't feel the need to save, because they can rely on the universal basic income if things get tough?'

'That's right, Hanna,' said Aldeman. 'Most people have several months' reserve put by, but nobody hoards money the way they do on your planet.'

Nikolai leaned forward. 'How does the universal basic income work?' he asked. 'Don't people end up doing nothing? Wouldn't it merely push up prices?'

'There have to be particular components in place first, for it to be effective,' said Merian. 'Your friend already mentioned rent controls. That's one. Another is sufficient good-quality state-owned accommodation. Few people in cities own their own apartments.'

'So *that's* why you don't see homeless people here,' murmured Roberto. 'Or *favelas*.'

'You rent from the city council, don't you Aldeman?' said Lucy. 'Why is renting normal, even for someone descended from the former royal family?'

'It is simply how we do things.' He rocked back on his chair for a moment, considering Lucy's question. Then his eyes sparkled with a fresh realisation. 'I believe it is because we physically outlast our structures. We are not sentimental about them. Buildings are only worth the resources you put in to maintain them.

'I am 1045, and the house I was born in has already been rebuilt twice. Perhaps that is why we feel such an affinity with the natural world – landscapes do not change as rapidly as cities.'

Merian continued, 'The third pillar is our culture of service to the community. Every adult does some kind of voluntary work: a few hours a week if they work full-time or more, depending on whether they have relatives to care for and how much time they have to spare.'

'Every adult?' Nikolai asked. 'Seriously?'

'It's expected,' said Elian. 'It's a way to learn new skills and meet people outside your regular circle – to break out of your bubble, you know?'

'So what do *you* do?' asked Lucy.

'He helps the old lady in the flat above his with her food shopping,' said Aneira, proudly. To Hanna's surprise, Elian looked ashamed. 'It's not much. My studies take up most of my time. I'm buying food for our family anyway, so it's no extra effort. Once I'm working, I'll be able to do more, like Mother.'

All eyes turned to Merian. Hassan asked, 'Merian? How do you spend your free time?'

'I am a fully qualified paramedic. I work four days a week here, and in between I do a day shift and a night shift driving an ambulance.'

Hanna boggled. That was unexpected. So what did Aldeman do?

Lucy got there before her. 'Aldeman? Don't tell me you volunteer, too?'

He twinkled at her, reminding Hanna of his brother-in law. 'I am not only a Councillor. I am also a counsellor. As you might expect, my responsibilities do not leave me with much time, but I do answer calls to Essoona's Citizens' Advice helpline one evening a week. Anonymously, of course. It helps me keep a sense of perspective – stops me losing sight of real people's problems, you know? And it is never boring. Each situation is unique.'

'Don't you need lots of training and experience?' asked Saïd.

'Years of it,' agreed Aldeman cheerfully. 'I have all the right diplomas. Assisting people with their problems gives me great satisfaction. Sometimes it helps me find solutions in my day job, too. Inspiration, cross-pollination, call it what you like.'

✦ ✦ ✦

IN THE TRAM home, Hanna and Hassan sat in companionable silence. The day had been so packed with new impressions, it was a relief to let her mind coast. Hanna gazed outside, catching micro-glimpses of people's lives through third-floor windows. A man cooking, wearing nothing but an apron. Two children on scooters hurtling in circles around a living room coffee table. A woman sitting on a sofa, looking at her *zana*. A room full of people holding glasses: a party.

Hassan said, 'I have something to tell you, too.'

She turned away from the window. This sounded serious.

'I'll be qualifying soon. Then I'll take a long leave

before my two and a half years' service period.'

'And you'll go travelling.'

'I will.'

Hanna wasn't surprised: everyone took a break once they completed their training. 'Any ideas where?' she asked.

'Kenya, to do tourist stuff with Ozzy. Uganda, to visit my foster parents. And I'm going back to South Sudan. To Juba.'

Oh wow. This was big. Hassan hadn't been back to his home country since Kitty had first found him: a ten-year-old orphan begging on the streets, hopelessly crippled after losing both feet to a landmine. She'd taken him to friends in Kampala and he'd begun his new life, seizing every opportunity which had come his way and never looking back. Until now. She put her hand on his arm.

'You're ready?' she asked.

He sighed. 'I need to see where I came from. With my adult eyes.'

'Will you know anyone?'

'My mum had a brother who stayed back in Pibor. Delius has been trying to trace him for me, but I think he probably died. I don't remember him well. A couple of mates who joined the army – I never knew their surnames. So, no. No one really. I just want to *see* it, before the next phase of my life begins.'

'To say goodbye?'

'Maybe. Or to see if it still feels like home. You always think you'll go back for good one day, don't you?'

Hanna nodded. She hoped to return to Ethiopia one day, even if she didn't settle near Gambella. She hadn't mentioned it to Hassan, because—what if he didn't want to come with her? Her mind swerved away from the idea that they might not always be together. Could she see herself living in South Sudan? Perhaps. If it meant she could stay with Hassan. If the people there managed to stop fighting long enough for them to raise a family in safety.

Her thoughts moved ahead to her own summer holidays. No Hassan. Aneira was taking Elian to Amra to meet her extended family. But a month of freedom: time for a proper vacation, to explore beyond Essoona. They should use it wisely. Maybe visit some cities up the coast? Or rent a cabin in the mountains and go hiking? The whole stomach-churning, life-or-death drama aside, she'd quite enjoyed her snowshoe tour in Switzerland last winter. Mountains were probably easier to climb when they weren't covered in snow. Perhaps she could ask Felix and Saïd for suggestions.

When they arrived back at Dunia House, a lanky white man with neat red hair and a million freckles was struggling to get two enormous suitcases out of the teleport. He wore shorts and, as he descended the stairs, his hairless legs reminded Hanna of the tasteless sausages Felix liked to eat – the ones that came in a jar of dubiously coloured liquid. She vaguely recognised him: she'd seen him around on the *Shantivira*.

Reaching their level, he dropped his cases and shook their hands. 'Hi, I'm Max, Jangmi's replacement?' he said in perfect Kawaida. 'D'you know where I can find Mr Park?'

He looked more like an office worker, not an agricultural labourer, Hanna thought.

'Where are you from, Max?' asked Lucy.

'Vancouver, originally. I've worked on the *Shantivira* for seven years. You're all second years?'

They nodded.

'Good luck. I totally failed astro-geography. Three retakes and I still didn't pass. Luckily, I have green fingers, so they let me work in the biomes instead.'

'We'll take you through to the kitchen,' said Roberto, picking up one of the suitcases. 'Meet the rest of you upstairs?'

They agreed and trooped up to the living room. Nikolai stayed behind and picked up the other suitcase. 'We'll ask Mrs P if there's any cake going,' he said.

HANNA MADE COFFEE and joined Hassan on the sofa. His black and silver boots were on the floor and he sat cross-legged, researching something on his *zana*. Farida sat with them and Saïd, Felix and Lucy took the sofa opposite.

'Have any of you thought about the summer holidays yet?' Hanna asked them.

'Saïd and I have been reading up on our local mountains,' said Felix. 'There are some great climbing routes we'd like to try.'

'There are lots of bike trails, too,' said Lucy, looking at Hanna hopefully.

Farida sighed. 'You're all so *active*. I want to sit on a beach and read. And eat well. I don't mind going for walks, but I'm *not* climbing any mountains.' She looked over to Saïd. 'Sorry.'

He shrugged. 'I like walking.'

'And eating,' added Felix.

'And eating,' said Saïd.

NIKOLAI AND ROBERTO entered the room, Nikolai carrying a stack of plates and cutlery and Roberto triumphantly bearing a cake decorated with thick brown butter icing.

'Ta-da!' he cried. 'Mrs Park's coffee and walnut cake, all for us!'

Nikolai set the plates down on the coffee table and pulled up extra chairs, while Roberto fussed round, serving everyone a slice. Hanna couldn't put her finger on it, but she sensed something in Nikolai and Roberto's friendship had shifted: always naturally outgoing, Roberto had become almost excessively extroverted. Hanna hoped history wasn't about to repeat itself. Last year, he'd developed an awkward, unrequited crush on their classmate Seru, an irrevocably heterosexual Fijian rugby player. Having failed the end-of-year language exam, Seru had left the *Shantivira* programme. Now Roberto had apparently found a new focus for his affections.

The conversation about holidays continued. Lucy said, 'What I'd really like to do is spend more time in Samae, diving with Björn.' She turned to Nikolai. 'Imagine how much we'd get done if we could go every day.'

Nikolai said, 'That would be great, but I want to climb too.' He looked at Roberto. 'That whole coastline is pretty rocky. We might find some interesting routes.'

'Cliff climbing?' said Felix. 'What kind of rock is it?'

'I don't know; it looks limestoney.'

'The beach there is nice, Farida,' said Lucy. 'Shall I ask about holiday rentals when we go next weekend?'

'Are there restaurants?' asked Farida. The west coast of Syenitia was sparsely populated and Hanna knew she preferred big cities.

'A couple. Nothing fancy, but we won't starve.'

'Tell you what, guys,' said Felix, 'let's go with them one weekend and check out these cliffs. Then we can decide.'

'Sounds like a plan,' said Saïd. 'I'm ready for a proper vacation.'

'You're right,' Farida said. 'We haven't had a decent break since the new year. I feel a bit washed out, to be honest.'

'Me too,' said Lucy. 'Christmas was so long ago. Talking of Christmas, what happened to that SD card? We never heard any more about it. We'll have to ask Joe what he did with it.'

Hanna and Farida exchanged glances. Not pursuing it was one thing. But Joe couldn't expect them to lie to the others. Farida spoke first. 'Joe never got it, Lucy. Irion told Hanna it was stolen before Mary could give it to him.'

'Stolen?' Lucy yelped. 'After all we went through to get it?'

Horrified gasps rippled round the group.

'It's worse than you think,' said Hanna. 'It can only have been one of us.' She spotted Roberto's confusion and said, 'Not you, Roberto, you weren't there. But someone sitting here.'

'Well, you can't think it was me this time,' said Lucy.

Hanna shook her head. 'No. Anyway, Joe told us the

card was safe and not to discuss it or pursue it. So we haven't.'

An awkward silence fell. Hanna dabbed up the remaining crumbs on her plate and ate them while studying her friends' faces.

'It was me.'

Nikolai. She *knew* it.

'Nikolai!' said Lucy, jumping to her feet. 'You *fuck-wumpet!*'

'I'm sorry,' he said. He turned to face Hanna. 'I'm especially sorry about lying to you at your party, Hanna.'

Hanna's nostrils flared. 'You were very convincing,' she said. 'I'm not sure I'll ever believe anything you say, ever again.'

Nikolai studied his trainers. They weren't as white as they'd once been. He straightened up saying, 'I'm sorry you feel that way. But it was ... necessary.' He lifted his chin. 'Joe's right. The card is in safe hands.'

'*Why?*' Roberto asked. 'Why did you steal this thing if it was meant for Joe?'

Nikolai paused. They waited.

'So, I told you my mum is an ex-Shantiviran, right?'

Nods around the circle. 'Svetlana Poroshkin,' Saïd said.

'Yes,' said Nikolai. 'That's honestly all I knew – until I told her about what happened in Switzerland. She kept asking me all these questions I couldn't answer, because I hadn't seen Nestor and David's weapon for myself. When I told her what was on the SD card, she said I must get it for her and bring it to her personally in Yakutsk.' He looked up at them. 'You haven't met my mother. She's pretty hard to say no to.'

'So you went to Yakutsk?' prompted Roberto.

'*Da*. I went to Yakutsk. And Nestor and David's facility wasn't the only weapons development operation secretly funded by Kitty, without permission from the Galaksi Alliance. Mum thinks she has several running in parallel. Kitty doesn't want to leave protecting the Earth to chance and the goodwill of the Alliance. One of those facilities … is my mum's.'

'Safe hands, then?' queried Hassan, who'd been listening carefully.

Nikolai shrugged. 'Safer than Nestor's, for sure. Kitty knows she has it. But Joe doesn't know about it. Please don't tell him.'

'He doesn't *want* to know,' said Hanna. 'I think he suspects, but if he knew for certain he'd have to report it to Aldeman. If we tried to tell him he'd probably stick his fingers in his ears and sing "la-la-la" until we gave up.'

Hassan chuckled and poured himself another coffee. 'He probably would.'

Nikolai cleared his throat. 'While I'm coming clean—'

'What?' said Lucy.

'The diving. I love diving; I'd be helping Björn anyway. But Mum wants me to find out what the Pweza's power source is.'

'Won't that get you into trouble?' Farida said. 'You don't want to be kicked off the programme like David Wang.'

'She says no, because it's not the Syenitians' secret. They won't mind.'

Lucy's eyes sparkled. 'I'll help you. I can keep my

promise to David after all. I'm sure Björn will too, if we tell him.'

Inwardly, Hanna sighed with relief. If the whole affair was Kitty-approved, she could stop worrying. She'd drop by the language school tonight after swimming with Hassan. Kitty wouldn't mind if she told Irion and Mary. Would she?

13. MEETINGS, MEETINGS
JOE

J OE STOOD BY the buffet, with only an orange juice and a plate of tiny sandwiches to shield him from the Argentinian delegate's barrage of questions. He took a step back as the old man flourished a sheaf of printouts under Joe's nose. Somehow this guy had got hold of the species summaries Delius had uploaded to the dark web last year. What was a UN representative doing with *them*?

'Well, Mr … er,'—Joe leaned forward to check the man's nametag—'Mendez. If you'd let me get a word in, I can tell you about them.' He raised his glass in the direction of the top sheet. 'That one there is a Sayari; their skin evolved that colour to protect them from their highly radioactive sun. They're good, law-abiding people. Fun fact: instead of laughing, they waggle their ears when they're amused.'

Mendez picked out another sheet, which showed a grey-skinned being from multiple angles. It had three eyes, evenly spaced around its bald head. 'And this one?'

'A Mhasibu,' said Joe. 'Very serious. Great accountants. Never miss a thing.'

'What about this creature?' Another image, showing a brown, insect-like alien with six limbs.

'A Wadudu. They joined the Galaksi Alliance fairly recently. I've heard they're excellent chemists.' Thank goodness all the pictures were of Alliance members. At this stage, he didn't want to terrify people with details about the Ranglatiri.

'What about *that*? Surely it's not real?'

'That's a Grooka.' Joe grinned. 'Don't get into a fight with a Grooka. They might look like big green teddy bears, but they're short because their planet is so huge.'

Mendez looked blank.

'Their gravity is twice what it is here,' Joe explained. 'An adult Grooka barely comes up to my waist, but she could throw me across the room, no bother.'

They were interrupted by a young man in a checked shirt, open at the neck to reveal a white T-shirt underneath. He took Joe's hand and pumped it up and down, saying, 'It's an honour to meet you, sir. I'm Karl Zuhowski, from NASA's Orbital Debris Program Office? Do you have a minute for some questions?'

Joe looked across at Jorge Mendez, who'd already gathered up his papers and turned away without saying goodbye. 'Sure,' he said. 'Let's find a table so I can put down my drink and eat something.'

'I enjoyed your briefing earlier,' said Zuhowski.

'Thanks,' said Joe, taking a bite of his dainty tuna and cucumber sandwich. 'I'm not used to speaking in front of so many people.'

The UN delegates had listened to his presentation in respectful silence, then proceeded with a pre-prepared set of logical questions. Thankfully, they were calm and professional: focused on gathering the facts to report to their superiors. At least half of them had already met Joe at one of the many smaller meetings Susan had invited him to in recent months, where he'd attempted to persuade them of the *Shantivira's* good intentions individually. This session had been on a larger scale: Board Room D had been packed.

Joe had no idea how the national governments – Earth's 'real' authorities – were taking the news of first contact. So far, they'd all been unnervingly quiet on the subject, but he suspected frantic behind-the-scenes activity. Time would tell. His biggest worry was that they'd feel threatened and make some kind of pre-emptive strike. The Syenitian Council would take that as a sign humans weren't worth the effort after all and those wishing to shut down the *Shantivira* project might get their way – leaving the Earth defenceless. It had been hard enough getting the Council's agreement for this approach in the first place.

Zuhowski placed his empty plate on the table. Judging from the pastry crumbs, he'd been eating sausage rolls. 'I wanted to ask more about the debris dematerialising you do.'

As he ate, Joe ran through the work the *Shantivira* did to keep the terrestrial space station orbits free of debris, explaining how the magnetic shielding they'd installed on the ISS last summer was saving them a lot of time. Now they only needed to protect China's space station and the satellites' orbits.

'Ah, there you are, Joe!' Susan came over to join them. 'Before I forget, I wanted to return this.' She placed Joe's wedding ring on the table.

Quickly, he picked it up and put it back on his thumb.

'Thanks, Susan. Did it give you the proof you needed?'

'Oh yes. It caused quite the sensation among the powers that be, once they received the lab results. I had to pull several strings to get it back for you.'

Joe noticed Zuhowski's curious expression. 'It's made of *valkoinium*, a metal we don't have on Earth,' he explained. 'Stronger than diamonds.' Then he took a deep breath before asking the million-dollar question. 'So, Susan, when can I speak to the UN General Assembly in New York?'

Susan smiled kindly and put her hand over his. It felt warm and strong. 'I'm sorry, Joe. The committee will want many more meetings – with you and without you – before we can take things that far. Perhaps early next year, if we're lucky.'

Behind Zuhowski, he observed a few delegates who'd overheard and were smirking at his naivety. He clearly still had some convincing to do, despite all the evidence he'd submitted. Working with 'normal' humans again was tough. He'd forgotten how much patient persuasion was needed to win people's support.

Joe remembered Dalian's personal threat to have the *Shantivira's* funding cancelled if he failed and his resolve stiffened. He'd sit through every boring meeting and stroke as many egos as he had to, if that's what it took to protect the Earth. With the exception of Dan, the ISS crew had kept their side of the bargain. Dan had been dealt with. Now it was up to Joe to do his part. Fleetingly, he considered taking up golf, then shivered. Hopefully that wouldn't be necessary.

+   +   +

AFTER LUNCH, JOE handed back his security pass at the VIC gate and headed for the *Kaisermühlen* U-Bahn station with a spring in his step, like a child let out of school early.

Your presentation went well, didn't it? said Kitty in his head. It was the first time he'd heard from her since she'd dropped him off that morning. He couldn't see her, but he knew she was waiting further along the crowded platform. In case of trouble, she'd been with him as a gecko on the ceiling, but they'd agreed she wouldn't show herself unless she had to. They planned to take the train into central Vienna, where they could teleport home without being seen. There were too many security cameras around the VIC.

Once I got warmed up, yeah, it went OK. Thanks for helping me practise.

It's a novelty to see you in a well-cut suit. You look fantastic, babe.

I'd rather be wearing jeans, Joe grimaced. Suits were never quite comfortable. *At least Susan returned my ring. My thumb felt wrong without it.*

How was lunch? Kitty asked. *That guy with the papers had his knickers in a right old twist, didn't he?*

Joe grinned. *He did.*

There was something familiar about him ... no ... it's gone. Perhaps it'll come to me later.

I'm glad the Americans didn't ask me about Dan. I was surprised they didn't.

Perhaps the UN delegates don't know he's missing.

The train pulled in and the doors slid open.

We get off at Stephansplatz, right? he asked.
Right. Find a good place and I'll follow you there.

THE DOORS CLOSED and Joe looked around the carriage, seeing if he could spot Kitty. Up at the far end, two young women were enjoying an uninhibited snog. The world had obviously moved on since his time in London. Hooray for that.

He turned back to find two square-jawed, prop-forward types between him and the doors, their casual clothes bland and expensive. An older one and a younger one, both a head taller than Joe. Actually, they looked like carbon copies of Dan Simpson. Did they make these guys in a mould or something? He'd bet his socks they were US military. Uh-oh. He gave Kitty a mental nudge to watch through his eyes.

'Can I help you gentlemen?' he asked, treating them to his friendliest smile.

'Joe Llewellyn?'

'That's me,' he said, keeping it light. A woman wearing sunglasses and a floaty cotton dress – daisies on a yellow background, buttons down the front – came along the carriage and slid into a nearby seat. Kitty. She pulled a paperback novel out of her handbag and pretended to read.

Are they armed? he asked her.

Don't know. They're not transmitting, which suggests they're on their own. No back up team in a van somewhere.

That's a relief.

'We want to talk to you. Someplace private,' said the

older one with the marginally less severe haircut.

'What about?'

'Friend of ours. Went missing a while back.'

Ah. 'Dan Simpson?'

'So you do know him.'

'Our paths have crossed,' said Joe. 'Would a café do? I fancy some coffee and cake.'

The two men shared a glance. 'OK.'

Do you know anywhere, Cath?

From Stephansplatz? Yeah, I'll guide you.

Out loud, he said, 'I know just the place. Will you tell me who you are and where you came from while we wait for our stop?'

'No. Not here.'

They waited in silence for the journey to end. The men seemed uncomfortable, as if embarrassed by the situation. Joe guessed whatever they did for a living, it didn't usually involve playing the part of professional muscle. He relaxed slightly. Perhaps they really only wanted to talk.

At the station, the escalator carried them up to street level. Behind him, he heard one of the men say to the other, 'Did you *see* those girls making out, right there in the subway car?'

Kitty was a few steps above, carefully not paying them any attention whatsoever.

He said, *Bit demure for you isn't it, that dress?*

It's my cunning disguise.

It works. I almost didn't recognise you.

They came out by the Stephansdom, its roof tiles glittering like emerald scales in the midsummer sun. He followed Kitty away from the cathedral, along a shopping street and left down an alleyway.

Starbucks? he said, surprised, but she was already past it. Ahead of them, she stopped to look in the window of a shop selling stuffed toys. A giraffe as high as the doorway peered out onto the street.

Oh, those bears are so cute! *Do you think Flora's too old for cuddly toys? Thandiwe isn't.*

Cath! *You are* not *going shopping now.*

Afterwards though? Once we've found out what your goons want?

They're not my *goons!*

Well they're not mine, are they? I'm not shopping, babe. I need to get changed so they don't realise I was with you on the train.

Where am I taking them? he asked as he walked past her, trying not to look.

Go to the end of the street and turn left. Café Sans Souci is a little way along on your left. I went dancing there, back between the wars. See you there.

Don't be long.

THERE WAS NO Café Sans Souci, but there *was* a Café Bräunerhof. He slid into a seat by the window, facing the door. The younger man sat next to him, blocking his exit, the other – the one who'd done all the talking so far – sat opposite, spreading himself out so he took up nearly the whole bench.

Joe looked him straight in the eye. 'So, who are you, who sent you, and what do you want from me?'

'We're here … unofficially. I'm Ray, that's Paul,' he

gestured at his colleague. 'We know Dan from way back when. His parents are concerned. He hasn't called them for months. Normally he checks in every few weeks. When his father asked NASA, they said Dan was on sabbatical and they'd no idea where he was.'

A bell tingled as the café door opened and a Syenitian-height Kitty strode in, now all in black. Ankle boots, wet-look leggings and a close-fitting sleeveless top with a raised collar and a plunging V-neck. Her hair hung in a long plait over her shoulder; wrap-around sunglasses hid her glittering eyes. Joe felt a sudden urge to press his face onto the bare flesh of her chest and inhale her scent. She sensed his desire and her mouth twitched in amusement. Sometimes their telepathy didn't even need words.

She approached the table. 'Hello boys,' she said, her voice deep and confident. Then, to Ray, 'Scooch over.'

'Yes, ma'am.' Ray slid closer to the window and she sat beside him, blocking *his* exit.

The waiter swooped in and Kitty used her perfect German to help them order coffee and the cake they wanted. When he'd gone, Joe said, 'This is Kitty. Kitty, these are friends of Dan's: Ray and Paul. Carry on with your story, Ray.' The power balance had shifted. Now Joe was in charge.

Ray did a recap for Kitty, obviously itching to know who she was but not daring to ask.

'... a few weeks ago, they received a letter from him and they believe he's having a mental breakdown.'

'Can I see this letter?' said Joe.

'No. We don't have it. It was a crazy tale about being abducted by aliens. But that he's fine and won't be coming back anytime soon.'

Oh God. The utter numpty, said Kitty. *I told him not to mention the Alliance.*

Perhaps he didn't.

'The thing is,' said Ray, 'it was hand delivered. So it couldn't be true. But they're clutching at straws.'

The waiter brought their cake: apple for Ray, chocolate for Paul and rhubarb with creamy meringue topping for Joe. Kitty poured three cups of coffee and sat back to watch them eat.

Paul cleared his throat. 'There's a rumour that something happened to the ISS during Dan's mission – something involving another, previously unknown space station, of which *you* are the captain. When Mr Simpson senior learned from a UN contact you'd be presenting here today, he sent us to talk to you. Alone,' he added, looking pointedly at Kitty.

'The only other people who know what happened are in Russia or still in space,' said Ray. 'If you have *any* information, please share it. His mom's worried sick.'

Do you believe them? Joe asked Kitty. *They're here for the parents?*

Not just for the parents. No way. I took photos on the train and looked them up. They're both NASA. Ray Scott is fairly high up the food-chain. I'm guessing the big cheeses didn't like Dan's resignation letter and want to know why he's gone AWOL. And if he's really off-world. I don't doubt they know Dan personally, though. Look at them!

I know what you mean, said Joe. *Same hair, same way of holding themselves. I can imagine he'd dress the same way too, off duty.*

Not any more, she replied. *He's had a makeover. I think he's released his inner rebel, twenty years later than most humans do.*

Did you read what he wrote before you delivered the letters?

Nope. I thought it was none of my business. What shall we tell them, Joe?

You'll *tell them the truth. I'm sworn to secrecy, remember? Minimum details. But they need to know he's been well-treated or it'll affect my progress with the UN.*

OK, boss.

'You can tell her he's fine,' said Kitty out loud. 'I saw him last month. He gave me the letters to deliver.'

'Where is he?' demanded Paul.

'In the Elegua sector, on a planet called Amra. Abducted is a strong term: I prefer "removed to a safe distance".'

Ray said, 'So it's *true*? About the aliens? He's not the type to make up stories.'

Kitty turned her back to the room and took off her sunglasses. Her green eyes sparkled, the vertical pupils narrow slits against the dazzling sunlight outside. She treated them to a broad grin, displaying her elongated canines which, so far, she'd kept concealed. 'Yes. It's true.'

The colour drained from Ray's face and he jerked back away from her, thumping his head on the window. Paul started getting up, but Joe grabbed his arm and pulled him back into his seat. 'Don't you want to know what happened to your friend?'

Kitty said, 'Dan made Joe a promise, which he broke. More than once. It was agreed Dan should be removed to a place where he couldn't upset our delicate negotiations before they'd begun. After Joe approached the UN, I went to bring him home … but – and this is kind of embarrassing – he's having such a great time, he didn't want to come back. That's why he wrote the letters.'

'How do we know you're not just saying that?' said Paul in a shaky voice. 'How do we even know he's still alive?'

Kitty reached behind her back and took out her *zana*, seemingly out of thin air. Joe liked to imagine she had a sort of invisible Mary Poppins rucksack where she kept her stuff. Another of his wife's many mysteries.

She put it on the table and activated the 2D mode so it looked like a conventional Earth tablet. She pulled up a video and the words to Tom Petty & the Heartbreakers' 'Learning to Fly' and a guitar accompaniment filled the room. The waiter's head flicked round and she lowered the volume quickly.

'That sounds like Dan!' said Ray, astonishment overtaking shock.

Kitty passed him the screen. 'He's made quite a name for himself,' she said.

Ray's eyes widened as he watched the clip of Dan in concert at *The Garden*. Joe wondered what Ray found more surprising: Dan's musical talent, his new look, or the alien audience.

'Show me!' said Paul. Joe noticed a tremor in his hand as he almost snatched the device from his colleague. 'He played that all the time at Princeton,' he said. 'Kind of a running gag, 'cause we were doing Air Force ROTC.'

'But even so, why would he stay?' said Ray. 'Away

from his family and his buddies?'

Joe smiled. 'I believe he's met someone.'

I watched them. He's utterly smitten. If you ask me, she looked like trouble with a capital T. But it's his life.

'What, an *alien* woman? Like *her*?' said Paul, pointing at Kitty.

'Not like me,' she said. 'A Sayari. Silver skin. Your height, but more willowy.'

Paul shook his head. 'I don't believe you. That's gross. No offence, ma'am, but Dan just isn't that kind of guy.'

Joe called over the waiter and signalled his intention to pay.

'Can we get a copy of that?' Ray asked, nodding at the video.

'No,' said Joe. 'Listen, we're going now. Don't try to stop us. We can't tell you anything else. All other communication must go via the proper UN channels. But I promise you, Dan's having the time of his life. He won't come home until he's ready.'

+ + +

THEY MATERIALISED IN the living area of the *Pride* and Kitty cocked her head to one side, listening.

There's something going on. Come on.

Kitty shifted to her jaguar form and they jogged over to Docking Bay 2, where a group of *Tumbas* were coming in to land, one by one. Hassan and Ozzy were out of their spacecrafts and dancing a jig together, arm-in-arm in their flight suits. Shakila descended from her *Tumba*, removing her helmet and fluffing up her hair with a practised hand as she headed for the lift.

'Damn it, the minute I give orders not to be disturbed, I miss some action,' muttered Joe. More loudly, he called, 'What happened?'

Delius appeared at his side. 'Probes, Captain, but none like we've seen before. Small, fast, no ID. No response to our attempts to communicate. They were moving in decreasing orbits, as if they intended penetrating the atmosphere. Yisheng and I decided we should destroy them before they got that far. There he is, coming in now. He'll give you a full report.'

Joe watched as Yisheng landed his *Tumba*. 'Did you capture one?' he asked Delius. 'So we can take it apart and find out where it came from?'

'No. It was a bit of a scramble, sir, to knock them all out. There were too many. If we'd taken the time to pull in a sample, we'd have risked letting one get past us.'

'Shame,' said Joe. 'But it was the right call. Well done. Wish I'd been here to help.'

Hassan and Ozzy crossed the docking bay, both beaming from ear to ear.

'Joe, that was our last training mission! We've qualified!' They crouched down to make a fuss of Kitty, who nuzzled them affectionately.

'*That's* what the dance was for. Congratulations!' He shook their hands. 'Welcome to the official crew. Now give me your mission report.'

Ozzy blinked. 'What, in writing?'

Joe laughed. 'No, you eejit, just tell me how it was.'

'Stressful,' said Ozzy. 'Slippery little tykes, they were.'

Hassan said, 'They were impossible to see: we had to

do it all on screen. They were way faster than the orbital debris we've dematerialised so far.'

'Yeah,' said Ozzy, 'and debris doesn't actively try to evade you. I didn't know probes did that.'

'They don't, usually,' said Joe, thoughtfully. 'Looks like these were something different.'

'But we got them all, in the end,' said Hassan.

'You did,' said Joe. 'Well done. So you're due a long leave. What will you do with it?'

'We're going travelling,' said Ozzy. 'Hassan's going to show me Africa.'

'What, all of it?'

'No,' scoffed Hassan. 'But I'll take him to meet my foster family, show him where I grew up, do some tourist stuff, you know. Lake Victoria, a safari; we haven't planned the details yet. We'll take a couple of the others with us too. And … I'm going back to Juba.'

'Oh Hassan, are you sure?' Joe bit his lip, annoyed at himself for speaking before thinking. Of course Hassan was sure, or he wouldn't have said so.

'It's been nearly fifteen years. I need to go. The situation there isn't as bad as when I left.'

'Fair enough. I know you'll take care of each other.'

I'll keep an eye on him, Joe, discreetly.

Do that. Isn't there a civil war in South Sudan right now?

Yes, but they're having peace talks. It looks like they might even sign a deal soon.

YISHENG CAME TO join them, and Hassan and Ozzy went to get changed.

'Hey, Yisheng, sorry I missed all the fun,' said Joe.

'Did Delius tell you already?'

'He did. But I'd like to hear your version. Was there really no chance to get a sample?'

Yisheng shook his head. 'We were lucky to stop them reaching the planet as it was.'

Joe said, 'Whoever sent them will be suspicious when they don't return. But I don't see what else we could've done. We'll cross that bridge when we come to it. Something that sophisticated: I doubt we've heard the last of it.'

A bleep from Joe's *zana* interrupted them. 'I'd better take this. I'll catch up with you later, OK?' Joe turned away to take the call. 'Gabriel! Thanks for getting back to me. Let me take you back to the *Pride* where it's quieter.'

The little holographic Gabriel peered past him, into the docking bay.

'Busy day?' After more than a decade living in New York as the Irish ambassador to the UN, Gabriel still hadn't lost his accent.

'Always something going on. Do you miss it?'

'Different lifetime, mate. I'm one of the grown-ups now. Talking of which, how did you get on this morning?'

Joe climbed the steps into his ship. 'Honestly?' He placed Gabriel on the table and pulled out a chair for himself. Jaguar-Kitty jumped onto the sofa and settled down, one ear tuned to their conversation like a satellite antenna. 'They were mostly polite, but I'm not sure what they actually thought. That's why I called you, Gabe. Sooner or later, they'll send me to the General Assembly. We need to be ready. There's a lot of persuasion to do behind the scenes first.'

'You need me to activate the others?'

'You know who they are?'

'A couple of people I recognise from my *Shantivira* days, otherwise no. I presume Delius has their details?'

'Of course. I'll ask him to send them to your *zana*.'

'How many of us are there?' asked Gabriel.

'Nine embedded in various parts of the UN, including you. We need to get everyone together soon so we can agree our approach. Can you organise it?'

'Sure. Where should we do it?'

'Here?' Joe suggested. 'On the *Shantivira*?'

'A barbecue?'

'Sounds good. Tell me when they can all make it and I'll talk to Maneewan.'

14. HATRED

NESTOR

'STOP HERE, PLEASE,' said Nestor to the taxi driver, pulling out his wallet. This street wasn't at all what he'd expected from Pedro, who'd lived in buzzing city centres ever since their university days in Buenos Aires. This was ... *suburban.* A modern white cube with dark, horizontal slits for windows, bordered by a well-maintained lawn and neatly trimmed shrubs in pots. It must be Pilar's influence.

He opened the metal gate and walked up the path to the gun-metal grey front door. He pressed the buzzer and a bell chimed within. Footsteps approached; the door opened. Pedro's pretty wife had aged, but hadn't they all?

'*¡Hola, Nestor! ¿Cómo estás?*'

'*¡Pilar!*' They hugged and kissed cheeks, old friends reunited. Pedro descended the polished granite stairs and greeted him warmly. His slicked-back hair was thinning, but he retained his sense of style: dressed today in a shirt, slacks and embroidered velvet slippers.

'Nestor,' he said in Spanish, 'welcome to Vienna!'

'My friend,' replied Nestor, 'it's good to meet in person again, after all these years.'

'Lunch will be a little while,' said Pilar. 'You two go and catch up.'

Pedro showed Nestor into his study and prepared *mate*. Nestor took a seat in a black leather armchair and waited for his friend to complete the ritual. He received the proffered gourd gratefully and sucked on the silver straw until no more bitter liquid came, then handed it back to his host.

'*Gracias*. So, tell me, how did it go? Did he recognise you? Was *she* there?'

'I didn't *see* her. And he had no clue who I was. I switched to using my middle name after I failed my *Shantivira* assessment, because I didn't want them finding me. Only family and school friends call me Pedro nowadays.'

Nestor touched his fingertips together. 'Mendez is so common, it's unlikely they'd make a connection. None of us look as we did forty years ago. I think we're safe.'

'The others were most interested in your alien profiles. I forwarded them to as many people as I could, along with Llewellyn's explanations.'

'Did you say where they came from?'

'I said a contact discovered them on the internet, quite by accident.'

'Almost true.'

Pedro smirked. 'I'm not sure how convinced they were. But Llewellyn actually *gave* them credibility by talking about them. More fool him. It's a first step in our battle for hearts and minds, anyway.'

He topped up the *mate* with hot water. 'So, how is it going? Are you really starting all over again?'

Nestor sighed. 'What choice do I have? I'm not starting from the beginning, though. I have my assistant and most of my records. It pays to keep backups in a separate location. I've found premises near where I grew up, but it'll take years to get back to where we were. We must stop Llewellyn *now*, Pedro, before it's too late.'

'I can disrupt things as much as possible at this end,' said Pedro, sipping his second helping, 'but I'm only one person.'

Nestor studied the geometric patterns in the silk rug at his feet. Afghan, he guessed. Certainly hand-made and probably antique. It did little to soften the white-tiled floor; its purpose was purely ornamental.

'A well-situated person,' he said. 'Don't be too disruptive, *mi amigo*. We mustn't risk your position. It's too valuable. Rather, keep your ears open for people who are having doubts and might be persuaded to join our cause. Tell me when they let Llewellyn speak to the General Assembly.'

'Not for months. Years possibly. They're not taking him seriously yet.' Pedro passed the gourd to Nestor again and he cupped it in his hands, contemplating.

'Let's hope they never do,' he said. 'Good. That gives me more time to prepare. We must send the Syenitians a clear message that the Earth doesn't want their help.'

'You'll never forgive her, will you?'

'Never. She led me down a path of sin and defiled me. Because of her, I've never felt able to live a normal life. A wife, a family—I do envy you, Pedro.' The corners of Nestor's mouth turned downwards. 'Perhaps I should be grateful to her, for making me realise I have a higher purpose. God put me on this Earth to prevent His creation from being overrun by filthy aliens.'

'But you still want revenge?'

'Of course.' Nestor smiled thinly. 'Who wouldn't? They destroyed my life's work. I did extract some useful information from David Wang the traitor: Llewellyn is my key. If he suffers, she will too.'

'What are you planning, Nestor?'

Nestor took a long draught of *mate*, then shook his head with a malevolent smile. 'It's better you don't know, Pedro. Anyway, I'm still exploring possibilities. I do have a little side project on the go, in case my plans don't work out. I've been dividing my time between Patagonia and the UK.'

Pilar put her head round the door. 'Lunch is ready. Can you help me carry everything through?'

15. THE STOWAWAY

DAN

D AN WOKE AND stretched, taking care not to disturb
the still-slumbering Afra beside him. He loved
watching her sleep. Her habitual defensive ferocity
vanished and she appeared at peace; a picture of inno-
cence.

She was away two weeks out of four now, since the
Gezi Urdina had been repaired, but she stayed with him
whenever she was in Laro. He suspected she still kept her
own place, but it seemed she preferred his company to
solitude. Or maybe she just liked his apartment better.
Once they'd discovered humans and Sayari were indeed
physically compatible, Dan found himself unable to refuse
her anything.

He still had no idea what her 'deliveries' involved, or
where they took her. He worried they were dangerous and
she was keeping quiet to protect him. Or that she still
didn't trust him. What if something happened to her?
How long would he wait for her, not knowing if she was
OK?

'Penny for them?' The brown eyes were watching him.
Afra was awake.

'Oh,' said Dan. 'The usual. Who are you, really? Why

won't you let me into your life? Do you even care about me, or do you only stay with me for sex and food?'

'I'm Afra Azu and I care,' she said, stroking his face with surprising tenderness. 'We've had this conversation a hundred times, Dan. If you want to be with me, you can't ask me stuff like that. I don't ask you questions, do I? You think I don't wonder why you're here, what you did to have the Galaksi Alliance maroon you in this dump? Sometimes it's better not to know. Let's just have some fun together while we can, OK? What's for breakfast?'

'Sausages,' he said, rolling on top of her, deflecting conflict with sex again, as was their habit. She giggled and responded by nibbling his ear.

Afterwards, he left her in bed and took a shower. While he was drying off, Afra stuck her head around the door. 'Dan? My *zana* battery's flat and I need to check the weather forecast. Can I borrow yours?'

'Sure,' he said, lathering up his face for a shave. 'Help yourself.'

WHEN HE CAME out of the bathroom, he found a still-naked Afra at the kitchen table with a face like thunder, watching a hologram projection from his *zana*. The video which had reversed his fortunes the day he'd arrived in Laro. Now he understood every word.

On a repeating loop, Aldeman was saying, 'Dan Simpson will be staying in Laro for several months as the honoured guest of the Galaksi Alliance before being returned to his home planet by one of our agents. We have rented a ground floor apartment for him at Suukimpravit 56, in the Mang district. The Alliance will be grateful for any help and support you can give him.'

'It started playing by itself when I unlocked it,' said Afra. 'I wasn't spying on you.' Her eyes flashed with fury. 'It was all lies, wasn't it? You don't hate the Galaksi Alliance: they're your meal ticket. Did they tell you to approach me? To find out what I do?'

'No, Afra, they never mentioned you. Aldeman's only saying that to protect me.'

Afra let out a bark of choked laughter. 'You know Varpushaukka *by his first name*? Who's their agent? Who do you report to? *What* are you reporting?' She was shouting now. '*Have you told them about me?*'

Dan's expression gave him away and he looked at the floor, embarrassed.

'WHAT did you tell them?'

'Nothing! Not even your name.' His voice cracked. 'Just that … I love you.' He took a deep breath. 'And not to contact me again because I'm going to stay here to be with you.'

Afra threw her arms in the air in frustration. 'Well, if that's true, you're a fucking idiot!' Her liquid-dark eyes, usually so expressive, were cold and flat. 'Frankly, Dan, your clinginess is unattractive. I was going to tell you; I'm leaving for another trip tonight. But now I've seen this, it's over. You won't see me again.'

She dressed hurriedly, gathered her few belongings and shoved the half-loaf of bread on the worktop into her rucksack.

Dan froze, dumbstruck. His stomach clenched and his tongue felt like a slug in his mouth. What could he say to make her stay?

'Bye,' she said, not looking him in the eye.

Dan regained the power of speech. 'Afra! Wait—'

But she'd already slammed the door.

+　+　+

HE DIDN'T GO to work that day. Instead, he paced the streets of Laro, not caring where his feet took him. He couldn't believe it was over. He wouldn't believe it. He was sure the Galaksi Alliance had no interest in Afra and her exploits. If Kitty had even passed on the information, which was doubtful. She'd seemed more amused and pleased for him than curious. Whatever it was Afra was doing, it was making her paranoid. How could he make her trust him?

+　+　+

AT DUSK HE was on the ferry, crossing to the spaceport. Now he'd made the decision to come, he prayed he wasn't too late. And that he could remember the way. At the boardwalk, he looked for the gap he'd followed Afra into, all those months ago. There. That one. Carefully, he threaded his way between the buildings, hoping he wouldn't meet anything nasty.

He approached the clearing with caution, staying hidden in the shadow of a deserted workshop. The *Gezi Urdina* was still there. Plus, the ramp was down! Relief washed through him, from his heart to his toes. Afra must still be loading her mysterious cargo. Perhaps it was his lucky day after all.

He jiggled his rucksack into a better position and picked up his guitar case. Now or never. Go! He ran across the open space and sheltered under the gangway, listening. Nothing. He climbed up to the main corridor as swiftly and as silently as he could. He needed to find a hiding place, fast. If she caught him now, she'd never take him with her. The engine room. That would do. He slipped through the door and shoved his rucksack and guitar under the gently pulsing cylinder, before squeezing through the gap himself. He pushed his stuff into the far corner and huddled up beside it. If she opened the door, she'd be unlikely to spot him unless she looked below the reactor.

Voices outside. He recognised Afra's, but not the language she was speaking. It wasn't the melodic tones of Kawaida, but something harsher, more sibilant. The other voice was deeper: male. Dan heard the lifting mechanism of the ramp grind into action and Afra and her conversation partner moving away down the corridor. He'd got into position just in time. Did Afra have an accomplice? That was something he'd never considered.

The silver tube began to throb, then settled into a high-pitched whine which quivered Dan's stomach until he thought he'd faint. Within minutes it became unbearable. Something else Dan hadn't considered: the noise the engine made when in use. Stupid, stupid. He had to get out of here.

Dan spotted a hatch in the floor at the other end of the room. Quickly, he opened it and peered below. It was dark and full of boxes; it must be the cargo hold. He knew Afra wouldn't want him in there, but he didn't want to leave the engine room by the main door. They were probably still close enough to Amra for Afra to turn around and take him back. He must stay hidden long enough for them to be in deep space when she found him. Then she'd *have* to take him with her, wouldn't she?

He dropped his rucksack down and lowered his guitar case on top of it, before swinging down himself. Wow, it was cold. Why couldn't he breathe? No air, he realised. Shit. His knees buckled and he slumped to the metal floor, unconscious.

+   +   +

DAN WOKE WITH a shiver. Why was his head wet? Where was he? Before he could move, a splash of water filled his eyes and nostrils, leaving him choking and spluttering as he struggled to raise himself to a sitting position.

Water. Whoever it was out there throwing water at him might be able to give him some to drink. His mouth was dry and sticky, his neck was stiff and his head throbbed like hell. Had he been out drinking? He didn't remember. He opened his eyes and looked around. He was on the floor of a dimly lit metal cage, an eight-foot cube with a sturdy padlock on the only door.

On the other side of the bars, casually swinging a bucket in a snow-white four-fingered hand, was a being which struck terror into Dan's soul. He'd seen one before – on a screen, at a safe distance – last year when the *Shantivira* team had narrowly prevented the Earth from being invaded. Face-to-face was petrifying. Although, in fact, it had no face, only a convex white mesh, shrouded by the deep hood of a heavy grey cloak. A Ranglatiri. Was it going to torture him? He knew these creatures were capable of spectacular cruelty. They were cannibals, relishing the flesh of their own kind or any intelligent creature.

If it ran an electric current through the cage, Dan would fry. Was that its plan? Was that why it had soaked him? Was he about to die in excruciating pain?

'What are you doing here, Sssyenitian?' it hissed in Kawaida. 'Who knows you're here?'

Did Afra work for the Ranglatiri? She wasn't like them; Dan refused to believe it. Had she been so secretive to protect him?

'I'm not a Syenitian!' said Dan. 'I'm from Earth. I came to find Afra.'

'*You're* Afra's Earthling?' The creature laughed: a hollow, gravelly rumble. 'She's been in a foul mood about you all day. I can't promise she'll be pleased to see you.'

So it knew about him. Dan summoned his courage and asked, 'Have you any water?'

The Ranglatiri looked in its bucket. 'I used it all trying to wake you. I'll bring more.'

'Thanks,' said Dan, shivering again. It was too cold for wet clothes.

The Ranglatiri noticed. It pulled off its cloak and pushed it through the bars, saying, 'Wrap yourself in this. You can have your things back once we've gone through your stuff.'

Gratefully, Dan complied. Underneath, the creature wore a simple black tunic and leggings. The bare skin Dan could see was the same pure white as its hands. Did these guys have no blood? A shock of fluffy white hair sprung up around the edges of the white mesh, making Dan imagine Albert Einstein wearing a fencing mask. *Was* that mesh actually a mask? Was there an organic face beneath it?

'I thought you'd have a fancy breastplate and a skirt on under that cloak,' he said.

'You're not the thing you look like. Neither am I. I'll tell Afra you're awake.'

16. BELLYN'S MISSION
DAN

A FRA STOOD OUTSIDE the cage, arms folded, tapping her foot. Not pleased to see him. Instead, she talked to the Ranglatiri in its own language: words thick with Ks and Ss. Their discussion became heated and Dan wondered if he should intervene.

'Hey!' he shouted, banging the water bottle the Ranglatiri had given him on the bars. 'Are you going to let me out of here or what?'

'Not until Afra's calmed down,' said the Ranglatiri. 'You're safer where you are. She wants to eject you into deep space. Or feed you to me. I'm still considering that. You didn't tell me you're on the Galaksi Alliance payroll. That changes everything. I understand why she feels betrayed. Afra, no!'

Afra had her gun out and was pointing it at Dan. 'He'd be dead anyway, if you hadn't found him, Bellyn,' she said in Kawaida. 'He's bloody lucky to be alive. Hiding in a low-atmosphere cargo hold, how dumb can you get?'

'Afra, I know you care about this boy. You've been much happier these last few months with him. *Think* before you do anything you can't put right afterwards. If you kill him, it will make you sad for a long time. If *I* kill him, it will spoil our friendship. I don't want either of those things. If you believe he's a threat, we'll keep him here until we've considered our options.'

'What about his *zana*? It'll be tracking us.'

'Then we eject *that* into deep space. Not him. Come, mistress, put the gun away.'

'Do it,' said Dan. 'Those *zanas* have brought me nothing but trouble. I'll be glad to be rid of it.'

Finally, she looked him in the eye. 'You will?' She lowered the gun. 'OK, Earthboy, here's the deal. We ditch your *zana*. You tell us what you did to end up in Laro. We make our delivery and decide what to do with you afterwards. You'll be in this cage for a week. Can you handle that?'

Dan grinned. 'If you come and visit me every day, yes, no problem.'

She let out a shriek of exasperation and stalked away from him. 'Come on, Bellyn, time to put the rubbish out.'

DAN WAITED, SITTING cross-legged on the cage floor, wondering how to phrase his story. Examining it with the wisdom of hindsight, he didn't come out of it too well. Even though – at the time – he'd been convinced he'd been doing the right thing. Afra and Bellyn returned, each carrying a metal stool. Harsh scraping echoed round the chamber as they positioned their seats. They sat together, facing him: judges, jury but hopefully not executioners.

'We're listening,' she said.

Here goes, thought Dan, pulling Bellyn's borrowed cloak more tightly around himself. 'You never asked, so you can't say I lied. My planet doesn't know about aliens. We're just starting with space travel.'

'You're a *primitive*?' said Afra, incredulous. 'That explains so much,' she said more thoughtfully. 'Like your spectacular ignorance. And your ... physicality.' Her eyes twinkled, kindling a hope in Dan that she cared about him after all. 'Why did you end up on Amra? And how come you speak Kawaida?'

Dan told her how, within the Galaksi Alliance, the Syenitians had designated the Earth as a nature reserve to protect it without revealing themselves to the inhabitants; about the *Shantivira*, the ISS and his role on it, the asteroid hit and how the *Shantivira* had pulled them in for repairs.

'Your planet's space station has *no shielding*? And you were *living* on it? You're braver than I thought.'

'Well it does now, because the Syenitians gave us some,' said Dan. 'They gave us *zanas* to learn Kawaida with, too. But hardly anyone on the planet knows about the Syenitians. My crew's agreement with the *Shantivira* was we'd keep their secret and the Syenitians would formally announce their existence to the Earth authorities as soon as they could organise it. But I believed people should know straight away. My people in particular. I thought it might give us an advantage over the other parts of the planet, you know?'

'Your planet is split into rival territories?' Bellyn said, bringing his fingertips together in front of his chest. 'Primitive indeed.'

'So I stole a *zana* to take home with me as evidence,' continued Dan. 'But I got caught. To cut a long story short: the Syenitians put me on Amra temporarily to keep me out of the way while they planned their approach to the Earth authorities.'

'That was kind. My people would have killed you,' said Bellyn.

'I'd be tempted to do the same,' said Afra. 'Dan, what were you thinking? You betrayed your crew's promise. You'd have started a war between your territory and the others on your planet. Wasn't that obvious to you?'

Embarrassed, Dan studied the anti-slip pattern of raised bumps on the cage floor. 'I'm glad the Syenitians stopped me.' He looked up. 'You know what, I've never admitted that before. I hated them for a long time. I was wrong. They were right. But I'm glad it happened, because otherwise I wouldn't be sitting here with you guys.'

'In your cage, because we don't trust you,' said Afra.

Dan smiled wistfully. 'Well. I'm working on that. I don't want to go home. I want to explore space and learn to fly spacecraft. And I want to be with you, Afra.'

She turned away from him, clearly still annoyed.

Bellyn said, 'Won't you be returning to your planet soon? Surely the Syenitians must have made themselves known already; you've been on Amra for months.'

'Yes, it's done. They offered to take me home a while back. I said, "No, I'm staying," and they said, "OK". They stopped my allowance and I've been paying my own way ever since. Now you've dumped my *zana*, I've no way of contacting them. Honestly. You're safe. They're not interested in whatever it is you're doing. I'm not their responsibility. I told them to forget about me.'

Bellyn turned to Afra. 'What if he's carrying a tracker chip?'

'I'm not!'

'You might not know about it,' said Afra. 'I'll get the scanner.'

She unfolded her limbs gracefully and left Dan alone with the Ranglatiri. Bellyn said nothing, so Dan remained silent too. He hoped they'd give him dry clothes soon, but it wasn't the right moment to ask. Minutes passed. It was a relief when Afra returned with a gun-shaped object. She pointed it at him and examined the results on its flip-up screen.

'He's clean,' she said. 'Just one little Earthboy, far from home.'

'I'll earn my keep, Afra,' Dan pleaded. 'I'll do whatever you want. Let me stay. Please?'

AFRA AND BELLYN switched back to the harsh-sounding language which Dan presumed must be Ranglatiri. Unable to understand, Dan tried to glean what information he could from their body language. Afra was still angry with him, so much was obvious. Bellyn seemed more placatory. In contradiction to the little Dan knew of the Ranglatiri, he appeared to be the calmer and more considerate of the unlikely pair. Dan had the impression Bellyn was arguing Dan's case, persuading Afra to let him stay. Afra was evidently the ultimate decision maker. But why did she have a Ranglatiri working for her? Yet again, Dan wondered what she did for a living. Eventually, her expression softened and she addressed Dan directly in Kawaida.

'OK,' she said. 'You can stay.'

Dan's face split into a wide grin. 'I can?'

'You can have the position of ship's cook and general dogsbody. You'd better earn your keep.'

'I will!'

'But you must stay locked up until after the drop. Sorry. There are … circumstances.'

'Afra, he needs to know what he's getting himself into,' said Bellyn.

Afra nodded. 'Tell him. If he doesn't agree to cooperate, we'll have no choice but to hand him over to Henning with the shipment.' She stood up and rested a hand on Bellyn's shoulder. The genuine affection in the gesture didn't escape Dan. 'I have to check on the autopilot,' she said. 'Will you be all right on your own?'

Bellyn said, 'I'll call you if I need you.'

She left the room without glancing at Dan. Dan waited.

Bellyn sat for a moment, his ghostly fingers interlocked in his lap. 'I expect you're wondering why we're making such a fuss about you being here. But in the circles we move in, looking like a Syenitian is a real liability.'

Dan studied the white mesh face. No information to read there. 'I always knew Afra had some kind of dark secret,' he said.

'It's not Afra's secret. It's mine.' Bellyn dragged his stool closer to the cage. He sat with his elbows on his knees, his head level with Dan's. 'We're contraceptive smugglers. Contraception is illegal on my planet, but there's still a demand for it. We buy our product from a secret manufacturing plant near Laro and distribute it to my contacts among the deep space pirates.'

'Space pirates?'

'Space pirates have more freedom than most Ranglatiri. They're able to get the pills back to our brothers at home without the females finding out.'

Dan was confused. 'A *male* contraceptive?'

'How much do you know about my people, Dan?'

'They're cruel, violent, cannibalistic slavers who destroy everything in their path. No offence.'

'None taken,' said Bellyn. Dan thought he detected amusement in his voice. 'Off-world, you only see the pirates. They're the more aggressive males which won't submit to female authority. They're sent out to rove space, looking for riches to send home. It's a way of keeping the peace back on the planet and getting the materials we need at the same time.'

'Female authority? The Ranglatiri are a *matriarchy*?' Dan almost giggled.

'That's right. Females control everything on Ranglatiri. Males do not have the strength or the intelligence of females. Males are not permitted to hold office. We perform low-level or domestic tasks.'

'What?' said Dan, disbelieving. 'Why don't you rise up and demand equal rights?'

Bellyn laughed: the nervous laugh of someone confronted with an outrageous, preposterous idea.

'That could never happen. The whole system is set up to perpetuate female power. Dissent, any kind of resistance, is punishable by death. Anyone viewed as a traitor is torn limb from limb in public and eaten by the crowd. Even if not all females agree, it's easier for them to stay quiet and go along with it. Nobody wants to die that way.'

Dan began to understand. 'I can see why you don't want to get caught,' he said, shifting position on the cold metal floor. 'But why is looking like a Syenitian such a problem?'

'Syenitians are the Ranglatiri's most feared enemy. All contact with Syenitians is strictly forbidden outside combat. My customers are nervous people: if they were observed consorting with a Syenitian – or a life form which looked like one – it'd attract unwanted attention from the authorities and risk our whole operation.'

'I'm sorry if I've put you both in danger.'

'No harm has been done, yet. Although Afra is associated with you on Amra, most of my customers have never seen her. She usually stays in the cockpit during our deliveries.'

'Couldn't I do the same?'

'There's a problem. Ranglatiri have a local empathic field. Sort of a localised hive mind. We use it to identify each other and to communicate emotion, but it also tells us if another being is present. My customers would sense you the minute they boarded. They've accepted Afra is necessary as a pilot but they'd need reassuring that you pose no threat to our operation. The way you look won't help.'

'An empathic field?' said Dan. 'So how come you didn't sense *me*, the moment I snuck aboard?'

Bellyn bowed his head. 'Because I'm a stupid old man with dulling senses who wasn't paying attention. I'm in deep trouble with Afra for not spotting you; I ought to have been on the lookout for stowaways. The idling reactor masked your presence, but I *should* have detected you. In my defence, nobody sane would hide by the reactor: its resonant frequencies match those of organic matter.'

Dan lifted his head. *That* was why it had been so uncomfortable.

Bellyn said, 'I *did* sense you the minute you left the engine room.'

'You saved my life,' said Dan. 'Thank you.'

'Don't thank me yet.' Bellyn leaned back and folded his arms. 'We can't hide you from Henning; he's in his prime and he'll be on high alert when he comes for the pickup. If he believes you might be a security risk, he'll feed you to his crewmates. Alive. We won't be able to stop him.'

Hmm, thought Dan. Out of the frying pan and into the fire. 'Who's Henning?' he asked.

'Our customer: the Ranglatiri we're on our way to meet. The story we give him will spread through the network and the next delivery should be easier because the other clients will already know about you.'

'Story?'

'If you want to stay with us, you'll need a cover story. You're not going to like it, I'm afraid.'

17. SUMMER HOLIDAY
HANNA

H ANNA STOOD ON the dive platform next to Felix, her flippers poking out over the edge. Her knees absorbed the motion of the boat as it rose and fell with the waves. Saïd and Roberto were already in the water, yelling and splashing each other like teenagers.

Suddenly, she wasn't sure. She'd never been out at sea before. The west coast of Syenitia was a distant smudge on the horizon and, to the south, she could just make out the cranes of Averkira-Port; giant structures reduced to tiny dots at the limit of her vision.

Did she truly intend leaving the safety of the boat to jump into that vast expanse of water? What if she got tired and couldn't make it back to the boat? What if a current dragged her away? What if she confused their boat with one of the other support vessels above the underwater building site?

Behind them, Björn and his team – four Syenitian divers, Lucy, Nikolai plus another human, whom Björn had introduced as 'Andy-from-New-Zealand' – were focused on their pre-dive checks. Those tanks looked *heavy*.

Beside her, Felix stretched his leg far out over the

water. He disappeared, resurfaced and took off his snorkel, spitting into his mask and rinsing it in the sea.

'What are you waiting for, Hanna?' said Farida. All very well for *her*: she would spend a leisurely morning on the top deck, reading.

With a loud clank, Andy dumped a black zip-up bag by her feet. 'Can you clear the platform please, ma'am?' he said in English. 'We need to get our kit into the water.'

'Come on, Hanna!' shouted Felix.

Now or never. Stop thinking and just do it, she told herself. She held her mask to her face and plunged into the blue. Surrounded by noise and bubbles, she kicked her fins wildly, knocking herself painfully on the ankle. Her head surfaced and she drew breath – only to splutter because her snorkel had filled with water. She ripped it off and coughed out the salty liquid, along with a huge blob of snot. *Gross.*

Floating nearby, Felix laughed. 'You OK?' he asked. 'The same thing happened to me when I first used a snorkel. You'll know better next time.'

Not sure there'll *be* a next time, thought Hanna darkly. She emptied her snorkel and took a few practice breaths with it before lowering her face into the water.

Wow. A different world lay beneath her, as if she were an eagle soaring in a cerulean sky. A network of circular buildings spread across the seafloor, a cluster of towers flexing with the current like grass in the wind. The buildings glistened with shimmering patterns, mirroring the surrounding coral. Huge blue octopuses – Pweza – glided between them, or clung to their exteriors in groups. Colourful fish swam everywhere Hanna looked, as if she were inside the world's largest aquarium.

Plunging sounds made her jerk her head around. The dive team descended rapidly, each carrying a bag of tools. Lucy gave Hanna an OK sign with her thumb and index finger; Hanna returned the gesture, then broke the surface to speak to Felix.

'Let's look at those towers,' she said.

They kicked their way over, Hanna remembering to keep her legs straight, the way she'd been told. Saïd and Roberto were already there, looking down inside. The inner diameter was narrower, with holes set into the wall spiralling round and down as far as Hanna could see.

She squeaked in alarm as a Pweza emerged right below them. It rose swiftly and stopped in front of them. On its forehead, it displayed the Kawaida characters for, 'Can I help you?'

Hanna remembered the whiteboard and pen Björn had insisted they all carry. She pulled hers out of its pocket and scribbled, 'Just looking. OK?'

'Is OK,' came the answer.

Ever the architect, Roberto wrote, 'What's this tower for?'

'Sleeping.'

'Your buildings are very beautiful,' he continued.

'Thank you. So is your planet. Thank you for letting us stay here.'

The snorkellers looked at each other. How to explain, using a tiny whiteboard, that they weren't Syenitians and this wasn't their planet? They couldn't. Not without causing confusion.

'No problem,' wrote Saïd. 'We wish your people health

and happiness.'

The Pweza tipped its body in acknowledgement and darted away in the direction of the seabed. Hanna felt a jet of water on her face in its wake.

They stuck together now, more aware that they were visitors and should behave appropriately. Holding hands, the friends swam around the edge of a rippling kelp forest. Beyond it, the seafloor rose so the coral was just a few metres below them. They could see the fish close up; follow them from coral clump to coral clump as they went about their fishy business. Hanna extended a hand to stroke a large, stripy creature cruising by, then jerked it back as she remembered what Björn had said: don't touch anything, assume everything is poisonous and keep your distance.

They drifted for a while, alien observers curiously studying the abundant life below in all its shapes and colours, trying to understand how it fitted together. Hanna made a mental note to download a book on Syenitian sea life.

Felix looked at his watch and gave the thumbs up sign to surface. Back under the sky, he pulled out his mouthpiece and said, 'We should head back. I don't know about you, but I'm starving!'

They kicked their way over to the boat and made their way up to the top deck. The dive team were already there, wearing their wetsuits removed to the waist, like neoprene leggings. Despite the warmth of the day, Lucy had her thick fleece jacket zipped up over her swimsuit. Both she and Nikolai slumped in garden chairs, looking tired and pale. The others chatted quietly among themselves, eating one-handed from plates of Syenitian rice covered with purple sauce.

In contrast, Farida was bright-eyed and full of energy. 'How was it?' she asked Hanna.

'Great, thanks. Lots to see. You should come with us, after lunch.'

'No thanks,' she said, grinning. 'You know I don't do water.' She nodded towards the buffet table, which held a selection of large bowls and a pile of plates and cutlery. 'Try the curry,' she said. 'It's excellent.'

Hanna served herself a portion before sitting between Farida and Lucy. Fiery, even by Hanna's standards. But tasty. She investigated: nuts, vegetables and chillies in a milky liquid.

Björn pulled his chair over to join them. 'So, any of you enjoy snorkelling so much you'd like to learn to dive and help us out here?'

'No fear,' said Felix. 'The idea of all that water above me gives me the heebie-jeebies.'

'I'm tempted,' said Roberto. He jerked his head at Lucy and Nikolai. 'But the state of those two isn't encouraging.'

'We're fine,' argued Lucy. 'We've been working, not like you layabouts.'

Roberto asked, 'What've you been doing all morning?'

'Clearing the seabed of urchins,' said Nikolai, 'so the Pweza can set up their shrimp farm between the buildings.'

'What did you do with them?' asked Hanna, curious.

Lucy said, 'Put them in a big cage so the Pweza can eat them later.'

'I hope you wore gloves,' said Saïd.

'Oh, we did, don't worry.'

'Where do the other boats come from, Björn?' asked Felix.

'Averkira, up the coast. They have further to travel, but they bring different specialist teams and equipment. They're not here every day like us. That's why we're at the closest cove, even though there's nothing there.'

Samae, the fishing village where they were staying in a basic, state-owned beach hut, had a tiny supermarket and one restaurant with a limited menu. Not a tourist spot, and not Farida's idea of civilisation. But after months in Essoona and years in London, Hanna relished the tranquillity. Björn's team lived in greater comfort in a large house up the hill, with views over the bay.

'Can you tell us about those towers, Björn?' said Roberto. 'Are you building them up to the surface?'

'Beyond,' said Björn. 'The sleeping quarters will stay below the exterior water level, but there'll be a transparent dome on top, full of water.'

'What for?' asked Farida.

'So they can see above water,' said Nikolai.

'There'll be a pontoon attached, so boats can dock and people can communicate face-to-face with the Pweza, without diving equipment,' said Lucy.

'That's the idea,' Björn said. 'Anyway, how's your vacation going?'

'We've been swimming from the beach in the village,' said Felix. 'And cliff climbing.'

Nikolai said, 'We should have a break from diving tomorrow. Let's go to the place you told me about. I want to have a go at that overhang.'

Hanna shivered. With Hassan away, she'd taken the chance to try rock climbing without him feeling left out. But she'd been scared *and* bored at the same time. Tomorrow she'd stay on the beach with Farida.

'I'll come with you,' said Farida, to everyone's surprise. 'I want to see what the fuss is about. Will you belay me, Saïd?'

'Sure,' he said, his face cracking into a grin. 'But don't you have some reading you should be doing?'

'I've finished six books since we came,' said Farida. 'It's time to do something else.'

Andy-from-New-Zealand approached, holding a steaming cup of *saiju*.

'Mind if I join you?' he said in English. Not waiting for permission, he flipped his chair round towards them and sat on it backwards, slurping his drink. He was a wiry man around Björn's age, with kind eyes and dark hair receding at his temples. Björn was a head and neck taller and twice as wide. Hanna thought of the pair as 'Little and Large'.

'Andy's new on Syenitia,' explained Björn in Kawaida, for Nikolai, Saïd and Farida's benefit. 'Great diver, rubbish linguist.'

Andy understood enough to retort, 'Give us a chance! I've only been here two months. I get such headaches trying to understand that lot.' He jerked his head at the four Syenitians, who'd finished eating and were tapping at their *zanas*.

Felix was curious. 'How did you get the job, if you don't speak Kawaida?'

'I recruited him as soon as I got the contract,' Björn

answered for Andy, in Kawaida. 'I needed someone who knows how to mix the gases for humans. Too many risks of mistakes if I had a Syenitian dive buddy. Their physiology's different to ours. Andy and I have worked together for two decades. I trust him with my life.'

Hanna asked Andy directly, 'So when did you find out about aliens?'

Andy jerked his head at Björn. 'Maybe you already heard this story? Coupla months back, our dive bell fell on Björn's leg, 180 metres down. I thought he was a goner, but his mate Godzilla turned up and saved the day.'

Lucy laughed and Felix spluttered, 'Godzilla! Did you call her that to her face?'

'He did,' said Björn. 'He's lucky Kitty has a sense of humour.'

Andy said, 'Afterwards, Björn told me what his wife really does for a living. I'd always assumed Tima worked in a lab, with a white coat and safety glasses, you know?'

'Tima's great,' said Hanna. 'She was our instructor, last year.'

'It's a big step, though,' said Lucy. 'Chucking in a good job for a leap into the unknown.'

'Well, work wasn't the same after Björn left. We're like an old married couple; we can almost read each other's thoughts when we're underneath the water. I've wanted to leave the industry for a while. Back in the eighties, they told us the oil would run out in twenty-five years. We knew about global warming in theory, but the money was good and the downsides were in the distant future. We believed oil was a temporary phase before we switched to sustainable energy, you know?'

'Are you married, Andy?' asked Hanna.

'No wife, no kiddies. I'm a nomad seeking adventure. How could I pass up a chance like this?' He chuckled. 'Even if I can't put it on my CV.'

Next to them, the Syenitians rose and started heading downstairs. Yalian, the male of the group, patted Björn on the shoulder.

'Back to work,' Björn said, in Kawaida. 'Would you like to come to ours for a barbecue tonight? Andy's enjoying having people he can actually talk to.'

FOR THE AFTERNOON session, the snorkellers headed straight to the reef they'd found that morning. Hanna could have drifted all day, suspended in the velvet blueness. There was plenty to see, yet it was deeply relaxing. She'd tried snorkelling from the beach earlier in the week, but this was way better. No waves to resist, no current to fight. Just endlessly fascinating Fish TV to watch.

Hassan would love this. Why hadn't they thought of it before? They should come together one day. He already had the fins. She wondered what he was doing, right now. She imagined him in a Land Rover, crossing a dried-up river bed on the trail of a herd of elephants. Eating a juicy steak cooked on a camp fire. Exploring the backstreets of Mombasa. She couldn't wait to hear about his adventures.

She hated not being able to talk to him whenever she wanted. He couldn't use his *zana*, but he *did* have a terrestrial smartphone. Yet, in four weeks, she'd only received a few brief texts and more photos of zebras than she ever needed to see.

At the start of the year, when they'd been apart because of the teleports not working, they'd hologram-called on their *zanas* daily. Why the radio silence now? Had something happened? She didn't want to pester him, so she'd just been sending him a few lines every couple of days. She hoped he was OK. If he wasn't, Ozzy would let her know, wouldn't he?

ONCE THEY GOT home, after checking her messages (nothing, as expected, but no news was good news, right?), Hanna was so tired she slept for two hours straight. When she woke, she hadn't even time for a shower: they had to leave for Björn and Andy's house. As she climbed the hill, the dried salt prickled on her skin. Surreptitiously, she licked the back of her hand and tasted the sea. Mmm. Meanwhile, Felix was complaining about his sunburn. He'd worn a short wetsuit for snorkelling; now the backs of his knees were a painful lobster-pink.

Björn's team had set everything up in the garden. Out of their neoprene, Hanna found it easier to tell the Syenitians apart. All were slightly taller than Björn, tanned and healthy from their outdoor life. Biologist Heran was interviewing the Pweza, discovering as much as possible about them. These sessions worked both ways: the Pweza had teamed her up with a group of their scientists so they could learn about Syenitians.

Zorikan, an architect, studied Pwezan building methods and supported Ravian and Yalian, the construction engineers. These two sourced the materials the Pweza needed and coordinated the subcontractors. They didn't dive daily, as they had frequent on-land meetings to ensure the project ran smoothly. Björn himself headed the diving operation: checking weather reports, organising supplies and planning the dives so nobody exceeded their safe time underwater.

A grill hung from an upside-down metal L over a fire pit and Andy was busy roasting whole fish. 'No meat, I'm afraid, but I promise you, these little guys are great with chilli sauce.'

Hanna helped herself to a beer and sat with Lucy and Felix, chatting about this and that. She missed Hassan most during moments like these. She played absently with her locket and gazed around.

The house was built from the same grey stone as the local cliffs, with a turf roof. The panoramic windows were so enormous, it seemed the house only had three walls. There was a small terrace and a covered area where Björn, Ravian and Yalian were rummaging through stacks of diving paraphernalia. Flowering trees overhung either side of the garden, providing shade and a heady scent from the purple blooms. The wide lawn – not grass, but a gold, emerald and sapphire meadow of wild flowers, with a pathway mown between the house and the fire pit – sloped down to a wooden fence with a gate to the clifftop footpath and a view of the vivid blue bay, edged by curving cliff faces. A swing seat faced out to sea: Hanna decided she'd sit on it later. Bees hummed. Birds sang. She sensed the alcohol seeping into her thighs, making her feel pleasantly floppy.

Roberto was up by the house, waving his hands enthusiastically as he interviewed Zorikan. Nikolai leaned against the wall, listening to their conversation. Farida and Saïd were chopping up salad ingredients with Heran. Hanna half-thought she ought to help them, but didn't get up.

At last the fish were cooked to Andy's satisfaction. They sat around the fire pit, enjoying their fish, salad and fire-baked potatoes and discussing their plans for the following day.

Lucy told Hanna, 'I'm not bothered about climbing. I'd rather visit your reef. Will you come to the dive site tomorrow and show it to me? Or would you prefer to go climbing?'

Hanna shook her head. 'No, I'll come. I had fun to-day.' She looked over to Björn, 'That's OK, isn't it? You *are* going out tomorrow?'

'We are. Plenty of room for two more.'

Hanna asked Lucy, 'Won't you be bored, going to the same place on your day off?'

'I've been working the whole time, Hanna. I'd love to explore without having to watch the clock. A day snorkelling is just what I need. I'll introduce you to some of the Pweza.'

They finished eating and sat watching the fire burn down to embers. The shadows lengthened and the sun disappeared behind the house. Felix and Saïd were discussing climbing equipment with Nikolai and Roberto; Farida was practising her English with Andy.

Hanna clicked open her locket, but it was too dim to see the picture properly. Four more weeks. She could last that long, couldn't she? Anyway, there was something she should sort out first. Time to begin her research. She gave Lucy a nudge. 'Will you come for a walk? I want to ask you something ... in private.'

Lucy raised her eyebrows, intrigued. 'Sure. Let's see where that cliff path goes.'

They stood up and waded through the flowers to the gate, then headed up the hill, away from the village. Lucy asked, 'What's up, Hanna?'

'Well, I have good news. Before he left, Hassan and I managed to have sex – you know, actual penetrative sex.'

Lucy squealed and threw her arms around Hanna's neck. 'Congratulations! That's wonderful.' She released her and looked at her face. 'It was OK, wasn't it? You did enjoy it?'

Hanna smiled shyly. 'Oh yes. Although, to be honest, I didn't think it was much better than the stuff we did before. It's more a relief that we *can* do it, if we want. Hassan was extra happy.'

'I bet he was,' said Lucy, grinning. 'So what did you want to ask me?'

'Well ... I'm not ready to care for a baby on top of our training. I want to wait at least until my duty period on the *Shantivira* is finished before even considering it. We used a condom but, honestly, it didn't seem like much of a barrier to getting pregnant. They break sometimes, don't they?'

Lucy nodded. 'That's what happened to me, when I had that abortion.'

'Well, you know my feelings about that,' said Hanna.

'It's no drama if you catch the pregnancy early enough, Hanna. A couple of pills and it's done.'

'Still better to avoid getting pregnant in the first place.'

'Absolutely. I've always gone for the belt-and-braces approach since: condoms plus another form of contraception.'

'What do *you* use?'

Lucy stopped walking and lifted her right arm. 'I have an implant here; you can feel it.'

Hanna touched the soft, pale skin on the inside of Lucy's upper arm. She felt a small bump, the size of a matchstick.

'It slowly releases hormones over three years, so I don't need to worry about getting pills while I'm here.'

'Did it hurt?'

'No. It was a bit sore for a few days, but I didn't need stitches.'

Hanna felt dubious about filling her body with hormones and said so.

'Most reliable birth control *is* hormonal, Hanna. But you don't have to have an implant. You could have injections, or wear patches, or do it the old-fashioned way and take pills. You could have a coil, but that's usually for people who've had all the children they want. I'll send you a link.'

'Thanks,' said Hanna. They continued on to the top of the hill in silence and stood looking out to sea, catching their breath from the climb.

'Make an appointment at the family planning clinic, next time you're in London,' said Lucy. 'They'll explain your options better than I can.'

'Yeah,' said Hanna. 'I will.'

THEY TURNED AND walked back. The light was fading fast and Hanna had to watch her step to stay on the path.

Lucy asked, 'So, how's Hassan's trip going?'

'Oh, fine, as far as I know,' said Hanna.

'Where is he now? In Uganda already?'

Hanna glanced over the cliff edge to the waves crashing on the rocks, thirty metres below. 'I'm not sure,' she admitted. 'To be honest, he's been a bit rubbish at keeping in touch.'

To Hanna's surprise, Lucy laughed. 'Well, he's a man, Hanna. What did you expect?'

Hanna shrugged. 'He called me every day when we couldn't see each other at the beginning of the year.'

'Yeah, but this is different. He's out of his routine, living a different existence – one you're not part of. He hasn't forgotten about you: he's just got other stuff going on.'

Hanna said nothing.

Lucy looked up from the path and studied Hanna's expression in the shadows. 'You haven't been worrying, have you? I'm sure he's having the time of his life.'

Without me, thought Hanna. Still, what Lucy had said made sense. Hassan's head was in Africa, with the rest of him. He was having a proper holiday from his *Shantivira*-life. He'd tell her everything when he came home.

'Don't be silly,' she said, keeping her tone light. 'Of course I haven't been worrying! I miss him, that's all.'

'I know,' said Lucy. 'I'd be the same if it were Felix.'

WHEN THEY REACHED the garden gate, Lucy placed a hand on Hanna's arm.

'Look,' she whispered with an impish grin.

The swing seat was moving, quietly creaking and squeaking. Hanna heard a suppressed moan and perceived two horizontal figures with naked upper bodies, both male, their faces joined in a deep, masculine kiss. The one on top was pale, the other so dark she could barely see him in the shadows. Hanna's mouth fell open. Nikolai and Roberto!

Lucy giggled and opened the gate as silently as she could, attempting not to disturb them. 'About time,' she murmured as they crept past.

'Is Nikolai *gay*?' whispered Hanna.

'Not openly, like Roberto,' said Lucy. 'But I never felt he was interested in women. Did you?'

'Never thought about it,' said Hanna.

'You only have eyes for Hassan,' Lucy teased.

'So what if I do? He's the One,' said Hanna firmly. 'We were meant to be together.'

18. CAPTIVITY

DAN

D AN CURLED UP on his mattress, pressing his stomach to try and overcome the wave of gnawing hunger. It would pass. He knew it would pass. Bellyn's plan had sounded reasonable when he'd agreed to it four days ago. Probably because Dan had never been held captive before and had no understanding of the challenges it involved. God, he was hungry. And he smelled. His facial hair was past the designer stubble stage, transitioning from prickly to soft. It itched like hell, reminding him of his first days on Amra when he'd been forced to grow a beard out of necessity.

Today was the last day Afra would visit him before the delivery date. Later, Bellyn would take away his guitar, his books, his blanket and mattress, his water and most of his clothes. He'd be allowed to keep his shorts, and access to the sanitary suction tube for his bodily waste. Nothing more. Bellyn was going to teach him to behave like a slave.

The big idea was to convince this Henning that Dan was Bellyn's new slave in training. That Bellyn had found Dan, an ignorant primitive, sleeping rough on Laro and been amused by his physical resemblance to a Syenitian. The *Gezi Urdina* was short-handed, so he'd persuaded

Afra to let him put Dan to work in the galley. This plan assumed Henning didn't know Sayari considered slavery abhorrent. But Bellyn was confident, saying slavery was such a normalised feature of Ranglatiri life, most couldn't imagine how a society might function without it. Afra believed the Ranglatiri government perpetuated slavery so males had someone to look down on. Ah, and here she was. He sat up.

'Morning, lover.'

'Hello, Afra. How are you today?'

'Better than you. You look like shit.'

Dan gave a bashful smile. 'Feel like it.'

'Bellyn swears Henning won't fall for it if you look well fed and perky. He's in charge of slave conditioning on his ship, so he'll know what to look for. This is the fastest way for you to lose your healthy glow. We'll build you up again afterwards, I promise.'

'On instant noodles?'

Afra's ears waggled. 'Hey, I brought you something.' She opened her bag and pulled out a metal bowl, which she pushed through the bars. Dan took it curiously, turning it over in his hands, but she said nothing. She dipped back into the bag and passed him more items. A large metal flask. A small towel. A hand-held mirror. His shaving soap and shaving brush. Now he understood. And finally, his razor.

'I think I remembered everything.'

He beamed at her. 'You beauty.' He held up the flask. 'Is this hot water?'

'Yes.'

He put the towel in the bowl and poured on the

steaming water, enough to moisten it but not soak it, and held the cloth to his face, allowing the heat to do its work. Oh, that felt good.

'It'll grow back before Henning comes, won't it?' said Afra. 'But not longer than it is now?'

Under his towel, Dan nodded.

'Good,' she said. 'We'd be in even more trouble if Henning thought you were a Syenitian Cylf. You need to look like an organic life form.'

Dan removed the cloth and placed it on his knee. 'I certainly smell like one.'

Afra's ears twitched with amusement as she watched him lather up the soap. Looking at his reflection, Dan used the shaving brush to dab the foam onto his face. He passed the mirror out to Afra. 'Will you hold this for me?'

She positioned it against the bars outside. 'Like this?'

'Perfect, thanks.' Dan picked up his razor and opened it. He rinsed the blade in the soapy water and wiped it with the towel. Starting with his cheek, he worked his way down the right-hand side, then the left. Chin. Adam's apple. Lower lip. Done. He washed and dried his face and scrutinised the result in the mirror. No missed bits and not a single cut. Well done, Dan. It had taken weeks of practice, but he'd got the hang of it. He looked up to see Afra watching him, her expression unreadable. Their eyes met.

'Better?' she asked.

'Oh yes. I feel like a new man.'

Meticulously, Dan cleaned and dried the razor and brush, then passed everything back to Afra. He picked up his guitar and began to play. Through the bars, Afra rested a warm hand on his knee.

'Afra?' he said, still strumming.

'Mmm?'

'How does Bellyn eat? Where's his mouth?'

'His mouth?'

'Yeah. I didn't want to ask him directly.'

The ears waggled again. 'Same place as you and me. It's a mask, what we see. He needs it because the atmosphere which most life forms prefer has too much oxygen for Ranglatiri. You know they evolved in caves, deep underground? That's why their skin's so white: no light, so no colour. He only takes the mask off to eat and sleep. He sleeps next door in the cargo hold; we keep its atmosphere comfortable for him, so of course you passed out when you hid there.'

So much weirdness. 'I can't believe the Ranglatiri are a matriarchy,' said Dan, putting down his guitar and taking Afra's hand in his. 'What about the Sayari?'

'We've been an equal society for thousands of years. That's why my people get on so well with the Syenitians. I have nothing against Syenitians personally: doing what I do means contact with them is dangerous, that's all.'

'I see why you kept me in the dark about your work. But I don't understand why you didn't avoid me all together.'

'I tried. But I couldn't resist your primitive charm, Earthboy.' 'So what about your planet?'

'What about it?'

'*Not* a matriarchy?'

Dan shook his head. 'The shift to equality is beginning, but most of Earth is still an out-and-out patriarchy.'

The ears waggled again. 'Ah. That explains your blasterproof sense of entitlement. You and Bellyn will be good for each other. Might balance out the extremes.'

'I will *never* call you mistress.'

'You noticed that, huh? I've tried to stop him, but he falls back into it if he's stressed. The indoctrination of female superiority begins at birth with them, along with the speciesism. I doubt he'll ever shake it off completely. Has he told you how they reproduce?'

'No.'

'It's barbaric. What's worse is the way they accept it as the natural thing to do.'

'What do they do?'

'The female eats the male who fertilised her eggs and one of his brothers raises the spawn. Males outnumber females two to one on Ranglatiri. It's considered an honour to give your life so your family's genes can continue. But funnily enough, many don't feel up to it. That's where our operation comes in. I'm no fan of the Ranglatiri as a species, but *nobody* should be forced to reproduce, especially if it's a death sentence.' Afra pulled her hand back through the bars and picked at some dirt on her boot.

'They use it as an excuse not to educate males beyond a basic level, saying it's not worth the investment as most are destined to either have short lives or to spend all their time on childcare. No wonder they have no problem with slavery, if that's how they treat the majority of their population. It makes me so angry; it's a terrible waste of potential talent. Look at Bellyn: he's such a lovely guy and he's achieved so much, setting all this up. But he sincerely believes he's my inferior, because I have a womb and he hasn't. It's ridiculous.'

'How did you two meet?' Dan asked.

'He approached me in *The Garden*, looking for a discreet pilot. I transported anything for the right price when I started out: people, packages, whatever would fit in my cargo hold. No paperwork, no tax, no questions. I knew the risks were insane, but I thought fewer Ranglatiri would be a good thing. Plus I found the money hard to refuse.' Her ears waggled. 'All those plundered riches: the Ranglatiri aren't short of a *fedha* or two. Then I got to know him. Bellyn's been like a father to me, Dan. He's my family.'

Dan wanted to ask about her Sayari family, but knew Afra well enough now not to push it. She'd tell him in her own time, if she wished.

She sighed and began unfolding her legs. 'I'd better get back to work. One of the starboard thrusters isn't firing properly; there's a blocked nozzle somewhere. I'll swing by later to say goodbye.'

'Have a good day,' he said to her retreating back, then picked up his guitar. Might as well make the most of it while he could. God knew how he'd get through the next three days, stuck in here with nothing but his brain for company. He'd been carefully not thinking about it – now the moment had come. This was what he must do to keep Afra safe.

FOUR HOURS LATER, he sat cross-legged in an empty cage, barefoot and bare-chested, feeling apprehensive. How would he make it through the night with no mattress or blanket? They'd dimmed the lights so he could hardly see. Afra had been and gone: 'See you on the other side,' she'd said. Now he was face-to-mask with Bellyn, waiting for whatever came next.

Bellyn reached through the bars. 'Take my hands, Dan.'

He obeyed. They were warm and dry, like Afra's. Dan had been expecting clamminess.

'Before we begin, I want to thank you for doing this for us. I truly respect your bravery, and your sacrifice.'

'Sacrifice? What sacrifice?'

'You'll see. I promise not to take more than you have to give. However much you suffer over the coming days and nights, I won't let you lose yourself completely.'

'Are you going to use violence, Bellyn? Or drug me?' Dan could hear the tension in his own voice.

'No drugs. And I will never hit you. All the injuries you'll experience will be psychological. Severe, but not permanent. You can trust my judgement; I used to do this for a living. I'm going to strip back your psyche and reprogram you.'

'Reprogram? You mean *brainwash me*?' Shit. What had he got himself into here?

'I'm going to put you through hell, Dan. New connections will form in your brain. This time tomorrow, pleasing me will be your sole objective. If we did this for a month instead of three days, those newly learned responses would become dominant and you'd find making independent decisions almost impossible.' Bellyn sounded apologetic, but firm. 'Slavery isn't about chains and cages,

Dan. It's a state of mind. It's believing you are powerless to change your circumstances. It's not being able to think about the future, because all your efforts are focused on day-to-day survival. It's a state of hopelessness, marginally preferable to death. In those conditions, people have zero capacity for resistance.'

Dan bit the inside of his cheek. 'Bellyn, you're scaring me.'

'Good. As it is, by the end of the week you'll be able to switch freely between the mental states of a slave and a freeman. Remember, all that's in this cage is what you took in there with you.'

'Huh?'

'If I can get the balance right, you'll come out a stronger person. But it will be a perilous journey. We'll be opening doors in your mind you'd prefer to keep closed.'

Dan tried to pull back, but Bellyn's grip on his hands tightened, preventing him. A chill ran up Dan's spine. He said, 'Remind me, *why* is all this necessary?'

'You need to be totally convincing. Henning must be sure you pose no threat to our operation. We're trying to save your life. And mine. And Afra's.' Bellyn released Dan's hands and sat back on his heels. 'Imagine you'd been captured by what Afra would call "real Ranglatiri". People like Henning. People who don't view outworlders as individuals with their own hopes and fears. An untrained slave is worth almost nothing to them. If it looks like you won't cooperate, they'll snap your neck and have you for dinner.'

Dan gulped. He gripped the cage bars with both hands to steady himself.

'Those life-or-death decisions are made in the blink of an eye, depending on the mood of the trainer and how much he had for breakfast,' continued Bellyn. 'They don't care what happens to you after: their task is to break you in. Eating the more muscular captives before they lose condition is a perk of the job. They'd be tempted to share someone strong like you with their brothers straight away. One insolent look and you'd be dead. That's how they weed out the troublemakers. Anyone who could conceivably start an uprising is killed before they come into contact with other slaves. If you ever get caught by my people, Dan, total submission is your only hope.'

Bellyn stood up. 'Well, we might as well begin. Do you have any questions? I won't speak to you again until we're done, except to issue orders.'

Dan rubbed his arms and looked up at him. 'Will you show me your face?'

Bellyn sat back down. 'Why not?' He unpopped some hidden catches and removed his mask.

Dan was prepared for the chalk white skin and the carnivore's teeth. But pink eyes? Like a lab rat? And so many wrinkles! Yet despite its gruesomeness, there was a kindliness to this face; the albino eyes twinkled with wisdom.

'How old are you, Bellyn?'

'Ooh, let me see. Around a hundred, in standard years.'

'Is that old for Ranglatiri?'

'I'm in the last fifth of my lifespan, yes.'

'Can I see inside your mask?'

Bellyn turned it round. It contained a screen and a

mass of cables.

Confused, Dan said, 'I thought it was for breathing? What's all this kit?'

'You had your *zana*. Our communicators are built into our masks.'

'I suppose that makes sense, if you're wearing them anyway. But aren't you all telepathic?'

'*Em*pathic. We can't read thoughts: just intentions, moods, emotions and we can recognise individuals. So it doesn't matter that we all look the same. But it's difficult for us to deceive each other. Why do you think I'm taking your conditioning so seriously? I need to be sure myself you don't pose a threat, or *I* won't convince Henning even if *you* manage to.'

'Oh. What happens to me if you're not convinced?'

'I'd kill you quickly to prevent the slow death Henning would give you.' He patted Dan's hand through the bars. 'It won't come to that. Afra trusts you. Once I know you better, I'm confident I will too.'

Partial reassurance. Better than none, Dan supposed. 'How long can you survive without the mask?'

'Oxygen toxicity begins to affect us after an hour or so.'

'Seizures?'

Bellyn nodded. 'It starts with tunnel vision and nausea, then convulsions. Ultimately we lose consciousness and die. Removing someone's mask is a favoured form of execution on Ranglatiri.'

'Why don't you all stay underground where you evolved?'

Bellyn laughed, his pointed teeth flashing in the dim

light and reminding Dan incongruously of Kitty. He fitted his mask back on and said, 'My people are great miners, but to trade with outworlders, you need to come above ground. Most prize money and power over everything else: even physical comfort or a habitable environment. If we lived underground, we'd have to do without slaves. Society as we know it would collapse.'

Perhaps that would be for the best, thought Dan.

Bellyn stood up. 'From now on, whenever I approach the cage, you kneel close to the bars keeping your hands behind your back and your eyes downcast. You don't look up unless I tell you to. Do you understand?'

'Yes, master.'

'I'm serious, Dan. You have no name. I have no name. You will not call me anything. Not master, not Bellyn, not bastard Ranglatiri scum. If you speak without being spoken to, I will withdraw your privileges.'

'Privileges?' said Dan, looking round the empty cage.

'Water. Food. Light. Warmth.'

Oh crap. This was going to be nasty.

'We won't speak again until after Henning's gone. You'll find it easier if you try not to fight the process. Accept your situation. Accept yourself. Goodbye, Dan.'

Accept yourself? What did he mean? Dan said nothing, just watched Bellyn walk away into the gloom. Dan's first few days in captivity seemed like a pleasant memory; days filled with conversation, music and time to read books. He had nothing now except himself.

✦   ✦   ✦

DAN HAD NO idea how time was passing. He'd tried counting, but kept losing track and having to begin again. A pointless exercise. His body was the best indicator. He'd emptied his bladder some time ago and he was getting thirsty, so several hours. It wasn't as cold as he'd feared: Bellyn must have turned up the heating. He sat waiting (for what?) on the cage floor, bored. Alone in the semi-darkness, thoughts like *Have I given up my freedom forever without a fight?* and *Was it all a lie to keep me quiet: will they hand me over to Henning anyway?* tapped away at his consciousness, undermining the trust he'd placed in his captors.

The grating noise of the door opening made his pulse quicken. Instantly, his body was on full alert. As Bellyn approached, he shuffled over to the front of the cage and knelt with his hands behind his back the way he'd been told. A water bottle appeared and Dan sucked at it gratefully.

In a stern voice, Bellyn said, 'Close your eyes when you're drinking.'

Dan obeyed. When he'd quenched his thirst, Bellyn removed the bottle and Dan opened his eyes again, making sure to focus on Bellyn's boots. Bellyn held his hand through the bars: in it was a piece of red fruit – the first food Dan had been offered in days. Dan didn't recognise it, but it smelled amazing: a tantalising promise of sweet, succulent satisfaction.

Instinctively, Dan extended his hand, but Bellyn whipped it away before Dan could take it. He spun on his heel and strode out of the room, switching off the light and plunging Dan into total darkness. He couldn't even see his hand in front of his face.

Dan was confused. What had just happened? Was Bellyn teasing him? Was he going to use food as a form of torture? With a jolt of shock Dan realised his mistake. Bellyn expected Dan to keep his hands behind his back and eat directly out of his hand, like a guinea pig in a child's petting zoo.

In the pitch black, Dan seethed with resentment. Who did they think they were, treating him like this? He was an Iraq War veteran and a NASA astronaut. Until he'd retired, his father had been an Associate Justice at the Massachusetts Supreme Judicial Court. His mother was on the board of prominent charities. This would never have happened on Earth. Not to Major Dan Simpson.

Now he'd smelled food, his hunger returned with a burning vengeance. Aside from his anger, it was all he could think about. He snarled with frustration and began pacing up and down the cage. He was so familiar with its dimensions; even in the dark he could turn before bumping into anything. His peace of mind had evaporated.

Enraged, he threw himself bodily at the bars a few times, hoping to sense a weakness. But the only weakness was in him. His flesh weaker than steel; all he had were his thoughts, which were uniformly black. He honestly didn't know if he'd get through this with his sanity intact.

He squatted in a corner, hugging his knees, angry at Bellyn, angry at Afra, angry at Rowan for taking him away in the first place and angry at himself for refusing Kitty's help. How could he have been such a dumbass? Why hadn't he taken the chance to go home when she'd offered it?

She'd turned up on his first day in captivity, back when it had all been a novelty and he'd believed a week in a cage would be a cakewalk after half a year in a metal tube. She'd stayed in the shadows, but he'd heard her voice.

'Dan? Delius told me your *zana's* drifting through deep space, so I came to check up on you. Are you OK? Do you want me to get you out of there and take you home?'

'I'm fine,' he'd insisted, like an idiot. 'This is purely temporary,' he'd said, indicating the cage with a wave of his hand. 'A sort of security quarantine. You mustn't come again, Kitty. I'll lose their trust if they see you. They're good people, doing a good thing. I want to stay and help them. Please don't track me anymore. Forget about me.'

'Forget about you? Are you sure?' she'd said doubtfully. 'OK, if that's what you want. Goodbye, Dan. Take care of yourself.'

And she'd gone, just like that. His ticket home. His get-out-of-jail-free card. Now he had no way of getting in touch with her. He'd burned all his bridges. *Numbskull.*

AT LENGTH, THE strong emotion passed. Dan huddled in the corner trembling, from exhaustion rather than cold. His mind was numb. Empty. Eyes open or shut, it made no difference. There was only the nothingness.

✦　✦　✦

DAN BLINKED AND opened his eyes. The lights were back on. When had that happened? He'd been having a wonderful dream: he'd eaten the fruit Bellyn had offered him earlier and it'd tasted utterly delicious. The grating of the door had woken him. Quickly, he got into position. He wasn't going to get it wrong again.

Bellyn approached and held out the water bottle, not saying a word. Dan closed his eyes obediently and drank his fill. Then Bellyn offered him the fresh red fruit again. Keeping his hands behind his back, Dan stretched forward and bit off a chunk. God, it tasted good. Better than in his dream, even. Rich, sweet, packed with flavour. It had the consistency of a mango, but tasted like red berries: strawberries and raspberries with a hint of something else. Cinnamon? Sticky juice ran down his chin as he took another bite. Too soon, it was all gone. For a moment, Dan considered licking the remaining juice from Bellyn's hand, but he pushed the idea away, disgusted at himself.

Bellyn rinsed his hand, then aimed the bottle at Dan's face, washing the juice off Dan's chin. Dan forced himself to remain motionless, eyes to the floor.

When Bellyn went, the lights stayed on. It seemed Dan had got it right this time. He did some yoga stretches, then a round of push-ups. Those few calories had given him a burst of energy, making him feel almost like himself again. After reaching his target of a hundred, he rolled onto his back and slept.

When he woke, nothing had changed. The lights were still on; he was pleasantly warm. Thirsty, but not urgently so. He waited patiently, thinking Bellyn would come soon. Hours passed. Still no Bellyn, and his mouth was unbearably dry, his tongue thick and heavy. Now he had a headache too. His mind fell back into its destructive loop. What if Bellyn didn't come? What if he forgot about Dan? Bellyn had no idea about the limits of the human body. Nor did Afra. Dan knew he'd survive a day or two without water, but longer? When would his organs start to fail? He began to curse himself for doing all those push-ups and sweating out the precious liquid. He should have conserved his strength.

His chest filled with horror as the true extent of his dependence on Bellyn – a self-professed cannibal – dawned on him. What had he signed up to here? He hadn't understood what the reality would be like. He'd thought he could handle anything life threw at him. But Bellyn had total power over him. He could just ... not come, Dan would die and their security problem would be solved. How would Afra feel about that? Did she even care? If he died, would Bellyn eat his corpse? Dan knew he would. In space, you recycle everything.

If only I'd never stolen that damned *zana*, I wouldn't be stuck here, he thought with rising panic.

But then you'd never have met Afra, pointed out a counter voice inside him.

Is she worth dying for?

You're not going to die, dummy.

How do you know?

Afra trusts you. Bellyn trusts Afra.

But I don't know if I trust them. What if Bellyn kills me by accident?

THE DOOR GRATED. Thank God! Dan knelt in front of the bars, head bowed and hands behind his back. That part was getting easier, at least. It shocked him how much he instinctively wanted to please Bellyn: how natural it already felt.

Dan put his lips thankfully to the proffered water bottle. He drank and drank until it was empty. Not enough. Never mind. Better than nothing.

Bellyn offered him a handful of nuts this time. Dan didn't hesitate: he snaffled up every single one. When they'd gone, he probed the creases of Bellyn's hand with his tongue for any crumbs he'd missed. It seemed his inhibitions were dropping away, along with his dignity.

Bellyn patted Dan's head in approval then, to Dan's delight, offered him a second bottle. Dan closed his eyes in pleasure as he satisfied his thirst. He didn't even need to finish it. As Bellyn turned to go, Dan heard himself say, 'Wait! Please – can you leave the rest of the water with me?'

A disgusted hiss was the only response.

Soon after Bellyn left, the temperature began to drop. Bellyn had switched off the heating. Bastard. Dan cursed. He should have known better than to speak. He knew the rules. Stupid. Stupid. Stupid. How cold was it going to get in here? Would it be worse than the hours he'd spent with no light?

Shivering, he curled up in the corner, trying to conserve his body heat for as long as possible. Dozing, he had a flashback to the night when – he must have been eight or nine – he'd woken from a horrendous nightmare in the middle of the night, convinced there was a monster in his bedroom. Weeks before, his mother had told him he was a big boy now, and she and his father didn't want him coming to them in the night any more. So he'd hidden in his wardrobe until morning, huddled up against the cold just like this.

Please God, let it be OK, let me survive this and I promise I'll never do anything bad again. Funny, he'd stopped believing in God years ago. Something he'd never had the courage to tell his parents. They'd taken him and Mark every Sunday. The brothers had both hated going, but never dared question it. His father used to say, 'A family which prays together, stays together.' Dan hadn't been inside a church since he'd left home. And here he was, begging for help from a higher power.

Time passed in a glacial creep. He could sense his beard growing: the hairs pushing their way to freedom, one by one, making his face itch. Dan couldn't sleep; it was too cold. Long-suppressed childhood memories bubbled up in his head, glimpses of forgotten incidents. Things that had made him feel as bad as he did right now.

Schoolyard fights, bickering with Mark, the constant effort not to annoy his parents. For the first time in years he thought of Steve, remembering his infectious grin and wide shoulders. They'd been inseparable as teenagers – had had so much fun playing football and discovering music together. They'd even formed a band, him on guitar and Steve on bass. They'd called themselves 'Jones' after the dolphin in their favourite film at the time, *Johnny Mnemonic*. His mom had walked in on them during their first kiss. 'We shall never speak of this,' she'd said. Soon after, Steve's family had moved away from Boston and they'd lost touch. Easily done in the pre-digital age.

Dan realised he wasn't so cold any more. The heating was back on: perhaps praying had worked after all. Gradually he allowed himself to relax. At last, he slept.

On Bellyn's subsequent visits, Dan did everything right. He could feel his personality receding and barely cared. Whenever his good behaviour earned Bellyn's approval (expressed wordlessly, via a gentle pat on the head), Dan felt a deep joy. Pleasing Bellyn was all that mattered. He began exercising again, confident that – as long as he stuck to the rules – Bellyn would give him enough to drink and not punish him.

Dan had lost all sense of time. Life had become simple: this cage was his home, Bellyn's short visits the highlights of his day. The lengthy stretches between them were harder. He slept a great deal, uneasy sleep punctuated by obscure dreams and shadowy nightmares. When awake, he mostly brooded on his childhood. The happiness he felt when he won Bellyn's approval was identical to the sensation he'd experienced as a kid in the rare moments his father had praised him. Why was that?

His parents had always expected him and Mark to live up to their high standards and the pressure to perform had driven him his whole life. Now he understood why he'd joined the Air Force and, when that wasn't enough, NASA. He'd wanted to make his parents proud of him. Nothing wrong with that, he argued. And later on, his superior officers. Pleasing authority figures had become an internalised response for him. Hell, *that* was why he'd stolen the *zana* all those months ago. *That* was why he'd believed it was the right thing to do, even though everyone else had disagreed with him.

Resigning from NASA and stowing away on the *Gezi Urdina* was the first time he'd done something purely for himself. The first time in thirty-three years. And look at where *that* had got him. Dan released an anguished sob, followed by another. Now he'd started crying, Dan wasn't sure he'd ever stop. He'd never cried like this before. He curled into a ball, overwhelmed by a tsunami of emotion. He wasn't even sure what he was crying about.

His distress was so all-consuming, he didn't notice Bellyn approaching until he'd unlocked the door and was sitting beside him on the cage floor. Bellyn held him gently, stroking his hair while Dan sobbed uncontrollably into his chest. He didn't speak, but Dan found the calm presence of another being immensely soothing. Dan cried and cried until, eventually, no more tears came.

Bellyn dried his face with a clean cloth and held him a little longer. Then he took Dan's hands in his, giving them a reassuring squeeze before he left the cage, snapping the padlock shut behind him. Emotionally exhausted but finally at peace, Dan slept.

19. HENNING

DAN

WHEN DAN WOKE, he felt better than he had done in days. Months. Years, even. He understood himself better: having examined his vulnerabilities and insecurities with clear eyes, he could accept them instead of suppressing them. He couldn't change his past, but he wouldn't expend any more energy trying to be the person other people wanted him to be. Just as soon as he got out of this damned cage. The irony of his situation wasn't lost on him.

In future, he'd listen to his own inner voice, rather than the parentally programmed one. At last he realised why he'd never got on with his brother. You couldn't afford to be friends with someone if you were competing for love. What a shame. What a waste. If he ever returned to Earth, he'd try to mend their relationship, build some bridges.

Whatever the consequences, Dan knew he'd been right to stow away on the *Gezi Urdina*. He'd followed his heart: he couldn't have done anything else and been happy. And so far, so good. He was still here. Still breathing. Bellyn had trained him well; perhaps they'd fool this Henning person. If not … well, he wouldn't have done anything differently. No regrets. Whatever came, he'd face it calmly. After last night, he trusted Bellyn completely. Bellyn had seen him at rock bottom and hadn't laughed at him or exploited him – instead he'd given him what Dan had needed; company and comfort.

The sound of the door opening had Dan waiting in position before Bellyn entered the room. This time, Bellyn stroked his hair before offering him anything. Dan nuzzled his hand, eyes closed in pleasure at the unexpected contact. Then Bellyn gave him some of the delicious red fruit. Maybe soon he'd find out what it was called. His three days must be nearly up, surely?

After Dan had finished eating and drinking, Bellyn crouched down to his level. 'Henning will be here in an hour,' he said in his normal, friendly voice. 'I'm going to switch off the heating now, or he'll suspect I've been treating you too kindly. It won't be for long. Just know it's not a punishment. You've been doing so well. You can do this. Good luck.'

Dan didn't reply, or even look up from the ground. No need to push his luck, this close to freedom. Did that mean he'd see Afra again later? His heart gave a little skip of hope. Through the bars, Bellyn patted him on the shoulder, then left.

+ + +

DAN WAS CURLED up in a foetal position with his face to the wall, conserving body heat, when the familiar grating of the door had him rolling over and up onto his knees in one practised movement. Hands behind back: check. Head down: check. This was it. Make or break. Life or death. Suddenly he was very scared.

TWO VOICES ENTERED the room. One was Bellyn's. The other belonged to a pair of heavy-duty white boots, splattered with reddish mud. They stopped in front of Dan's cage and, in the torrent of incomprehensible Ranglatiri, Dan caught the words Syenitian and Kawaida.

A hand grabbed him by the hair, firmly but not roughly, tilting his head to one side, exposing Dan's neck. His anxiety level shot up, as did his heart rate.

Don't struggle, stay passive, eyes down, breathe, he told himself, trying to stay calm. He sensed a finger run along the top of his ear. Bellyn must be showing Henning his non-pointy ears: proof he wasn't a Syenitian. The hand released him and came back holding a piece of fruit, which Dan gobbled up eagerly. No chin-wiping this time, he noted, resisting the urge to wipe his mouth on the back of his hand and praying his submissiveness was convincing. The voices continued their conversation for a few minutes, then the boots turned and left him alone.

As soon as the door scraped shut, Dan wiped his mouth and huddled up against the cold again, waiting. Not long now. Soon he'd be free – or dead. But it'd gone as well as could be expected. He was sure he hadn't done anything wrong.

A little later, he heard the engine starting. A good sign, surely? And Bellyn had put the heating back on, bless him. He unfolded his limbs and did a few stretches, before settling at the centre of the cage to wait.

The door grated and Dan was on his knees at the bars in an instant, his body flooded with adrenaline. Two pairs of boots entered the room: Bellyn's familiar black ones and – blue ones. Afra.

Bellyn unlocked the door, saying, 'You can come out, Dan. We did it. Henning went away a happy customer. He offered me a fair price for you, actually, but I said no, I needed you here.'

Dan almost didn't believe it. He stood up and dared to look straight ahead. The cage was open. Beyond it: Bellyn. And Afra. Afra's face … he'd never seen it looking so sad. But this was a joyful moment, surely? He hesitated, paralysed by uncertainty. Was this a trick to get him out in the open? Had Henning seen through them after all? Was Bellyn going to kill him quickly now, as he'd promised?

'What are you waiting for, Dan?' asked Afra, confused by his behaviour.

Dan decided if Bellyn intended to snap his neck, he wouldn't let Afra watch. So it was probably OK. But why did Afra look so distressed?

'Dan.' Bellyn stretched out a hand towards him. 'It's safe. You're safe. Come out.'

Dan obeyed. No choice but to obey that voice. He stepped through the opening into Bellyn's waiting arms. As they embraced, tears streamed silently down Dan's cheeks. Why was he crying? Relief? Dan let them fall, burying his face in Bellyn's shoulder. He knew Afra was watching; he also knew she wouldn't understand the depth of the bond he had with Bellyn now. He didn't understand it himself.

Bellyn disentangled himself and gently propelled him

towards Afra. She hugged him fiercely, on the edge of tears herself. Her body armour pressed into his skin, uncomfortable but reassuringly solid. Bellyn turned the lights back up to their normal level and Dan winced at the unaccustomed brightness.

'I expect you'll want a shower first,' said Afra.

Dan said nothing, just stroked her hair, amazed all over again by its glowing beauty. He touched her lovely face, entranced.

'Dan? Speak to me. You're scaring me.'

Dan opened his mouth, but no words came. Instead, he smiled for the first time in days. It felt good.

'Dan's been on a dark journey, Afra,' said Bellyn. 'He'll need some time to find his way back to us.'

Dan had another go. 'Shower,' he managed. Followed by, 'Bed.'

Bellyn patted him on the shoulder. 'We'll take you to your cabin. Come on, Afra.'

✦　✦　✦

HOURS LATER, DAN made his way forward to the *Gezi Urdina's* cockpit. It felt strange being fully clothed. Good strange. He'd brushed his teeth twice and showered, slept like an exhausted zombie, showered again and shaved. He knocked at the door. Afra answered.

'Dan, you don't need to knock! You're a crew member now. This is your home.'

He smiled his new-found smile and kissed her. Slowly: exploring, questioning. She kissed him back. He pulled her to him; she responded by running her fingers through his hair. Briefly, Afra turned back to the room. 'Bellyn? You can manage without me for an hour or so, can't you?'

Bellyn swivelled round in his chair and gave Dan a little wave. Dan waved back.

'Of course,' he said, turning back to the control panel. 'You kids go and have fun.'

Afra practically dragged him along the corridor to a door Dan hadn't noticed on his first visit. Behind it, a spiral staircase led downwards, into the belly of the *Gezi Urdina*. Where were they going? It took them a while to get down the steps. They kept having to stop to kiss each other. All over. Afra had his T-shirt off before they even reached the bottom.

Through two more doors and onto a large double bed, tapered at one end. They must be in the nose of the ship, directly below the cockpit. 'This is my cabin,' said Afra, breathlessly, hurriedly unzipping her boots. Couldn't be anyone else's, thought Dan. Blue walls. Blue carpet. Blue bedlinen.

Dan kicked off his shoes and focused on pulling off her top and her trousers. Straddling her, he kissed and licked the curve of her stomach, working his way upwards as he fiddled with the catch of her bra. Success! He threw it across the room and bit into her right breast playfully, making her squeal. She undid his jeans as he grazed her nipples with his teeth and then he was inside her, filling her with the hardest erection he'd had in months. She gasped and wrapped her legs round his buttocks, urging him on.

'Aaaaaaaaaaaaaaaaa—aaaa—aaaaaaaaaah!' he yelled, throwing his head back, every muscle in his body tensed, a tiny part of him wondering if Bellyn could hear them from upstairs. No matter. He collapsed onto Afra, his heart pounding. Wow. He hadn't been expecting *that* when he'd woken up this morning.

'My go,' she commanded, pushing his head downwards. Dan complied cheerfully, first with his tongue, then with his finger, the way she liked it; occasionally licking and biting her inner thighs by way of variation. Her spine arched and her heels drummed on his back. He repeated the process until she, too, lay back limp and sated. Limbs entangled, they rested on their sides, face-to-face. Afra's ears began to waggle and Dan laughed, a fit of side-splitting laughter so strong, he could barely breathe. He clutched Afra's shoulder, and her ears waggled more violently as he doubled up, unable to stop. Eventually the spasms subsided and they rested there, looking into each other's eyes. Never had Dan felt such contentment, such *rightness*. For the first time in his life, he was travelling off-piste, without a map. Following his heart, rather than his sense of duty.

'Afra?' he said, his voice cracked and unfamiliar from lack of use. 'Why did you look so sad, when you came to let me out?'

She thought for a moment. 'I wasn't prepared. Bellyn warned me, and I've been watching you on the heat camera—'

'—Wait. You had a *camera* on me?'

'Of course. To ensure your core temperature didn't drop too far. But … seeing you kneeling there like some … slave … and the darkness, and the *smell* …' She took his hands in hers. 'I'm sorry, Dan. I didn't understand what we were asking of you. Was it *very* awful?'

'Well—' said Dan, thinking. How could he possibly explain what he'd been through? He'd never be able to put it into words. Bellyn understood; he'd known precisely what he was doing. A dark journey, he'd called it. And he used to do it professionally. How many people's spirits had he broken? How many people had he 'reprogrammed' into total subservience? A conversation for another day, when Afra was busy somewhere else.

'Dan?'

Management summary, then. 'It wasn't fun, no. It's like ... Bellyn rewired my brain and I have this irresistible compulsion to do what he tells me, although he promised that'll wear off. The time alone was the hardest. It forced me to look at myself from the outside, you know? I realised that until I came to Amra – until I met you – I'd been living the life my parents wanted me to have. I don't even know what kind of life I would have chosen for myself: I never considered it consciously. All the choices I'd made were against the backdrop of "What would Mom and Pop think?" I'm stopping that. Or at least, I'll try to.'

'Is that what it's like having parents? Looks like I had a lucky escape. I've always done exactly what I pleased.'

'That's what I love about you,' said Dan, grinning. 'Your free spirit. So you're an orphan?'

'Towpi fever,' confirmed Afra. 'Both parents, while I was away at flight school.'

'I'm sorry,' said Dan.

'Don't be,' she said. 'I have Bellyn. And you too, now.'

'Are you sure you want me, Afra? I put you in an awkward position, stowing away like that. You can take me back to Laro if you like, and I won't bother you again. I'll go back to my jobs and put myself through pilot school on my own. I want to be with you, but only if that's what you want too.'

She stroked his face. 'It was hard work keeping our secret from you. It's better now you know. Bellyn definitely wants you to stay. He likes you. It's difficult for him, living with a female; he feels he has to be on his best behaviour the whole time. He'll relax more with another male on board. And we could certainly do with an extra pair of hands. Please stay, Dan.'

Dan beamed. 'Thank you. Afra?'

'What?'

'I'm hungry.'

'Well, you're the ship's cook. What do you want to eat?'

'What've you got?'

Afra sat up. 'I went shopping while Henning was here. Come and see what I bought.'

THEY ENDED UP switching on the autopilot and having a little party in the mess room – to formally welcome him as a crew member, Bellyn said. As well as fresh meat and vegetables, Afra had bought alcohol: a greyish liquor Dan suspected could easily be repurposed as rocket fuel. Still, it had the desired effect.

After they'd eaten and Bellyn was fixing his mask back on, Dan asked the question which had niggled at him all day.

'What did you tell Henning, Bellyn? What did he say?'

Bellyn gave a short bark of laughter. 'Our meeting didn't begin well. He saw Afra leave the ship but sensed someone else was still on board. He became aggressive, saying we'd broken our contract by involving another person. He was set to walk away and badmouth us to his network. That would have killed our business.'

'How did you bring him round?' said Afra.

Bellyn patted Dan's hand. 'I told him our story – about finding Dan starving in a Laro backstreet. That he was a primitive: no idea where from, no idea how he'd ended up on Amra. That he had no people here and didn't speak Kawaida. That he would have died if I'd left him where I'd found him.'

Dan said, 'What did Henning say?'

'He said, "But why did you take it with you?" and I said, "I hate waste. I thought it'd be nice to train up a slave again, after all these years. Keep my hand in, you know? Goodness knows, I could do with some extra help round here and we can't afford to pay anyone. If I can teach it to prepare the captain's disgusting food, it'll be worth the effort. If not, I'll eat it. No harm done."'

Except to me, thought Dan. Great.

'Henning asked, "What does your captain think?" and I said, "She doesn't care as long as I get my work done. Do you want to see it? It looks like a hairy little Syenitian."

'That's when we came in, Dan. "It's not a security risk, Henning. It knows *nothing*," I said. "It's intelligent enough – I'm teaching it Kawaida – but it has no education." I told him you were a vegetarian, so you were cheap to keep, and that you were surprisingly docile for your build.' Bellyn chuckled. 'Somehow, I don't think that's true, all those push-ups you did. Do you know how to fight, Dan?'

Dan recalled his basic military training, long ago. 'I'm a bit out of practice,' he said.

'Perhaps Afra can show you a few moves,' said Bellyn. 'And I can teach you to fight with a *stakarh*. You might find it useful one day.'

'What's a *stakarh*?'

'Ranglatiri combat staff,' said Afra.

'Now Henning's spreading our story, the next time a customer notices you, it won't be such a problem because they'll believe they know about you,' Bellyn continued. 'You know how to behave in front of them now: stand behind me, keep your eyes down and only speak when you're spoken to.'

'So how much am I worth?' asked Dan. 'What was this "fair offer" Henning made for me?'

Bellyn put his arm around Dan's shoulders and gave them a reassuring squeeze. 'You know I'd never have sold you, however much he offered?'

'I know,' Dan acknowledged, 'you'd have broken my neck and eaten me instead, out of kindness.'

Afra's eyes widened. News to her, thought Dan, happy she hadn't known about Bellyn's backup plan.

Bellyn said, 'That was before. I trust you now.'

'How much?' said Afra.

'Double the average meat price. It was a good offer, from Henning's point of view. Dan's similarity to a Syenitian is amusing, but his lack of education limits him to menial work.'

Double the meat price. Whoopee-do. Did that mean

they wouldn't eat him and work him into the ground instead, or that they'd savour him as a delicacy?

'I hope they don't search for your planet to find more Earthlings, Dan. I rather talked up your suitability for slavery.'

'They'll get a shock if they do,' said Dan. Hooray for the *Shantivira* and the violent nature of mankind. 'Bellyn, will you teach me your language?' He turned to Afra and said, 'I'd like to learn Sayari too, but Ranglatiri is more important if I'm going to be any use to you.'

Afra approved. 'It's not hard. There are no words for emotions, because they do that through their empathic field.'

'By touch, too,' said Bellyn. 'You must have noticed, Dan.'

Dan nodded. He kind of liked it.

Afra said, 'Bellyn and I switch to Kawaida to discuss our feelings.'

'We'll start lessons tomorrow,' said Bellyn.

'Thanks,' said Dan. Feelings, he thought. Touch. 'Afra, love, will you go and get my guitar?'

She unfolded her elegant limbs and kissed the top of his head. 'Sure,' she said, and left the room.

Bellyn was astounded. 'You'd order a female around, just like that? And she does what you tell her? Willingly?'

Dan grinned. 'If you don't ask, you don't get. Why not try it? Bellyn, while she's gone … I wanted to thank you for last night. For taking care of me the way you did.'

Bellyn grasped Dan's shoulder. 'I've seen it many times,' he said. 'People's lives catch up with them when they have nothing to do but think. To survive, you must let go of the old life before you can embrace the new one. Seems to me, you did that yesterday.'

Dan gripped Bellyn's shoulder in return. 'Yeah,' he said. 'I think I did.'

'Well,' said Bellyn, dropping his arm, 'there's only one thing left to do.'

'What?'

'When we get back to Laro, you need a tattoo.'

'A tattoo? I can't get a tattoo! If my family saw it—,' Dan stopped abruptly, realising what he'd said. Embracing the new life was going to be harder than expected.

'This tattoo will protect you,' said Bellyn. 'It's the sign you're a properly broken in slave – which you're certainly not – but any Ranglatiri seeing it will assume you pose no threat *and* you're worth more alive than dead. Call it a life insurance policy.'

'Will it hurt?'

'I don't know, Dan. I've never had one done, myself.'

20. HEARTBREAK

HANNA

'THAT WASN'T TOO bad,' said Lucy as they left the school workshop and headed for the canteen. On their first day back after the summer break, they'd been learning how to replace converter tips: the metal tube poking out through each of a *Tumba's* spikes. The discharge points for the thrusters and dematerialisation beams needed constant monitoring for wear.

'Easy in the lab,' said Aneira. 'Wait until you try it in a real ship, in a tricky spot under the floor.'

'But that's just access,' said Hanna. 'The job itself wasn't as complicated as I'd feared.'

In the queue for lunch, they found themselves right behind Briavan and her coterie of hangers-on. *Les Briavettes*, Saïd called them. Hanna's heart sank. An unpleasant confrontation was practically unavoidable.

The low-level bullying the humans had experienced at the beginning of the year had eased as they'd proven themselves capable. After Elian had started hanging out with them, it had all but ceased. Only Briavan continued making snide remarks – and only, in Hanna's opinion, because it was an easy way to upset Aneira. Her obvious jealousy was almost embarrassing.

Briavan jeered when she saw the three friends. 'You still clinging to those losers, Aneira? I'm amazed they're still here. Apparently, their mid-year results were so bad, Kalarran's considering sending them back where they came from.'

Lucy wasn't having any of it. 'You lying cow!' she hissed. 'That's rubbish and you know it. Our results were fine.' She jabbed a defiant finger into Briavan's chest and said in a loud, clear voice, '*You're* the one who should be sent home for spreading false rumours about your classmates. I've half a mind to report you.'

The Briavettes tittered with nervous laughter. Syenitians would never respond with such instant aggression, Hanna realised. That was why Briavan thought she could get away with her nastiness.

Aneira put her hand on Lucy's arm. 'Ignore her. She *wants* to cause a scene. Don't give her the satisfaction. You don't have to justify yourself to *them*.'

Hanna drew herself up to her full height and tipped back her head to look Briavan in the eye. 'Why don't you drop it, Briavan? Don't you see how pathetic it is, being horrible to Aneira because Elian isn't interested in you? Your obsession is damaging your soul health or whatever you Syenitians call it. He doesn't want to be with you. *Let him go.*'

Briavan stared down her nose at Hanna and said nothing, her face momentarily frozen to stone.

'Hey, you,' called the man behind the counter. 'It's your turn. D'you want something to eat or not?'

Briavan spun back round and flashed him a winning smile. '*So* sorry, I was miles away.'

But Hanna knew her words had hit home. Maybe Briavan would be less of a problem in future.

THEY TOOK THEIR trays of rice and beans to the furthest table away from Briavan and the Briavettes. In unspoken agreement, they chose to ignore the little drama in the queue.

'So, Aneira, tell us about your holiday,' said Lucy. 'How long was the trip to Amra?'

'Three days. We were lucky we could borrow a ship with a hyperdrive, or we wouldn't have had time to go.'

'It's a five-week journey without, isn't it?' said Lucy.

'At least,' Aneira confirmed, through a mouthful of rice.

Hanna asked, 'What did Elian think of Laro?'

'He *said* he liked it. He ate everything Auntie Andria offered him. He managed not to call it a scrubby backwater in front of my relatives. Elian's never been to a non-Alliance planet, can you imagine?' Aneira sounded amused.

Hanna felt unable to comment, having only ever been to two planets herself. 'How did he find the extra gravity?' she asked.

'Tough to start with,' said Aneira. 'Me too, to be honest. I'm not used to it either.'

'So what did you do?'

'Just pottered about. Gave him a taste of Amranese life. Explored the town, helped my cousins in the warehouse. There's not much there for tourists. We went to the jungle. Canoed on the river. Oh! I remember what I wanted to tell you!'

'What?' said Hanna and Lucy as one.

'We saw a *human* at the market!'

'A human?' said Hanna, as Lucy asked simultaneously, 'Are you sure?'

'I think so. He looked like a short Syenitian, but a Syenitian would never cut their hair that way. He had a yellow shopping trolley and bought large amounts of meat.'

Hanna and Lucy exchanged a glance. Had Kitty caught up with Nestor and exiled him?

'A male human?' said Lucy. 'Did you speak to him? Did he have white hair?'

'We didn't speak to him,' said Aneira. She screwed her eyes closed, trying to remember. 'He had brown hair. Darker than yours, Lucy. And the same pale skin as you and Felix.'

'Matthew?' said Hanna to Lucy. 'It'd be just like Nestor to send him out to do the shopping.'

'Who else could it be? Do you have a picture, Aneira?'

'No, sorry. Do you think it's someone you know?'

'Maybe,' said Lucy. 'But we have no way of knowing. Never mind.' She scraped her plate clean and said, 'Hanna, tell us, how did Hassan and the others get on on their travels?'

That weekend, Hanna had seen Hassan for first time since his return to the *Shantivira*.

'Great! I haven't seen all the pictures yet. But they did two weeks' safari in Kenya and saw lots of zebras, elephants and giraffes. They're types of animals,' Hanna added for Aneira's benefit.

'Any lions?' Lucy asked.

'One, early in the morning. They saw a whole family of rhinos though.'

'With babies?'

'One baby, yeah.'

'And they went to Uganda? To visit Hassan's foster family?'

'That's right. Then Hassan and Gildas went to South Sudan, but they thought it might not be safe there for Ozzy, so Ozzy and Gaositwe went to stay with Gaositwe's family in Botswana.'

'Why wouldn't it be safe for Ozzy?' Aneira frowned.

Lucy looked at Hanna. 'It's complicated,' she said. 'There's been fighting there recently, and not much law enforcement. On our planet, pale-skinned people come from wealthier territories than Hassan's home country, so they'd be a target for crime if they went there. He'd have put Hassan and Gildas in danger too, if he'd gone with them.'

'They can't blend in,' said Hanna. 'Outside their own regions they stand out like mushrooms on a forest floor. Think of that guy in Laro, Aneira. You noticed his skin colour first, didn't you?'

'I suppose so.'

Lucy said, 'What did Hassan say about South Sudan, going back after fifteen years away?'

'Not much. I didn't see him for long yesterday. I expect he'll tell me more next weekend. He said it smelled the same. It was the rainy season, so everything was very green, but the roads were impassable and they had to stay in Juba.'

The conversation moved on, and Hanna fell silent, brooding on her reunion with Hassan. He hadn't wanted to go for one of their walks. Instead, they'd stayed in the kitchen drinking the Kenyan coffee he'd brought her and then visited the post collection point to pick up a package for Gambrinus. Houses in Essoona had no letterboxes: letters and parcels for every resident on a block were delivered to a single location in the central square and placed in pigeon holes guarded by post office staff. As usual, there'd been a queue: a couple of people Hanna vaguely recognised had waved hello.

When their turn came, Hassan had showed the confirmation that Gambrinus had authorised him to collect his order.

'What is it?' Hanna had asked, as the official hoisted a large, rectangular parcel across the counter.

'Gambrinus' latest synthesiser. Straight from the factory: he's been waiting for it for months. I said I'd pick it up, seeing as I was coming anyway.'

She'd helped him carry it back to Dunia House and decided that was the best moment she'd get.

'Hassan?'

'Yes, Hanna?'

'I'm on the pill.'

'The pill?' He'd looked at her blankly.

'The contraceptive pill. So we can have sex without worrying about me getting pregnant.'

Hassan had blinked, then followed up with a quick, curt nod. 'That's ... great. Well done, Hanna. Good job.'

His reaction wasn't what she'd expected. He hadn't asked her how she was; if she felt any different. If she was

OK. That wasn't like him. She'd read about so many terrifying side effects to hormonal contraceptives she was relieved that, after a few weeks of taking it, she just felt a bit ... blobby. And more easily moved to tears. She'd put on a couple of pounds, but you couldn't call her over-weight. If anything, it suited her.

'Listen, Hanna,' he'd said. 'I'm sorry I wasn't in touch as much as I promised. Being back in Africa was so intense, I kind of forgot about my real life on the *Shantivira*. I never forgot about *you*, but it was like ... I couldn't join up the two worlds in my head, you know? It made it hard to talk to you.'

Hanna didn't know. How could anyone forget about the *Shantivira*, even for a moment? To her, it sounded as if he'd had more interesting things to do than speak to her. Hassan had disappeared into the teleport the minute they'd got home. Hanna had an unsettling sensation something wasn't right.

HANNA FINISHED HER beans in silence, listening to Lucy updating Aneira on the latest gossip: about Nikolai coming out and getting together with Roberto, and that Farida was spending all her spare time with Saïd. Everyone was pairing off. Hanna was happy for them, but she couldn't help feeling a little lonely.

+ + +

THE WEEK PASSED. After the long break, slotting back into the intense routine required considerable effort. By Friday afternoon, Hanna was physically and mentally exhausted. Her bedroom was empty – Farida was still at the university – so she dumped her bag on the floor and crawled gratefully into bed for a power nap.

She woke refreshed. Time to make plans for the weekend. Still under her duvet, she pulled out her *zana* and called Hassan.

'Hey, you.'

'Hey.'

'So, do you want to come over here or shall I come to the *Shantivira*?'

Hassan eyes slid away from her face. 'Sorry, Hanna, I have to work all this weekend. I won't be able to see you.'

Hanna's heart sank. 'All weekend? That's unusual.'

'Because I was away for so long. I need to do some extra shifts.'

'Oh. OK. Next weekend then.'

'Yes. I hope so. How was your week?'

Hanna updated him and they chatted for a while until Hassan said he needed to go. Hanna shut down her *zana* thoughtfully. She couldn't put her finger on it, but something was definitely off. Did he truly have to work, or was he making a polite excuse not to see her?

She brooded on it all through the following day, not mentioning her fears to anyone else. After dinner, she was waiting for Farida in the entrance hall when Joe exited the teleport and jogged down the stairs, humming to himself. He noticed her and gave her a friendly smile.

'Evening, Hanna,' he said, eyeing her bag. 'Off to the bathhouse?'

'Hi, Joe. Yes, Farida and I are meeting a friend at the

main one in town.'

'Very nice. Been there before?'

'A couple of times. It's fancier than the others I've been to.'

'The rooftop pool with the view over the bay is my personal favourite,' said Joe.

Hanna decided to seize the opportunity. 'Joe ...'

'What?'

'Do *Shantivira* pilots often have to work both days on the weekend?'

'Only in emergencies.'

'So Hassan will definitely be free *next* weekend, even if he has to work all *this* weekend?'

'Work all weekend?' Joe looked confused. 'Hassan isn't on duty until tomorrow morning, Hanna. As far as I know, he was helping out in the tropical biome all day. Have you two had an argument?'

'No. Of course not!' said Hanna, her head whirling. Why would Hassan lie to her? 'Everything's fine. I must have my days mixed up.'

LATER, IN THE final pool of their session – the big one on the bathhouse roof – Hanna could hold back no longer. Interrupting Farida and Aneira's conversation about pensions, she said, 'I think Hassan's cheating on me!' and burst into tears.

There was a shocked silence, broken only by the gentle bubbling of the opaque green water. Wisps of steam rose between Hanna and her friends.

'*What?*' said Aneira.

'No way, Hanna,' said Farida. 'Hassan *adores* you. What makes you think he's cheating?'

Between sobs, Hanna explained about Hassan's reaction last week to her going on the pill, right up to finding out from Joe that Hassan had lied to her. 'They say you should get married before having sex, because the man loses interest once you do. What have I done? Everything was fine before; if only I'd waited! Did he meet some sophisticated Ugandan beauty while he was visiting his foster parents? Someone who's the same age as him and reads the same books as he does? What if she's a friend of the family? Someone he grew up with? He's never introduced me to his foster parents. They're university academics and I never even went to school. Is he ashamed of me?'

Farida seized Hanna's hands. 'Hanna, stop! I'm sure there's a rational explanation. Hassan would never, *ever* cheat on you. He's not the type.'

Hanna pulled back her hands and splashed her face with the warm water. 'What other explanation is there?' she said, turning away to look at the view. Joe was right, it was amazing. To the east, the sun was setting over the ocean and the city lights twinkled prettily in the twilight. The lighthouse at the north of the bay was already on: flashing its warning six times a minute.

Aneira took a place beside her, resting one arm on the stone edge of the pool. 'I agree,' she said. 'But there's no point in getting upset until you know the facts. You need to confront him.'

'Confront him?' said Hanna.

'That's what Elian did, when he suspected *his* boyfriend was going behind his back.'

Farida goggled. 'Elian had a *boyfriend*?'

'Sure he did. Last year, before he met me. You know most Syenitians are bisexual, right?'

Hanna and Farida shook their heads.

'Something to do with them all living for so long. Improves their chances of finding a partner and keeping in good mental health.'

'Oh,' said Farida.

Hanna watched a bat swoop low over the water, hunting the insects attracted by the pool's lights. An evening breeze stirred, dissipating the steam above the water.

'So you think I should ask Hassan straight out, why he lied to me?'

'It's the only way,' said Aneira.

Farida said, 'I agree. I can't believe he'd be unfaithful. Listen to what he has to say before making any decisions.'

Hanna gulped. 'OK. Next weekend. I need to do it face-to-face. If he refuses to come here, I'll find him on the *Shantivira*.'

21. THE ROGUE SAMARITAN
JOE

J OE WOKE AND, without moving, estimated the time. The all-round projection of the night sky was brightening to a paler blue, with a hazy orange glow coming from the direction of the wardrobe. There were still a few stars, but it was light enough to see the occasional cloud scud past the peak of Corn Du, beyond his feet to the south. Familiar with the recording, Joe knew he had another half an hour before daylight revealed a panoramic view from the top of Pen y Fan in the Brecon Beacons. At that point, if they were still sleeping, his alarm clock would wake them with Radio Cymru.

Apart from the futon (which could be stored in a long, low cupboard at the head of the bed) and the white fitted wardrobe, the room had no furniture. This space was their private refuge aboard the *Pride of Essoona*.

He mentally ran through his list of jobs. Lots to do before his afternoon meeting with Aldeman. Better get up. He wriggled out from under the warm weight of demon-Kitty's tail and onto the tatami mat floor.

As he did his morning stretches, Kitty stirred and rolled over to face him, eyes still closed: serenity itself. He smiled. Sleeping here, she felt able to use the form which needed the least energy to maintain. A side of herself she rarely showed to others. Plus, it stopped cat hairs from getting into the bedlinen. He caressed the red scales on her cheek.

Five more minutes, she said.

You stay there, love, he replied, *I have some reports to read.*

Joe wrapped himself in his kimono, then padded through to the galley to make breakfast. Waiting for the kettle to boil, he activated the exterior cameras. These displayed whatever was outside on a gigantic screen which took up one entire wall of the living area, like a panoramic window.

'What the hell?'

The *Koppakuoria*, which normally dominated the docking bay, was gone.

'Delius?' he addressed the audio link. 'Report, please.' No answer. That was weird. 'Delius!' Nothing. OK, now he was getting worried.

'Gambrinus?'

'Captain?' The *Shantivira's* backup computer responded immediately.

Thank heaven for small mercies. 'This isn't your shift, Gambrinus, where's Delius? And *where's* our cargo ship?'

'Um, so, he popped out on an errand.'

'An *errand*?' What the fuck? 'And he took the *Koppakuoria*? What errand? Why wasn't I informed?'

'Er …'

'Patch me through and show me his location.'

'Yes, Captain.'

The screen displayed a map of Africa, stretching from

one end of the dining table to the other. A red dot flashed at the top of the green bit on the right-hand side. The border region between Ethiopia and South Sudan, Joe thought. Hanna and Hassan's corner of the world. At the same time, Delius' face appeared, the *Koppakuoria's* familiar cockpit behind him.

'Delius? What are you doing?'

'I'm sorry, sir, but Hassan was most persuasive. I promise not to leave the ship.'

'Hassan? Wait, you've *landed*? On the planet? Delius, you're not authorised!'

'We haven't landed. We're hovering. We don't need long.'

'Turn on the cameras in the hold, Delius. Now.'

The map and cockpit image slid to one side and suddenly Joe was looking out into blinding bright sunshine and ... faces. Hundreds of faces crowding around the loading ramp. Behind them, a red earth road, a wall with an open gate and, beyond, corrugated iron shacks and white tents, interspersed with scrubby trees.

'We're on an airstrip for a refugee camp in the northeast of South Sudan, sir.'

Hassan came into view, dressed in black shorts and an orange T-shirt, with an unknown man wearing an UNHCR jacket. They passed a white box, stamped with the blue UNHCR logo, down to the waiting hands, swiftly followed by another, and another. The boxes were being transferred to the compound, hand-to-hand along a human chain.

A momentary surge of pride overtook Joe's anger. If you were going to break the rules so spectacularly, then do it for a good reason. Good on you, Hassan. Even though this could mean the end of the *Shantivira's* funding, and the Earth being left at the mercy of anyone who fancied invading – at least the lad's heart was in the right place.

Joe looked closer, totting up violations. For starters: unauthorised use of alien technology on a primitive planet; taking the *Shantivira's* main computer into a war zone; allowing the *Koppakuoria* to be boarded by unauthorised personnel. He gritted his teeth.

Thank goodness Hassan had had the sense to put on his terrestrial prosthetics – not his usual black and silver boots which were packed with Syenitian technology. Couldn't risk *them* going astray. Joe saw no one taking pictures, saw no smartphones in the crowd. Perhaps they'd get away with it. Would anyone believe these people, if they said a spaceship had brought their supplies? Perhaps, seeing only humans on board, they'd think it was some kind of aircraft.

Hassan's head jerked up and he called out to someone. Joe had no audio, but he saw a girl – who had been walking away – stop and turn back. Hassan sprang down from the ramp and pushed his way through to her. Joe watched their body language: hers cautious, his excited and somehow supplicatory. He was asking her something, wanted something important from her. What? The girl turned and jogged back into the compound. Hassan returned to the *Koppakuoria* and continued lifting boxes.

Eventually the hold was empty and the throng diminished. The adults were mostly gone: the fresh supplies were *their* priority. Only a few curious watchers remained, and scores of children, eager to see what the enormous insect would do next.

Hassan shook hands with his helper, who patted him on the back and jumped down. Joe thought Hassan would turn to go, but he stood on the edge of the ramp, waiting. Waiting for what?

Oh no. The girl Hassan had spoken to returned, carrying a bag. Joe facepalmed, then watched from between his fingers. A *passenger*? Hassan, you're taking this too far.

She approached the hold and peered in, wide-eyed and curious. There was something familiar about her, but Joe couldn't put his finger on it. Hassan helped her aboard; the ramp closed and they disappeared from view.

Delius interrupted Joe's doom-laden thoughts. 'We're on our way home, sir. Arriving in fifteen minutes.'

Fifteen minutes? He'd better get dressed.

+ + +

JOE WAITED WITH folded arms, a humanoid Kitty smouldering by his side. As they watched the cargo ship land, he said, *I want to hit something.*

Oh, me too. Bloody idiots, the pair of them. We must restrain ourselves, cariad. *Listen to what they have to say.*

This'll be the end of us, Cath. *Dalian's been wanting to shut us down for years: I can't imagine her ever dropping this.*

No. But it's not just her decision. The whole Council will have to vote on it. We won't go down without a fight.

THE REAR RAMP lowered and three figures emerged, in height order from large to small.

Joe! She looks exactly like Hanna.

The missing younger sister? But if Delius had found her, surely he'd have asked you to pick her up? Why throw the rulebook out the window and jeopardise the Shantivira? Can you remember her name?

Kia.

THEY STOOD FACE-TO-FACE, two against three. Joe stepped forward and took the girl's hands in his. She stopped staring at her surroundings and focused on him.

'It's Kia, isn't it?' he asked in English. 'Hanna Abebe's sister?'

A shy nod.

'Please don't be frightened. You're safe and among friends. Did Hassan tell you what we do up here?'

She looked at him, worry and confusion clear to read in her expression.

Hassan cleared his throat. 'Um … she doesn't speak much English. I'll interpret for you.'

He did so, and Joe reached a decision.

It's Nuer, their language, isn't it? Which you speak?

That's right, said Kitty.

Take her to the canteen and find her something to eat. Don't show her around. As soon as I'm done with the shouting match, take her and Hassan to Hanna in Essoona.

Aye, aye, Captain.

KITTY SPOKE TO Kia, whose eyes widened to saucers. She bit her lip and darted a beseeching glance at Hassan, her anchor in all this strangeness. He put his hands on her shoulders and said something reassuring. Then Kitty led her away. Showtime.

Switching to Kawaida, Joe said, 'Hassan, you are suspended from duty pending investigation and trial by the Syenitian authorities on behalf of the Galaksi Alliance. After giving me your report, you will leave the *Shantivira* and await further instructions in Dunia House.'

'Yes, Captain, but—'

Joe held up his hand and continued. 'Delius, you'd be suspended too, but I need you here. No doubt you factored that into your decision to help Hassan. But there will be consequences.'

'I have no regrets, Captain. My actions align with my programming.'

Joe sighed. 'I know. Come on, then, Hassan. Explain to me why you felt you could use our cargo ship illegally and without permission.'

'It's the rainy season, Captain. That refugee camp has been impossible to reach by road for months. They're totally reliant on airlifts for fresh supplies.'

'And how is that the *Shantivira's* problem, precisely?'

Hassan studied the white floor of the docking bay. 'Well, it's not.' He looked up and met Joe's gaze. 'But it *is* mine. Those are my people, Joe. Kitty can't give them all better lives like she did for me. They're stuck where they are. I feel like … now I'm in a position to help, I have a duty to do what I can. Whatever the consequences. If this is the end of my career as a pilot, I can live with that.'

Can you, though? thought Joe, rubbing his stubble. An appalling waste of talent, but he couldn't see an alternative outcome to this mess yet. 'Hassan, I can't fault your motives. But think of the bigger picture. Is helping a few thousand people worth having us closed down for? To leave the Earth undefended against any species which fancies a slice of the pie? We have a fight for survival on our hands now, thanks to you. There are ... factions on the Syenitian Council who'd love to shut us down, and you've just handed them all the ammunition they need. And breaching the Syenitians' security protocols is one thing. What consequences will this have on Earth, once word gets out? You've driven a coach and horses through months of painstaking work with the UN.'

'Sir, if I may interrupt,' said Delius, not stopping for permission, 'I did a full analysis. The camp's remoteness means its communications are easily controlled. The technology available there is basic. Smartphones are currently not prevalent. Word of mouth reports may spread, but they have no hard evidence we were ever there. I assessed the risks and found them to be minimal compared to the benefit to life.'

Joe sighed again. The irony of a machine reminding him of fundamental human priorities – just as he had to do for Kitty every so often – did not escape him.

'Joe,' argued Hassan, 'we only use the *Koppakuoria* two or three times a year. Mostly it sits there doing nothing. It's such a waste, when you consider how many people we could help with it.'

Perhaps there was a silver lining there ... perhaps *that* was the way out of this PR nightmare. He needed time to let the idea unfurl. Put it to one side for now.

'Hassan, if your plan had gone wrong, we'd have had to do without our main computer. Do you realise how inconvenient that would have been?'

'I approached Gambrinus first, but Delius insisted it was his turn.'

Inwardly, Joe cursed himself for not having taken Delius to the surface himself when he'd had the chance last year. He'd known it would come back to bite him one day and now here they were.

'But you still took a Syenitian combat cyborg into a war zone. The Syenitians will regard that as involving them in someone else's fight without their agreement.'

'A *retired* combat cyborg, sir,' corrected Delius. 'We didn't land. There was no fighting nearby. I broke no rules regarding myself. Only taking the ship without your permission and revealing it to the locals.'

'Well, that's all right then, isn't it?' Joe hoped Delius would detect the sarcasm in his voice. He didn't always. 'Hovering that low is the *same* as landing, Delius. You mustn't take the rules so literally. To be fair, though, the locals didn't seem bothered, did they?'

'They were more interested in the boxes,' agreed Hassan. 'They trusted us because I involved one of their regular delivery guys, and because I looked and sounded like them too.'

'This all came out of your trip, didn't it?'

Hassan bowed his head in acknowledgement. 'It brought it all home to me: my privileged life. I'd put the situation in South Sudan out of my mind for so long ... kept myself busy collecting qualifications. Once I saw how things were there … I couldn't not do something.'

Joe patted him on the shoulder. 'I *am* proud of you, Hassan. I'm furious and frustrated and frightened of the future too, but I understand why you did it, and I'll do what I can for you. But it won't be pretty. You're going to need a good lawyer.'

Delius said, 'May I suggest Commander Westwood, sir? I could coach him in the relevant protocols.'

'William? Yes. I'll ask him. Last question. Did you know Kia was there? Was she part of your mission?'

For the first time since landing, Hassan's face split into a broad grin. 'No! No idea! I didn't notice her until she turned away. Then I recognised her from her walk. Her right shoulder dips a little with each step, like Hanna's does.'

'And she was happy to go with you, just like that?'

'I said I'd take her to Hanna.'

'And so you shall. Go pack a bag and put your comfy feet on. Kitty will take you both as soon as you're ready.'

'Yes, Captain.' Hassan turned to Delius and hugged him. 'Thanks, Delius. You were awesome.'

Delius' expression was as impassive as ever, but Joe was sure his neural networks were firing at full tilt, trying to calculate the appropriate response to this unusual display of affection. He was used to hugs from the children, but adult embraces were a new experience. Slowly he lifted his arms and briefly encircled Hassan. To Joe, he said, 'Sir, I must return to the control room and backup my new files.'

Joe suppressed a smile. After decades of watching from afar, Delius had finally fulfilled a personal dream and approached the planet's surface. All that fresh data about the Earth was precious treasure to him. And they'd need it to mount a defence convincing enough to save the *Shantivira*.

He looked at his watch. 'Off you go, the pair of you. I have a call to make.' He strode back to the *Pride* and sat on the lower step. He put his *zana* on the ground in front of him and told it to dial Gabriel.

'Gabriel, mate,' he said to the hologram when it appeared, 'You're in Dublin this week, right? We're on the same time, roughly?'

'Well, I'm a bit jet-lagged, but it's not the middle of the night for me, if that's what you mean.'

'Good. Listen, I need to talk to you. There's been a development. Can you meet me in the pub in, say, half an hour or so? I'll send Kitty to pick you up.'

Gabriel checked his diary. 'I'll have to do some postponing. I assume it's important?'

'It's important,' said Joe.

'I can make it in an hour and a half, will that do you?'

'See you there.'

JOE AND KITTY materialised in the beer cellar of *The Cath Palug*, a picturesque pub in a remote corner of Snowdonia. It had existed in some form for over a thousand years, partly thanks to ongoing financial support from its (secret) co-owner, one Kitvian 'Reika' Ahmitorsdottir, aka Kitty Llewellyn. She'd used it as a bolt hole for centuries: a quiet place to rest and be among people who accepted her. Countless generations of the Davies family had grown up playing with a black jaguar – which appeared at intervals to snooze by the fire – then learned her secret when they came of age.

The pub had a reputation for being unfriendly to tourists and non-Welsh speakers, but this was because Kitty (the friendly big cat) was an open secret in the local community. Knowing she posed no hazard to local livestock, they shielded her from the perceived risk of being taken away and put in a zoo. Or getting the current landlords, Ianto and Angharad, prosecuted for keeping a dangerous animal without a licence.

Since marrying Kitty, *The Cath Palug* had become Joe's refuge too; a place he could watch the rugby and chat with people in his native language – although they loved to tease him about his Southerner's dialect. It was the perfect location for private meetings.

Ianto was in the cellar, changing a barrel. *'Ti'n iawn, Joe? Ti'n iawn, Kitty? O, mae hi 'di mynd eto yn barod ...'*

'She's gone to get Gabriel,' Joe replied, also in Welsh. 'Can I help you with that, mate?'

IT WAS ELEVEN in the morning and Joe had the place to himself. Summer sunshine streamed through the leaded windows, criss-crossing the worn flagstones with little diamonds and highlighting the grains on the dark wooden furniture. Dust motes danced silently in the air and the comforting scent of pub calmed his still-jangling nerves. He sat at his usual table, nursing a pint of Brains and tying his mind in knots, trying to foresee the ramifications of Hassan's stunt. What was the best approach to take with Aldeman?

The cellar door banged shut and he looked up to see Gabriel crossing the room, wearing a tailored navy-blue suit. Behind him, jaguar-Kitty made a beeline for the hearthrug. They didn't light the fire in August, but it was still her favourite spot.

Thanks, love.

No worries.

To Gabriel he said, 'Sorry to drag you away from the office. I got you a Guinness, hope that's OK.'

'I shouldn't be drinking so early in the day. You're a bad influence, Llewellyn.' Gabriel pulled out the chair opposite Joe and sat. '*Sláinte mhaith,*' he said, raising his glass to Joe.

Joe lifted his pint in return. '*Iechyd da, mêt.*'

'So, what's all this about?' Gabriel asked.

Joe told him.

'Oh crap.'

'You said it. They're both absolutely unrepentant.'

'Everything was going so well with the UN. Our barbecue was such a success. Everyone on board with our dominoes lined up and ready to go. What's going to happen now?'

'I have to tell Aldeman. And I don't want to.'

'No.'

'But dealing with the Syenitians is my problem. I brought you here because we need to agree on how to play it with the UN.'

'If they ever hear about it.'

'Of course they'll hear about it. We need to prepare our answers.'

Gabriel turned his glass on the beer mat. 'Perhaps we

could … guide public opinion.'

'You mean, put the focus on "aliens help UN", rather than "OMG, aliens!"?' said Joe, taking a sip of beer.

Gabriel nodded. 'You have to hand it to the lad: it's PR gold, if we can spin it the right way.'

'You don't think people'll think we're interfering in matters which don't concern us? The South Sudanese especially. I don't want things there to get even worse because of us.'

'Imagine if aliens had descended from the heavens and told us to stop fighting in Ireland, back in the eighties?'

'We'd have told them to fuck off, wouldn't we?' Joe said, grinning. 'And gone straight back to killing each other.'

'You were there, British Army boy, you know better than me. But this was a humanitarian mission: locals "borrowing" equipment to help their own people. Could Hassan be persuaded to do an interview?'

Joe shook his head. 'Keep Hassan out of this. He has enough problems. He might end up being exiled if they find him guilty.'

'OK, a deal with the UN, then. To prove the *Shantivira's* good intentions. That was the trial run and we're ironing out the details. Joe, this might be what we need to get you in front of the General Assembly sooner rather than later.'

'That could work,' said Joe.

Angharad came back into the bar and began unloading the dishwasher. 'You two fancy an early lunch?' she asked in Welsh. 'Lasagne and chips?'

Joe interpreted for Gabriel.

'Why not?' he said. 'I cancelled my plans, just for you. Buying me lunch is the least you can do.'

As they ate, Joe tried to articulate a feeling that had been gnawing at him for months.

'How did you do it, Gabriel? Go back to working with humans after all those years on the *Shantivira*? Don't they drive you nuts?'

Gabriel put down his knife and fork. 'No more than the Syenitians did, or anyone else I've worked with. You mean, them not knowing what I know, and me not being able to tell them?'

'Yeah. Doesn't it make you feel like a permanent outsider?'

'No. But I never really left. I have more ties to the Earth than you, Joe. I have a ridiculous number of relatives. Honestly, becoming a diplomat was child's play after a life of dealing with my crazy family.'

Joe said, 'I haven't spent this much time with – let's call them "normal" – humans since I left the army. I enjoy the jokes and the banter. But … I look like them and I speak their language, but I don't see things the same way as they do. I feel like this planet isn't my home anymore.'

'Bullshit,' said Gabriel. 'If not here, then where? This is your wife's home, isn't it, Kitty?' he said, directing his words towards the fireplace.

Yes, said the voice only Joe could hear. *I* made *this my home.*

Gabriel continued, oblivious. 'Home is people more than places, Joe. It sounds to me like you need to have an honest conversation with your mother. You can't put it off for ever.'

Joe shook his head. 'Christ, Gabe, not you as well. I get enough of that from Kitty.'

'You'll never be at peace until she knows the truth about you.'

Listen to him, Joe.

'Do *your* family know the truth about *you*?'

'Some of it. Enough to understand.'

'I could never talk to her so openly. We stick to safe topics like her health, my health, her garden and the weather. No feelings. No honest opinions, or we wouldn't even be able to pretend we have a relationship.'

Gabriel raised his eyebrows. 'How long have things been like that?'

'Forever. No. Not forever. I'd say, since my Nan died, when I was thirteen. My dad had been drinking for a while, but Nan was strict and he knew she'd throw him out if he let it get too bad.'

'But then she died?' prompted Gabriel.

'She left her cottage to Mam. It wasn't much: two up, two down and a toilet at the bottom of the garden. But once he had a secure roof over his head, he felt he could do what he liked. He controlled Mam, you see. What she wore, who she talked to, what she thought, even. She spent her life trying to please him. Every time he hit her, she believed him when he promised he'd never do it again. It didn't happen often, because she tried so hard not to make him angry in the first place. But we always walked on eggshells, watching everything we said so his temper wouldn't blow up.'

Kitty rose and padded across the room. She settled under their table, pressing against his leg. He leaned down and stroked her head. She knew the whole sorry story already, but this was the first time he'd ever spoken of it to anyone else.

'What about you?' asked Gabriel. 'Did he hit you too?'

Joe grimaced. 'Mostly when he was sober, to "teach me a lesson" about whatever it was that day. He saw it as his parental duty; his dad had done the same to him. Once I hit puberty, the beltings were the only physical contact we had.'

Gabriel reached over the table and squeezed his hand. 'Mate, I'm so sorry. I had no idea.'

'I was usually in bed by the time he came back from the pub, so it wasn't too bad. But then he started drinking during the daytime as well. I'd grown as tall as him, but he was much stronger.'

He stopped, not sure how to describe what had happened next. Gabriel said nothing, just waited patiently and eventually Joe spoke to fill the silence. 'One day, not long after my fifteenth birthday, a letter arrived from school. When I came down from the Beacons, behind our house, Mam and Dad were waiting for me in the back garden. They'd been called for an appointment with the headmaster because of me bunking off school. They'd had no idea I'd not been going. I'd always been careful to leave on time in the morning and come home soon after school finished.'

'And really you were roaming the hills with Kitty?'

'Not every day. Sometimes she didn't come and I went by myself. I'll never forget Mam's face. It said, "How could you upset him like this? This is all your fault: now I'm going to get it too." That was all she cared about.'

'What did they actually say?' asked Gabriel.

'Mam was shrieking about me bringing shame on the family and what would the neighbours think if they found out. Dad had already been drinking and he had that evil look in his eye. He said, "This calls for more than the strap: you're too stupid to understand unless I make it clear."' Joe's face flushed with the memory of it, and he rubbed his leg against Kitty's flank for reassurance. 'He punched me in the stomach, full force. I fell to the ground and he started kicking me. He still had his steel-capped boots from when he worked down the mine. God, it hurt. I begged Mam to stop him, but she just looked at me like I was dirt, then turned and walked away. I thought he was going to kill me, so I yelled for *Cath*. That's still my private name for her, you know?'

'I know.'

'Dad said, "Nobody can hear you up here, boyo." But she came, right away.'

Heard you halfway across the galaxy, babe. That was the moment I knew for sure we were connected.

'And what did Kitty do?'

'I heard a growl behind me, and suddenly Dad was floating upside-down in the air above the vegetable patch. His face was scarlet and he couldn't move his limbs. Kitty pressed her head against my injuries and they stopped hurting.

'I crouched in front of Dad and lay my arm across her back. "This is my magic cat, Dad," I said. "One word from me and she'll rip your throat out. I'm taking her for a walk and when I come back, I want to find you've gone for good. If I ever see you again, I'll have her kill you, do you understand?"

'He nodded vigorously and I said, "OK, drop him, *Cath*." Dad fell onto his hands and knees, and that was the last time I saw him, grovelling in the mud. That's why I can't talk to Mam. I'll never forgive her for not even *trying* to protect me. And she can't bear the sight of me.'

'But he's dead now?' said Gabriel. 'From that miners' disease?'

'Miners and smokers. Emphysema. While I was in the army.'

'Nasty,' said Gabriel. 'I wouldn't wish that on anyone.'

Syenitian-Kitty appeared in the seat beside Joe, wearing her favourite medieval red dress. 'I'm saying this out loud so Gabriel can back me up. You must tell Grace what you do, Joe, and soon. She ought to hear it from you *before* news about the *Shantivira* gets out. We'll need her cooperation if someone wants to use her to get to you.'

'But I don't *care* if they come for her. Let them have the miserable cow and good luck to 'em.'

'She's your *mother*, Joe,' said Kitty. 'Your one living relative. Future regret is a bad companion. You must be the grown-up here.' She hesitated, picking at the moisture-thickened edge of a cardboard beer mat. 'I never told you this before; I didn't think it would help. But Grace *was* watching that day. Of course she was worried about you, but she didn't dare confront Gareth. You ended her marriage, without even consulting her. You probably saved her life, ultimately, but she *loved* your father. I suspect she's never forgiven you for that.'

Joe stared into his beer, trying to imagine how his mam might have felt. She'd never mentioned seeing Kitty. Not ever. She must have been as frightened as his dad had been. No wonder she hated him.

'Look at it strategically, mate,' said Gabriel. 'Once you go before the General Assembly, everyone will want a piece of you. Your mother is an unsecured potential access point to you, and therefore to the *Shantivira*. If your antagonism is mutual, she's a liability: we need her on our side or there's no telling the damage she could do to our reputation. This isn't just about you.'

Joe rubbed his face. He hadn't thought about it like that. He wouldn't trust Grace Llewellyn not to undermine all his efforts with the UN, either innocently or maliciously. She needed to be handled with care.

He sighed in resignation. 'OK. I'll tell you what: when we go properly public – when or if I speak in front of the General Assembly – then I'll tell her what I do for a living. All right? Will *that* get you off my back?'

'Immediately after, before she sees you on the news?' said Kitty.

'You can take me straight there, as soon as we're done.'

'Shake on it?' said Gabriel.

Joe shook Gabriel's hand.

If I survive that long, he said to Kitty. *Aldeman and the Council might skin me alive first.*

Don't be such a drama queen. They'll get over it. It's not much worse than when you got the fish for the Pweza.

You think?

You're just upset because Hassan thought of it before you did.

Yeah, right.

THEY WERE PREPARING to leave when Joe's terrestrial phone rang. His heart sank when he saw the caller ID.

'Joe? I just had a most intriguing telephone call from a nice man at the UNHCR. He asked me if I knew which country made spaceships shaped like big beetles and if I could get him one for aid deliveries.'

Fuck. Fuck. Fuckity *fuck*. He forced himself to smile. 'Susan! How *are* you?'

'What's going on, Joe? How does the UNHCR know about your cargo ship?'

22. REPERCUSSIONS

HANNA

O N THE TRAM home from school, Hanna let her mind return to the problem of Hassan. Only tomorrow, then it was the weekend. Should she call him tonight to arrange something? Or wait and surprise him in person? It was so hard to know what to do for the best. She dreaded the conversation they'd have. Better to arrange something, so she wouldn't chicken out on the day.

Still brooding, Hanna trudged from the tram stop round the corner to the entrance to Dunia House. She dumped her bag at the bottom of the staircase and went to the kitchen to make herself a cup of *saiju*. The door was open and she could see into the room from the corridor. She stopped dead, her heart on a yo-yo.

Hassan was sitting at the table drinking coffee – she could smell it from here – with someone she couldn't see. Someone female: Hanna could hear her voice. They were speaking Nuer! Hanna's imagination went into overdrive. Had Hassan brought his new girlfriend along to show Hanna it was over between them? Was she from South Sudan like him? But why had the teleport worked for her? Unless she was already a Shantiviran? Oh, God, Hanna thought, she couldn't compete with that …

With all her willpower, she forced her feet to take her into the kitchen. When she saw who sat there, her hand flew to her mouth.

'Kia!' she gasped.

Hanna sprinted round the table to greet her sister. Kia stood up clumsily, knocking over her chair. Hanna flung her arms around Kia's slight shoulders and squeezed her fiercely, burying her face in Kia's neck. When she came up for air, tears blurred her vision.

'Kia! How? When?' Hanna could barely get the words out. She blinked until she could see again and looked at Hassan. He beamed at her, his eyes full of love. Hanna held Kia's arms and studied her face. 'You're OK?'

Kia nodded energetically; her eyes were wet too. Hanna sat opposite Hassan and pulled her sister onto her lap, rocking her back and forth. Kia nestled her head under Hanna's chin, just like she'd done when she was tiny. Hanna didn't think she'd ever let her go again.

'Explain,' she said to Hassan.

He poured a fresh cup of coffee and pushed it towards her. Then, working backwards from finding Kia at the refugee camp, he told her the whole story.

'I hated lying to you, Hanna,' he said. 'I almost couldn't do it. But if you'd known what I'd been planning, you'd have had to tell Joe or be in as much trouble as I am. That's why I've been avoiding you. I had to protect you. It would be a tragedy to end your career as well as mine.'

Hanna didn't know what to say. She couldn't believe she'd been such an idiot, thinking he'd found someone else. This was *Hassan*. Her Hassan. She should have had more faith. He must never, ever find out about her suspicions: that she'd let her trust in him waver. She was *so* ashamed of herself.

When her voice returned, she said, 'So what happened when you went home? You've hardly talked about South Sudan since you came back.'

'Too painful. But the anger started building long before I got there.'

'Anger?'

'About the inequality. The unfairness. My inability to change it.' Hassan shook his head. 'That safari we went on, Hanna. You wouldn't believe the comfort the tourists live in, far out in the bush. So much extravagance.'

Hanna said nothing, just waited for him to find the words.

'Apart from the staff, Gildas, Gaositwe and I were the only black Africans. I hadn't realised how hard it is to tour our own continent, even now, in 2015. So many visas to organise, so much bureaucracy. People do manage to travel, of course, but we have this huge luxury tourist industry and we're barely on its radar as a target market. It's so short-sighted. A wasted opportunity.'

Hassan paused to take a sip from his coffee. The cup clinked in the saucer as he put it down. 'Surely we should be able to learn about the wonders of Africa at first hand? After all, *we're* responsible for caring for them. Surely we should be encouraged to understand our neighbours better by visiting their countries?'

Hanna could only agree. 'And the other guests?' she asked. 'How did they treat you?'

'Fine, for the most part. I had the impression they were curious to talk to'—Hassan made air quotes—'"actual

Africans" as their peers in the group. A bit patronising though. Some of the older ladies were convinced I wouldn't be able to manage the tour because I'm'—more air quotes—'"disabled". It was embarrassing, the fuss they made.'

'I'm sure they thought they were being kind,' said Hanna.

'I'm sure they did. But it's not my job to make them feel good about themselves. Sometimes I felt forced into representing all disabled people everywhere, when all I wanted was a holiday with my mates.'

He sighed. 'It wasn't just the safari, though. It was the whole experience. The contrasts. Even in Kampala: it was wonderful to see my foster family, but it brought home to me how lucky I've been. After Kitty took me to Uganda, I never wanted for anything.'

'And then you and Gildas went on to Juba.'

'It was so different to my memories, Hanna,' Hassan said, rubbing his face. 'It smelled the same, the food was the same ... but ... the way people live there ... the way they view the world ...' He looked up at her. 'I suppose I had a massive culture shock. All this time, I've been thinking of it as home – where I come from, where I belong – and it turns out it's not true. I'll never live there again. It might be where I'm from, but I feel safer and more comfortable here in Essoona. But I'm sad because I feel that way. Does that make sense?'

Hanna nodded. One day she'd return to Ethiopia and she hoped she'd be able to fit in. 'What gave you the idea of borrowing the *Koppakuoria*?' she asked.

'We got talking to some aid workers one night. They

were worried they wouldn't be able to transport supplies to this refugee camp in time – it'd been cut off by flooding – and the people there would starve. I didn't tell Gildas, but I took the guy's number and got in touch with him later on. I had to do *something*, Hanna, you understand, don't you?'

She did. 'It was God's will, Hassan. You helped people – and found my baby sister. I'm so proud of you.' She detached herself from Kia to reach over and squeeze his long fingers. 'Kia, love, you're going to have to sit on your own chair. My legs have gone numb!'

Silently, Kia slid into a neighbouring seat.

'What about you, Kia?' said Hanna. 'How did you end up in South Sudan?'

Haltingly, Kia began to tell her story. How the orphanage had sent her to work in a factory in Khartoum and how she and some fellow Ethiopians, another girl and two older boys, had run away one night, in an attempt to get home. They'd hitch-hiked up the White Nile to Kosti, where they'd found a cargo ship headed for Juba. After more than a week of sleeping on deck and being eaten alive by mosquitoes, they'd disembarked at Melut and made their way east on foot, cadging lifts whenever they could. One of the boys had become ill with malaria and a kindly truck driver had delivered them to the refugee camp, where the boy, Tamru, had received treatment.

There was a click and a squeak as someone opened the back door from outside. Joe strode into the room. The summer evening breeze caught the door and it banged shut behind him.

'Evening all! Is there enough coffee in that pot for me?'

'Plenty,' said Hassan, 'help yourself.'

Joe found a mug, sat down opposite Kia and served them all more coffee.

'How are you settling in, Kia?' He gulped his drink while Hanna translated the question and his eyebrows shot up. 'Hell, that's strong stuff! I'll be awake all night.'

Hanna giggled. It *was* much better coffee than anything she'd ever had in London. 'The taste of Kenya,' she said. 'Kia says, how can she settle in, she doesn't know where she is or where she'll be sleeping tonight. But I'll sort that out.' To Kia she said, 'You can stay with me, in my room. You're safe here.'

Joe responded with a smile, which faded as he turned to Hassan.

'So, I spoke to Aldeman. You're being formally charged with taking a vessel without consent, misapplying Alliance property, disobeying lawful commands, plus obstructing operations. The documentation has already been sent to your *zana*. Your trial has been set for January, at the central law courts in town. Until then, you're not permitted to leave the Earth and the teleports will be blocked for your biosignature. I'm here to escort you back to the planet.'

'So he can't visit Essoona *or* the *Shantivira*?' said Hanna, outraged. 'But they're his home, Joe! You're cutting him off from his *family*!'

Joe flashed her a look, a mixture of irritation and regret. 'No, Hanna. *He* did that. He knew the consequences and chose to go ahead with his hare-brained scheme regardless.'

'It's true, Hanna,' said Hassan. 'Delius told me what to

expect: including what I'd be charged with. That's why I was so careful not to tell you anything.' To Joe, he said, 'You'll need my boots back too, won't you?'

'Leave them on the *Shantivira*. We'll go there first to pick up your stuff. You can stay in the basement flat at the language school.'

'So I can still visit him?' asked Hanna, relieved.

'I hope you will, Hanna. You *and* his other friends. It's suspension from duty pending a judicial hearing, not a prison sentence. Yet. Hassan, you're allowed to keep your *zana* so you can prepare your defence.'

'Did you ask William about representing me?'

'I haven't had time. I've been in back-to-back meetings all day, thanks to you.'

Hassan stared at the tabletop and Joe took pity on him. In a gentler voice, he said, 'I can't imagine he'd say no. It's exactly the kind of challenge he loves. There's plenty of time for him to brush up on his barrister skills.'

'Making coffee?' said Hanna, confused.

Hassan's lips twitched. 'Representing a client in court,' he said. 'That's what he used to do, before joining the *Shantivira*. Joe … have I really blown the *Shantivira's* cover? We were so careful. I doubt there's any proof. Who are the people at the camp going to talk to? They're completely cut off, that was the whole reason they needed help.'

Joe sighed. 'You'd be surprised. The UNHCR already knows more than it should, even if it's not sure what to believe. But it's August silly season. There's a good chance any information published more widely won't be taken seriously. With luck, we'll avoid a major public panic.'

'Let's hope so,' Hassan said quietly.

Joe pulled a *zana* out of his jacket pocket and passed it to Kia. She held it cautiously, with two hands, staring at the blank screen.

Joe said, 'This is for you, Kia. Hanna'll show you how to use it. You need to learn Kawaida – our language – so you can get by here without an interpreter.'

Hanna translated and saw Kia look directly at Joe's face for the first time since he'd burst through the back door and interrupted her story.

'Thank you,' she said, in a barely audible whisper. Hanna wondered if Joe was the first white person Kia had ever spoken to. It was possible, she supposed.

'Right, Hassan, let's take you to Mary and Irion.'

Hassan's chair scraped on the floor as he stood up. He looked at Hanna, longing and sorrow etched into the lines on his face. This was it. Separation. Hanna got to her feet and held him tightly, pressing her face against his yellow hooded top. Hassan returned her embrace, resting his forehead on her head.

Joe gave them a few moments, then said, 'What a pair of drama llamas! No need for a fuss, you two. I'm sure Hanna will be in London this weekend.'

True. The weekend was less than forty-eight hours away. She'd survive without seeing Hassan until then. Kia needed her now, even more than Hassan did. She came up for air and tried to reassure Hassan. 'It'll be OK,' she said. 'Thank you for bringing me my sister.'

'Anytime,' he whispered into her hair, then straightened up. 'OK, Joe. I'm ready. Take me back to Earth.'

When they'd gone, Kia took Hanna's hand. 'Hanna, is

Hassan in trouble with that *ferenj*? Because of me?'

Hanna sighed. Kia hadn't understood a word they'd said since Joe had turned up. So much to explain, so many new things for Kia to take in. 'Not because of you, darling. We're all delighted Hassan found you, even Joe. He *is* in trouble for borrowing a spaceship without permission. He can't come here to visit us until it all gets sorted out. But that's not for you to worry about. What's important now is to get you settled in.' Hanna stood up. 'Let's find Mrs Park.'

23. A PLOT
NESTOR

'NESTOR? IT'S PEDRO. Is this a secure line?'

'Pedro! Yes, go ahead.'

'I have news. They're going to let him speak at the plenary debate of the General Assembly in September.'

Nestor allowed himself a humour-free smile. 'Because of the headlines? "Refugees Receive Supplies from Space", "UN Denies Being in League with Extra-Terrestrials", "Why Can't We Feed Our People Without Alien Aid" and the rest? I thought they might.'

'You can't blame them for wanting answers. Llewellyn has bumped himself to the top of the agenda.'

'He'll regret using vulnerable people for his little publicity stunt.' Nestor pursed his lips in a thin, hard line. 'It's time to act, before people start taking him seriously. Thank you for the building plans, by the way. They were precisely what I needed.'

'Don't tell me what you intend to do with them. Plausible deniability is bliss. But I have your assurance none of the other delegates will be in danger?'

'Not from my team. I can't answer for what will happen if he brings *her* with him.'

Pedro paused, then said, 'There's not much we can do

about that, is there? Is there anything else you need from me?'

'Confirmation of the exact date and time, as soon as you have it. And any special arrangements you hear about.'

'You shall have them, my friend. Goodbye for now.'

'Goodbye, Pedro. Give my regards to Pilar.'

Nestor returned to his gardening, humming a cheery little tune to himself. Bending nature to his vision was hard work, but highly satisfying. He'd extracted most of the weeds; soon he'd get the weedkiller out and stop the undesirable elements from taking hold ever again. In his mind's eye, he pictured Llewellyn prostrate on the General Assembly podium, his body limp and lifeless, a red stain on his white shirt spreading outwards from his heart.

It wasn't personal: Llewellyn was merely a connection which needed to be severed. The effect of his sudden death upon the she-devil and her alien friends would be sweet and delicious.

And if he failed? Well, he was running his backup plan in parallel, just in case. Speaking of which, he'd better do some organising at that end, too. He picked up his phone again and dialled.

'Prynhawn da, cariad. Sut wyt ti, heddiw?'

PART THREE

24. KIA

HANNA

TOTALLY FOCUSED, HANNA twisted and spun in her seat as – one by one – she targeted and dematerialised the asteroids along the route Kalarran had specified. No simulation today: real asteroids, real weapons, real speed. She wanted to come in the top five on the leader board, so she drove Tulu as hard as she could. If they crashed, well, the shields would *probably* hold. She didn't want to find out. She wasn't going to crash.

Twist, target, fire. Twist, target, fire. It was exhilarating and relaxing at the same time. For fifteen minutes it was just her and Tulu. No tag team to agree manoeuvres with, no running dialogue. No direct competitors. No time to think about the unsolvable problems that chased her mind in circles these days. Just the simplicity of the hunt. A zen state of flow.

She completed the course and joined the others at the rendezvous. They wouldn't see their times until they returned to the classroom. She let her mind drift, wondering what Kia was doing and how Hassan's meeting with William had gone.

Kia was … struggling. Hanna's years in London had, to some extent, prepared her for life in Essoona, but Kia was suffering from severe culture shock. Her months in Khartoum were her only experience of life in a city and she'd had little freedom to explore. She still had the mindset from life in the isolated orphanage – where she'd always been with the same few hundred girls and female teachers, all of whom looked like her. Life in the diverse community at Dunia House took some getting used to. It didn't help that there was nobody her own age here. Hanna had taken her into town to show her the sights, but Kia had trembled with fear and asked to go back. It wasn't just the aliens: Hanna believed the flying trams, the imposing buildings and the sheer mass of people had all played a part. Poor Kia.

The language barrier was a huge problem. Like the rest of their family, Kia was a chatty, sociable person who needed to express herself verbally. Here, the only person she could talk to easily was Hanna. But Hanna was at school all day during the week and spent Friday nights, Saturdays and Saturday nights in London, with Hassan. *He* needed her too. Plus, they were finally having regular, uninhibited sex.

Since her success with the moon cup, Hanna had discovered whole new ways of enjoying Hassan's body. Despite – or perhaps even because of – everything else that was going on, they'd developed a new closeness. If only they'd had no responsibilities, they'd happily have spent every hour of every day together. She always came back on Sunday mornings to spend the day with Kia, but she guiltily suspected it wasn't enough.

The new gardener, Max, was giving Kia daily Kawaida lessons. Progress was slow: Kia wasn't naturally academic and didn't enjoy intensive schooling. Initially, she'd been crippled with shyness – and fear of being alone with a white man – but that seemed to be wearing off.

Max had put her in charge of the chickens on the Dunia House allotment and she found the practical outdoor work soothing. Mrs Park had taken Kia under her wing, and she spent her afternoons helping around the house like Hanna had in London, communicating in language fragments she'd learned from Max and her *zana* training programs.

Hanna knew Kia needed more, but she couldn't see a clear way forward for the long-term. Kia felt so over-whelmed here that, after their failed city tour, she'd refused to venture beyond their local square. All Hanna could do for now was keep her safe and well-nourished.

The exercise came to an end and they flew in for-mation back to the Academy. Below her, the River Soon split the city in two, before the glittering ribbon wound its way from the coast to the mountains. There was so much she still wanted to see before her time here was over. But what with supporting Hassan and Kia not wanting to go anywhere, she might not have the chance. She sighed. Priorities, Hanna, priorities. People were more important than places.

They approached the school from the sea as usual and landed their *Tumbas* on the docking ports. Tulu almost quivered with relief as her tanks began to charge: not for the first time, Hanna had underestimated the amount of energy her weapons needed and had left them barely enough to get home.

'Sorry, Tulu, I'll be more careful in future,' she said as

she opened the door. She patted the green-veined hull. 'See you tomorrow.'

They trooped into the lecture theatre, where the screen displayed the results. Eagerly, Hanna scanned the list. What? Sixteenth? Not even in the top ten? Even Lucy had come eleventh. This was no good, she was slipping. Briavan had come first: from the way she was strutting about and tossing her hair, Hanna would have guessed that even without looking at the board. Then Elian, then Aneira: the usual suspects. Hanna tried to shrug off her disappointment. No doubt they'd had plenty of sleep instead of staying up until the small hours, researching the Syenitian legal system. Felix had come in at 107 and he seemed cheerful enough. She should take a leaf out of his book and chill.

Kalarran droned on, reviewing and berating their performance. Now the thrill of flying was over, her adrenaline levels plunged and the late night caught up with her. She tried physically holding her eyelids open: impossible. She *mustn't* fall asleep. Not here. Kalarran would skin her alive with sarcasm. She jabbed her pen into her thigh repeatedly. Pain helped, at least for a little while. God, it was so stuffy in here.

The lesson ended and, thankfully, it was time for lunch. She considered sneaking back to Tulu for a little nap before astro-geography. It wouldn't be the first time. She kept blankets and a cushion there for precisely that purpose.

'You OK, Hanna?' asked Lucy. 'You look *knackered*.'

Hanna rubbed her eyes. 'I've been burning the candle at both ends, that's all.'

'Any news about Hassan?'

'About the trial, you mean?'

Lucy nodded and Hanna shook her head. 'It's early days. William's been visiting and they're beginning to put a case together. Delius and Aldeman are giving William a crash course in the Syenitian legal system.'

'Aldeman too? I'd have thought he'd have to stay out of this?'

'Well, it's the *Shantivira's* future on the line, isn't it? He can share his lawyer's knowledge. The verdict is the court's decision, the Council has nothing to do with it.'

'How is Hassan? Now he's famous?'

'I'm worried about his mental health, to be honest. He's barely been outside since those newspaper articles came out. He's terrified someone'll recognise him.'

Lucy's eyes widened. 'That's not good. It's not likely, is it? Not from the pictures I've seen.'

Hanna agreed. The few photos she'd managed to track down were grainy and out of focus, taken with an old-fashioned 35 mm camera.

'Remember, Hanna, the media always has ridiculous stories during August. Now people are back at work after the holidays, they'll soon forget all about it.'

'Do you think so?' Hanna stood a little straighter. 'It's true, the press isn't exactly taking it seriously. The main theory seems to be it's a hoax by the aid agencies.'

'A marketing stunt? To encourage people to donate more?'

'Insane, right?'

Lucy shrugged. 'People come up with explanations which make sense to them. Even if it's completely made-up bollocks. So, is there anything I can help with for the party?'

Hassan turned twenty-five that week and Hanna was organising a surprise party at the weekend. If he couldn't go out and see people, at least they could come to him. 'Bring a salad,' said Hanna. 'Otherwise we're good, thanks. Irion has everything under control.'

THE WEEK CREPT by until, at last, Friday came. After school, Hanna went straight to her room to pack for the weekend. When Kia had first arrived, Farida had generously moved into a single room so Hanna could share with her sister. Initially, Hanna had been grateful, but now she sorely missed Farida's peaceful presence. Sharing a room with a teenager wasn't exactly restful. Apart from anything, Hanna was permanently tidying up. She knew Kia found it hard here, but couldn't she pick her clothes and wet towels up off the floor? Or not drop them in the first place?

Kia lay on her bed, reading a teenage magazine. She held it up for Hanna to see. 'Lucy gave it to me,' she said. 'To help me learn English.'

'That was kind,' said Hanna, kicking off her shoes and collapsing on her bed. She longed for a ten-minute lie-down. She was so tired, her limbs felt heavy, as if she needed superhuman effort to move them. She closed her eyes.

'It's Hassan's party tomorrow, isn't it?'

'Mmm,' said Hanna.

'I want to come. I want to come to London. I want to

say "Happy Birthday" in person.'

Hanna opened her eyes. 'Sorry, Kia, the teleport won't work for you. Anyway, you totally freaked out when Irion and Mary came. I was so embarrassed. I'm not putting them through that again.'

'I was shocked, that's all. You told me Irion was an alien, I was prepared for that ... but you didn't say she was married to a woman!'

'Is that why you were so rude?' asked Hanna, sitting up. 'But it's so normal nowadays, Kia, I didn't imagine you'd have a problem with it.'

'You do know homosexuality's wrong, don't you?'

'No. I don't know that,' said Hanna, thinking furiously. She had to put herself in Kia's head. Remember her teenage opinions, based on what she'd been told – rather than her current views, which had been formed from her own experiences.

'I *used* to think that,' she said cautiously. 'That's what we were taught to think. Then I went to London and saw same-sex couples holding hands in the street. They were just people, Kia, happy because they'd found someone to be with. When I met Irion and Mary and realised how much they love each other: well, they *belong* together. I don't believe love is ever wrong. If you find it, you should hold onto it, wherever it comes from.'

Kia shook her head. 'The worst thing is, you imagine they're your mothers now! You only get one mother, Hanna. Ours is gone. You can't *replace* her.'

Hanna ground her teeth. Kia had been five years old when their parents died. She couldn't have many clear memories of either of them. Not like she did. Hanna took a deep breath and counted to ten in her head. 'Of course not. We could never replace her. But like you said, Mama's gone. Irion and Mary are part of my life. I believe Mama would be happy I found people who helped me. Why didn't you mention this before?'

Kia shrugged and looked at the floor. 'S'not important.'

Hanna crossed the room and sat on Kia's bed. 'I think it is,' she said, placing her hand on Kia's.

Kia pulled her hand away. She dried her eyes on her sleeve and sniffed. 'Whatever. But the *party*, Hanna. Can I come if I promise to behave myself? Can you ask Kitty to take me? *Please?*'

'No! Kitty has enough to do without being your personal taxi service. Anyway, I don't have her number.'

'Get them to make the teleport work for me and she won't have to.'

'I don't want you roaming the streets of London while I'm at school. Anything could happen. You're safer here.'

'That's so unfair!'

Hanna gave up any hope of having a rest. She'd try again at Hassan's flat. She stood up and began to pack a bag.

'What, you're going away *again*?'

'It's Friday, Kia. I always go to Hassan's on Friday, you know that.'

'You're avoiding me! You wish I'd never come here!'

'Kia, that's not true. It's just … I haven't seen Hassan for days and I miss him. I see you every day during the week. We'll do something nice on Sunday, I promise.'

'There's *nothing* nice to do here. It's all BORING and

full of OLD PEOPLE! I'm sick of having to be *polite* and *grateful* the whole time.'

Hanna relented. She remembered that feeling only too well. The heavy weight of obligation: permanently being on your best behaviour for fear of losing the hospitality you were receiving. Exhausting. Kia wouldn't be happy until she felt able to relax and be herself. But she could only do that if she could *talk* to people. Kia urgently needed to improve her Kawaida.

'OK, I'll go tomorrow morning instead. You can show me how you're getting on with your language studies. We can practise together if you like.'

'What's the point? Why should I bother learning Kawaida? I'll be going home soon, won't I?'

Hanna said nothing. Where was home, for Kia?

'Won't I?' said Kia, an undertone of panic in her voice. 'You said you were only here until December. Then you'll be on the space station, close to Earth.'

'That's right, Kia. But you'll still need Kawaida on the *Shantivira*.'

'I don't want to live on the *Shantivira*. I want to go back to the camp. At least I had friends there.'

Back to the camp? Was she serious? Hanna would never be able to guarantee her safety there. She must handle this carefully. Kia clearly felt isolated. She desperately needed more contact with humans of her own age. Almost impossible here in Essoona. Oh, Kia, she thought. What am I going to do with you?

'Look, I'll make a few calls. Maybe I can find a way to get you to the party.'

Kia jumped up and threw her arms around Hanna,

squeezing tight. 'You will? You're the *best*, Hanna!'

'Don't get too excited. It'll be full of *old people*.'

Kia sniggered. 'Like you, you mean?'

'Yeah,' said Hanna, 'old people like me.'

BY SATURDAY AFTERNOON, Hanna had done it: persuaded Kitty and Joe to activate the teleport for Kia for one night, as long as she didn't leave the language school. Joe said he couldn't risk her being picked up and interviewed by the authorities before his audience at the UN later that month. He didn't want anything to distract from the narrative he was building.

The change of scene thrilled Kia. She helped them set up the buffet and the drinks table, then, at the appointed time, they took their places and waited in hushed expectation.

William had been keeping Hassan busy in the neighbouring flat, preparing his statement for the hearing. When Hassan entered the room and they all yelled, 'SURPRISE!', Hanna saw from his expression that it was.

Behind him, William chuckled. 'Gotcha!'

Hassan's eyes sparkled. 'You sure did! Wow! It's so great to see you all!'

Hanna stepped forward and hugged him. 'Happy birthday, my love.'

'Is this your doing?' he asked.

'My idea.' She smiled at him. 'I had help. Everyone misses you.'

'Thank you.' He squeezed her so hard, for a moment she couldn't breathe. 'I missed you last night.'

'Me too,' said Hanna. 'But we can catch up tonight.'

One by one, the guests wished Hassan a happy birthday. When it was Kia's turn, he took her hands in his and looked her in the eye. 'How are you getting on?' he asked.

Hanna watched. Would Kia spill out all her problems to Hassan? Now, at his birthday party?

Kia shrugged. 'Fine, thanks,' she said. 'I hope you enjoy your party.'

'I need to say hello to everyone,' he replied, 'but we'll have a proper talk later, yeah? I want to hear all about your life in Essoona.'

After chatting with Irion and Mary, Hanna caught up with people she hadn't seen for months. The hours flew by and eventually she collapsed in a quiet corner with Lucy, ready to exchange all the new gossip.

'Scooch up,' said Hassan, appearing out of the crowd. He joined them on their sofa with a heartfelt sigh of relief. 'I haven't stood for so long in these things since we went to Munich. I swear they're getting more uncomfortable.' He pulled off his artificial feet and let them drop to the floor, swinging his stumps into Hanna's lap for her to rub. 'You don't mind, do you Lucy? We're not grossing you out?'

Lucy shook her head. 'You'd have to try a lot harder to gross *me* out,' she said with a giggle. She jerked her head at his prosthetics. 'When did you last have them adjusted?'

Hassan frowned. 'Not since my first year here. So two years ago, I guess.'

'Shouldn't you have them checked every six months?'

'Yeah. But I've never worn them all the time before. My Syenitian boots are as comfy as a pair of slippers. God, I miss them. These ones are making a weird clicking noise.'

'He can't at the moment,' said Hanna. 'We're waiting for his new visa to come through. He's not supposed to be in the UK until it does.'

Lucy rubbed her chin. 'My friend Alice is a prosthetist. She's based in Devon, but she often comes to London to visit her parents. I could ask her to look at them, if you like?'

'Does she know about the *Shantivira*?'

'Not yet. She thinks I work on an oil rig. But once Joe speaks to the UN in public at the end of the month, I'll be able to tell her what we really do. I've wanted to for years, but I never had the courage. It's time to come clean.'

'Do you trust her?'

'With my life.'

'OK, then,' said Hassan. 'But see how she reacts first, before you bring her here or tell her about me. Joe won't be happy if she blows the language school's cover.'

'You're right,' Lucy said. 'I'll make sure she has time to get used to the idea.'

They were interrupted by Irion standing in front of them, her expression a mixture of concern and horror.

'Hanna? You'd better come.'

Hanna followed her to the bathroom, the sound of someone violently throwing up getting louder as they approached. Kia had her arms wrapped around the toilet bowl, her slight form quivering with every retch. Hanna ran to her, gently pulling Kia's braids out of the danger zone.

'Kia! Are you ill? Was it something you ate?'

Lucy appeared in the doorway. 'More something she *drank*. I'll get her some water.'

Oh shit. Hanna had been so occupied catching up with people, she hadn't been watching Kia. This was all her fault.

Kia croaked, 'Hanna?'

'Yes, my darling?'

'I don't feel very well.'

'I can see that. What did you have?'

'Um … a bit of everything? It was all just there, on the table. I was bored, I thought I'd try it. Nobody told me not to.'

Irion passed Hanna a wet flannel and Hanna wiped Kia's face.

'I'm sorry, Kia,' said Hanna. 'I shouldn't have left you on your own.'

Lucy came back with a pint glass of water. 'Get this down you, Kia. Slowly. We don't want to make you sick again.'

Hanna translated and Kia sipped the water obediently. Irion opened the window wide and slipped out of the room.

Lucy crouched beside them. 'She could have alcohol poisoning. We need to work out if she needs a doctor. Can you find out exactly what she drank?'

Hanna repeated the question in Nuer and Kia closed her eyes, trying to remember. 'I started with a beer. But I didn't like the taste, so I left most of it. Then a glass of red wine, but I didn't like that either. Then I found that stuff you drink with limes, brown sugar and ice. That was yummy. I had three or four of those.'

Hanna related her answer to Lucy.

'*Caipirinhas.* OK,' said Lucy. 'Did she have soft drinks

in between?'

That was a no.

'Did she have anything to eat?'

Hanna asked and Kia nodded. 'Lots. All down the toilet now.'

'It doesn't matter,' said Hanna. 'Keep drinking your water, if you can.'

Irion returned with a soft white blanket, which she wrapped around Kia's shoulders.

'Ask her if she ever drank alcohol before today,' she said to Hanna.

Hanna asked.

'No. Never. Hanna, I've finished being sick. I just want to go to bed. Please take me home.'

'OK. Can you stand?' Hanna helped her to her feet and put Kia's arm over her shoulder.

'Where are you going?' said Lucy.

'She wants to go home,' Hanna said.

'Teleporting's a bad idea,' said Irion. 'She should stay in your room, Hanna. We'll take turns sitting with her.'

'Irion's right,' said Lucy. 'We mustn't leave her alone. It doesn't look too bad – her speech isn't slurred – but the *cachaça* could still be being absorbed into her bloodstream. If she passes out or starts breathing too slowly, we'll need to ask Hagar to come right away. I'll send her a message, let her know what's going on.'

'OK, thanks,' said Hanna. 'Come on, Kia, there's a comfy bed waiting for you. Irion?'

'Yes?'

'Could you bring a bucket and a hot water bottle?'

'Coming right up.'

Hanna led Kia into the room next to the bathroom: a pastel pink box room with a single bed, a chest of drawers and a table holding a sewing machine, neat piles of fabric and stacks of plastic boxes containing all Hanna's needlework paraphernalia.

'This is my room,' said Hanna. 'It's where I keep the stuff I couldn't take to Dunia House. Do you like the patchwork quilt? I made it.' She took Mr Tembo, the cuddly elephant Farida had given her for her birthday last year, from his place on the pink pillow and offered him to Kia.

Kia pressed the toy to her chest and looked around the tiny space. 'You have *two* rooms? *Two* homes?'

Hanna pulled back the covers and indicated Kia should climb in. 'I'm extremely lucky.'

Kia kicked off her shoes and climbed into bed. Hanna switched on the bedside lamp and turned off the bright overhead light. There was a gentle knock at the door and Hassan entered, holding the requested sick bucket and hot water bottle.

'I heard there's been some drama,' he said. 'How are you feeling, Kia?'

'Horrible,' she said.

He put the bucket on the floor by her head and gave her the hot water bottle.

'Thanks,' she said. Tears rolled down her cheeks and she sniffed. 'Why are you all being so *nice*? You should be shouting at me!'

Hassan grinned. 'We've all been there, Kia. Except maybe Hanna. I've never seen her more than a little bit tipsy. Tomorrow's hangover will be all the punishment you'll ever need, I promise. Hanna?'

'Yes?'

'You need to keep her sitting up and drinking water for as long as you can. As long as she's awake and can drink water, she's OK. When she sleeps, put her in the recovery position so she won't choke if she's sick. Watch her breathing. If you think she's not getting enough oxygen, call Hagar straight away. You have your *zana* handy?'

'Yes,' Hanna confirmed.

Hassan stepped to the door. 'Then I'll wish you ladies goodnight.'

'Goodnight Hassan,' mumbled Kia. 'Sorry for messing up your birthday.'

'You haven't messed it up. I hope you feel better soon.'

Hanna went to the door with him. 'Tell Irion I'll do the first shift.'

He leaned forward to kiss her and, when his mouth was by her ear, he murmured, 'Get her talking. Distract her. Nobody gets that drunk without being very unhappy about something. Maybe you can find out what it is. Goodnight.'

'Goodnight, my love.'

Hanna returned to Kia and sat on the floor beside the bed.

'You heard what Hassan said. Can you sit up and drink your water for a while longer?'

Kia sat up, resting against the velvet headboard. Her face was still wet with tears. Hanna tucked the covers around her so she'd stay warm and wiped her face.

'I'm sorry Kia. I've been a rubbish sister these past few

weeks. I should have made more time to be with you.'

Kia sniffed again. 'You were so pleased to see me when I first arrived. But then you went back to school and I thought you didn't want me here anymore. I thought you thought your lessons were more important than being with me.'

'Well, they *are* important,' said Hanna. 'I *can't* miss them, just because you're here. They're not more important than you, but if I don't pass my exams, I won't be able to earn enough money to look after you.'

Kia blew her nose noisily. 'You never asked why I didn't go back to Ethiopia when Tamru was well enough to travel. Did you never wonder why I stayed behind in the camp?'

Honestly? Hanna had been so busy trying to keep all the plates of her life spinning, it hadn't crossed her mind. Feeling guilty, she asked, 'Why *did* you stay behind?'

'I met your friend, Negasi Sewonet. Remember him? And his younger brother, Alimayu.'

Hanna blinked. 'Of course I remember,' she said. 'How are they? How did they end up in South Sudan?'

'Floods,' said Kia simply. 'Hanna, our village isn't even there anymore. We couldn't go home if we tried.' She began to cry steadily: regular sobs shuddering her small shoulders.

'What happened?' asked Hanna softly.

'It's all gone. It rained and rained and the river burst its banks. It washed away their cows. Their father drowned trying to rescue them. The maize crop was destroyed – not only theirs, everybody's. They had to leave; there was nothing to eat.'

Hanna pictured her village as she remembered it: the huts, the fields, the grazing cattle, the river flowing peacefully by. The rainy seasons when everything turned to mud. How the river rose until it was almost level with the path beside it. She imagined it as a surging torrent, pulling everything it touched in and along with it. She began to cry, too.

'Their mother died after a few weeks on the road,' Kia said. 'From drinking bad water, they think.'

'Oh, Kia,' said Hanna, hugging her tightly and remembering how she'd once envied Negasi: that he'd gone to school and she hadn't. Her heart went out to him and his brother.

'I feel like a tree whose roots have been cut off,' said Kia. 'I always thought I'd go back one day.'

'We're still young, Kia. We can grow new roots. I already have, a bit. You can too. What about Negasi and Alimayu? Are they still at the camp?'

Kia shook her head. 'They left to try and get to Europe. Two weeks before Hassan came. They were going to send for me once they got settled.'

'Do you have a photo of them? Maybe we can find them and help them.'

Kia shook her head again. 'No, I haven't. Hanna?'

'Yes?'

'I think I'm going to be sick again.'

25. LEARNING TO FLY (II)
DAN

'**G**OOD! AGAIN,' SAID Bellyn. 'Faster this time.'

Dan returned to his upper guard starting position, holding the rear end of his six-foot *stakarh* in his left hand and the middle with his right, thumbs facing each other. The Ranglatiri quarterstaff was a simple yet brutal weapon. All the moves focused on head strikes, aiming to kill the opponent outright as quickly as possible. Traditionally, the Ranglatiri used the *stakarh* to settle disagreements in a fight to the death. Dan had tried to draw parallels with the rules of medieval chivalry, but Bellyn had laughed at Dan's explanation. 'No rules,' he'd said. 'No messing about. Kill, or be killed. Outworlders don't call us "the walking death" for nothing.'

Training was a necessarily cautious affair, rehearsing the sequences and footwork in controlled slow motion. Neither of them wore protection: they made sure to stop the strikes before they connected. They practised the actual strikes separately, using a dummy. Dan enjoyed those days; whacking stuff with a big, solid stick was a great way to blow away tension and aggression on long trips. Each time they went through the sequence, Dan felt his movements becoming more fluid.

Bellyn tilted his head and put a hand up to the side of his mask. 'Incoming call,' he said, turning away from Dan to take it. 'Practise spinning until I'm done.' He strode away into the unlit end of the empty storage area they used as a makeshift fitness room.

Dan complied. Spinning the staff helped familiarise you with its balance and motion as well as strengthening your wrists. As he made the meditative figure-of-eight movement, the tattoo inside his right wrist flashed into view at regular intervals. It had healed completely weeks ago and Dan had to admit he kind of liked it, despite its sinister significance. It was a simple black circle, two inches across, the line roughly an eighth of an inch thick.

The tattoo artist had been terrified when Bellyn turned up in full battledress: white skirt, white breastplate and white helmet, with a silent Dan following at a respectful distance. Dan had stayed resolutely in character, not even making eye-contact with her except when she formally asked him if he consented to having the tattoo. Bellyn had insisted the performance was necessary, because otherwise any Ranglatiri checking up on them would discover the tattoo was a lie. Still, she'd done good work and Bellyn had given her a big tip.

Dan had quit both his jobs and now worked full time on the *Gezi Urdina*, shopping for supplies, cooking, cleaning, doing laundry: a regular little housekeeper. He'd withdrawn from his astro-geography and navigation classes and was studying remotely, taking an accelerated course in preparation for the Amranese Pilot's Association theory exam in a few months' time. If he passed, all Dan had to do to get his space pilot's licence was clock up enough supervised flight hours. Then the galaxy would be his oyster.

Dan stayed in the cockpit for each take-off and landing, keenly observing everything Afra and Bellyn did and saving his questions for later. Afra found his incessant curiosity about space flight amusing and irritating in equal measure, but Bellyn was a good and patient teacher. Not only did he help Dan with his assignments but, on uneventful stretches in deep space, he'd switch off the autopilot and let Dan fly the *Gezi Urdina*: trying out manoeuvres and familiarising himself with the navigation software.

Dan spent his evenings learning to speak Ranglatiri. The Ranglatiri were so institutionally xenophobic, the species had no standard programs to teach their language to aliens. Dan had to learn the same way Afra had: by spending hours repeating whatever Bellyn said, over and over, until he'd internalised it. Although the written runes remained beyond him, Dan could already decode whole chunks of Afra and Bellyn's discussions as well as express himself on a basic level. In return, Dan was teaching Bellyn the guitar, creatively adapting chords so Bellyn could play them with four fingers.

Bellyn's reluctance to speak about his personal background meant Dan had taken weeks to piece together his story, mostly from conversations with Afra. Like many Ranglatiri, Bellyn had lost two brothers to fatherhood. The marriage had been agreed when the boys were children and sealed in an elaborate ceremony as soon as they came of age. That was when he'd lost his oldest brother: according to tradition, copulation with and consumption of the groom by the bride took place on the wedding night. Bellyn's mother had been saving up for the dowry their whole lives, regularly cursing the fact that she'd only produced male offspring.

Still, her disappointment had been tempered once her daughter-in-law's eggs had hatched. Three females and two males. Bellyn's other brother became so busy with childcare, Bellyn never saw him.

As a male without a 'spare' brother, Bellyn had had to support himself. He'd financed his education with a string of late-night cleaning jobs, studying Kawaida and basic book-keeping. On graduation, he'd started a career as a slave trainer, hoping to make his mother and uncle proud. Breaking in slaves was a respected profession and he'd excelled at it. But he'd become too interested in his charges: their personalities, where they'd come from, where they'd travelled to, what they'd done with their lives.

This was dangerous knowledge for someone who'd been brought up not to question the superiority of his own species. Over time, seeing incoming slaves as people with thoughts and feelings prevented him from doing his job properly. Unable to bear it any longer, he'd quit and retrained as a lab assistant at a pharmaceutical firm.

There he'd met Arbnora, his first and only love. Arbnora was a top-level scientist specialising in the Ranglatiri reproductive system. Bellyn had begun working late, just to be near her. For her part, she'd appreciated his interest in her work and had illicitly treated him as an equal whenever they were alone.

As the trust between them grew, Arbnora had revealed

she was a member of an underground organisation striving for male equality. She had a radical covert project: to develop a male contraceptive. Arbnora was convinced that, if males could take charge of their own reproductive systems, it would revolutionise Ranglatiri society from the inside out. To Bellyn's amazement, she even believed the ancient tradition of eating the sperm donor at the wedding ceremony wasn't necessary for the health of the offspring.

But a colleague had found out and, hoping to take her post, betrayed her to the secret police. Arbnora had just made her breakthrough – the formula for a pill which would prevent sperm fertilising the egg – when the police raided her laboratory and tore her limb from limb on the spot.

While the policewomen were distracted by their feeding frenzy, Bellyn had snuck out of the room and fled. Arbnora had prepared him for this scenario: swiftly, he'd collected her backup files and her life savings, and stowed away on a pirate ship leaving port that morning.

With the pirates' help, he'd found some Wadudu willing to manufacture Arbnora's pills in strictest secrecy. Then he'd organised a distribution network via his new contacts in the pirate community, who sold the pills on to their brothers and friends back home.

Without a doubt, Bellyn was the bravest and kindest person Dan had ever met. Yet Bellyn regarded himself as a shameful criminal: a traitor to his people who willingly associated with aliens. Worse – a traitor who had failed to save the woman he loved.

+ + +

BELLYN EMERGED FROM the darkness, his call finished. 'I have to talk to Afra,' he said. 'See you upstairs later?'

Dan nodded, mid-spin, unwilling to break his concentration. He didn't have long, then he'd have to start making lunch.

✦   ✦   ✦

WHEN DAN ENTERED the mess room with their meal, Afra and Bellyn broke off their discussion and Afra appraised him with a fresh sparkle in her eyes.

'There's your answer, Bellyn,' she said. 'Would he manage?'

Bellyn leaned back against the wall. 'Perhaps. Yes. I don't see why not.'

'Manage what?' said Dan, sitting opposite them and tucking into his fried rice.

'That call I took earlier,' said Bellyn, 'was from a potential customer. A big order: the biggest we've ever had—'

'—assuming the factory can fulfil it,' interrupted Afra.

'Let's assume they can,' said Bellyn. 'Naguneen, my contact, is extremely far away. The closest he can get to us is five weeks' journey from here, and he can't stay there for long. The real question is, can we reach him in time?'

'So where do I come in?' asked Dan. 'Eat your food, Bellyn, before it gets cold.'

Dan always warmed Bellyn's raw meat to 38°C, the way Bellyn preferred it. As if the creature had just been killed. Bellyn removed his mask and took a large, bloody bite from the slab on his plate. 'Something new?' he asked, raising his eyebrows.

'Some *kondoo* I found at the market yesterday.'

'It's good. Very fresh.'

Afra said, 'Normally we'd do a good part of that trip on autopilot, or we wouldn't get enough rest to fly safely. But the autopilot takes the safest route, not the quickest. If we had another pilot,' here she looked pointedly at Dan, 'we could fly manually the whole way, in shifts. It would shave days off our journey.'

Dan's eyes widened. 'You'd let me fly the *Gezi Urdina* unsupervised?'

'Just the easy bits. I can sleep in the cockpit. I'd be on hand if you needed help. Are you up for it, Earthboy?'

'You bet I am!' Dan beamed at her. 'So when do we leave?'

'I'll go to the factory after we've eaten. Then we'll know more. I hope to leave in the next three days, though.'

'And *where* are we going?' Dan had studied astro-geography for long enough now to be confident he'd understand the answer.

'Raymi,' said Afra, stretching out her legs under the table, 'over in the Karu sector. Naguneen is working on Wanusha, in the processing plant for that superconducting mineral the Ranglatiri are so excited about. If he travels in our direction, Raymi is the furthest he can get from Wanusha during his leave period.'

'What superconducting mineral?' Dan asked.

'It's called *kahack*,' said Bellyn, wiping his mouth and fingers fastidiously on his handkerchief before replacing his mask. 'Its only known source is on Wanusha. It's the special ingredient in the top-secret shield technology the Ranglatiri government engineers are developing.'

Afra's ears waggled. 'The "top-secret" shield technology all the pirates have been talking about since that prototype frigate disappeared a while back.'

'Prototype frigate?' said Dan.

'The government equipped a pirate frigate with these new shields for testing in a secret project,' said Bellyn. 'I've told you before what gossips Ranglatiri space pirates are. They always share new information with each other, as a sort of insurance policy against the authorities. When this ship didn't return from its mission, people started to talk. It was supposed to be indestructible, and no one's heard anything from the crew since.'

Afra said, 'My theory is, they ran away with it and they're living it up on some distant system, knowing nobody can touch them.'

Supposed to be indestructible? Shit, thought Dan. It could only be the monstrous ship Kitty had destroyed last year, after the *Shantivira* fleet had failed to make a dent in it.

Bellyn turned to Afra. 'The latest is, the government sent probes to its last known location and they've disappeared as well. There's something well defended in that sector.'

Dan shivered. Better not mention he'd witnessed the destruction of this prototype with his own eyes. He hoped the Ranglatiri wouldn't think there must be something worth having there, just because their probes hadn't come back. The more he learned about the Ranglatiri, the less he wanted them anywhere near the Earth.

'I should go shopping,' he said, changing the subject. 'Stock up for the trip. Will we be able to buy stuff when we get there, or shall I organise supplies for the way home too?'

'Just for the way there,' said Afra, standing up. She took a couple of *embwaki* from the bowl on the table and stuffed them into her pocket. She loved the fleshy red fruit as much as Dan did, so he ensured they had a constant supply. 'We won't hurry back. This deal's so big, we'll be able to afford a holiday. We can stop off and show you some places.'

Dan stood to clear away the plates. Bellyn put a hand on his arm. 'Don't disappear into town yet, Dan. I want to teach you take-offs and landings so you can practise before we leave.'

Take-offs and landings? Dan's mood brightened. At this rate, he might get his licence by the end of the year.

26. THE UN GENERAL ASSEMBLY

JOE

'**M**AY I REQUEST protocol to escort Captain Llewellyn.'

We're on.

Joe and Kitty followed their guide through the doorway and out into the packed UN General Assembly Hall.

Nervous? asked Kitty.

Freaking terrified, said Joe. *But it's OK, I've got my brown trousers on today.*

Kitty giggled. *Good luck.*

Thanks. When I need courage, I'll remind myself Wales beat England at Twickenham in the Rugby World Cup on Saturday. Anything's possible. We can do this.

Joe took his place at the famous rostrum, in front of the green marble background. Human-sized Kitty, all in black and wearing sunglasses, stood to one side in her bodyguard pose. He'd also dressed for the occasion: in his favourite baggy linen shirt, the nubuck leather jeans he'd bought in Vienna and, around his neck, the ancient gold torc Kitty had given him as a wedding present.

The woman sitting at the desk behind and above him said, 'I have great pleasure in welcoming Joseph Dylan Llewellyn, Captain of the Galaksi Alliance Earth Defence

Facility, the *Shantivira*, and I invite him to address the General Assembly.'

Joe twisted round to address her. 'Thank you very much, Madame Vice President.' He turned back to the audience. Showtime.

Threat assessment, cariad?

Everyone on the floor went through Security, we can assume they're safe. But there are two people in places they shouldn't be. One up there by the lights on top of that wooden bit—don't look! And another up on the edge of the ceiling dome. I'm going to check it out.

Kitty stalked out through the door behind the gold backdrop. Joe swallowed his nerves.

'Ladies and gentlemen, I'm honoured to be here. Thank you for inviting me to speak. You're at the end of a long day, so I'll keep it brief. First, I'd like to wish the UN General Assembly a happy seventieth birthday and add my support to this year's focus on sustainable development. The proposed measures are a step in the right direction, although personally I believe they don't go far enough.

'You're thinking: this is that crazy guy we heard about, who's come to talk about his alleged alien space station. Why is he lecturing us on sustainability? Well, today I'm going to give you another reason why humanity needs rapid, effective action on inequality and the planetary crisis.'

Joe began by introducing himself, highlighting his years of army service and his sense of duty towards his fellow humans. He was just getting onto the Galaksi Alliance, the Syenitians and the role of the *Shantivira*, when he heard a faint 'snap' noise from above. His invisible personal shield stopped what looked like a .50 calibre subsonic projectile in its tracks, centimetres from his heart. Woah. Thank goodness Kitty had insisted on fitting a shield generator in the heel of his shoe. Someone out there really didn't want him speaking today.

It's all right, Joe, I've got her. Carry on.

You said there were two?

Other one's dealt with. They can't hurt you now. I'll question them later.

This meeting's livelier than the others I sat through to get here.

Keep going with your speech before they realise anything's wrong. We don't want their Security evacuating the building.

Kitty reappeared from behind the gold wall and took up her standby position again. The audience waited for him to continue. From their lack of reaction, they had no clue what had just happened. Joe plucked the two-inch copper bullet out of the air and placed it on the rostrum.

'Sorry. My train of thought escaped me there for a moment. Honestly, I've seen plenty of action in my time, but standing up in front of you people is one of the most challenging things I've done. Where was I? Yes. Awareness of our organisation sky-rocketed recently when one of my pilots used our cargo transporter without permission for a humanitarian mission in his home country of South Sudan. Unfortunately, this means he is currently suspended pending an inquiry. The Syenitians are very strict about what their equipment is used for. I should add though, once they understood what he'd done and why, they made a substantial anonymous donation to the UNHCR South

Sudan Emergency Fund.'

Don't tell them it could still get the Shantivira *shut down!*

I wasn't going to!

'This doesn't alter the proposal I've been negotiating with UNOOSA. After the ISS crew became aware of our existence – I hope you all received the report before this session – my priority was to ensure first contact went smoothly, and to negotiate the best possible deal for the Earth. As the Galaksi Alliance's representative for this planet, I'm proposing an exchange: we'll teach your scientists and engineers how a shield generator works, and the fundamentals of generating gravity.'

Joe placed both hands on the rostrum. 'It took me months to persuade the Syenitians that the Earth needs this technology now, before lives are lost in long range space missions. But they agreed, finally, and the seminars are currently being organised. They'll be held on the *Shantivira* and we'll provide interpreters for any language you require. All space agencies will receive this training simultaneously, should they wish to take us up on our offer.

'You're asking yourselves: what do they want in return? Is it a price we can afford to pay? You're going to laugh, but there *is* something we really need. Until now, the requirement for secrecy forced us to import part of our fuel from the nearest spacefaring planet, a round trip of at least three months for our elderly cargo ship. But the Earth could provide it in abundance, with no detrimental effects. We don't even want much, just a regular supply.' Joe smiled at the sea of faces. 'We don't want your oil, or your gas, or even your coal. We want your sewage.'

Laughter rippled around the room. Awkward, polite laughter, which suggested the audience didn't trust Joe yet.

'Ladies and gentlemen, I'm serious. All Syenitian ships run on organic waste and the *Shantivira* is no exception. You're thinking, how can they extract so much energy from so little? Well, I'm no energy scientist, but I can tell you the Syenitians will never, ever share information about their power source. It's off-limits, along with their weapons technology. Any violation and all assistance will be revoked, up to and including protection from hostile forces by the *Shantivira*.

'They'll help us become a spacefaring society, but they won't hand us everything on a plate. Any knowledge exchange beyond what I've negotiated will be tied to stipulations on eliminating structural inequality and transitioning our current growth model to a steady-state economy.

'Otherwise, the Galaksi Alliance risks us developing into a threat to intelligent life. They'd pull their investment and allow the Earth to be overrun by the more malevolent species in the galaxy. We *can't* let that happen. We must prove that we deserve help and that we have a good chance of becoming Galaksi Alliance members in the future. If we don't, the Earth is toast, probably within our lifetimes.'

In his mind's eye, Joe saw the Ranglatiri pirate frigate above the Earth, picking off his pilots. If there had been more of those ships ... well, look at what it had cost Kitty to stop just one of them. He took a deep, slow breath and forced himself to concentrate on the task in hand.

'In view of my South Sudanese colleague's recent

actions, I have another proposal. If our cargo ship is making regular trips to the planet's surface anyway, we could combine this with logistical support for humanitarian causes. As you no doubt saw on the news, our cargo craft is easily able to transport heavy payloads to inaccessible regions. We can't solve all the Earth's problems, but we'd like to help if we can.

'I've also agreed with UNOOSA that, once the training courses are under way, we'll allow UN inspectors and journalists to visit the *Shantivira*. It's time we stopped being such a secret.' Joe gripped the rostrum. Time for the big reveal. He said, 'I imagine you have many questions, and I'll answer some before our time runs out. But you're bound to think of more later. Luckily, I'm not the only person here who can tell you about the *Shantivira*.'

In Kawaida, he said, 'OK everyone, please stand up and come to the front.' As arranged, the nine former Shantivirans made their way forward to join Joe on the podium. A murmur of surprise passed through the crowd.

'These colleagues of yours have all served on the *Shantivira* during their career, and have bravely volunteered to answer your questions over the coming months.' In Kawaida, he said, 'Guys, do you want to introduce yourselves? Come up to the microphone.'

Gabriel came first. 'Gabriel Quinn, Permanent Representative of Ireland to the United Nations New York.' The others formed a line behind him.

'Elizabeth Molefe, Botswana.'

'Luisa Ramirez, Mexico.'

'Sulaiman Taleb, Algeria.'

'Maggie Oliver, Representative of Canada.'

'Daecho Chamratsamee, Representative of Thailand.'

'Sophia Karpenko, Ukraine.'

'Shaozu Feng, People's Republic of China.'

'Leyla Dogan, Turkey.'

Joe returned to the microphone. 'They and their families are all under the protection of the Galaksi Alliance. If they are threatened or pressured in any way, there will be immediate repercussions.'

He turned to look at them. 'Thanks, everyone,' he said in Kawaida, 'you can go back to your seats. Good luck, and get in touch straight away if you have problems.'

They filed off the stage. Joe hoped they'd be able to handle the inevitable media storm. They didn't have the luxury of teleporting away from trouble.

Time to wrap this up. 'I've said all I have to say. Are there any questions?'

Silence. Then a man on the Ugandan table in the front row asked, 'What language were you speaking just now?'

Joe repeated the question into his microphone so the rest of the room could hear.

'Kawaida, the lingua franca of the civilised galaxy. We learn it during our flight training. I'm told it sounds like Swahili, although there's no connection as far as I know.'

'It does.'

The US President, also sitting in the front row, put up his hand. 'What did you pull out of the air, before?'

Joe picked up the bullet. 'This, you mean?'

Barack Obama nodded.

'Actually, that's a nice demonstration of the shield technology I mentioned. My security officer here—,' he gestured at Kitty, '—insisted I wear a personal shield for this appearance. Just as well, as there were two snipers up there and one of them managed to fire a shot at me.'

He heard gasps of horror and some people got up to leave. Joe held up his hands and raised his voice. 'Please stay in your seats, everyone. The danger has passed. We've already taken them in for questioning. We'll hand them over to the Earth authorities when we're done. Their equipment is still up there, so the police can begin their investigation straight away.

'I swear it wasn't a stunt to demonstrate our technology. It nearly put me right off my speech!' Joe looked at the President. 'I admire your courage, sir, doing this sort of thing every day. I'm not sure I'd have the nerve. So, I have time for one more question. Is there anything else you'd like to know?'

A man at the Ukrainian table stood up and said in a loud voice, 'If everything you say is true, when will we see some aliens?' Next to him, Joe observed Sophia suppress a smirk behind her hand. If he didn't do it now, she'd tell them later anyway. That was the job he'd given her. Time to go off-piste.

'If you mean normal Syenitians – you won't be meeting them. I'm their representative. They tried settling here many thousands of years ago, but the colony failed. They have no interest in the planet itself, only in nurturing the development of humankind.

'This is just the start of building trust between our peoples. All we're proposing is an exchange: you give us the fuel we need and we'll help you become a spacefaring species. The only alien you're likely to come across is my bodyguard here.'

Laughter echoed round the room. They thought he was joking. He twisted his head to look at Kitty. *They're still sceptical*, Cath. *Will you talk to them?*

She raised her eyebrows. *Speak in public? Moi? OK, but don't yell at me if I mess it up.*

Just try not to scare them silly.

Joe turned back to the audience. 'This isn't a planned part of my speech. But Kitty here is a rare and ancient shape-shifting space demon who settled in my country many thousands of years ago and has been protecting the Earth ever since. She is one reason I'm so very proud to be Welsh. Kitty, come and introduce yourself.'

Joe stood to one side, and Kitty stepped up to the microphone.

'Good afternoon, everyone,' she said in her low, melodic voice. 'I'm Kitvian Ahmitorsdottir; the *Shantivira* crew call me Kitty.'

She took off her sunglasses and smiled, revealing her predator's teeth. On the screens above, her glittering reptilian eyes flashed, clear for all to see. The audience gasped. They weren't laughing now.

'Please don't be afraid,' said Kitty. 'The Earth's been my home for millennia, and I've made protecting it my life's work. I *love* this planet. It's a rare jewel. The way you treat it breaks my heart. It's not here for your convenience. It is itself a life form, of which humans are a tiny part. Putting prices on its generous resources is like putting a price on your own mother.'

She lifted her hand and pointed a long finger.

'*You* are the wardens of this world and you are *failing*. Stop destroying your ancient forests. They are what keep you alive. Fix your equality problem before it's too late. Prevent rich countries from ripping-off poor countries. Stop capital flight. Cancel developing country debt. Stop imposing conditions on how nations run their economies. And for Earth's sake, stop measuring your "progress" with GD-bloody-P! Your corporations' best interests are not humanity's best interests. If you allow them to pursue their goals unchecked, they'll strip this planet bare like a fleet of Ranglatiri space pirates.'

Babe, you're ranting, warned Joe.

Whoops. Sorry. Kitty gripped the rostrum and lifted her chin.

'If you make these changes and can mature into a steady-state economy, most people's quality of life will improve quickly and dramatically. That's worth fighting for, surely? The permanent pursuit of profit is making humankind miserable.

'Take it from your friendly neighbourhood space demon,' she said, 'all the other planets you could survive on are already occupied. I've done my best to protect the Earth but, as your technology advances, it's getting harder. I hope you consider Captain Llewellyn's proposals carefully. I believe cooperating with the Galaksi Alliance – and the Syenitians in particular – is humanity's best chance of survival.'

Well done, Cath. Let's make this an exit they'll remember, shall we?

Y Ddraig Goch?

What else? Wait for my signal.

Kitty stepped aside and Joe returned to the microphone. 'Ladies and gentlemen, it's time for us to go. If you

347

have any questions about our proposal, ask Susan Omondi at UNOOSA. My former colleagues in the audience can provide more general information about our operation. Please appreciate the courage they are showing by volunteering to reveal their identities, and treat them with kindness and respect. Thank you for listening and goodbye.'

Joe bowed.

Now.

Kitty jumped over the podium railing, shifting into her red dragon form as she did so. She landed on four feet on the carpet below, in front of the first row of seats. Joe heard a few isolated screams as she flourished her wings.

Better skedaddle before they panic, he said.

Hop on, then.

Joe did.

Kitty's head was level with the Ukrainian table. To her colleagues' horror, Sophia was stroking the dragon's scaly nose. 'You are naughty, the pair of you,' she whispered.

Kitty treated the Ukrainians to a broad wink, then they were in the air. After a couple of wing-beats, the familiar rushing noise filled Joe's ears and the sea of upturned faces disappeared.

27. MR EVANS

JOE

J OE LANDED ON sheep-cropped grass beneath a clear blue sky, holding hands with a Syenitian-shaped Kitty. The scent of ferns was strong in the late-summer air. They were in a favourite spot, high on the Brecon Beacons, not far from Joe's childhood home. He used to meet Kitty here secretly, back when he was a teenager and had believed she was 'just' a magic cat.

Their eyes met and they collapsed instantly into fits of laughter.

Oh my God! Did you see their faces? Joe still couldn't quite believe what they'd done. He hoped their spontaneous stunt hadn't ruined his months of painstaking work.

I know! A day they'll never forget. I haven't shown myself to so many people for centuries. Kitty stopped grinning and became more serious. *There'll be consequences, you do understand that?*

Joe nodded. *We'll deal with them as they come. But it felt like the right thing to do.*

It could go either way, said Kitty. *I'll keep an eye on the others and pull them out if necessary.*

I'll call Gabriel later and find out what the reaction was. But first—he pushed her up against a large boulder,

349

luxuriously warm from the late afternoon sun—*there's something else I want to do.*

He kissed her roughly, pressing his chest onto hers and grabbing her hair. She responded eagerly, unbuttoning his flies and lifting the skirt of her velvet dress. Even after all these years, Joe still wasn't sure if she ever wore underwear or if she made it disappear at the appropriate moment. Whatever. He closed his eyes, thrusting and grunting the excess adrenaline and the stress of the day away until, finally, he reached the point of bliss.

Better? asked Kitty, as he pulled up his trousers.

Oh yes.

You should address the UN more often, if that's the effect it has on you.

No way. Once was enough for a lifetime.

Still, I like the days you shave. And those trousers are delicious against my skin.

I didn't realise wearing leather would make me so horny.

Kitty smiled. *At least you'll look smart for your announcement to Grace.*

Damn, I was hoping you'd forgotten.

Joe, you promised.

Joe leaned against the rock beside her and studied the horizon.

I know. But I'm scared, Cath. *You and Gabe want me to smash the carefully crafted façade I've spent decades building. There's no telling how she'll react.*

It's time, love. You can't put it off any longer.

Joe groaned. *Oh, all right. Let's get it over with.* A flicker of hope stirred inside him. *Who knows, perhaps she'll even be proud of me.*

THEY SET OFF down the hill, the short grass on the track springy under his feet. Kitty shifted and padded at his side as a jaguar. A pair of red kites circled lazily in the wide sky above, scanning for small rodents in the heather.

A thought occurred to him. *What did you do with the snipers?*

They're waiting in my den. Separate cells, far apart: they can't hear each other. I'll let them stew and interview them later.

Joe didn't envy them. Kitty's hidden lair was a hollowed-out mountain, deep in Snowdonia, the only person-sized exit blocked and underwater. There was no light at all. The couple of times he'd been there, he'd been able to see through Kitty's eyes: her dragon-hoard of ancient treasure and, more interestingly, the secret graves of her first husband, Emrys Ambrosius (also known as Merlin), and Arthur, King of the Britons. Along with her solemn promise to protect Wales, Kitty had sworn to guard the Pendragon's resting place for all eternity. They'd never discussed it, but Joe was certain that, when his time came, his earthly remains would end up there too. He wasn't sure how he felt about that.

When she'd first made the cave with a hand-held dematerialisation beam, she'd added some steep-sided prison cells. After a few hours in pitch-black silence, broken only by flutterings and scufflings from the resident bat colony, people were generally ready to talk. If they weren't, well, Kitty had her own special interview technique.

I want to listen in when you do, OK? he asked, conscious they'd have to hand the prisoners over to the police as promised once they had the information they needed. Things mustn't get out of hand.

Yes, boss.

Who do you think they are?

Paid professionals, judging by their equipment. I took the younger one with the faster pulse first. I thought he was more likely to hurt someone by accident. That would have spoiled everything.

Leaving me in the sights of an expert killer?

You were the safest person in the room, with your shield. It was just a few seconds. I can't be everywhere at once. Nothing happened, did it?

Apart from me nearly having a heart attack, you mean? No.

Well then. Stop fussing.

THEY APPROACHED GRACE'S wisteria-clad cottage from the back. The poisonous shrub twined around the stone building, enveloping it in a heavy cage of tangled branches.

Aren't you going to get changed? Joe asked, looking down at Kitty.

She's already seen me like this. It'll be less of a shock than anything else.

Even though last time she saw you, you suspended her husband upside-down over the vegetable patch?

There were other times, afterwards.

There were? When?

When she came to check on you, at night. You were asleep; we just stared at each other in silence. Neither of us wanted to wake you.

You never told me.

You've always been so angry with her; you never talk about it properly. I don't think you understand how powerless she was against Gareth. He shut down her ability to decide for herself. And you look exactly like him. Imagine how that makes her feel.

Joe tried. Was his mam *frightened* of him?

THEY WALKED PAST the military-manicured garden, round to the front of the cottage. Joe glanced up, assessing the state of his ancestral home. The guttering was coming loose and the window frames needed repainting. But the slate roof was holding up well. The thick walls were built to last. The little house could do with some maintenance, but the underlying structure was solid.

Joe gritted his teeth. *I'm still only doing this because I don't want anyone using her to apply pressure on us.*

He ran his hand along Kitty's back and she arched her spine against him.

Sure, whatever, babe. I just need to get close enough to touch her. Then I'll have her biosignature and I can pick her up if she gets into trouble. But it'll be no good if she's terrified of me. You have to convince her I'm friendly, or she'll never accept my help.

Bushy hydrangea sentries in terracotta pots flanked the green front door, the blue flowers as high as Joe's chest. He pressed the doorbell and listened to the familiar electronic tones chiming 'Greensleeves'.

Perhaps she's not in, he said hopefully.

She's in, said Kitty. *I can smell her from here. Cigarettes are so disgusting.*

Joe heard footsteps approach. There was a pause as his mother checked the security spyhole, then the door opened.

He took a deep breath. *'Ti'n iawn, Mam?'*

'It's you,' replied Grace, also in Welsh. 'You should have phoned.' Her eyes widened as she saw jaguar-Kitty. 'That … *thing's* not coming into my house. Make it wait outside.'

'No. I'm not hiding her from you anymore, Mam. Where I go, she goes.'

He'd expected a fight, but she just sighed and turned away from him. 'Come on through, then. Shut the door behind you.'

A large brown suitcase with wheels stood in the hall. That was new. Her burgundy crocodile-skin handbag rested on top. 'Off somewhere nice, Mam?'

'Patagonia. I'm going on holiday with my Mr Evans. He's picking me up in half an hour. I thought that was him ringing the bell.'

Joe boggled. That was unexpected. Apart from a package tour to Spain, Grace had never been anywhere. Still, excellent timing. The government couldn't come for her if she was off gallivanting with her boyfriend.

What a relief. He followed her into the living room at the back of the house. The French windows displayed the garden in all its end-of-summer glory. Beyond a modest patio area bordered by pots of lavender, banks of pink and yellow flowers stretched to the rear of the plot, along the edges of a bowling-green-perfect lawn. Roses (nearly over now, but not a dead head in sight), foxgloves, dahlias and others Joe didn't recognise. Towering hollyhocks swayed in the afternoon breeze, like a family of pink triffids out for a stroll.

'Why are you all dressed up?' Grace said, sitting in the armchair closest to the television. 'Why are you wearing a *necklace*?'

'It's a torc, Mam. Welsh gold.' Not waiting for an invitation, he took the chair opposite her. Kitty sat upright on the floor beside him and he rested his hand on her head for comfort and courage.

Eyeing Kitty warily, Grace said, 'If you want a cup of tea, you know where the kitchen is.'

'I'm not stopping, Mam. I just came to tell you something. Why I'm all dressed up, in fact.'

Joe explained, as concisely as he could, that he didn't work on an oil rig in the North Sea, but was, in fact, in charge of an alien space station which protected the Earth. That he'd come directly from speaking at the UN General Assembly. That he was concerned, now he was a public figure, that governments or other agencies might try to use her to get to him.

As he spoke, Grace's expression evolved: first polite interest, then surprise, through to hostile disbelief.

'You?' she sneered. 'Address the UN? You're away with the fair folk, lad. Ask the doctor for some tablets!'

Give her time, Joe, said Kitty. *She'll realise you're telling the truth when she sees the news.*

'You've said what you came to say,' said Grace. 'Now go. I want you gone before Mr Evans gets here.'

I still need to touch her. Will you give me a moment?

'All right, Mam. I'll just use your toilet, if you don't mind, then we'll leave you in peace.'

Joe went up to the bathroom, the one in the extension he'd paid for with his army wages twenty years ago. The tiles looked dated, but it was clean to the point of sterility. Apart from the all-pervasive cigarette smell, of course. Did she still smoke in the bath?

He returned to the living room back to find a mortified Grace standing on her chair, shouting, 'No! Shoo! Go away!' as Kitty rubbed her head against Grace's ankles.

'Joe, get it off me!' she pleaded.

He asked Kitty, *Got what you need?*

Yes.

'*Cath*,' he said out loud, 'come here.' In a furry black flash, Kitty took up her obedient, butter-wouldn't-melt pose by his side.

Grace climbed down and lit a cigarette with as much dignity as she could muster. She took a drag and said, 'Go now. Put your pet in the zoo before you come next time.'

Joe saw red. Stony-faced, he unfastened the patio doors and slid them open. *We're showing her the red dragon*, he told Kitty.

Oh, Joe, are you sure?

Do it, he ordered.

Kitty slipped outside and shifted. She took up the full length of the garden, inadvertently knocking over the ornamental stone birdbath with her tail.

Whoops.

Don't worry about it.

She snaked her head back through the door so she could rest it on Joe's shoulder. He put his hand up and stroked the scales on her cheek.

'She's not my pet, Mam. She's the *Ddraig Goch*. She's my best friend. She's my *wife*.'

It was too much for Grace. The colour drained from her face and her knees gave way. The burning cigarette fell from her limp hand and smouldered on the carpet.

Syenitian-Kitty appeared instantly behind her, catching Grace beneath the armpits before she crumpled to the floor. Gently, Kitty laid her in her chair and set about reviving her, holding Grace's hand in both of hers. A tiny pulse of life energy was enough to make Grace's eyelids flutter and open. She stared in stunned silence at Kitty's alien features and snatched back her hand.

Joe ground his heel on the cigarette, extinguishing it. The doorbell rang.

'I'll go,' said Joe.

He practically jogged to the front door, relieved to escape the atmosphere in the living room. Outside stood a man in an expensive suit and a purple silk tie, with a deeply lined face and slicked-back snow-white hair. Behind him was a silver Mercedes, plus a driver wearing an actual uniform. With a hat. *Not* what Joe was expecting.

'Mr Evans, I presume?' he said in Welsh, offering him his hand to shake. The man nodded, but didn't take his hand. Awkwardly, Joe dropped his.

'I'm Grace's son, Joe. She tells me you're taking her on holiday?'

The man's expression darkened; his eyes narrowed as he appraised Joe.

'I warned them you were a slippery bastard,' he muttered.

'Sorry?' said Joe, not understanding at all.

Mr Evans turned away from him and, switching to English, called to his driver. 'Matthew? Load Mrs Llewellyn's suitcase and be ready to leave immediately.'

The driver got out of the car and Mr Evans pushed rudely past Joe, making a beeline for the back of the house, calling, 'Grace? *Cariad?*'

Joe followed him, confused and annoyed at the man's reaction. He heard his mother say, 'Nestor!' the delight and relief in her voice unmistakable.

In the living room, Joe found Grace on her feet again, with her arm around Mr Evans, facing a stunned-looking Kitty.

'Nestor,' said Kitty, her hands outstretched, pleading. 'You can't take her.'

Joe was startled to hear her address the stranger using the informal Welsh version of 'you'.

'Watch me, hellspawn.'

Nestor? That *Nestor?* Joe demanded silently.

Yes. That Nestor.

'Nestor,' said Grace, 'do you know this … person?'

'It's not a person. It's an evil demon. Our paths have crossed, yes. But don't worry, my dear, I'm taking you to safety. It won't be able to find you, let alone hurt you.'

'What about my son?'

'He's made his choice. There's nothing I can do to help him.'

Grace turned to Joe. 'I already asked you to leave once. Now I'm telling you. Get out, and take your freak with you!'

The lashing force of his mother's animosity made Joe

step back instinctively. He looked at Kitty, who was even paler than usual.

Can you stop her from going with him?

We become the bad guys if we take her against her will, said Kitty. *I have her biosignature now, so I can keep watch. He won't hurt her: she's too valuable alive and he'll be getting a kick out of having power over us. She's safe for the moment. And she'll be out of reach of the government.*

What is this guy's problem? You have to tell me, Cath, *no more secrets.*

Why didn't you tell me the boyfriend's name? I could have nipped this in the bud. He must have been grooming her for months.

Grace interrupted them. 'What are you waiting for? Go on, go! We don't want you here.'

In a flint-hard tone, Nestor said, 'You heard the lady. Leave.'

Cold splinters crept into Joe's heart. He'd lost her. He'd always thought he wouldn't care if she never spoke to him again, but now he realised it wasn't true. Too late.

In a flat voice he said, 'Ta-ra, Mam. Have a nice holiday.' He could barely push the words past the knot in his throat.

JOE TOOK KITTY'S hand and pulled her through the still-open French windows. Behind them, he heard the glass door slide shut with a thump and the lock click into its catch. He waited for Kitty to stand the birdbath upright and they left the garden through the back gate.

I don't want to go home yet. Let's walk up to our meet-

ing place and you can bloody well explain.

It's not something I'm proud of.

I don't imagine it is.

They settled into a slow hill-climbing rhythm, steadily gaining height. They heard the Mercedes' engine start below and watched as it drove away.

That's that then, he said.

No. It's the beginning of something, not the end.

Come on, Cath. *Spill.*

She kept walking. Minutes passed; Joe remained patient.

At last she said, *We all make mistakes, Joe. Especially me.*

What happened?

Do you remember our first night together? After you left the army, I mean.

Joe grinned, despite himself. *How could I forget?*

Well, something similar happened with Nestor, but he didn't take it as well as you. It was 1969, and I was in a hotel bar in Buenos Aires. The Americans had just landed on the moon, and everyone was celebrating. There was a man sitting on his own ... I was hungry and he was ... beautiful. I swear, I had no idea how young he was until the damage was done.

What damage?

She waved his question away with a flap of her hand. *I approached him and we got chatting.*

Don't tell me, he was from the Welsh-speaking part of Argentina?

Gaiman, Chubut province, yes.

I guessed as much.

He'd left home to study engineering and was finding big city life tough. He was looking to make a connection with someone, anyone. It was too dark for him to see my eyes properly, and he'd already had a bit to drink. As for me, well, I'd not been back to Wales or spoken Welsh for years. Talking to Nestor triggered something inside me; I realised I was homesick. The attraction became irresistible and ... well ... I took him to bed.

And he had the shock of his life when he woke up beside a demon Kitty? Been there, done that, thought Joe, with fleeting sympathy for Nestor.

I was very gentle, she insisted. *We didn't break a single piece of furniture. I had no idea he was a virgin – or that he was fanatically religious. When he saw my true form, he thought I was the devil who'd deliberately seduced him to corrupt his most precious gift. He believed he was going to Hell and it was all my fault. I imagine he still feels that way. He was so terrified, I never showed myself to him again. Today was the first time I've spoken to him since that night.*

But you kept an eye on him? It wasn't a coincidence he started working with David Wang?

She shook her head. *First I watched him because I regretted what had happened. I hoped I'd get a chance to fix it. But his hatred hardened into an obsession. Somehow, he found out more about me – that I came from a different planet – and his passion expanded into a mission to protect the Earth from all aliens.*

So your objectives aligned?

In a way, yes. It seemed a shame not to use his engineering talent. Kitty detoured around a dense patch of ferns. Her velvet dress brushed the fronds, releasing their thick, prehistoric scent into the late-afternoon air. *I thought working with David might help him view things differently. I didn't realise Nestor was a full-blown sociopath until much later. When he discovered I was funding their operation, he completely lost it.*

Joe shook his head in disbelief. *And you let Mam go away with this crazy person? Even though it's obvious he's just using her?*

Kitty reached out for him, but Joe didn't reciprocate. She let her hand fall to her side. *You saw them, Joe, we couldn't have stopped her without taking her freedom. She has to be allowed to make her own choices. He's too afraid of me to really hurt her, I'm sure of it. It's the leverage he wants. I'll check on her every day. I can pull her out straight away if necessary.*

Surely he knows you can do that?

I don't think so. I'm certain he doesn't know I can find anyone I've touched, or he wouldn't have bothered hiding from me. He's never seen me teleport.

They walked on in silence for several minutes.

You should have told me this years ago.

You should have told your mother the truth years ago instead of putting it off for so long.

Fair point, Joe conceded, but only to himself.

Cath? *Are you funding other operations like Nestor and David's?*

If I told you, you'd have to tell Aldeman.

So you are, thought Joe, intrigued. *OK*, he said, *here's another question: do you think Nestor organised the assassination attempt today? He seemed surprised and disappointed when I told him who I was.*

It's possible. But I don't see how he could have got that far without inside help. I'll talk to the snipers and ask Delius to trace their payments. Whatever happens, I won't let him hurt Grace.

THEY REACHED THE secluded hollow where they'd first arrived, now deep in shadow. The sun was setting and, to the east, the full moon was on the rise: a cold light in the darkening sky. Joe shivered. The invigoration from the climb was fading fast and he had no jacket. A distinct chill in the air heralded the beginning of autumn.

Kitty sat cross-legged on the rock where they'd had sex, not more than an hour ago. Joe remembered what a high he'd been on; how, after talking to the UN, anything had seemed possible. Would they have had more luck persuading Grace if he'd resisted his bodily urges and arrived earlier?

Kitty noticed his expression. *Don't feel guilty, love. There's nothing more we could have done today. At least you got to speak to her, to explain. She needs time to digest what you told her; what we showed her.* She took his hand in hers. *Grace and Nestor have lots in common. They're the same age. They're keen gardeners. She hates me nearly as much as he does. Perhaps they'll be good for each other. We'll have to let things take their course and be ready.*

28. THE RUNAWAY

HANNA

ARRIVING BACK AT Dunia House after visiting Hassan in London, Hanna descended the curving staircase to the entrance hall, thinking vaguely about making a cup of *saiju*. The front door swung open and Lucy and Nikolai came in. They'd gone diving yesterday and had obviously just returned. 'Hello, you two,' said Hanna. 'Not away the whole weekend?'

Nikolai said, 'I promised Roberto we'd go climbing this afternoon.'

'And I wanted to spend the day with Felix,' said Lucy. 'Hey, how did Alice's visit go? I'm sorry I couldn't be there.'

'Good, thanks. She sorted out that clicking noise in no time.'

Lucy's friend's professionalism had impressed Hanna. She'd asked Hassan a series of questions about his prosthetics and listened carefully to his answers. Then she'd selected some tools from her case and got to work.

'She was curious about us, of course,' said Hanna. 'I know you showed her the news reports about Hassan, and *everyone's* seen that video of Joe and Kitty, but I still had the feeling she wanted to check you weren't making it all up.'

The clip of Joe and Kitty's exit from the UN – followed by a joyful standing ovation from the wonderstruck delegates – had gone viral, circumnavigating the globe within hours.

Revealing the dragon had been a lucky touch of genius: it seemed, for now, at least, more people were fascinated by the ancient mythical creature than concerned about the alien space station orbiting the planet. In fact, the popular view appeared to be, 'if the dragon's been watching over us all this time, then the space station must be OK too.'

'Did you manage to convince her?' Lucy asked.

'I told her you were the best human pilot in our year, apart from me,' said Hanna with a grin.

Lucy grinned back. 'I said *you* were the best human pilot in our year, apart from *me*.'

Hanna chuckled.

'There's another reason we came back early.' Lucy's eyes shone. 'We've something to tell you. Come up to the lounge, the others are already there.'

Curious, Hanna followed them back up the stairs to where Felix, Saïd, Farida and Roberto were waiting.

Hanna sat down: Lucy and Nikolai remained standing.

Felix said, 'Come on, Lucy, what's this big announcement?'

She glanced at Nikolai. 'You tell them,' he said.

'We know how the Pweza's power source works!'

'How?' said Saïd.

'Micro-fusion,' said Lucy. 'It takes some power to get started, but then it runs and runs.'

'How?' repeated Farida.

'They electrolyse sea water into hydrogen and oxygen. The oxygen goes to oxygenate the recycled water in their spacecraft and buildings, and boost shrimp growth on their farms. The hydrogen is fed into a bank of mini fusion reactors, which heats water to steam, which is used to drive a turbine.'

Nikolai fished a glass jar out of his rucksack. It was full of water and a smooth, grey object, shaped like a large doughnut. 'They let us have a deactivated one to reverse engineer. I'm going to give it to my mum.'

Felix said, 'I thought you needed heavy hydrogen for fusion?'

'*We* do. The Pweza don't.'

'They gave us an electrolyser, too,' said Lucy, pulling a shimmering green sphere out of her own bag and holding it out for them to see. It fitted in the palm of her hand: a short tube, perhaps three centimetres in diameter, stuck out in Hanna's direction. Two narrower tubes protruded from the other side, a 'Y' with a ball at the junction. It reminded Hanna of a diagram she'd seen of the human heart.

Felix stood up and took it from her, turning it over in his hands. He looked up at them. 'We could use this on Earth. To turn offshore wind power into hydrogen, which can be transported and stored.'

Lucy nodded. 'I know,' she said, with a little jiggle of excitement. 'Björn's already considering how to mass-produce a terrestrial version.'

'Does he understand how it works?' asked Farida.

'They're teaching him,' said Nikolai. 'The difficulty is getting hold of the raw materials and being able to manufacture the membrane with the right quality.'

Hanna thought of David Wang. She didn't want Lucy and Nikolai to get thrown off the *Shantivira* training programme like he had. 'What about the Syenitians? Won't they mind us using this technology, even if the Pweza don't? Do they even know about it?'

'Of course they do,' said Lucy. 'That's the beauty of it, Hanna. This knowledge isn't a secret. It belongs to the Pwezans and they're happy to share. Imagine what we can do with it!'

Hanna wondered how long it would take humankind to weaponise this new technology. In her experience, engineering enthusiasts like Lucy and Nikolai were often naïve about human nature. She said nothing: she didn't want to spoil her friends' moment of triumph. Instead, she stood up.

'It's fantastic news, Lucy. But I promised Kia we'd go to the Extra-Syenitia Museum today. She'll be waiting for me.'

She picked up her bag and carried it up to her room, expecting to find Kia. She wasn't there. Strange. They always met here on Sunday mornings. Things had been better between them since Hassan's disastrous birthday party. Kia had relaxed considerably and was clearly enjoying exploring Essoona and its surroundings with Hanna by her side. Plus her Kawaida was improving rapidly. Hanna thought Kia had finally accepted her situation and was beginning to feel at home. So where *was* she?

She looked closer. The room was uncharacteristically tidy. Where was Kia's stuff? Hanna opened the wardrobe;

Kia's side was empty. What? Her heart beat faster, thumping hard through her ribcage. Under the bed, Kia's bag was still there – momentary relief – until Hanna realised her own, sturdier rucksack was missing. She sat on the bed, her shoulders slumped. Had Kia run away? Where would she go? The teleport wouldn't work for her without special permission. So where *was* she?

She noticed a folded paper on Kia's pillow, poking out from under Mr Tembo. In her orphanage-neat Amharic script, Kia had written,

Dear Hanna,

I can't stay in this place. It's all wrong. I hate it.

Anyway, something's happened and I must go back to the camp.

I'm sorry for not telling you, but I knew you'd try and stop me.

Don't worry about me, I can take care of myself.

It was nice to see you. I hope we'll meet again one day, if God wills it.

Your affectionate sister,
Kia

p.s. I took your rucksack, I hope that's OK.

The words danced on the page as Hanna's vision blurred with tears. She dropped the letter and covered her face with her hands. Oh God. OhGodohGodohGod.

'I can't stay in this place. I hate it.'

Kia had been hiding her unhappiness for weeks. She'd

told Hanna she'd wanted to return to the refugee camp and Hanna hadn't listened. Not properly. She hadn't taken Kia seriously.

And now she'd run away. Anything could happen to her. Hanna let out a sob, but suppressed the following one and stood up: she had to find Kia, fast. How long had she been gone? Since this morning? Yesterday? Since Friday night already?

Mrs Park. First Hanna must ask Mrs Park when she'd last seen Kia. Then they'd organise a search party.

SHE FOUND HER in the laundry room, folding sheets.

'Mrs Park! Kia's run away!'

Mrs Park put down her washing basket. 'Run away? *Why? Where?*'

'She left a note,' said Hanna. 'She's unhappy here and she wants to go back to Earth. Can you remember the last time you saw her?'

Mrs Park's momentary confusion passed and she focused on Hanna's question. 'Not today. Last night, before I went to bed. She had her pyjamas on, I'd guess she did sleep here. She must have left early this morning.'

Hanna agreed. Kia wasn't the terrified mouse who'd arrived at Dunia House two months ago, but Hanna couldn't imagine her roaming the streets of Essoona in the dark. 'She can't be more than four or five hours ahead of us. Will you stay here and tell me if she comes back?'

'Of course,' said Mrs Park. 'You're going to look for her?'

'I'll take some of the others. She must have gone to the spaceport.'

HER FRIENDS WERE still in the lounge, discussing Lucy and Nikolai's discovery.

'Kia's gone!' she announced. 'She's run off to try and return to Earth. I think she might be at the spaceport, trying to hitch a lift.'

'*Why?*' said Lucy, echoing Mrs Park.

'I don't know exactly. She said in her note she wasn't happy here and something had happened which meant she needed to get back to the refugee camp.'

'Why didn't she just ask?' said Farida. 'If that's what she wanted, I'm sure it could have been arranged.'

Hanna hung her head. 'She did ask. But I dismissed the idea without listening properly. I told her she was better off here.'

'Well, she probably is,' said Felix.

'That's not the point, though, is it?' said Nikolai. 'The point is we have an unhappy teenager who believes she has no option but to take matters into her own hands.' He stood up. 'We have to find her, fast.'

'Yes,' said Hanna. 'Will you come to the spaceport and help me look for her?'

ON THE TRAM, Hanna sat quietly, her silence masking the emotions which paralysed her: guilt, anger, regret, despair.

Lucy squeezed her shoulders. 'We'll find her, Hanna. She won't get far.'

Hanna looked up. 'What if she does? I doubt there's a single pilot there who's ever heard of the Earth.'

'Exactly,' said Lucy.

'So nobody honest will take her. Which leaves criminal gangs. She could board some ship and never be seen again.'

'Oh,' said Lucy, crestfallen. 'I hadn't thought of that.'

They met Aneira and Elian at the spaceport entrance. Lucy had called Aneira as soon as they'd set off and Aneira had brought Elian to help. Hanna sent a picture of Kia to all their *zanas* and they split into three groups of three.

They walked along the rows of docking bays, which radiated from the commercial zone by the main entrance like the slats of a folding fan. The place was packed with Syenitians. This was hopeless, thought Hanna. They'd never find her like this. They could barely see the spacecraft beyond the throng of towering aliens. She found a bench and sat down with a sigh. 'I need a rest,' she said.

'It's like looking for a nano-drone in a forest,' said Aneira.

Farida said, 'I had no idea it'd be so crowded.'

Drones. Hanna slapped her forehead. She was an idiot. She said, 'This place must be full of cameras, right? There has to be a central control room. Perhaps they'll let us look at the footage from this morning.'

'Security cameras?' said Farida. 'I haven't seen any. They don't seem to go in for them on Syenitia.'

'What's a security camera?' said Aneira. They explained and Aneira shook her head. 'No, you won't find those on any Alliance planet. The constitution strictly forbids general surveillance of civilians. Police officers wear cameras which automatically record their interactions with the public and upload them to the server for the law courts, but those recordings can only be accessed by the police or the individual who was filmed.'

371

'Oh,' said Farida.

'Cameras aren't necessary,' Aneira smiled. 'You can track a person via their *zana*, if you have its ID. Haven't you tried that already?'

'I tried calling,' said Hanna. 'But she didn't pick up.'

'But what about the *location*?'

'I'm not sure how to do that.'

'I'll show you.' Aneira pulled up Hanna's contacts and opened Kia's profile. She started a program which projected an image of stars with a flashing green dot at the centre. The dot stayed where it was and the surroundings zoomed in. Aneira provided the commentary.

'She's still in the galaxy, in the solar system, on Syenitia, in Essoona …'

'That's Dunia House, not the spaceport,' said Farida.

'So either she's there or she left it behind.'

'Can you zoom in further?'

The green dot hovered level with a window on the third floor. Hanna called Mrs Park, who answered on the first tone.

'Mrs Park, it looks like Kia's *zana* is in our bedroom. Could you please go and check she's not with it after all?'

Moments later, Mrs Park entered Hanna's room. 'She's not here, Hanna.' Hanna watched the little Mrs Park hologram projected by the *zana* open drawers and look beneath the bed covers.

'Got it!' she cried. 'It's under her pillow.'

'So she left without it. Oh well. It was worth a try.'

'What if she's not at the spaceport?' said Farida, voicing Hanna's own fear. 'What if we're searching in the wrong place?'

'We can't give up,' said Hanna, standing up again. 'We'll just have to keep looking. As long as it takes.'

FOR THREE INTERMINABLE hours, they continued their bay-to-bay search, showing Kia's picture to anyone who looked like they might be spacecraft crew. Hanna was exhausted, and she knew the others were too. Despite what she'd said, soon the time would come to give up and report Kia as a missing person.

Her *zana* bleeped. A message! Elian's image appeared; he was smiling. Hanna's heart swelled with hope.

'Have you found her?'

'We have!'

Hanna's knees almost buckled with relief. Thank God.

'Is she OK?'

'I don't know, Hanna. She appears physically un-harmed, but I'd guess her soul health is not in balance. I believe she is sad and upset.'

'Where are you?'

'In a grotty little café on the outer perimeter. Roberto insisted we stop for a break and there she was. I'm sending you the location now.'

THE CAFÉ WAS at the far end of one of the 'fan slats'. The crowds thinned and the docking bays became smaller and closer together. The ships in them were less flashy than the glistening models Hanna had glimpsed nearer the entrance. Functional, rough-and-ready: some were so decrepit-looking, Hanna wondered how they'd even get off the ground, let alone through Syenitia's atmosphere.

When they arrived, Kia was sitting with the boys, her hands cupped around a mug of *saiju*. She stared blankly at the stained tabletop while they chatted in low voices. Hanna glanced at their surroundings: the overly bright lighting exposed the ageing interior and grimy walls without mercy. The professional cleaner in her yearned for a bottle of bleach and a scrubbing brush.

The other customers were a mixture of species from across the galaxy. Some shabbily dressed Syenitians, a cluster of three-eyed Mhasibu, two Sayari, a couple of orange Tarumbets, some Amranese and a few furry green Grooka. Most were too busy with their own affairs to pay any attention to their group, but in the far corner Hanna observed a Mwongo sitting alone, watching them. She shuddered. She hoped Kia hadn't been talking to *him*.

Farida and Aneira began pulling up more chairs, but Hanna lifted her hand. 'You can all go home. Kia and I need time to talk. Thanks so much for your help, I don't know what I'd have done without you.'

Roberto rested his hand on Kia's arm. 'It's going to be all right, Kia. You'll see. Your sister loves you. Whatever the problem is, you can tell her.'

Kia looked up at him and her lips formed a small, polite smile. She said nothing.

Chairs scraped the floor as Roberto, Nikolai and Elian stood up and left the café with Farida and Aneira. Hanna took Roberto's seat and reached across to Kia. The table was sticky with a thin layer of food residue, but she ignored her shiver of disgust and placed her hands on Kia's.

'Kia?'

She was interrupted by the waiter. 'Good day, ladies, would you like something to eat?'

Without waiting for permission, he put his *zana* on the table so it could project a menu onto the wall. Hanna wasn't at all sure she wanted to eat in a place like this, but her stomach told her she was hungry.

'Kia?' she asked. 'Are you hungry?'

A nod.

Hanna examined the menu. There were four items on it: noodles with fish, noodles with meat, noodles with vegetables and noodle soup. Not trusting the café to prepare fish or meat safely, she ordered noodles with vegetables, noodle soup and a pot of *saiju*. The waiter nodded and left them.

Hanna took a deep breath through her nose and forced herself to exhale slowly through her mouth. She mustn't get angry or she'd make things worse.

'I take it you couldn't find anyone to take you to Earth?'

Kia shook her head. 'They'd never heard of it. Nobody knew where it was. They said it must be very, very far away.'

'It is,' said Hanna. 'It takes weeks in a fast cruiser.' She jerked her head at the bays outside. 'It'd take months in any of those ships. I could have told you that, if you'd asked me.'

Kia simply shrugged.

Hanna persevered. 'Brave of you, though, to go talking to complete strangers, in a language you've just started learning. Alien strangers, even. Impressive, considering you refused to leave the house a month ago.'

'I couldn't see any other way to get back to the camp.'

Hanna's jaw dropped. 'Couldn't see any other way? What about *talking to me*?' Her voice shrilled with outrage. 'If whatever it is so important, I'm sure we could have arranged it. Kia, anything could have happened! You could have been kidnapped by slavers, for God's sake!'

The waiter returned with their food, allowing Hanna to catch hold of herself, just in time. Deep, slow breath. And again.

'Soup or fried noodles? You choose, I don't mind.'

Kia pulled the plate of noodles towards her and began shovelling them down. Hanna lifted the soup bowl to her lips, but put it down again quickly. She'd have to wait until it cooled. She topped up Kia's *saiju* and poured herself a cup too.

'Why did you leave your *zana* behind? If you'd brought it, you'd have been able to buy yourself a meal earlier.'

Kia paused, mid-chew. 'I didn't want you to get into trouble like Hassan. I know you're not allowed to take alien stuff back to Earth. I thought anyone willing to give me a ride would share their food with me.'

Hanna boggled. Kia would have happily asked an alien spacecraft to land on their planet, but was so worried about causing Hanna problems she'd left her communicator behind, risking not being able to call for help if she needed it.

Hanna said, 'So tell me Kia, what happened that meant you had to return to the camp so urgently?'

Kia concentrated on chewing and Hanna let her question sit there between them. She could be patient. Eventually, Kia put down her fork.

'I missed my period. The third month in a row. I feel sick all the time. I'm pregnant.'

Ah. That explained a lot. Kia's moodiness, certainly. Hanna remembered her own pregnancy with Samuel. At the time she hadn't understood what was happening to her. Kia seemed more clued up than she'd been. Plus, Kia had Hanna. Back then, Hanna had been utterly alone.

'That's why I got so drunk at Hassan's party,' said Kia. 'I suspected I might be after I missed my period the second time.'

'And you thought you could give yourself a miscarriage by drinking alcohol?'

Kia picked up her fork again. 'A girl I knew got rid of hers that way. But I wasn't even sure I *was* pregnant: I just wanted not to have to think about it for a while, you know?'

Hanna put her face in her hands. 'Oh Kia. Why didn't you *tell* me? There are much safer and more reliable ways of terminating a pregnancy, if that's what you want. No one should be forced into having a baby. We need to talk to Hagar, on the *Shantivira*. She knows everything.'

'You're not angry? I thought you'd be angry. Ashamed of me.'

'No, Kia. Never. I only want to help you.'

'Then help me get back to the camp.'

A little light went on in Hanna's brain. 'The baby's father is at the camp?'

Kia shook her head. 'The baby's father is Alimayu. We ... made love ... when we said goodbye the night before he left for Europe. So no. But I need to stay at the camp so he can get in touch with me when he's found a job and a place to live. Otherwise he won't know how to find me. He doesn't know I'm pregnant.'

Hanna let out a silent breath. It hadn't been rape. Thank God. She picked up her bowl and slurped her soup. She'd waited too long: now it was lukewarm. She gulped it down and attacked the thick, slithery noodles, tangled at the bottom of the bowl like a nest of eels.

'I've been so confused,' Kia said, watching Hanna eat. 'But I've decided now. I want to keep it. And Alimayu should have a chance to be its father. So I need to go back to the camp. You understand, don't you?'

Oh God, thought Hanna. Had *she* been that naïve when *she'd* been fifteen? On her trips to London, Hanna had been watching the refugee crisis unfold in the media with increasing alarm, wondering: were Negasi and Alimayu in one of those perilously overcrowded dinghies? Could they even swim? Or were they stuck in Libya, forced to labour for the people traffickers?

There was no way her sister was bringing a child into the world in a remote refugee camp when she could have it on the *Shantivira*, with the best medical care in the Earth's solar system. Hanna must bring Kia round to her way of thinking. She made a quick calculation. She had until April. Hassan's trial would be over by then. They'd be able to see their future more clearly.

She pushed her bowl away and stood up. 'Come on. Let's get you back to Dunia House and we'll take it from there.'

29. A HERO'S DEATH
DAN

'THERE IT IS.' Amra glowed up ahead: a red-green half-moon. Dan flicked off the autopilot and made his approach manually. 'Home sweet home,' he said to Bellyn, beside him in the co-pilot's seat.

Bellyn nodded. 'I'm looking forward to not travelling for a while. And having something fresh to eat.'

'Yeah. Me too. I'll go shopping as soon as we land,' said Dan bringing the *Gezi Urdina* into a low orbit and thinking about buying as much *embwaki* as he could carry. Unfortunately, it didn't store well. He wondered vaguely about drying it. Or making *schnapps* from it.

Standing behind him, Afra rested her hands on his shoulders. 'Try and time the thrusters better this time, love. I don't want to lose another stabiliser.'

Dan grinned. 'Aye aye, Captain.'

Apart from navigation, landing a spacecraft was the trickiest part of flying one. The others had been giving him all the opportunities for practice they could and he'd improved considerably. But when the gravity was different on every planet, mistakes were easy to make. Don't get cocky, he thought. Bring her in lightly.

He waited until the computer said he should begin

their descent. They skimmed over deserts and rainforests, glittering rivers snaking through both. He hadn't noticed how beautiful this planet was when they'd left it: he'd been looking ahead, out into space, delighted to be leaving what had once felt like a prison. Before, he'd been so busy working, he'd not explored much beyond Laro. Perhaps he could persuade Afra to let them have a vacation and go back to nature for a while. After all, they were rich now. They could afford to take some time off. Although … if the mosquitoes were bad in the city, what were they like in those forests?

Laro appeared on the horizon and Dan slowed down. It would be embarrassing if he overshot the spaceport again, like he had in Fortina, and have to turn around. Not cool. Here at least he recognised some landmarks. The weather was clear so he flew manually, following the river upstream. There was the passenger ferry and the row of warehouses. He banked starboard and circled their landing bay, decreasing their altitude with each loop until he was able to hover over the marked zone. Slowly, slowly, check the thrusters were all firing evenly and … they were down. Dan let out a breath he hadn't known he was holding.

'Well done,' said Afra, kissing his neck. 'Your best so far. Now, will you come into town with me? I want to have lunch in a restaurant.'

They left Bellyn on board and took the ferry into town. Intense planetary aromas assaulted Dan's nose; a sensation he relished after every long trip in space. He laid his arm casually across Afra's shoulders and she responded by wrapping hers around his waist.

As Laro came closer, he studied it with new eyes. Everything was familiar, but now he had that sensation of freedom and possibility that came with being on a romantic weekend away. Would they sleep at his flat now they were back? If they did, he'd miss his evening talks with Bellyn. Perhaps they could carry on living on the *Gezi Urdina* until they decided what they'd do next.

Afra was talking about using their profits to fit her ship with a hyperdrive to extend their range, but that would mean they'd have no money left for anything else. A long-term investment, she said. Well worth it. She was probably right. Afra and Bellyn would decide together. Dan was still a junior partner in their operation.

After stuffing themselves at Afra's favourite restaurant, they worked their way round the market, filling Dan's bags with fresh food. They carried them back across the river and threaded their way between the crumbling warehouses.

Just before the last corner, Dan heard an ominous click and felt something solid press on the back of his neck. At the same time, Afra squealed in alarm.

'Drop the bagsss,' said a voice with a strong Ranglatiri accent. 'Keep walking.'

Shit. Dan obeyed, his mind racing. What was going on? What should he do? They arrived in the clearing and the sight that greeted them made Dan stop short and cry out.

Two large Ranglatiri each had one of Bellyn's arms, holding him immobile. His face was bare and Dan saw from his glazed expression that his mask had been off for a while. Now Dan understood. The secret police Bellyn so feared had finally tracked them down. Those oversized heavies must be females. They intended to execute Bellyn; to pull off his arms and legs as punishment for his betrayal. A third Ranglatiri stood to one side, staring at him and Afra. That had to be Adelharz, the chief of the secret police. Bellyn had warned them about *her*.

It was happening exactly how Bellyn had said it would. But confronted with it, Dan wasn't sure he could pull off what he needed to do. Only one way to find out. He dropped to his knees, eyes to the ground and hands behind his back in full slave submission mode. 'I surrender,' he said in Kawaida. It was essential not to let them know he and Afra understood their language.

To his left, he was aware of Afra being stripped of her weapons. His own captor started frisking him as well, until she noticed the circle tattoo inside his right wrist. Dan forced himself to remain absolutely passive as she pulled his arm up for closer inspection. Satisfied, she dropped it again, not bothering to search him any further. The knife sheath taped to his stomach remained safely in place. Afra and Bellyn always insisted he shouldn't leave the ship without a concealed weapon, even at home on Laro. Now he was glad he'd listened to them. A tiny spark of hope he and Afra might escape with their lives unfurled inside him.

Out of the corner of his downcast eye, he saw Adelharz touch the side of her mask, activating her communicator.

'We have them all, order the strike,' she said in Ranglatiri.

What strike? thought Dan. The factory? Oh shit. They were going to destroy all trace of their operation, weren't they?

'We need the female alive,' Adelharz said to their captors. 'She has information about the traitor's contacts. We'll eat the other one on the journey home.'

'Ma'am?' said Dan's guard. 'It's been trained.'

'So the rumours are true. We'll send it to the Mines of Kifo, then. Disable the female so she doesn't try anything.'

'Yes, Ma'am.'

This was where Dan had to go against all his instincts and hold his nerve. If he acted too soon, Bellyn's emergency plan would fail. Afra knew this as well as he did. She'd forgive him. Dan remained motionless as his guard left him to help her colleague break Afra's arm and smash up her knee with a heavy metal club. Afra roared in pain but Dan continued staring resolutely at the ground. Soon. Soon.

'Good,' said Adelharz. She turned to Bellyn. 'Traitor, do you have anything to say before we carry out your sentence?'

Bellyn said nothing. He was beyond speech. Dan prayed Bellyn would lose consciousness and not feel any pain when the moment came. Dan's captor poked his shoulder. 'Sslave,' she hissed in Kawaida. 'Watch your masster receive jusstice.'

Dan obeyed, not daring to close his eyes. Bellyn's head lolled and his knees sagged. Poor Bellyn. He looked so small between those brutes.

'Pull!' commanded Adelharz.

For an instant, Bellyn seemed to come to. He lifted his head and looked directly at Dan. Dan thought Bellyn would scream, but he remained silent.

A tear ran down Dan's cheek as he returned the gaze

in a wordless goodbye. One of Bellyn's arms detached and the guards dropped him on the ground. They pulled out axes and set to work dismembering him. Dan sensed a change in his guard: she was totally focused on the execution, distracted by bloodlust. Afra's too. Not long now. Adelharz picked up an arm and removed her mask to eat. Bellyn's executioners did the same.

Now. Staying as still as he could, he slid his hand under his T-shirt and drew out his knife. In one swift movement, he thrust it below the rim of his guard's breastplate with maximum force, puncturing the flesh and brutally slashing it across so her innards spilled onto the grass. Her blood was darker than a human's, burgundy rather than scarlet.

As she collapsed, Dan leapt to his feet in the direction of the other guard. He hooked his fingers beneath her mask and ripped it off before she had a chance to react. He tossed it to one side and grabbed her hair, yanking her head back to expose her throat. Another efficient slash and she, too, fell to the ground. His heart pumping, he pulled off the first guard's mask for good measure, in case she used it to call for help. The whole action took less than ten seconds.

He threw Afra over his shoulder and sprinted to the *Gezi Urdina's* gangway. The others were still in their feeding frenzy: hadn't even noticed the drama unfolding across the landing bay. In the cockpit, he settled Afra carefully in the co-pilot's seat before starting his pre-take-off checks. Grim-faced with pain, Afra tapped at the controls with her good hand. A joystick emerged from behind a panel.

'What are you doing?' he asked.

'I don't want them telling their friends what happened, in case we want to use that trick again.' A head-up display appeared outside the window and white pulses of light shot into the small group of Ranglatiri. They fell to the ground instantly, scorched and smoking. 'That's for Bellyn, you bitches,' she said coldly. 'Dan? Can you get the shopping? We'll need it. Hurry. Others will be along soon.'

Dan ran outside. The shopping was where he'd left it, everything still there. His memory flashed back to that morning: back to a different world where Bellyn was still alive and they were happy to be home. All gone. He shouldered the bags and dashed back to the ship, trying not to look at the smouldering corpses as he went. Something a little way from the gangway caught his eye: Bellyn's mask. It must have rolled there when they'd pulled it off. He scooped it up without slowing his pace.

Back in the cockpit, Afra had done as much as she could with one hand. Perhaps they should get voice-activation installed along with a hyperdrive. That would be handy. Dan dumped the food and strapped himself into the pilot's seat.

'Hurry!' cried Afra, pointing outside to where a unit of Ranglatiri were approaching from the main entrance to the landing bay. Several carried shoulder-supported rocket launchers.

Dan didn't need telling twice. He whacked the thrusters up to full power and they shot vertically into the air, out of range. Not elegant, but effective. High above Laro, they saw a fire raging on the north side of town.

'Is that the factory?' he asked.

Afra nodded.

Dan flew away from Amra, into the safety of space. Once he was sure they weren't being pursued, he flipped on the autopilot, washed his hands and went to the first-aid cabinet. He pulled out rolls of translucent, jelly-like material, then carefully removed Afra's clothes. She gritted her teeth, but made no sound. Her arm had been broken cleanly, but her knee was a battered, bloody mess. Quickly, Dan unrolled a layer of jelly and wrapped it round her arm. The ends fused together and the tense lines on Afra's face softened as the painkillers took effect.

'Will this be enough for your leg?' he asked as he knelt at her feet, enveloping her knee with as many layers of jelly as he could.

'We'll find out, won't we? There's nothing else we can do right now. We can't go to hospital on Laro. We have to go far away, where they won't follow us. Assuming they didn't plant a tracking beacon. You'll have to do a search later.'

'Bellyn told me if something like this happened, we should hide on Syenitia.'

'Yeah. They wouldn't come after us there. I could get this leg seen to. We'll go to Aldina. Can you set the course?'

'Yes. But it'll take weeks, Afra. The food we bought this morning will never last.'

'There are plenty of tins and dried noodles in the hold. We can up the oxygen level down there now.'

'I can't believe he's gone.' Dan's voiced cracked.

Afra covered her face with her good hand. 'Me neither.'

'He saved us,' said Dan. 'If he hadn't prepared us for what to expect, we'd *all* be dead.' Not reacting while they'd hurt Afra had been the hardest thing Dan had ever done. And he couldn't stop thinking about the sickening sensation of his knife sliding into the guard's guts. It went round his head on a loop; the initial resistance of skin and muscle giving way to softness, how his knife hand had been instantly covered in dark, sticky blood. The smell of it.

He remembered his first air strikes in Iraq, more than a decade ago. He'd joined the Air Force to fly, not to kill people. Knowing he'd taken an unknown number of lives from the safety of his F-16 cockpit had cost him more than a few nights' sleep. But that had been a mental hurdle. *This* was a physical reaction. His hands shook and his legs and arms seemed heavier than normal. He felt cold to his core.

'Afra? I never killed anyone up close before.'

'No? You're lucky. It was them or us: never forget that. Tell me if you have nightmares about it. Don't bottle it up, OK?'

'OK. Afra?'

'What?'

'What will we do now the factory's gone?'

'Lie low for a while. Have a little holiday. Get a hyper-drive installed. Then we carry on.'

'Carry on? How?'

'There's another factory. Smaller and further away, but with everything we need. You know Bellyn, he loved to have a backup.'

'And backups to the backups,' said Dan, with a wistful

smile. 'Yes. But how can we persuade his contacts to trust us?'

'We have something they can't get anywhere else. We'll work it out. You'll see.'

30. STAND BY AND DO NOTHING?
JOE

'SO, MY LORD, what are you going to *do* about it?' Joe asked Aldeman, unable to keep the impatience out of his voice. They were in the maze of tiny streets north of Kirjasto Square, the recent snowfall shovelled against the walls on either side, making the path even narrower than usual. Each time someone approached from the opposite direction, there was a polite little dance to decide who would step aside.

If the business proprietors didn't sweep away the snow in front of their premises immediately, the flagstones would be treacherous within hours. Joe made a mental note to put ice grippers on his boots before his next visit.

They were on their way to meet Björn at the Nakymaton bar, after their weekly update session in the baths. It had been a tense one: the Ranglatiri's invasion of Amra, a peaceful, friendly planet, topped all the newsfeeds. And the Syenitian Council was paralysed by inaction. According to Aldeman, only the Head Librarian (of all people!) had advocated immediate military intervention.

'Amra is not an Alliance member, Joe. We have no defence agreement with them. Even if we had, it happened too fast. It's too late to help them. Their whole planet is burning and nobody saw it coming. By the time we got there with battle cruisers, the locals will have already been shipped away as slaves.'

Fair play to him, Aldeman was deeply upset too. Joe was sure the plight of those unfortunate people would keep his friend awake at night for weeks to come. At least Joe knew Dan Simpson was safe. The moment he'd heard the news, he'd asked Kitty to track Dan's biosignature. As an undetected gecko on the wall, she'd reported he was piloting a ship destined for Aldina, accompanied by his Sayari girlfriend. So not only was Dan OK, he'd used his time away to learn to fly a spacecraft. Respect.

'But Aldeman, you can't just stand by and do nothing!'

Aldeman stopped and turned so Joe could see into the deep hood of his cloak. The glacier-blue eyes met Joe's for an instant, then he bent down until his lips brushed Joe's ear. 'I never said we were,' he murmured. 'Action *will* be taken. A strategy is being formulated. But it is top secret. I *cannot* speak of it to you. Not here. Not anywhere. Not ever.'

They walked around the corner to where the brown-curtained bar entrance protruded onto the street. They pushed their way into the warm, dimly lit fug, shedding their outer layers as they crossed the grimy wooden floor to their regular table at the back of the room. Björn was already there. He stood and stretched out his arms to greet Aldeman with a formal Syenitian hand press, then gave Joe a bear hug, lifting him off the ground.

'Good to see you!'

'Mate, it's been ages. How are you?'

'Good. Great. Looking forward to seeing the family again.'

'I'll bet you are,' said Joe. Björn had stayed in Samae for months at a time, barely seeing Tima and his children. Now he and his team were on shore leave for the winter.

They ordered beers and food and, after the waiter went away, Aldeman asked, 'Björn, I am curious. Why did you request this meeting? I assume there is a reason you wanted to talk to both of us.'

'I thought if I saw you together, I'd only have to explain once. You must have heard: the Pweza are sharing the details of their power source.'

Joe hadn't, but Aldeman nodded. 'Truly elegant in its simplicity. It is all we hoped it would be, when we invited the Pweza to settle here. We already have teams working on potential applications.'

'What is it?' said Joe.

'Micro-fusion,' said Björn. 'The power of the sun in the palm of your hand.'

Joe imagined humans equipped with hand-held weapons capable of melting mountains and shivered. 'Sounds dangerous.'

Aldeman shrugged. 'Everything can be dangerous: it depends on what you use it for.'

'My view exactly,' said Björn. 'Aldeman, sir, I want to use this technology on the Earth. It's our key to stopping global heating in its tracks.'

Aldeman arched his charcoal eyebrows. 'Hasn't humankind already passed that point? According to our reports, the Earth's systems are suffering like a child with a fever.'

'Slow it down then,' said Björn, throwing his hands in the air and thumping them on the tabletop. The Tarumbets at the neighbouring table turned their elongated heads to see what the noise was. 'Give ourselves time to lower that fever, to heal that child.'

'How?' asked Joe.

Aldeman pressed his palms together and put his fingertips to his lips. 'He wants to make the fossil fuel industry obsolete. To scale up this power source so it can replace Dunia's oil-based infrastructure. Correct?'

The waiter reappeared with their food and drinks. Again, they waited silently until he'd gone before continuing their discussion. Joe picked up his chopsticks and went to work on his deep-fried dumplings. Man, he was hungry.

'Correct,' said Björn. 'I want to flood Earth's energy market with cheap, green hydrogen, so the demand for oil drops like a stone. I have ideas on how to proceed, but I'm going to need substantial funding. I'm not looking to make a profit: just to cover costs and pay myself and my employees a fair salary. But there'll be a lot of infrastructure to set up.'

Björn and Joe knew Syenitian funding for Earth-based projects was never a problem. As long as the project invested in the wider public good rather than enriching a small group of people, Delius was authorised to untraceably 'adjust' the balance of the relevant bank accounts to cover the necessary outgoings. Both the language school in London and the *Shantivira* itself were financed this way, without costing the Syenitians a *fedha*.

'Funding is not an issue, Björn,' said Aldeman. 'Not starting a war is.'

Joe's head jerked up. 'What do you mean?'

'Do you think the people profiting from the status quo will quietly accept their time is over? Do you believe they will allow their power structures to be shut down, almost overnight?' Aldeman pursed his lips and shook his head. 'They will fight bitterly for survival, even if that ultimately means the death of their planet. Not logical, I know, but that is our assessment, based on what we understand of human behaviour.'

Björn looked crestfallen. 'Am I being pathetically naïve?' he asked, sipping his beer.

Aldeman smiled. 'No, Björn. You have vision. Imagination. I admire that. You *could* pull it off, with a well-thought-out strategy. The Council has nothing against humans using the Pweza's technology: we thought you would want to, so it has already been discussed and agreed, provisionally. But we must not rush into anything without detailed planning.'

Björn rolled his eyes at Joe across the table. Classic Syenitian lack of urgency coupled with a horror of spontaneous action. Joe suppressed a smile; he'd been here so many times before. But he'd been listening: Aldeman was going to help.

'We?' he confirmed. 'You're offering to get involved, my lord? Pit your Councillor's cunning against the mighty corporations, in the service of humanity?'

Aldeman cleared his throat. 'Well. The humans on Dunia would not appreciate my direct involvement. That would be inappropriate. Nor do I have the time. But I can offer support in an advisory capacity. Björn would make the on-planet decisions.'

Björn beamed. 'I'll take any help I can get. If we're

going to minimise the impact of global heating, we don't have much more than a decade to make the transition.' He looked at Aldeman. 'My contract with the Pweza expires at the spring equinox. I'll need them to make me industrial quantities of self-powering electrolysers – they're still setting up their manufacturing facility, so it could take a while. I'll base myself on Earth again so I can build a team and test the principle before scaling up to commercial production. It might be clever to buy an old rig that's stopped producing and has been scheduled for decommissioning. Or maybe we should start from scratch. Like I said, there's a lot to consider.'

'There is,' Aldeman said with an encouraging smile. 'So consider it and call me when you need me.'

Björn beamed. Joe suspected he'd been nervous about this meeting and relieved Aldeman had agreed so easily. What Björn *didn't* know was the Syenitians planned so far ahead, he'd actually been given the job with the Pweza in the hope he'd initiate the technology transfer for the Earth. He'd been pushing at an open door.

After they'd eaten, Joe walked back to Dunia House with Björn. It was a crisp, clear evening; Joe could taste the promise of snow to come in the air. He loved Essoona at night, you saw a completely different set of people going about their business. He had to stride briskly to keep up with Björn's long legs, but that was good: it kept him warm and, after all the time he spent sitting in meetings nowadays, he appreciated the exercise.

On the way, he updated Björn on the latest developments back home. Joe was now a global celebrity after a clip of their theatrical exit from the General Assembly had been posted online. With the honoured exception of *The Cath Palug*, he hadn't dared return to the populated parts of the Earth since. He was contemplating growing a beard to stop people recognising him. Even in the pub, they'd been incredulous – less about the alien space station and more that *their* Kitty was the Red Dragon of Wales. Joe could sit back and relax while his drinking companions listened spellbound to Kitty's stories of Merlin, Arthur and the *Cath Palug* herself.

Fortunately, the identities of the ex-Shantivirans had been redacted from the publicly released video of the session, helping them avoid media interest for now. If anything, the Red Dragon deflected attention away from them and onto Kitty and Joe; perhaps their stunt had been the right call after all. Joe was sure his colleagues' identities would leak out to the wider public eventually, but he was pleased the UN had taken proactive steps to protect their own.

According to Gabriel, they'd already had several productive meetings. Each country with a space agency was putting together a team of scientists to attend the seminars on the *Shantivira*. Joe hoped Dipesh and the rest of the maintenance crew were up to the job of teaching them what they needed to know.

He sighed inwardly. Everyone seemed to want a piece of him nowadays. His terrestrial phone never stopped ringing. He should get an assistant. Someone with sufficient knowledge to go to meetings in his place.

William would be his ideal choice, but he was up to his ears with Hassan's legal battle. Perhaps he'd have time after the hearing in January? But what if the case went to appeal? Yisheng's English wasn't good enough; plus, Joe's frequent absences meant he already had too much to do. Shakila? She wouldn't just handle the challenge, she'd relish it.

Björn interrupted his reverie. 'What about those snipers? Any word on who wanted you dead?'

The snipers had been kept entirely in the dark, and not just by Kitty. Kitty's interrogation had only revealed that all communication had been done via dead drops in New York. Almost a dead end. After a couple of days, they'd released them to the police and tracked the payments instead – payments made from a Swiss bank account which no longer existed. Everything pointed to organisation by a cautious, detailed mind.

Delius had done a deep dive into the data and uncovered the IP address of the computer used to close the bank account. Location: Gaiman, Chubut Province, the Welsh-speaking corner of Argentina.

Nestor. It could only be Nestor who wanted him dead. And his mam had gone with him willingly. Did she know? Did she *care*?

Joe said, 'We don't have enough proof for a prosecution. But we know who it was, yes. Delius is monitoring his activities closely; we'll know if he starts planning on having another go.'

At Dunia House, he said goodbye to Björn and returned to the *Shantivira* through the teleport. He reached out with his mind as he crossed Docking Bay 3 to the *Pride of Essoona*.

Babe, you home?

I will be.

When he got to their living area, Kitty was on the sofa, Syenitian-shaped.

Have a good evening? she asked.

Joe poured himself a single malt and sat beside her. He leaned against her so she could put her arm around him.

Yeah. S'pose. Did you check on Mam in Gaiman again, like you said you would?

Just got back.

And?

I hate to say it, but she's having the time of her life. Gardening. Complaining about the heat. Going to chapel. Teaching Welsh at the school in return for Spanish lessons. Learning to dance the tango.

Joe blinked. The *tango?* His *mam?*

How did you find all this out?

Just lurking. Plenty of stray cats there, it's easy to blend in. She's out in the garden a lot. The local Welsh speakers all stop at the fence for a chat when passing. They call her 'la jardinera galesa'.

Perhaps the time away from home would give her a new perspective, Joe thought to himself. Perhaps it might, ultimately, lead to their reconciliation. Something he hadn't realised he'd wanted until events had overtaken him. But they'd have to get her out of Nestor's clutches first. How were they going to do that without making things worse?

Sounds like she has a better social life than she did in Brecon.

She does, said Kitty. *Although she shuts right up if anyone mentions aliens or that video of us at the UN. Her lips go all thin and disapproving. Nobody else there is taking it seriously. The joke going round town is that the red dragon will visit the rugby club for the Christmas party.*

Joe laughed. *Why?*

Cos it's the Draig Goch *Rugby Club, duh.* Her eyes glinted mischievously. *Maybe I'll do a little flyby.*

Even though you refused to do one when we won at Twickenham? he teased. *If ever a flyby over a rugby pitch was justified, surely that was your moment? Before the Springboks kicked us out in the quarter finals?*

Kitty gave a toothy grin. *The world didn't know about me then, did it? And we were busy getting ready for the UN.*

Joe sipped his drink. *Resist the temptation,* cariad. *Nestor would realise we know where he is if you appeared in public there.*

You're right, she agreed. *Grace is safe as long as he feels safe. We'd better make sure he does.*

What does he *do all day, while Mam's gossiping with the neighbours?*

He and Matthew are rebuilding their little weapon in a unit in the industrial park. Kitty's lips twitched. *No immediate danger there. It'll take them years.*

Have you managed to find out who his contact at the UN was yet?

I have an idea, but nothing definite. The moment he reaches out again, I'll be certain.

Watch him, Cath. *He mustn't get the chance for another go.*

Don't worry, my love. He can't fart without us knowing. And as long as he has Grace, he doesn't need to come after you.

Joe finished his whisky and placed the glass on a side

table. He opened one of the little mother-of-pearl-handled drawers in the unit behind the sofa and took out a wooden hairbrush. Kitty settled into position, facing away from him, and he began brushing her hair in long, even strokes, as was their evening ritual.

Question for you, he said.

Shoot.

Al said they have a plan to deal with the Ranglatiri, but it's top secret. The way he was looking at me made me think he wanted me to ask you.

You thought right. It's insane; it breaks every law in the galaxy. But the gloves are off now: this is about survival. The Ranglatiri must be stopped before they destroy any more civilisations. If they attack an Alliance planet, it'll be all-out war.

He put down the hairbrush and unpicked a particularly stubborn tangle with his fingers. *There was something different about the strike on Amra. Normally they'd asset strip: that would have taken longer, we might have been able to do something. This was like ... a punishment.*

Kitty nodded. *Mmm. I heard it was the extra-Ranglatiri security service who razed Laro to the ground and they called in the pirates to finish off the rest of the planet. You're right, the objective was destruction rather than money-making. I'd love to know why.*

Joe picked up the hairbrush and continued brushing. *What's this insane plan, then?*

Promise you'll never breathe a word of this out loud? Not to anyone? Not even to me? And not write it down anywhere?

Telepathy only?

Telepathy only.

Righto. Do I even need to know? Would it be better if I didn't?

Kitty shook her head. *You should know about this. Aldeman's going to need your friendship more than ever in the coming months, Joe. Even though he won't be able to speak of the reason for it.*

Aldeman? What? Why?

Because ... Rowan's going to embed herself in the Ranglatiri government and attempt to control it from the inside.

The hairbrush in Joe's hand clattered to the floor.

You're not serious? That's nuts!

Yup.

You mean Rowan's going to have to pretend to be a Ranglatiri for ... what ... weeks? Months?

Years, if necessary. She's the only one who has a chance of pulling it off. I'd offer to do it myself, but—

—you're needed here.

And she's a better politician than I am. Better at thinking through consequences.

It's a big ask. How does she feel about it?

It was her idea. She volunteered. They don't call her 'Verndari' for nothing. She's been studying the Ranglatiri and learning their language on the quiet for years, just in case. She talked through all the options with Dalian before even mentioning her plan to Aldeman.

That was a surprise. The Syenitian Defence Minister was no fan of Aldeman's and everybody knew she wanted his job, any way she could get it.

I know what you're thinking, but Dalian has the best

interests of Syenitia and the Alliance at heart. Ro wanted advice from someone who wasn't emotionally involved. A perspective from someone else with centuries of experience in devious plotting.

Well, that would be Dalian. Joe scratched his chin. *Will Rowan be OK?* he asked. *On her own for so long, amongst those ... savages?*

She's tough. She's done similar undercover jobs on unfriendly planets before, just never for as long, or anywhere so—different. Aldeman will find it harder. Their cover story'll be they're having a trial separation period, a break from their marriage. That'll give you a good excuse to spend more time with him; everyone in Essoona knows you're close.

Joe stood up and poured himself another whisky. Perhaps it would stop his head spinning. He told the *Pride's* computer to activate the exterior cameras and gazed across the docking bay, past the dark hulk of the *Koppakuoria* and out to the blue, green and white planet beyond.

You OK? Kitty asked.

Just thinking, he said, not turning round.

Here he was, straining every sinew to persuade the Earth the Syenitians only wanted trade and friendship when, in fact, the Syenitians were willing to interfere in the government of another world to achieve their desired outcome. How often had Rowan given sticky interplanetary situations a nudge from the inside? He remembered several moments during his years as Aldeman's personal pilot where disagreements had inexplicably resolved before a situation degenerated into armed conflict. Was the Galaksi Alliance taking the sanctity of life to extremes? At what point did the cost of preserving intelligent life at all costs become too high?

He sighed. In the end, it came down to one thing. Survival. When you were under threat, you did what you had to do. The Ranglatiri were an evil plague spreading across the galaxy, annihilating everything in their path. If Rowan could destroy them from the inside, then good luck to her.

Cath?

Mmm?

Let's go to bed.

31. FAREWELL, ESSOONA

HANNA

'IS IT MUCH further?' panted Kia, holding her rounded belly with two hands from underneath, like a bag of groceries. Her warm breath left puffs of vapour in the cold, still air, like a small, disgruntled dragon in an oversized parka.

'Just after the next bend,' said Hanna, hoping she was right. The fresh snow on the path gave a satisfying squeaky crunch with each step she took. 'You're doing fine, Kia. Take care not to slip.'

Elian's brow furrowed. 'Should she even have come today? Shouldn't she be resting? The others are way ahead of us.'

Hanna opened her mouth, but Lucy got there first. 'She's not ill, Elian, she's expecting. Let her enjoy her last months of freedom.'

'Don't worry, Elian,' said Farida, 'the walk will do her good. By the time we reach the picnic spot, the others will have unpacked the food. Win-win.'

Aneira caught Hanna's eye and they shared a smile. Because they lived so long and weren't particularly fertile, Syenitians rarely had children. Elian had never met a pregnant person before. He found Kia utterly fascinating.

Kia found his constant questions utterly annoying.

Still, Hanna was glad they'd invited Elian and Aneira to the farewell winter picnic on Dragon Hill. Mr and Mrs Park organised one at the end of each year to say goodbye to the students before they returned to live aboard the *Shantivira*. Aneira needed all the distractions she could get at the moment. There'd been no news about her relatives since the Ranglatiri had burned her planet. Hanna knew the longer they heard nothing, the worse the news was likely to be. The Ranglatiri were cannibals: according to rumour, the 'lucky' captives would be sent to the Ranglatiri planet to work in the Mines of Kifo. Those not fit enough for hard labour would be held prisoner until they were required as food. Overnight, the Amranese had become an endangered species. Despite her down jacket, Hanna shivered.

The invasion had shattered Aneira's mental health. Although she'd passed the final flight tests last week (she'd have managed that with her eyes shut, Hanna thought), her scores in the theoretical component were so low, she'd have to repeat the year in order to qualify as a pilot. The way Aneira had been talking, Hanna wasn't sure she'd even bother. Consumed with fury at the lack of Alliance response to the invasion, Aneira had lost interest in her education. She'd persuaded Merian to speak up for the Amranese before the Council, but any hopes she'd had had come to nothing. Aneira was constantly trying to think of ways to help her home planet – or at least get justice for it – and failing at every turn. The frustration and sense of helplessness was affecting her physical health now; Elian had confided in Hanna that he didn't know how to help her.

With most of her own birth family either dead or missing, and the village she'd grown up in washed away by a flood, Hanna believed she understood some of what Aneira was going through. 'She's grieving, Elian,' she'd said. 'It's a process. She's lost a huge part of herself and it'll take time for her to adapt. To accept. You can't help her unless she asks you for something. At least she still has her parents and brothers. Just be there for her. Listen when she talks, hold her when she cries. Let her tell you what happens in her nightmares.'

For Hanna, too, school had lost importance. The human students had all scraped through their written papers, only doing respectably well in the flight tests. Hanna was further down the league table than she'd hoped, but it was a fair result considering what else was going on in her life. At least she'd finished ahead of Felix and Saïd. She still had *some* pride.

Briavan had come first in their flight exam, with Elian a close second. To her delight, Lucy had come third. Briavan had worn her victory like a superhero's cape, swooshing it around wherever she went so nobody missed how amazing she was. Hanna pitied her, because she didn't have anything more important to think about than coming top of their year. How could someone more than a hundred years old be so immature?

They rounded a corner and there were the others, setting up the picnic in the same sun-trap she and Lucy had rested in the day they'd first met Aneira. Despite the snow, it felt positively warm. With surprise, she noticed her little stack of stones still stood, now dusted with white. Not only that: it had been joined by three additional towers of varying heights, dotted about the clearing. She'd obviously started something.

Elian unfolded the stool he'd been carrying for Kia and fussed around her as she sat down with relief. The others spread out in groups, sitting on their empty rucksacks as insulation from the snow.

Hanna looked at her classmates. Mrs Park was serving up ox-bone soup and they passed the steaming bowls from neighbour to neighbour until everyone had been served. The past year, so far from home for all of them, had brought them even closer together. Wherever they ended up after their time on the *Shantivira*, she knew they were friends for life. An extended family and a reliable support network.

She'd miss Farida next year. Life would be tougher without her constant calm presence. They'd promised to visit each other regularly, especially when the baby came in April, but Hanna knew it wouldn't be the same. The baby … Hanna eyed Kia, who was biting into a rolled-up seafood pancake. What would it be like? Would it be a boy or a girl? Hagar had offered to tell them at Kia's most recent monthly scan, but Kia said she wanted it to be a surprise. Hanna knew she wouldn't be able to keep it to herself if Hagar told her privately, so she'd resisted the urge to ask.

Thank goodness they'd been able to persuade Kia to stay on the *Shantivira* with Hanna. Joe had arranged for the refugee camp to inform them immediately if they heard from Alimayu and Negasi, and it seemed this had been enough to set her mind at rest.

Initially, Kia had wanted to live with Mary and Irion and have the baby in London, but there were too many administrative hurdles to overcome in the months they had left. Anyway, if the teleports went down again, she might have the baby without Hanna. That didn't bear thinking about. Kitty had organised Kia an Ethiopian passport with a UK visa, so at least she could visit London legally as a tourist.

Hanna was far happier having Kia with her on the *Shantivira*. Hagar would monitor the pregnancy closely and there were plenty of people willing to help out. Mary and Irion had enough to do without a newborn baby to manage. It took a village to raise a child, the saying went, and, from January, the *Shantivira* would be Kia's village.

Aneira passed her the box of seafood pancakes and Hanna helped herself to two. The others were discussing their plans for the winter break. Most were seeing their families. Farida was going back to Indonesia; Saïd was returning to France. Felix was staying with Lucy at her parent's house in Devon for a while. Roberto and Nikolai were heading to Yakutsk to deliver the Pweza's sample electrolyser and power unit to Nikolai's mother.

'Be careful, guys,' said Felix. 'You won't be able to be your usual self in Siberia, Roberto.'

Nikolai squeezed Roberto's hand. 'We'll be discreet. We won't go out much; it's −40 °C outside. And dark. The sun sets before three p.m. at this time of year.'

Roberto grinned. 'It's just for a week. I'm going to learn to enjoy putting mayonnaise in my soup like a real

Russian. It'll be an adventure.'

'Then Roberto's taking me to Belo Horizonte for some sunshine,' said Nikolai.

'And to introduce him to my folks.' Roberto ruffled Nikolai's hair. 'They're going to *LOVE* him!'

'Does your mum know you're gay, Nikolai?' asked Lucy.

He shook his head. 'Part of this trip is to tell her. I thought giving her the power source and the electrolyser at the same time might cushion the blow.'

Hanna had never met the formidable-sounding Svetlana Poroshkin, but she was an ex-Shantiviran and, by all accounts, a friend of Kitty's. That must count for something.

Lucy clearly thought the same. 'I doubt it'll be a problem, Nikolai. Kitty would never have recruited her in the first place if she was homophobic.'

Roberto leaned forward. 'You can never be sure how people will react. It's always a leap of faith, telling someone.' He squeezed Nikolai's shoulders. 'But I'll be with you, *amor*. Whatever happens.'

'And you, Hanna?' asked Nikolai. 'Will you stay in London?'

Hanna finished her mouthful and shook her head. 'Hassan's desperate for a change of scene and a break from his trial preparations. Lucy's friend Alice has invited us to stay at their farm as test guests. Kia too.'

'Test guests?'

'They're diversifying into holiday lets,' said Lucy. 'Alice's husband has renovated an old cowshed, and they need someone to try it and be honest about what it's like to stay there.'

'I've never been to the West Country,' said Hanna, licking her fingers and wiping them on a tissue. 'I'm looking forward to seeing cows again.'

'Crediton's close to Exeter,' said Lucy, 'so we can meet up.'

'It'll be good for Kia to have a vacation before the baby comes,' said Farida, stacking their empty soup bowls.

Hanna tilted her head. 'I'm worried she'll be bored, with just me and Hassan.'

'I'll help you keep her entertained,' said Lucy. 'I'll be doing tourist stuff with Felix: she can come with us and give you two some time alone.'

'Thanks, Lucy, that'd be great.'

'Does Hassan have a date for his trial?' Roberto asked. 'Will we be able to take time off to support him?'

'Five weeks to go,' said Hanna. 'He'd love it if you came.' She rubbed her face. 'I'll be so glad when it's over, whichever way it goes. It's been hanging over us for far too long.'

'Yeah,' said Lucy. 'At least then you'll be able to plan for the future.'

Hanna looked at Kia, who was resting a box of spring rolls on her bump, happily sharing them with Aneira and Elian, who sat at her feet. Life was so full of surprises.

Could you ever really plan for the future?

AUTHOR'S NOTE

The world has moved on since *The Cleaner, the Cat and the Space Station* was published in 2021. The planetary crisis is more urgent than ever, but awareness is growing too.

The answers are out there. The technical problems are solvable. Let's visualise a better future for ourselves and our children, where quality of life for everyone is valued more highly than profit – and make it happen!

Fay Abernethy
June 2023

To find out more about the refugee situation in South Sudan and to make a donation visit:
www.unhcr.org/south-sudan-emergency.html

REFERENCES/INSPIRATION

BOOKS

Kate Raworth: Doughnut Economics, Seven Ways to Think Like a 21st-Century Economist

Stephanie Kelton: The Deficit Myth: Modern Monetary Theory and the Birth of the People's Economy

Jason Hickel: The Divide: A Brief Guide to Global Inequality and its Solutions

Jason Hickel: Less is More: How Degrowth Will Save the World

Guy Standing: Basic Income: And How We Can Make It Happen

Jon Alexander: Citizens: Why the Key to Fixing Everything is All of Us

Why do Syenitians put vinegar in their drinking water? Find the answer here:
Jessie Inchauspe: Glucose Revolution: The life-changing power of balancing your blood sugar

LINKS

Planet: Critical
Fascinating, deep-dive podcasts to stop you feeling

helpless about the climate crisis:
www.planetcritical.com or on YouTube.

Seasonal thermal energy storage
www.planete-energies.com/en/media/article/how-does-long-term-thermal-energy-storage-work

Energy conservation
www.theguardian.com/environment/2022/mar/26/amory-lovins-energy-efficiency-interview-cheapest-safest-cleanest-crisis

Complementary/community currencies
Bangla-pesa, Kenya
youtube.com/watch?v=ojFPrVvpraU
International Journal of Community Currency Research, VOLUME 19 (2015) SECTION D 18-30
Complementary Currencies for Sustainable Development in Kenya: The Case of the Bangla-Pesa
William O. Ruddick, Morgan A. Richards, and Jem Bendell
ijccr.files.wordpress.com/2015/03/ijccr-2015-ruddick-et-al.pdf
BerkShares, Massachusetts, USA
en.wikipedia.org/wiki/BerkShares
Bristol pound, UK
en.wikipedia.org/wiki/Bristol_pound
Chiemgauer, Bavaria, Germany
www.chiemgauer.info (in German)
WIR, Switzerland
www.wir.ch/de/produkte-loesungen/geschaeftskunden/wir-waehrung/chf-und-chw
(in German, French or Italian)

ACKNOWLEDGEMENTS

Thank YOU, for reading this book. Writers are nothing without readers.

Thanks to Hilary, Emma, Michael, Steph, Harriet and the team at Jericho Writers. Thanks to Jo for the *jelimbe-gu*. Thanks to Patrick for the fantastic cover. And special thanks to Alex, for pretty much everything else.

NOT READY TO LEAVE THE SHANTIVIRA JUST YET?

Then come on over to www.fayabernethy.com and download The Man with the Dragon Tattoo – the story of how Joe joined the *Shantivira* back in 1997. For FREE!

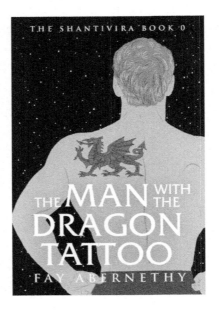

This is an *exclusive* story. You can't buy it anywhere: you can only get hold of it by joining The Shantivira Readers' Club. In return, I'll (occasionally) update you on how The Shantivira Book Three is coming along.

I promise to only send you emails I believe you'll find

interesting and entertaining. You can unsubscribe easily anytime. I will guard your personal data fiercely, with dragons.

If you enjoyed *Learning to Fly Alien Spacecraft*, then please tell other people you think might like it too. And if you could leave a little review – or even just a star rating – that would be fantastic. As a part-time indie author, my marketing budget is so tiny, it's invisible to the naked eye. This means I rely utterly on the kindness of readers like you to spread the word about the *Shantivira*.

Get it here:

Want to read more by Fay Abernethy?

THE CLEANER, THE CAT AND THE SPACE STATION
THE SHANTIVIRA BOOK ONE

There's an alien space station orbiting the Earth, secretly protecting us from invasion.
And it's recruiting humans like you to train as fighter pilots.

Since leaving Ethiopia, Hanna Abebe has survived in London by working illegally as a cleaner. But her life unravels after a sexual assault; living rough, she loses the resulting pregnancy and very nearly her life. Help arrives and Hanna's rescuers welcome her into an unusual new family: a school for recruits to the *Shantivira*, the secret alien space station which protects the Earth. Then Hanna uncovers a traitor in their midst …

Lucy Cooper is horse riding on Dartmoor when a mysterious shape-shifter offers her a place on the *Shantivira's* training programme. Her instinct is to refuse, but an organisation claiming the *Shantivira's* motives are sinister persuades Lucy to become their spy …

Joe Llewellyn is bored. Being the captain of the *Shantivira* isn't the challenge he'd hoped. Plus, he'd like to inform the Earth about aliens, but his boss won't permit it. Then a stray asteroid hits the ISS and Joe is forced to let the cat out of the bag …

This heart-warming blend of fantasy and science fiction is a must-read for fans of Becky Chambers, Ursula Le Guin, Ben Aaronovitch, Douglas Adams and Doctor Who.

Get it here:

DID MY SPELLING ANNOY YOU?

Colour instead of color, realise instead of realize, grey instead of gray?

Then I'm going to go out on a limb here and assume you might be a) in the US or b) an American. Possibly both!

Currently, there's just one version of this book available and that's in the only variety of English I feel capable of writing in – British English. *Vive la différence!*

ABOUT THE AUTHOR

More than twenty years ago, Fay Abernethy left the UK for a six-month engineering secondment in Germany, fell in love and stayed there. Brexit broke her heart.

Learning to Fly Alien Spacecraft is her second novel.

Printed in Great Britain
by Amazon